# Circle of Friends

Maeve Binchy was born in Dublin and was educated at the Holy Child Convent in Killiney and at University College Dublin. After a spell as a teacher in various girls' schools, she joined the *Irish Times*, for which she wrote feature articles and columns. Her first novel *Light a Penny Candle* was published in 1982, and she went on to write more than a dozen novels and short-story collections, each one of them a bestseller. Several have been adapted for cinema and television, most notably *Circle of Friends* in 1995. Maeve Binchy died on 30 July 2012. She is survived by her husband, the writer and broadcaster Gordon Snell.

To find out more visit www.maevebinchy.com

Also available by Maeve Binchy

# Maeve Binchy

# Circle of Friends

arrow books

19 20

Arrow Books
20 Vauxhall Bridge Road
London SW1V 2SA

Arrow Books is part of the Penguin Random House group of companies
whose addresses can be found at global.penguinrandomhouse.com.

Penguin
Random House
UK

First published in the United Kingdom in 1990 by Century
First published in paperback in 2000 by Arrow Books
This edition reissued by Arrow Books in 2020

www.penguin.co.uk

A CIP catalogue record for this book is available from the British Library.

ISBN 9780099498599

Typeset by SX Composing DTP, Rayleigh, Essex
Printed and bound in Great Britain by Clays Ltd, Elcograf S.p.A.

*For my dear love Gordon Snell*

# INTRODUCTION

Oh, how I envy anyone reading *Circle of Friends* for the very first time! You are in for such a treat, and are about to enter a world brought vividly to life by one of the most skilled storytellers of our age.

I was lucky enough to meet and interview Maeve Binchy a number of years ago, and it was such a joy. Behind her wise and warm eyes was a sharp intellect, a keen sense of right and wrong, and a deep humanity. She was also incredibly funny, and in a world divided into 'fountains' and 'drains' – people who can refresh, revive and give life to those around them, and people who draw upon and leech away the energy of others – Binchy was, without question, the Trevi Fountain of fountains.

*Circle of Friends* is a story of love, friendship, loss and betrayal, but it's also so much more than that. Maeve Binchy was never afraid to deal with the most important and universal emotions, and she knew exactly what makes us tick. She had a keen emotional intelligence, and a magical ability to immerse you completely in any world she created.

The world of *Circle of Friends* is one in which you feel so connected with the characters that you simply cannot stop yourself from turning the pages. No matter how many times I read it, I always find myself galloping through it, even though I try my hardest to take my time and savour it. Despite already knowing how the novel ends, I always *have* to race through and read what happens next!

The first time I reached the end, I was surprised, and satisfied, but I was also left feeling bereft. Finishing the book felt like I was saying goodbye to dear friends who I had come to love, even the ones whose choices and actions, at times, exasperated and frustrated me!

Whenever I return to read *Circle of Friends*, I can always picture each character so vividly – I feel I know exactly what they all look like – and I can effortlessly empathise with their sorrows and joys, feeling their emotions right alongside them. I most strongly identify with the socially awkward, slightly plump Benny, whose journey is at the heart of this coming-of-age story. Although Benny might end up being bruised, belittled and betrayed, she always has hope in her heart.

Benny is one of my favourite characters in all of fiction and, when you read *Circle of Friends*, it may not come as a surprise to learn that Maeve drew on her own experience of being a student at University College in Dublin where – like Benny – she was also a bit insecure and awkward around boys. Both Maeve and Benny share those admirable qualities of decency, honesty and sheer likeability.

There are no gimmicky plot twists in *Circle of Friends*,

and there are no explicit sex scenes (for which I am secretly grateful), because Maeve Binchy didn't need such easy distractions to grab and hold your interest. Her work is always completely absorbing and relatable, and she had the rare ability to make the ordinary extraordinary. Her writing feels totally authentic, and Binchy's gift for authenticity is what made her such a rare talent and a genuine treasure.

I absolutely adore *Circle of Friends* – my 'fave Maeve' – and, over the years, I have returned to read it time and time again. We are so blessed that this incredible woman left us so many brilliant novels, so many incredible characters, and such an important legacy.

Thank you, Maeve.

LORRAINE KELLY
November 2019

# Circle
# of Friends

# 1

## 1949

The kitchen was full of the smells of baking. Benny put down her school bag and went on a tour of inspection.

'The cake hasn't been iced yet,' Patsy explained. 'The mistress will do that herself.'

'What are you going to put on it?' Benny was eager.

'I suppose Happy Birthday Benny.' Patsy was surprised.

'Maybe she'll put Benny Hogan, Ten.'

'I never saw that on a cake.'

'I think it is, when it's a big birthday like being ten.'

'Maybe.' Patsy was doubtful.

'And are the jellies made?'

'They're in the pantry. Don't go in poking at them, you'll leave the mark of your finger and we'll all be killed.'

'I can't believe I'm going to be ten,' Benny said, delighted with herself.

'Ah, it's a big day all right.' Patsy spoke absently as she

greased the trays for the queen cakes with a scrap of butter paper.

'What did you do when you were ten?'

'Don't you know with me every day was the same,' Patsy said cheerfully. 'There was no day different in the orphanage until I came out of it and came here.'

Benny loved to hear stories of the orphanage. She thought it was better than anything she read in books. There was the room with the twelve iron beds in it, the nice girls, the terrible girls, the time they all got nits in their hair and had their heads shaved.

'They must have had birthdays,' Benny insisted.

'I don't remember them,' Patsy sighed. 'There was a nice nun who said to me that I was Wednesday's child, full of woe.'

'That wasn't nice.'

'Well, at least she knew I was born on a Wednesday . . . Here's your mother, now let me get on with the work.'

Annabel Hogan came in carrying three big bags. She was surprised to see her daughter sitting swinging her legs in the kitchen.

'Aren't you home nice and early? Let me put these things upstairs.'

Benny ran over to Patsy when her mother's heavy tread was heard on the stairs.

'Do you think she got it?'

'Don't ask me, Benny, I know nothing.'

'You're saying that because you *do* know.'

'I *don't*. Really.'

'Was she in Dublin? Did she go up on the bus?'

'No, not at all.'

'But she must have.' Benny seemed very disappointed.

'No, she's not long gone at all . . . She was only up the town.'

Benny licked the spoon thoughtfully. It's nicer raw,' she said.

'You always thought that.' Patsy looked at her fondly.

'When I'm eighteen and can do what I like, I'll eat all my cakes uncooked,' Benny pronounced.

'No you won't, when you're eighteen you'll be so busy getting thin you won't eat cakes at all.'

'I'll always want cakes.'

'You say that now. Wait till you want some fellow to fancy you.'

'Do you want a fellow to fancy you?'

'Of course I do, what else is there?'

'What fellow? I don't want you to go, anyway.'

'I won't get a fellow, I'm from nowhere, a decent fellow wouldn't be able to talk about me and where I came from. I have no background, no life before, you see.'

'But you had a *great* life,' Benny cried. 'You'd make them all interested in you.'

There was no time to discuss it further. Benny's mother was back in the kitchen, her coat off and down to business with the icing sugar.

'Were you in Dublin at all today, Mother?'

'No, child, I had enough to do getting things ready for the party.'

'It's just I was wondering . . .'

'Parties don't run themselves, you know.' The words sounded sharp but the tone was kindly. Benny knew her mother was looking forward to it all too.

'And will Father be home for the cake bit?'

'Yes, he will. We've asked the people for half past three, they'll all be here by four, so we needn't sit down to the tea until half past five, and we wouldn't have got to the cake until your father has the business closed, and is back here.'

Benny's father ran Hogan's Outfitters, the big menswear shop in the middle of Knockglen. The shop was often at its busiest on a Saturday, when the farmers came in, or the men who had a half day themselves were marched in by wives to have themselves fitted out by Mr Hogan, or Mike the old assistant, the tailor who had been there since time immemorial. Since the days when young Mr Hogan had bought the business.

Benny was glad that her father would be there for the cake, because that was when she might be given her present. Father had said it was going to be a wonderful surprise. Benny *knew* that they must have got her the velvet dress with the lacy collar and the pumps to go with it. She had wanted it since last Christmas when they went to the pantomime in Dublin and she had seen the girls on the stage dancing in pink velvet dresses like this.

They had heard that they sold them in Clery's, and that was only a few minutes from where the bus stopped when it went to Dublin.

Benny was large and square, but she wouldn't look like that in the pink velvet dress. She would be just like the fairy dancers they had seen on the stage, and her feet wouldn't look big and flat in those shoes because they had lovely pointy toes, and little pom-poms on them.

The invitations to the party had been sent out ten days ago. There would be seven girls from school, farmers' daughters mainly from outside Knockglen. And Maire Carroll, whose mother and father owned the grocery. The Kennedys from the chemist were all boys so they wouldn't be there, and Dr Johnson's children were all too young so they couldn't come either. Peggy Pine who ran the smart clothes shop said that she might have her young niece staying with her. Benny said she didn't want anyone they didn't know, and it was with some relief that they heard the niece Clodagh didn't want to go amongst strangers either.

Her mother had insisted she invite Eve Malone and that was bad enough. Eve was the girl who lived in the convent and knew all the nuns' secrets. Some people at school said look how Mother Francis never gives out to Eve, she's the real pet; others said the nuns had to keep her for charity and didn't like her as much as they liked the other girls whose families all contributed something to the upkeep of St Mary's.

Eve was small and dark. She looked like a pixie sometimes, her eyes darting here and there, forever watchful. Benny neither liked Eve nor disliked her. She envied her being so fleet and lithe and able to climb walls. She knew

5

that Eve had her own room in the convent, behind the curtain where no other girl was allowed to step. The girls said it was the room with the round window that faced down the town and that Eve could sit at the window and watch everyone and where they went and who they were with. She never went on holidays anywhere, she stayed with the nuns all the time. Sometimes Mother Francis and Miss Pine from the dress shop would take her on an outing to Dublin, but she had never stayed away a night.

Once, when they had gone on a nature walk, Eve had pointed to a small cottage and said that it was her house. It stood in a group of small houses, each separate and surrounded by a little stone wall. They looked down into the big disused quarry. When she was older she would live in it all on her own and there would be no milk allowed in the door, and no clothes hangers. She would put all her things on the floor because it was hers to do what she liked with.

Some of them were half afraid of Eve, so nobody denied the story, but nobody really believed it either. Eve was so strange, she could make up tales and then, when everyone had got interested, she would say, 'Fooled you'.

Benny didn't really want her to come to the party, but for once Mother had been insistent.

'That child has no home. She must come to this one when there's a celebration.'

'She *has* a home, Mother, she's got the run of the whole convent.'

'That's not the same. She's to come here, Benny, that's my last word.'

Eve had written a very neat correct letter saying that she accepted the invitation with pleasure.

'They taught her to write nicely,' Benny's father had said approvingly.

'They're determined to make a lady out of her,' Mother had said. No one would explain why it seemed so important.

'When it's her birthday she only gets holy pictures and holy water fonts,' Benny reported. 'That's all the nuns have, you see.'

'God, that would turn a few of them over in their graves up there under the yew trees,' Benny's father had said, but again there was no explanation of why.

'Poor Eve, what a start for her,' Benny's mother sighed.

'I wonder was she born on a Wednesday like Patsy?' Benny was struck by something.

'Why would that matter?'

'She'd be miserable. Wednesday's child is full of woe,' Benny parroted.

'Nonsense.' Her father was dismissive.

'What day was I born on?'

'A Monday, Monday September 18th, 1939,' her mother said. 'At six o'clock in the evening.'

Her parents exchanged glances, looks that seemed to remember a long wait for a first and, as it turned out, an only child.

'Monday's child is fair of face,' Benny said, grimacing.

'Well, that's true certainly!' her mother said.

'You couldn't have a fairer face than Mary Bernadette

Hogan, spinster of this parish, almost ten years of age,'
said her father.

'It's not really fair, I mean I don't have fair hair.' Benny
struggled to fit in with the saying accurately.

'You have the most beautiful hair I have ever seen.' Her
mother stroked Benny's long chestnut locks.

'Do I really look nice?' she asked.

They reassured her that she looked beautiful, and she
knew they had bought the dress for her. She had been
worried for a bit but now she was certain.

At school next day, even the girls who hadn't been
asked to the party wished her a happy birthday.

'What are you getting?'

'I don't know, it's a surprise.'

'Is it a dress?'

'Yes, I think so.'

'Ah, go on, tell us.'

'I don't know yet, really. I won't have it till the party.'

'Was it got in Dublin?'

'I think so.'

Eve spoke suddenly. 'It might have been got here,
there's lots of things in Miss Pine's.'

'I don't think so.' Benny tossed her head.

Eve shrugged. 'Okay.'

The others had gone away.

Benny turned on Eve. 'Why did you say it was got in
Miss Pine's? You don't know, you don't know anything.'

'I said okay.'

'Have *you* got a frock?'

'Yes, Mother Francis got one at Miss Pine's. I don't think it's new. I think someone gave it back because there was something wrong with it.'

Eve wasn't apologetic. Her eyes flashed, she was ready with the explanation before anyone else could make the accusation.

'You don't know that.'

'No, but I think it. Mother Francis wouldn't have the money to buy me a new frock.'

Benny looked at her with admiration. She softened in her own attack.

'Well, I don't know either. I think they got me this lovely velvet one. But they mightn't.'

'They got you something new anyway.'

'Yes, but I'd really look great in this,' Benny said. 'It would make anyone look great.'

'Don't think about it too much,' Eve warned.

'Maybe you're right.'

'It's nice of you to ask me. I didn't think you liked me,' Eve said.

'Oh, I do.' Poor Benny was flustered.

'Good. Just as long as you weren't told to, or anything.'

'No! Heavens no!' Benny was far too vehement.

Eve looked at her with a measured glance. 'Right,' she said. 'See you this afternoon.'

They went to school on Saturday mornings, and at 12.30 when the bell went they all poured out of the school gates. All except Eve, who went to the convent kitchen.

'We'll have to feed you up with a good meal before you go,' said Sister Margaret.

'We wouldn't want them to think that a girl from St Mary's would eat all before her when she went out to tea,' said Sister Jerome. They didn't want to spell it out too much for Eve, but it was a big event, the child they had brought up being invited out to a party. The whole community was delighted for her.

As Benny had walked down the town, Mr Kennedy called her into the chemist.

'A little bird told me it was your birthday,' he said.

'I'm ten,' Benny said.

'I know. I remember when you were born. It was in the Emergency. Your Mam and Dad were so pleased. They didn't mind at all that you weren't a boy.'

'Did they want a boy do you think?'

'Everyone with a business wants a boy. But I don't know, I've three of them, and I don't think one of them will ever run this place for me.' He sighed heavily.

'Well, I suppose I'd better be . . .'

'No, no. I brought you in to give you a present. Here's a pack of barley sugar all for you.'

'Oh, Mr Kennedy . . .' Benny was overwhelmed.

'Not at all. You're a grand girl. I always say to myself, there's that little barrel Benny Hogan coming along.'

A bit of the sunlight went out of the barley sugar. Moodily Benny tore the corner off the packet and began to eat a sweet.

Dessie Burns, whose hardware shop was next door to Kennedy's, gave her a shout of approval.

'That's it, Benny, like myself, always head in the nosebag. How are you in yourself these days?'

'I'm ten today, Mr Burns.'

'Jaysus isn't that great, if you were six years older I'd take you into Shea's and put you up on my knee and buy you a gin and it.'

'Thank you, Mr Burns.' She looked at him fearfully.

'What's your father doing over there? Don't tell me he's after hiring new staff. Half the country taking the emigrant ship and Eddie Hogan decides to expand.'

Dessie Burns had small piggy eyes. He looked across the street towards Hogan's Gentleman's Outfitters with huge unconcealed interest. Her father was shaking hands with a man – or a boy, it was hard to see. He looked about seventeen, Benny thought, thin and pale. He had a suitcase in his hand. He was looking up at the sign over the door.

'I don't know anything about it, Mr Burns,' she said.

'Good girl, keep your mind out of business, let me tell you it's a heart scald. If I were a woman I wouldn't have the slightest interest in it either. I'd just get myself a fine eejit of a man to keep me in barley sugar all day.'

Benny went on down the street, past the empty shop which people said that a real Italian from Italy was going to open up. She passed the cobbler's shop where Paccy Moore and his sister Bee waved out to her. Paccy had a twisted leg. He didn't go to Mass, but it was said that the priests came down to him once a month and heard his confession and gave him Holy Communion. Benny had heard that they had sent to Dublin and maybe even Rome for him to have a dispensation, and it wasn't a question of his being a sinner or outside the Church or anything. And then she was home to Lisbeg. The new dog which was half collie, half sheepdog, sat sleepily on the step loving the September sunshine.

Through the window she could see the table set for the party. Patsy had cleaned the brasses specially, and Mother had tidied up the front garden. Benny swallowed the barley sugar rather than be accused of eating sweets in the public view, and let herself in the back.

'Not a word out of that dog to let me know you were coming,' her mother said crossly.

'He shouldn't bark at me, I'm family,' Benny defended him.

'The day Shep barks for anything except his own amusement there'll be white blackbirds. Tell me did you have a nice day at school, did they make a fuss of you?'

'They did, Mother.'

'That's good. Well they won't know you when they see you this afternoon.'

Benny's heart soared. 'Will I be getting dressed, like in anything new, before the party?'

'I think so. I think we'll have you looking like the bee's knees before they come in.'

'Will I put it on now?'

'Why not?' Benny's mother seemed excited about seeing

the new outfit herself. 'I'll just lay it out for you above. Come up and give yourself a bit of a wash and we'll put it on.'

Benny stood patiently in the big bathroom while the back of her neck was washed. It wouldn't be long now.

Then she was led into her bedroom.

'Close your eyes,' said Mother.

When Benny opened them she saw on the bed a thick navy skirt, a Fair Isle jumper in navy and red. A big sturdy pair of navy shoes lay in their box and chunky white socks folded nice and neatly beside them. Peeping out of tissue paper was a small red shoulder bag.

'It's an entire outfit,' cried Mother. 'Dressed from head to foot by Peggy Pine . . .'

Mother stood back to see the effect of the gift.

Benny was wordless. No velvet dress, no lovely soft crushed velvet that you could stroke, with its beautiful lacy trim. Only horrible harsh rough things like horse hair. Nothing in a misty pink, but instead good plain sensible colours. And the shoes! Where were the pumps with the pointed toes?

Benny bit her lip and willed the tears back into her eyes.

'Well, what do you think?' Her mother was beaming proudly. 'Your father said you must have the handbag and the shoes as well, it would make it a real outfit. He said that going into double figures must be marked.'

'It's lovely,' Benny muttered.

'Isn't the jumper perfect? I'd been asking Peggy to get something like that for ages. I said I didn't want anything shoddy . . . something strong that would stand up to a bit of rough and tumble.'

'It's gorgeous,' Benny said.

'Feel it,' her mother urged.

She didn't want to. Not while she still had the velvet feel in her mind.

'I'll put it on myself, Mother, then I'll come and show you,' she said.

She was holding on by a thread.

Fortunately, Annabel Hogan needed to go and supervise the shaking of hundreds and thousands on the trifle. She was just heading off downstairs when the telephone rang. 'That'll be your father.' She sounded pleased and her step was quicker on the stair.

Through her sobs which she choked into the pillow, Benny heard snatches of the conversation.

'She loved it, Eddie, you know I think it was almost too much for her, she couldn't seem to take it all in, *so* many things, a bag and shoes, and socks, on top of everything. A child of that age isn't used to getting all that much at once. No, not yet, she's putting it on. It'll look fine on her . . .'

Slowly Benny got off her bed and went over to the mirror on the wardrobe to see if her face looked as red and tearstained as she feared. She saw the chunky figure of a child in vest and knickers, neck red from scrubbing, eyes red from weeping. She was not a person that anyone would ever dream of putting in a pink velvet dress and little pumps with pointed toes. For no reason at all she remembered Eve Malone. She remembered her small earnest face warning her not to think about the dress from Dublin too much.

Perhaps Eve knew all the time, maybe she had been in the shop when Mother was buying all this . . . all this horrible stuff. How awful that Eve knew before she did. And yet Eve had never had anything new, she knew that whatever dress *she* got for today would be a reject. She remembered the way Eve had said 'They got you something new anyway'. She would never let them guess how disappointed she was. Never.

The rest of the day wasn't very clear to Benny because of the heavy cloud of disappointment that seemed to hang over the whole proceedings. For her anyway. She remembered making the right sounds and moving like a puppet as the party began. Maire Carroll arrived wearing a proper party dress. It had an underskirt that rustled. It had come from America in a parcel.

There were games with a prize for everyone. Benny's mother had bought cones of sweets in Birdie Mac's shop, each one wrapped in different-coloured paper. They were all getting noisy but the cake had to be delayed until Mr Hogan returned from the shop.

They heard the angelus ringing. The deep sound of the bells rolled through Knockglen twice a day, at noon and at six in the evening, great timekeepers as much as reminders to pray. But there was no sign of Benny's father.

'I hope he wasn't delayed rameishing on with some

customer today of all days,' Benny heard her mother say to Patsy.

'Not at all, Mam. He must be on his way. Shep got up and gave himself a good stretch. It's always a sign that the master is heading home to us.'

And indeed he was. Half a minute later Benny's father came in full of anxiety.

'I haven't missed it, we're not too late?'

He was patted down and given a cup of tea and a sausage roll to bolster him up while the children were gathered and the room darkened in anticipation.

Benny tried not to feel the rough wool of the jumper at her neck. She tried to smile a real smile at her father, who had run down the town to be here for the big moment.

'Do you like your outfit . . . your first entire outfit?' he called over to her.

'It's lovely, Father, lovely. Do you see I'm wearing it all.'

The other children in Knockglen used to giggle at Benny for saying 'Father'. They used to call their fathers Daddy or Da. But by now they were used to it. It was part of the way things were. Benny was the only one they knew without brothers and sisters, most of them had to share a Mam and a Dad with five or six others. An only child was a rare occurrence. In fact they didn't know any, except for Benny. And Eve Malone of course. But that was different. She had no family at all.

Eve was standing near Benny as the cake came in.

'Imagine that's all for you,' she whispered in awe.

Eve wore a dress that was several sizes too big for her. Sister Imelda, the only nun in the convent who was good with the needle, had been in her sick bed so a very poor job had been done on taking up the hem. The rest of it hung around her like a curtain.

The only thing in its favour was that it was red and obviously new. There was no way that it could be admired or praised, but Eve Malone seemed to have risen above this. Something about the way she stood in the large unwieldy garment gave Benny courage. At least her horrible outfit fitted her, and though it was far from being a party dress, let alone the dress of her dreams, it was reasonable, unlike Eve's. She put her shoulders back and smiled suddenly at the smaller girl.

'I'll give you some of the cake to take back if there's any left over,' she said.

'Thanks. Mother Francis loves a slice of cake,' Eve said.

Then it was there, the blurry light of the candles and the singing Happy Birthday and the big whoosh . . . and the clapping, and when the curtains were open again Benny saw the thin young man that her father had been shaking hands with. He was far too old for the party. They must have brought him back to tea with the grown-ups who would come later. He was very thin and pale, and he had a cold hard stare in his eyes.

'Who was he?' Eve asked Benny on Monday.

'He's the new assistant come to work with my father in the shop.'

'He's awful, isn't he?'

They were friends now, sitting on a schoolyard wall together at break.

'Yes, he is. There's something wrong with his eyes, I think.'

'What's his name?' Eve asked.

'Sean. Sean Walsh. He's going to live in the shop.'

'Ugh!' said Eve. 'Will he go to your house for meals?'

'No, that's the great thing. He won't. Mother asked him to come to Sunday lunch and he made some awful speech about not assuming, or something.'

'Presuming.'

'Yes, well whatever it is he's not going to do it and it seems to mean coming to meals. He'll fend for himself he said.'

'Good.' Eve approved of that.

Benny spoke hesitantly. 'Mother said . . .'

'Yes?'

'If you'd like to come any time . . . that would be . . . it would be all right.'

Benny spoke gruffly as if fearing the invitation would be spurned.

'Oh, I'd like that,' Eve said.

'Like to tea on an ordinary day, or maybe midday dinner on a Saturday or Sunday.'

'I'd love Sunday. It's a bit quiet here on Sundays, a lot of praying, you see.'

'Right, I'll tell her.' Benny's brow had cleared.

'Oh, there is one thing though . . .'

'What is it?' Benny didn't like the intense look on Eve's face.

'I won't be able to ask you back. Where they eat and I eat, it's beyond the curtain, you see.'

'That doesn't matter at all.' Benny was relieved that this was the only obstacle.

'Of course, when I'm grown up and have my own place, you know, my cottage, I could ask you there,' Eve said earnestly.

'Is it really your cottage?'

'I told everyone.' Eve was belligerent.

'I thought it might only be a pretend cottage,' Benny said apologetically.

'How could it be pretend? It's mine. I was born there. It belonged to my mother and my father. They're both dead, it's mine.'

'Why can't you go there now?'

'I don't know. They think I'm too young to live on my own.'

'Well, of course you're too young to live on your own,' Benny said. 'But to visit?'

'Mother Francis said it was sort of serious, my own place, my inheritance she calls it. She says I shouldn't be treating it as a doll's house, a playing place when I'm young.'

They thought about it for a while.

'Maybe she's right,' Benny said grudgingly.

'She could be.'

'Have you looked in the windows?'

'Yes.'

'Nobody's gone and messed it all up on you?'

'No, nobody goes there at all.'

'Why's that? It's got a lovely view down over the quarry.'

'They're afraid to go there. People died there.'

'People die everywhere.' Benny shrugged.

This pleased Eve. 'That's true. I hadn't thought of that.'

'So who died in the cottage?'

'My mother. And then a bit later my father.'

'Oh.'

Benny didn't know what to say. This was the first time Eve had ever talked about her life. Usually she flashed back with a Mind Your Own Business, if anyone asked her a question.

'But they're not in the cottage, they're in Heaven now,' Benny said eventually.

'Yes, of course.'

There seemed to be another impasse.

'I'd love to go and look through the window with you some time,' Benny offered.

Eve was about to reply when Maire Carroll came by.

'That was a nice party, Benny,' she said.

'Thanks.'

'I didn't know it was meant to be fancy dress though.'

'What do you mean?' Benny asked.

'Well, Eve was in fancy dress, weren't you, Eve? I mean that big red thing, that wasn't meant to be ordinary clothes, was it?'

Eve's face tightened into that hard look that she used to have before. Benny hated to see the expression come back.

'I thought it was quite funny myself,' Maire said with a little laugh. 'We all did when we were coming home.'

Benny looked around the schoolyard. Mother Francis was looking the other way.

With all her strength Benny Hogan launched herself off the wall down on Maire Carroll. The girl fell over, winded.

'Are you all right, Maire?' Benny asked in a falsely sympathetic tone.

Mother Francis came running, her habit streaming behind her.

'What happened, child?' She was struggling to get Maire's breath back, and raise her to her feet.

'Benny pushed me . . .' Maire gasped.

'Mother, I'm sorry, I'm so clumsy, I was just getting off the wall.'

'All right, all right, no bones broken. Get her a stool.' Mother Francis dealt with the panting Maire.

'She did it purposely.'

'Shush, shush, Maire. Here's a little stool for you, sit down now.'

Maire was crying. 'Mother, she just jumped down from the wall on me like a ton of bricks . . . I was only saying . . .'

'Maire was telling me how much she liked the party, Mother. I'm so sorry,' Benny said.

'Yes, well Benny, try to be more careful. Don't throw yourself around so much. Now, Maire, enough of this whining. It's not a bit nice. Benny has said she was sorry. You know it was an accident. Come along now and be a big girl.'

'I'd never want to be as big a girl as Benny Hogan. No one would.'

Mother Francis was cross now. 'That's quite enough, Maire Carroll. Quite enough. Take that stool and go inside to the cloakroom and sit there until you're called by me to come away from it.'

Mother Francis swept away. And as they all knew she would, she rang the bell for the end of break.

Eve looked at Benny. For a moment she said nothing, she just swallowed as if there were a lump in her throat.

Benny was equally at a loss, she just shrugged and spread out her hands helplessly.

Suddenly Eve grasped her hand. 'Some day, when I'm big and strong, I'll knock someone down for you,' she said. 'I mean it, I really will.'

'Tell me about Eve's mother and father,' Benny asked that night.

'Ah, that's all long ago now,' her father said.

'But I don't know it. I wasn't there.'

'No point in raking over all that.'

'She's my friend. I want to know about her.'

'She used not to be your friend. I had to plead with you to let her come to the party,' Mother said.

'No, that's not the way it was.' Benny couldn't believe now that this was so.

'I'm glad that child's coming here to dinner on Sunday,' Eddie Hogan said. 'I wish we could persuade that young skinnymalinks above in the shop to come too, but he's determined not to trespass, as he calls it.'

Benny was pleased to hear that.

'Is he working out well, Eddie?'

'The best you ever saw, love. We'll be blessed with him, I tell you. He's so eager to learn he almost quivers like Shep there, he repeats everything over and over again, as if he's learning it off by heart.'

'Does Mike like him?' Benny's mother wanted to know.

'Ah, you know Mike, he likes nobody.'

'What does he object to?'

'The way Sean keeps the books. God, it's simple to understand, a child could do it, but old Mike has to put up a resistance to everything. Mike says he knows everyone's measurements, and what they paid and what they owed. He thinks it's like a kind of insult to his powers to write things down.'

'Couldn't you keep the books, Mother?' Benny suggested suddenly.

'No, no, I'd not be able to.'

'But if it's as simple as Father says . . .'

'She'd well be able to but your mother has to be here, this is our home, she runs it for you and me, Benny.'

'Patsy could run it. Then you wouldn't have to pay Sean.'

'Nonsense, Benny,' her father said.

But she wasn't to be stopped. 'Why not? Mike would like Mother being in there. Mike loves Mother, and it would be something for Mother to do all day.'

They both laughed.

'Isn't it great to be a child?' said her father.

'To think that the day isn't full already,' agreed her mother.

Benny knew very well that her mother's day was far from full. She thought that it might be nice for Mother to be involved in the shop, but obviously they weren't going to listen to her.

'How did Eve's parents die?' she asked.

'It's not a thing to be talking about.'

'Why? Were they murdered?'

'Of course not.' Her mother sounded impatient.

'Why then . . . ?'

'Lord, why, why, why,' her father sighed.

'At school they're always telling us to ask why. Mother Francis says that if you have a questioning mind you get to know all the answers.' Benny was triumphant.

'Her mother died giving birth, when Eve was being born. And then a bit later, her poor father, may the Lord have mercy on him, went out one evening with his wits scattered and fell over the cliff into the quarry.'

'Wasn't that desperate!' Benny's eyes were round with horror.

'So, it's a sad story, all over long ago, nearly ten years ago. We don't start bringing it all up over and over.'

'But there's more to it, isn't there . . . there's a kind of secret.'

'Not really.' Her father's eyes were honest. 'Her mother was a very wealthy woman, and her father was a kind of handyman who helped out in the convent, and did a bit of work up at Westlands. That caused a bit of talk at the time.'

'But it's not a secret or a scandal or anything.' Annabel Hogan's face was set in warning lines. 'They were married and everything in the Catholic Church.'

Benny could see the shutters coming down. She knew when to leave things.

Later she asked Patsy.

'Don't ask me things behind your parents' back.'

'I'm not. I asked them, and this is what they told me. I just wanted to know did you know any more. That's all.'

'It was before I came here, but I heard a bit from Bee Moore . . . Paccy's sister, she works above in Westlands you see.'

'What did you hear?'

'That Eve's father did a terrible act at the funeral, cursing and shouting . . .'

'Up in the church, cursing and shouting . . . !'

'Not *our* church, not the real church, in the Protestant church, but that was bad enough. You see Eve's mother was from Westlands – from the big house beyond. She was one of the family and poor Jack, that was the father, he thought they'd all treated her badly . . .'

'Go on.'

'That's all I know,' Patsy said. 'And don't be asking that poor child and upsetting her. People with no parents don't like endless questions.'

Benny took this as good advice not only about Eve, but about Patsy herself.

Mother Francis was delighted to see the new friendship developing, but far too old a hand in dealing with children to say so.

'Going down to the Hogans again are you?' she said, sounding slightly put out.

'Do you mind?' Eve asked.

'No, I don't mind. I can't say that I mind.' The nun tried hard to conceal her enthusiasm.

'It's not that I want to be away from here,' Eve said earnestly.

Mother Francis felt an urge to take the child in her arms as she used to do when Eve was a baby given into their care by the accident of her birth.

'No, no, of course, child. Strange though this place is, it is your home.'

'It's always been a lovely home.'

The nun's eyes filled with tears. 'Every convent should have a child. I don't know how we're going to arrange it,' she said lightly.

'I wasn't a nuisance when I arrived?'

'You were a blessing, you know that. It's been the best ten years St Mary's ever had . . . you being here.'

Mother Francis stood at a window and watched little

Eve go down the long avenue of the convent out to Sunday lunch on her own with the Hogans. She prayed that they would be kind to her, and that Benny wouldn't change and find a new friend.

She remembered the fights she had had to keep Eve in the first place, when so many other solutions were being offered. There was a cousin of the Westwards in England who would take the child, someone who would arrange Roman Catholic instruction once a week. The Healys who had come to start the hotel were reported to be having difficulty in starting a family. They would be happy to have Eve in their home, even after their own children came along, if they did. But Mother Francis had fought like a tiger for that small bundle that she had rescued from the cottage, on the day she was born. The child they had reared until some solution could be found. Nobody had seen that Jack Malone's solution would involve throwing himself over the quarry one dark night. After that there had been no one with better claim to Eve than the nuns who had reared her.

It was the first of many Sunday dinners in Lisbeg for Eve. She loved coming to the house. Every week she brought something which she arranged in a vase. Mother Francis had shown her how to go up the long windy path behind the convent and pick leaves and wild flowers. At the start she would rehearse arranging them with the nun so that she would do it well when she got to the Hogans, but as the weeks went by she grew in confidence. She could bring armfuls of autumn colours and make a beautiful display on the hall table. It became a ritual. Patsy would have the vases ready to see what Eve would bring today.

'Don't you have a lovely house!' she would say wistfully and Annabel Hogan would smile, pleased, and congratulate herself on having brought these two together.

'How did you meet Mrs Hogan?' she would ask Benny's father. And 'Did you always want to run a business?' The kind of questions Benny never thought to ask but was always interested in the answers.

She had never known that her parents met at a tennis party in a county far away. She had never heard that Father had been apprenticed to another business in the town of Ballylee. Or that Mother had gone to Belgium for a year after she left school to teach English in a convent.

'You make my parents say very interesting things,' she said to Eve one afternoon as they sat in Benny's bedroom, and Eve marvelled over being allowed to use an electric fire all for themselves.

'Well, they've got great stories like olden times.'

'Yes . . .' Benny was doubtful.

'You see, the nuns don't have.'

'They must have. Surely. They can't have forgotten,' Benny said.

'But they're not meant to think about the past, you know, and life before Entering, they really start from when they became Brides of Christ. They don't have stories of olden days like your mother and father do.'

'Would they like you to be a nun too?' Benny asked.

'No, Mother Francis said that they wouldn't take me, even if I did want to be a nun, until I was over twenty-one.'

'Why's that?'

'She says it's the only life I know, and I might want to join just because of that. She says when I leave school I have to go out and get a job for at least three years before I even think of Entering.'

'Wasn't it lucky you met up with them?' Benny said.

'Yes. Yes, it was.'

'I don't mean lucky that your mother and father died, but if they had to wasn't it great you didn't go somewhere awful?'

'Like in stories with wicked stepmothers,' Eve agreed.

'I wonder why they got you. Nuns usually don't get children unless it's an orphanage.'

'My father worked for them. They sent him up to Westlands to earn some money because they couldn't pay him much. That's where he met my mother. They feel responsible, I think.'

Benny was dying to know more. But she remembered Patsy's advice.

'Well, it all turned out fine, they're mad about you up there.'

'Your parents are mad about you too.'

'It's a bit hard sometimes, like if you want to wander off.'

'It is for me too,' Eve said. 'Not much wandering off above in the convent.'

'It'll be different when we're older.'

'It mightn't be,' Eve said sagely.

'What do you mean?'

'I mean, we have to show them we're terribly trustworthy or something, show them that if we *are* allowed to wander off, we'll wander back in good time.'

'How could we show them?' Benny was eager.

'I don't know. Something simple at the start. Could you ask me to stay the night here, for one thing?'

'Of course I could.'

'Then I could show Mother Francis that I'd be back up in the convent in time for Mass in the chapel, and she'd get to know I was to be relied on.'

'Mass on a weekday?'

'Every day. At seven.'

'No!'

'It's quite nice. The nuns sing beautifully, it's nice and peaceful. Really I don't mind it. Father Ross comes in specially and he gets a lovely breakfast in the parlour. He says the other priests envy him.'

'I didn't know that . . . every day.'

'You won't tell anyone will you?'

'No. Is it a secret?'

'Not a bit, it's just that I *don't* tell anything, you see, and the Community likes that, they feel I'm part of them. I didn't have a friend before. There wasn't anyone to tell.'

Benny smiled from ear to ear. 'What night will you come? Wednesday night?'

*

'I don't know, Eve. You don't have any smart pyjamas or anything to be going to stay with people. You don't have a good sponge bag, things that people who go visiting need.'

'My pyjamas are fine, Mother.'

'You could iron them, certainly, and you have a dressing gown.' She seemed to be faltering. 'A sponge bag though?'

'Could Sister Imelda make one for me? I'll do extra clearing up for her.'

'And what time will you come back?'

'I'll be at my prie-dieu in time for Mass, Mother.'

'You won't want to get up that early if you're visiting people.' Mother Francis's face was soft.

'That's what I'd want, Mother.'

It was a great evening. They played rummy with Patsy in the kitchen for a long time because Mother and Father went across the road to Dr and Mrs Johnson's house. It was a supper to celebrate the christening of their new baby.

Eve asked Patsy all about the orphanage, and Patsy told more details than she had ever told Benny. She explained how they used to steal food, and how hard it was when she came to the Hogans, her first job, to realise she didn't have to take any stray biscuit or a fistful of sugar and put it into her apron.

In bed that night Benny said in wonder, 'I don't know why Patsy told us all that. Only the other day she was saying to me that people with no parents didn't like being asked questions.'

'Ah, it's different with me,' Eve said. 'I'm in the same boat.'

'No you're not!' Benny was indignant. 'Patsy had nothing. She had to work in that awful place and get nits and steal and be beaten for wetting the bed. She had to leave there at fifteen and come here. It's not a bit like you.'

'No. We are the same, she has no family, I don't. She didn't have a home like you do.'

'Is that why you told her more than you told me?' Benny had been even more astounded at the questions Patsy felt free to ask. Did Eve hate the Westwards who were so rich for not taking her into the big house? Eve didn't, they couldn't, they were Protestants, she explained. Lots more, things Benny wouldn't have dared to ask.

'You don't ask things like that,' Eve said simply.

'I'd be afraid of upsetting you,' Benny said.

'You couldn't upset a friend,' Eve said.

Benny and Eve, who had lived all their lives in the same village, were each amazed at the things the other didn't know about Knockglen.

Benny didn't know that the three priests who lived in the presbytery had been given the game of Scrabble, which they played every night, and sometimes rang the convent to ask Mother Francis questions like how you spelt 'quixotic' because Father O'Brien was going to get a triple word score.

Eve hadn't known that Mr Burns in the hardware shop was inclined to take to the drink or that Dr Johnson had a very bad temper and was heard shouting about God never putting a mouth into the world that he didn't feed. Dr Johnson was of the view that there were a lot of mouths, especially in the families with thirteen children, that God had forgotten to feed.

Benny didn't know that Peggy Pine was an old friend of Mother Francis, that they had been girls years ago and that when she came to the convent she called Mother Francis Bunty.

Eve hadn't known that Birdie Mac who ran the sweet shop had a man from Ballylee who had been calling for fifteen years, but she wouldn't leave her old mother and the man from Ballylee wouldn't come to Knockglen.

It made the town far more interesting to both of them to have such insights. Particularly because they knew these were dark secrets not to be shared with anyone. They pooled their knowledge on how children were born, and hadn't any new enlightenments to offer. They both knew that they came out like kittens, they didn't know how they got in.

'It's got something to do with lying down one beside the other, when you're married,' Eve said.

'It couldn't happen if you weren't married. Suppose you fell down beside someone like Dessie Burns.' Benny was worried.

'No, you have to be married.' Eve knew that for certain.

'And how would it get in?' It was a mystery.

'It could be your Little Mary,' Benny said thoughtfully.

'What's your Little Mary?'

'The bit in the middle of your tummy.'

'Oh, your tummy button is what Mother Francis calls it.'

'That must be it,' Benny cried triumphantly. 'If they all have different names for it, that must be the secret.'

They practised hard at being reliable. If either said she would be home at six o'clock then five minutes before the hour struck and the angelus rang she would be back in place. As Eve had anticipated, it did win them much more freedom. They didn't allow their hysterical laughing fits to be seen in public.

They pressed their noses against the window of Healy's Hotel. They didn't like Mrs Healy. She was very superior. She walked as if she were a queen. She always seemed to look down on children.

Benny heard from Patsy that the Healys had been up to Dublin to look for a child to adopt but they hadn't got one because Mr Healy had a weak chest.

'Just as well,' Eve had said unsympathetically. 'They'd be terrible for anyone as a mother and father.' She spoke in innocence of the fact that Knockglen had once thought that she herself might be the ideal child for them.

Mr Healy was much older than his wife. It was whispered, Patsy said, that he couldn't cut the mustard. Eve and Benny spent long hours trying to work out what this could mean. Mustard came in a small tin and you mixed it with water. How did you cut it? Why should you cut it?

Mrs Healy looked a hundred but apparently she was twenty-seven. She had married at seventeen and was busy throwing all her efforts into the hotel since there were no children.

Together they explored places where they had never gone alone. To Flood's, the butchers, hoping they might see the animals being killed.

'We don't really want to see them being killed do we?' Benny asked fearfully.

'No, but we'd like to be there at the beginning so that we could if we want to, then run away,' Eve explained. Mr Flood wouldn't let them near his yard so the matter didn't arise.

They stood and watched the Italian from Italy come and start up his fish and chip shop.

'Weel you leetle girls come here every day and buy my feesh?' he asked hopefully of the two earnest children, one big, one small, who stood watching his every move.

'No, I don't think we'll be allowed,' Eve said sadly.

'Why is that?'

'It would be called throwing away good money,' Benny said.

'And talking to foreign men,' Eve explained to clinch matters.

'My seester is married to a Dublin man,' Mario explained.

'We'll let people know,' Eve said solemnly.

*

35

Sometimes they went to the harness maker. A very handsome man on a horse came one day to enquire about a bridle that should have been ready, but wasn't.

Dekko Moore was a cousin of Paccy Moore's in the shoe shop. He was very apologetic, and looked as if he might be taken away and hanged for the delay.

The man turned his horse swiftly. 'All right. Will you bring it up to the house tomorrow, instead?' he shouted.

'Indeed I will sir, thank you sir. I'm very sorry sir. Indeed sir.' Dekko Moore sounded like a villain who had been unmasked in a pantomime.

'Lord, who was that, I wonder?' Benny was amazed. Dekko was almost dead with relief at how lightly he had escaped.

'That was Mr Simon Westward,' Dekko said, mopping his brow.

'I thought it must be,' Eve said grimly.

Sometimes they went into Hogan's Gentleman's Outfitters. Father always made a huge fuss of them. So did old Mike, and anyone else who happened to be in the shop.

'Will you work here when you're old?' Eve had whispered.

'I don't think so. It'll have to be a boy, won't it?'

'I don't see why,' Eve had said.

'Well, measuring men, putting tape measures round their waists, and all.'

They giggled.

36

'But you're the boss's daughter, you wouldn't be doing that. You'd just be coming in shouting at people, like Mrs Healy does over in the hotel.'

'Um.' Benny was doubtful. 'Wouldn't I need to know what to shout about?'

'You could learn. Otherwise Droopy Drawers will take over.'

That's what they called Sean Walsh, who seemed to have become paler, thinner and harder of the eye since his arrival.

'No, he won't, surely?'

'You could marry him.'

'Ugh. Ugh. Ugh.'

'And have lots of children by putting your belly button beside his.'

'Oh, Eve, I'd hate that. I think I'll be a nun.'

'I think I will too. It would be much easier. You can go any day you like, lucky old thing. I have to wait until I'm twenty-one.' Eve was disconsolate.

'Maybe she'd let you enter with me, if she knew it was a true vocation.' Benny was hopeful.

Her father had run out of the shop and now he was back with two lollipops. He handed them one each proudly.

'We're honoured to have you ladies in our humble premises,' he said, so that everyone could hear him.

Soon everyone in Knockglen thought of them as a pair. The big stocky figure of Benny Hogan in her strong shoes and tightly buttoned sensible coat, the waif-like Eve in the clothes that were always too long and streelish on her. Together they watched the setting up of the town's first fish and chip shop, they saw the decline of Mr Healy in the hotel and stood side by side on the day that he was taken to the sanatorium. Together they were unconquerable. There was never an ill-considered remark made about either of them.

When Birdie Mac in the sweet shop was unwise enough to say to Benny that those slabs of toffee were doing her no good at all, Eve's small face flashed in a fury.

'If you worry so much about things, Miss Mac, then why do you sell them at all?' she asked in tones that knew there could be no answer.

When Maire Carroll's mother said thoughtfully to Eve, 'Do you know I always ask myself why a sensible woman like Mother Francis would let you out on the street looking like Little Orphan Annie,' Benny's brow darkened.

'I'll tell Mother Francis you wanted to know,' Benny had said quickly. 'Mother Francis says we should have enquiring minds, that everyone should ask.'

Before Mrs Carroll could stop her Benny had galloped out of the shop and up the road towards the convent.

'Oh, Mam, you've done it now,' Maire Carroll moaned. 'Mother Francis will be down on us like a ton of bricks.'

And she was. The full fiery rage of the nun was something that Mrs Carroll had not expected and never wanted to know again.

None of these things upset either Eve or Benny in the slightest. It was easy to cope with Knockglen when you had a friend.

## 2

*1957*

There hadn't been many teddy boys in Knockglen, in fact no one could ever remember having seen one except on visits to Dublin where there were groups of them hanging round corners. Benny and Eve were in the window of Healy's Hotel practising having cups of coffee so that they would look well accustomed to it when they got to the Dublin coffee houses.

They saw him pass by, jaunty and confident in his drainpipe trousers, his long jacket with velvet cuffs and collar. His legs looked like spider legs and his shoes seemed enormous. He seemed oblivious of the stares of the whole town. Only when he saw the two girls actually standing up to peer at him past the curtains of Healy's window did he show any reaction. He gave them a huge grin and blew them a kiss.

Confused and annoyed they sat down hastily. It was one thing to look, another to call attention to themselves.

Making a show of yourself was high on the list of sins in Knockglen. Benny knew this very well. Anyone could have been looking out the window seeing them being cheap with the teddy boy. Her father maybe, with the tape around his neck, awful sleeveen Sean Walsh, who never said a word without thinking carefully of the possible effect it might have. He could have been looking. Or old Mike, who had called her father Mr Eddie for years, and saw no reason to change.

And indeed everyone in Knockglen knew Eve as well. It had long been the nuns' ambition that Eve Malone be thought of as a lady. She had even joined in the game herself. Eve didn't want it to get back to the convent that she was trick acting in Healy's Hotel and ogling teddy boys out of the window. While other girls with real mothers resisted all the attempts to gentrify themselves, Eve and Mother Francis studied books on etiquette and looked at magazines to see how nice people dressed, and to pick up any hints on behaviour.

'I don't want you to put on an artificial accent,' Mother Francis had warned, 'nor do I want you sticking out your little finger when you're drinking tea.'

'Who are we trying to impress?' Eve had asked once.

'No, look at it the other way. It's who you're trying not to let down. We were told we were mad and we couldn't rear you. It's a bit of human, non-saintly desire to be able to say "I told you so" to the begrudgers.'

Eve had understood that immediately. And there was always hope that the Westward family would see her one day as an elegant lady and be sorry they hadn't kept in touch with the child who was after all their own flesh and blood.

Mrs Healy approached them. A widow now, formidable as she had always been, she managed to exude disapproval at fifty yards. She could not find any reason why Benny Hogan from the shop across the road and Eve Malone from the convent up the town should not sit and drink coffee in her bay window, but somehow she would have preferred to keep the space for wealthier and more important matrons of Knockglen.

She sailed towards the window. 'I'll adjust the curtains – they seem to have got all rucked up,' she said.

Eve and Benny exchanged glances. There was nothing wrong with the heavy net curtains of Healy's Hotel. They were as they always were: thick enough to conceal those within while giving a perfect view out.

'Well, isn't that a terrible poor ibex!' exclaimed Mrs Healy, having identified easily what the girls had been looking at.

'I suppose it's only his clothes really,' Eve said in a sanctimonious tone. 'Mother Francis always says it's a pity to judge people by the garments they wear.'

'Very admirable of her,' snapped Mrs Healy, 'but of course she makes sure that the garments of all you pupils are in order. Mother Francis is always the first to judge you girls by the uniforms you wear.'

'Not any more, Mrs Healy,' Benny said happily. 'I dyed my grey school skirt dark red.'

'And I dyed mine black, and my grey jumper purple,' Eve said.

'Very colourful.' Mrs Healy moved away like a ship under full sail.

'She can't bear us being grown up,' Eve hissed. 'She wants to tell us to sit up straight and not to put our fingers on the nice furniture.'

'She knows we don't feel grown up,' Benny said gloomily. 'And if awful Mrs Healy knows then everyone in Dublin will know.'

It was a problem. Mr Flood the butcher had looked at them very strangely as they walked up the street. His eyes seemed to burn through them in disapproval. If people like that could see their awkwardness, they were indeed in a bad way.

'We should have a rehearsal – you know, go up for a couple of days ahead of everyone else so we won't look like eejits.' Eve was hopeful.

'It's hard enough to get up there when we have to. There's no point in asking to go up there in order to waltz around a bit. Can you see them agreeing to that for me at home?'

'We wouldn't call it waltzing around,' Eve said. 'We'd call it something else.'

'Like what?'

Eve thought hard. 'In your case, getting books listed and timetables – there's endless things you could say.' Her voice sounded suddenly small and sad.

For the first time Benny realised properly that they were

43

going to live separate lives though in the same city. Best friends from the age of ten, now they would go down different roads.

Benny was going to be able to go to University College, Dublin, to study for a BA degree because her parents had saved to pay for her. There was no money in St Mary's Convent to send Eve Malone to university. Mother Francis had strained the convent's finances already to provide secondary education for the daughter of Jack Malone and Sarah Westward. Now she would be sent to a convent of the same order in Dublin where she would do a secretarial course. Her tuition fees would be waived in exchange for some light housework.

'I wish to God you were coming to college, too,' Benny said suddenly.

'I know. Don't say it like that, don't let your voice get drippy or I'll get upset.' Eve spoke sharply, but without harshness.

'Everyone keeps saying that it's great, we have each other, but I'd see more of you if you were still in Knockglen,' Benny complained. 'Your place is miles across the city, and I have to come home on the bus every night, so there'll be no meeting in the evenings.'

'I don't think there's much of the night life planned for me either,' Eve said doubtfully. 'A few miles of convent floor to polish, a few million sheets to hem. A couple of tons of potatoes to peel.'

'They won't make you do that!' Benny was horrified.

'Who knows what light housework means? One nun's

light could be another nun's penal servitude.'

'You'll need to know in advance, won't you?' Benny was distressed for her friend.

'I'm not in much of a position to negotiate,' Eve said.

'But they never asked you to do anything like that here.' Benny nodded her head up in the direction of the convent at the end of the town.

'But that's different. This is my home,' Eve said simply. 'I mean, this is where I live, where I'll always live.'

'You'll be able to get a flat and all when you get a job.' Benny sounded wistful. She didn't think she would ever see freedom.

'Oh yes, I'm sure I'll get a flat, but I'll come back to St Mary's, like other people come home from flats on holidays,' Eve said.

Eve was always so definite, Benny thought with admiration. So small and determined with her short dark hair and white elfin face. No one had ever dared to say that there was anything different or even unusual about Eve living in the convent, sharing her life with the Community. She was never asked about what life was like beyond the curtain where the nuns went, and she never told. The girls also knew that no tales would be told of their own doings. Eve Malone was nobody's spy.

Benny didn't know how she was going to manage without her. Eve had been there for as long as she remembered to help her fight her battles. To deal with the jibes of those who called her Big Ben. Eve had made short work of anyone who took advantage of Benny's gentle ways.

They had been a team for years: the tiny wiry Eve with her restless eyes never settling long on anything or anyone; the big handsome Benny, with her green eyes and chestnut-brown hair, tied back with a bow always, a big soft good-quality bow a bit like Benny herself.

If there had only been some way they could have gone in the doors of University College together and come home on the bus each night, or better still got a flat together, life would have been perfect. But Benny had not grown up expecting life to be totally perfect. Surely it was enough to have got as much as she had.

Annabel Hogan was wondering whether to change the main meal of the day to the evening. There were a lot of arguments for this and a lot against.

Eddie was used to his dinner in the middle of the day. He walked back from the shop and the plate of meat and potatoes was put in front of him with a regularity that would have pleased an army officer. As soon as Shep started his languid stroll out to meet the master at the turn of the road, Patsy began to heat the plates. Mr Hogan would wash his hands in the downstairs cloakroom and always profess pleasure at the lamb chops, the bacon and cabbage, or the plate of cod and parsley sauce on a Friday. Wouldn't it be a poor thing to have the man close his shop and walk back for a kind of half-hearted snack. Maybe it might even affect his work and he wouldn't be able to concentrate in the afternoon.

But then think of Benny coming back from Dublin after

a day in the university: wouldn't it be better if they saved the main meal for her return?

Neither husband nor daughter had been any help. They both said it didn't matter. As usual the burden of the whole house fell on herself and Patsy.

The meat tea was probably the answer. A big slice of ham, or grilled bacon, or a few sausages, and they could put a few extra on Benny's plate in case she felt the need of it. Annabel could hardly believe that she had a daughter about to go to university. Not that she wasn't old enough – she was well old enough to have seen a family through university. She had married late, at a time she had almost given up hope of finding a husband. She had given birth at a time when she thought miscarriages would be all she ever knew.

Annabel Hogan walked around her house: there was always some little thing to be done. Patsy was in the big, warm kitchen, the table covered with flour and crockery, but it would all be swept away and scrubbed by meal time.

Lisbeg was not a big house, but there was plenty to do in it. There were three bedrooms and a bathroom upstairs. The master bedroom looked out over one side of the front door and Benny's bedroom was on the other. At the back of the house, the dark spare room and the big, old-fashioned bathroom with its noisy pipes and its huge wood-surrounded bath.

Downstairs if you came in the front door (which people rarely did) you would find a large room on each side. They were hardly ever used. The Hogans lived in the back of the house, in the big shabby breakfast room that opened off the kitchen. There was hardly ever a need to light a fire in the breakfast room because the great heat of the range came through. There was a big double door kept permanently open between the two rooms, and it was as comfortable a place as you could imagine.

They rarely had visitors, and if ever anyone was expected the front drawing room in its pale greens and pinks with damp spots over the wall could be aired and dusted. But in the main, the breakfast room was their home.

It had three big red plush armchairs, and the table against the wall had three dining chairs with plush seats as well. A huge radio stood on the big sideboard, and shelves of ornaments, and good china and old books were fixed precariously to the wall.

Now that young Eve had become such a regular guest in the household, a fourth chair had been found, a cane chair rescued from one of the sheds. Patsy had tied a nice red cushion to it.

Patsy herself slept in a small room beyond the kitchen. It was dark and had a tiny window. Patsy had always told Mrs Hogan that it was like being dead and going to Heaven to have a room of your own. She had always had to share with at least two other people until the day she came to Lisbeg.

When Patsy had walked up the short avenue and looked at the square house with its creeper and its shabby garden it seemed to her like a house on the front of a calendar.

Her small room looked out on the back yard, and she had a window box. Things didn't grow very well in it because it was in shadow and Patsy wasn't much of a gardener, but it was her own, and nobody ever touched it, any more than they ever went into her room.

Patsy was as excited as any of them about Benny going to university. Every year on her annual holidays, Patsy paid a dutiful visit of one half day to the orphanage which had reared her, and then she went to stay with a friend who had married in Dublin. She had asked her friend to take her to see where Benny would be a student. She had stood outside the huge pillars of University College, Dublin, and looked at it all with satisfaction. Now she would know where Benny went and studied; she would know the look of the place.

And indeed it was a big step for Benny, Annabel Hogan realised. No more safe trotting to and fro from the convent. It was life in the big city with several thousand other students from all kinds of places, with different ways and no one to force you to study like Mother Francis. It was not surprising that Benny had been as excited as a hen walking on hot coals all summer long, never able to keep still, always jumping up with some further excitement.

It was a relief to know that she was with Eve Malone for the morning, those two could talk until the cows came home. Annabel wished that there had been some way young Eve could have been sent to university too. It would have made things more fair somehow. But things rarely turned out nice and neatly in this life. Annabel had said as much to Father Ross the last time he had come to tea, and Father Ross had looked at her sternly over his glasses, saying that if we all understood the way the Universe was run what would there be left for God to tell us on the Last Day.

To herself Annabel thought that it wouldn't interfere with the running of the Universe if enough money could be found somewhere for the university fees and accommodation for Eve Malone, the child who had no home except the big bleak convent with the heavy iron gates.

Mother Francis had asked God very often for a way to send Eve Malone to university but so far God had not seen fit to show her one. Mother Francis knew it must be part of his divine plan, but at times she wondered had she prayed hard enough, had she examined every possibility. She had certainly been up every road as far as the Order was concerned. She had written to the Mother General, she had put Eve's case as persuasively as she could. The girl's father, Jack Malone, had worked all his life for the convent as handyman and gardener.

Jack had married the daughter of the Westward family, as unlikely a match as was ever known in the country, but necessary since a child was on the way. There had been no problem in having Eve brought up as a Catholic, since the Westwards had never wanted to know about her at all, and didn't care what faith she was raised in just as long as they never had to hear her name.

Mother General's view was that enough had been done for the child already. To provide a university education for her might mark her out as a favoured pupil. Would not others from needy backgrounds expect the same?

It had not stopped there. Mother Francis had taken the bus to their convent in Dublin and spoken to the very difficult Mother Clare who held sway there. With so many young nuns starting university education in the autumn and lodging in the Dublin convent was there not a chance that Eve might join them? The girl would be happy to do housework to earn her place among the students.

Mother Clare wouldn't even consider it. What an extraordinary suggestion, to put forward a girl – a charity child who was not a Sister, a novice, a postulant, nor anyone with the remotest intention of becoming a nun – and raise her up above the many Sisters in the Community who were all hoping and praying for a chance of higher education . . . what would they feel if a girl who had already been pampered, it seemed, by the convent in Knockglen, were put in to study, over their heads? It would be an outrage.

And perhaps it was outrageous of her, Mother Francis thought sometimes. It was just that she loved Eve as much as any mother could love a daughter. Mother Francis the celibate nun who had never thought she could know the joy of seeing a child grow up in her care had loved Eve in a way that might well have made her blind to the feelings and sensitivities of other people. Mother General and Mother Clare were indeed right, it would have been preferential treatment to have financed Eve's university education from the convent funds.

But when all was said and done, Mother Francis wished she could be sure that they would treat Eve well up in Mother Clare's convent. St Mary's had always been a home for Eve; the fear was that she might find the sister house in Dublin more like an institution, and worse still she might find her own role there not that of an honoured daughter, but more that of a maid.

When Benny and Eve came out of Healy's Hotel, they saw Sean Walsh watching them from the doorway of Hogan's across the street.

'If you keep talking to me he might think we haven't seen him,' Benny hissed out of the corner of her mouth.

'Not a chance. Look at him standing there with his thumbs in behind his braces, copying the way your father stands.'

Eve knew only too well Sean Walsh's expectations: he had a long-term career plan, to marry the daughter of the house, the heir to Hogan's Gentleman's Outfitters, and inherit the lot.

They had never been able to like Sean Walsh, not since the very first day he had turned up at Benny's tenth birthday party. He had never smiled. Not once in all those years had they seen a real smile on his face. There were a lot of grimaces, and a little dry bark sometimes, but never a laugh.

He didn't throw his head back like Peggy Pine did when she laughed, or giggle into his fist like Paccy Moore; he didn't make big gestures like Mario in the fish and chip shop, or even get wheezing and coughing fits like Dessie Burns often did. Sean Walsh seemed watchful the whole time. Only when he saw others smiling and laughing did he give the little barks.

They could never get him to tell anything about the life he had lived before he came to Knockglen. He didn't tell long stories like Patsy did, or wistful tales like Dekko Moore about the time he made harnesses for the Lords of the Soil somewhere down in Meath. Sean Walsh would not be drawn.

'Oh, dear, you don't want to hear my stories,' he would say when Benny and Eve plagued him for some information.

The years had not improved him: he was still secretive and insincerely anxious to please. Even his appearance annoyed Benny, although she knew this was unreasonable. He wore a suit that had seen a lot of pressing, and was obviously carefully looked after. Benny and Eve used to tell each other in fits of laughter that he spent hours in his little room above the shop pressing all his ambitions into the suit with a damp cloth.

Benny didn't really believe Eve about Sean having ambitions to marry into the shop, but there was something deeply unsettled all right about the way he looked at her. She had so much wanted to be fancied, it seemed a cruel blow to think that if it ever happened it might only be by someone as awful as Sean Walsh.

'Good morning, ladies.' He made an exaggerated bow. There was an insult in his voice, a sneer that he hadn't intended them to notice. Other people had called them 'ladies', even that very morning, and had done so without any offence. It was a way of acknowledging that they had left school and would shortly start a more grown-up life. When they had been in the chemist's buying shampoo, Mr Kennedy had asked what he could do for the two young ladies and they had been pleased. Paccy Moore had said they were two fine ladies when they had gone to have heels put on Benny's good shoes. But with Sean Walsh it was different.

'Hallo, Sean.' Benny's voice was lacklustre.

'Surveying the metropolis, I see,' he said loftily. He always spoke slightly disparagingly of Knockglen, even though the place he came from himself was smaller and even less like a metropolis. Benny felt a violent surge of annoyance.

'Well, you're a free agent,' she said suddenly. 'If you don't like Knockglen you could always go somewhere else.'

'Did I say I didn't like it?' His eyes were narrower than ever, almost slits. He had gauged this wrong, he must not allow her to report his having slighted the place. 'I was only making a pleasant remark comparing this place to the big city. Meaning that you'll have no time for us here at all soon.'

That had been the wrong thing too.

'I'll have little chance of forgetting all about Knockglen considering I'll be coming home every night,' said Benny glumly.

'And we wouldn't want to anyway,' Eve said with her chin stuck out. Sean Walsh would never know how often she and Benny bemoaned their fate living in such a small town which had the worst characteristic any town could have: it was actually within striking distance of Dublin.

Sean hardly ever let his glance fall on Eve, for she held no interest for him. All his remarks were directed to Benny. 'Your father is so proud of you, there's hardly a customer that he hasn't told about your great success.'

Benny hated his smile and his knowing ways. He must know how much she hated being told this, reminded about how she was the apple of their eye, and the centre of simple boastful conversation. And if he knew why did he tell her and annoy her still further? If he did have designs on her, and a plan to marry Mr Eddie Hogan's daughter and thereby marry into the business, then why was he saying all the things that would irritate and upset her?

Perhaps he thought that her own wishes would hardly be considered in the matter. That the biddable daughter of the house would give in on this as she had on everything else.

Benny realised she must fight Sean Walsh. 'Does he tell everyone I'm going to college?' she asked, with a smile of pleasure on her face.

'Only subject of conversation.' Sean was smug to be the source of information but somehow disconcerted that Benny didn't get embarrassed as he had thought she would.

Benny turned to Eve. 'Aren't I lucky?'

Eve understood. 'Oh, spoiled rotten,' she agreed.

They didn't laugh until they were out of sight. They had to walk down the long straight street past Shea's pub with its sour smell of drink coming out on to the street from behind its dark windows, past Birdie Mac's sweet shop where they had spent so much time choosing from jars all their school life. Across the road to the butcher's where they looked in the window to see back at the reflection of Hogan's Outfitters and realise that Sean Walsh had gone back inside to the empire that would one day be his.

Only then could they let themselves go and laugh properly.

Mr Flood, of Flood's Quality Meat Killed On The Premises, didn't appreciate their laughter.

'What's so funny about a row of gigot chops?' he asked the two laughing girls outside his window. It only made them laugh more.

'Get on with you then, do your laughing somewhere else,' he growled at them. 'Stop making a mock and a jeer out of other people's business.'

His face was severely troubled and he went out into the street to look up at the tree which overhung his house.

Mr Flood had been staring into that tree a lot lately, and worse still having conversations with someone he saw in its branches. The general thinking was that Mr Flood had seen some kind of vision, but was not ready yet to reveal it to the town. His words to the tree seemed to be respectful and thoughtful, and he addressed whatever he saw as Sister.

Benny and Eve watched fascinated, as he shook his head

sorrowfully and seemed to agree with something that had been said to him.

'It's the same the whole world over, Sister,' he said, 'but it's sad it should come to Ireland as well.'

He listened respectfully to what he was hearing from the tree, and took his leave. Vision or no vision, there was work to be done in the shop.

The girls only stopped laughing by the time they had reached the convent gates. Benny turned to go back home as usual. She never presumed on her friendship with Eve by expecting to be let in to the inner sanctum. The convent in holidays was off limits.

'No, come on in, come in just to see my room,' Eve begged.

'Mother Francis? Wouldn't they think . . . ?'

'It's my home, they've always told me that. Anyway, you're not a pupil any more.'

They went through a side door; there was a smell of baking, a warm kitchen smell through the corridors, then a smell of polish on the big stairway, and the wide dark hall hung with pictures of Mother Foundress and Our Lady, and lit only by the Sacred Heart lamp.

'Isn't it desperately quiet in the holidays?'

'You should be here at night. Sometimes when I've come home from the pictures and I let myself in, it's so quiet I'd nearly talk to the statues for company.'

They went up to the small room where Eve had lived for as long as she could remember. Benny looked around with interest.

'Look at your wireless, right beside your bed!' The brown bakelite electric radio, where, like every other girl in the country, Eve listened at night to Radio Luxembourg, was on her night table. In Benny's house, where she was considered a very pampered only child, she had to borrow the kitchen radio and then perch it on a chair because there wasn't any socket near enough to her bed to plug it in.

There was a neat candlewick bedspread and a funny nightdress case shaped like a rabbit.

'Mother Francis gave me that when I was ten. Isn't it awful?'

'Better than holy pictures,' Benny said.

Eve opened a drawer in which there were piles of holy pictures, each one bound up with a rubber band.

Benny looked at them, fascinated. 'You never threw them away!'

'Not here. I couldn't.'

The small round window looked down over Knockglen, along the tree-lined drive of the convent through the big gates and down the broad main street of the town.

They could see Mr Flood fussing round the window of his shop as if he were still worried about what they could have found so amusing in its contents. They saw small children with noses pressed against the window of Birdie Mac's, and men with caps pulled well down over their faces coming out of Shea's pub.

They saw a black Morris Cowley pull up in front of Hogan's and knew it was Dr Johnson. They saw two men walking into Healy's Hotel, rubbing their hands. These would be commercial travellers, wanting to write up their order books in peace. They could see a man with a ladder up against the cinema putting up the new poster, and the small round figure of Peggy Pine coming out of her dress shop to stand and look admiringly at her window display. Peggy's idea of art was to put as much in the window as could possibly fit without falling over.

'You can see everything! Benny was amazed. 'It's like being God.'

'Not really, God can see round corners. I can't see your house; I can't see who's having chips in Mario's; I can't see over the hill to Westlands. Not that I'd want to, but I can't.'

Her voice was tight when she spoke of her mother's people in the big house. Benny knew from old that it was a thorny subject.

'I suppose they wouldn't . . .'

'They wouldn't.' Eve was firm.

They both knew what Benny was going to say: that there was no chance of the wealthy Westwards paying for a university education for Eve.

'Do you think Mother Francis might have approached them?'

'I'm sure she did, lots of times over the years, and she always got the door slammed in her face.'

'You can't be certain,' Benny said soothingly.

Eve looked out of the window down the town, standing as she must often have done over the years.

'She did every single thing to help me that anyone could. She *must* have asked them, and they must have said no. She didn't tell me because she didn't want me to feel worse about them. As if I could.'

'In a fairy story one of them would ride up to the avenue here on a white horse and say they'd been wanting you as part of their lives for years,' Benny said.

'And in a fairy story I'd tell him to get lost,' Eve said, laughing.

'No, I wouldn't let you, you'd say thank you very much, the fees are this price, and I'd like a nice flat of my own with carpets going right up to the wall and no counting how much electric fire we use.' Benny was gleeful.

'Oh yes, and a dress allowance of course, so much a month put in Switzer's and Brown Thomas for me.'

'And a holiday abroad each year to make up for not seeing you much over the past while!'

'And a huge contribution to the convent building fund for the new chapel to thank the nuns for doing the needful.'

Benny sighed. 'I suppose things like that *could* happen.'

'As you said, in a fairy story,' Eve said. 'And what would be the best happening for you?'

'Two men to get out of a van down there in a minute's time and tell my father that Sean Walsh is a criminal wanted for six murders in Dublin and that he has to be handcuffed and out of there this instant.'

'It still leaves the business of you having to come home from Dublin on the bus every night,' Eve said.

'Listen, don't go on at me. For all that you've been in and out of our house a thousand times you don't know the way they are.'

'I do,' Eve said. 'They idolise you.'

'Which means I get the six ten bus back every night to Knockglen. That's what being idolised does for you.'

'There'll be the odd night surely in Dublin. They can't expect you home every single night.'

'Where will I stay? Let's be practical – there'll be no nights in Dublin. I'll be like bloody Cinderella.'

'You'll make friends, you'll have friends with houses, families, you know, normal kinds of things.'

'When did you and I have anything approaching a normal life, Eve Malone?' Benny was laughing to cheer them up and raise the mood again.

'It'll soon be time for us to take control, seriously.' Eve refused to laugh at all.

Benny could be equally serious.

'Sure it will. But what does it mean? You're not going to hurt Mother Francis by refusing to go to this place she's sending you. I'm not going to bring the whole world down on us by telling my mother and father that I feel like a big spancelled goat going to college and having to come back here every night as if I were some kind of simpleton. Anyway, you'll be out of there and you'll get a great job and be able to do what you like.'

Eve smiled at her friend. 'And we'll come back to this room some day and laugh at the days when we all thought it would be so dreadful.'

'We will, we will, and Sean Walsh will be doing penal servitude . . .'

'And the Westwards will have lost all their money and their land.'

'And Mrs Healy will have thrown away her corsets and be wearing a short skirt.'

'And Paccy Moore will own a fleet of shoe shops throughout the country.'

'And Dr Johnson will have learned to smile.'

'And Mother Francis will be the Reverend Mother General of the whole Order and can do what she likes, and go to see the Pope, and everything.'

They laughed, delighted at the thought of such wonders.

## 3

Emily Mahon stood in front of the gas cooker and grilled the ten rashers that she served every morning except Friday. Her white blouse hung neatly in the corner of the room. She wore a nylon jacket to make the breakfast lest her clothes gets spattered before she went out to work.

She knew that Brian was in a mood this morning. He hadn't a word to throw to a dog. Emily sighed as she stood in the shabby kitchen. Theirs must be the least improved house in Maple Gardens. It was always the same – they say that the shoemaker's children are never shod. So it was logical that the builder's wife would be the only one in the road without a decent kitchen to work in. She had seen the jobs that were done on other people's houses. Kitchens that were tiled so that they only needed a wipe down the walls and a quick mop of the floor. There were units that all fitted together like a continuous counter rather than the cupboards and tables of different sizes that Emily had lived with for twenty-five years. It was useless trying to change him. 'Who sees it but us?' was the reply.

Very few visitors came into 23 Maple Gardens. Brian's builder's yard was the centre of his social activities, such as they were. The boys, Paul and Nasey, had never brought their friends home, and now they too worked with their father in the yard. That's where fellows called to pick them up, or to take them over to a pub for a pint.

And Nan, the baby of the family, eighteen years old and about to start at university today, Nan had not been one for inviting friends home either.

Emily knew that her beautiful daughter had a dozen friends at school, she had seen her walking down the street when classes were over, surrounded by other girls. She went to the houses of friends, she was invited everywhere, but not one of her schoolmates had crossed the door of Maple Gardens.

Nan was not just beautiful in Emily's eyes. This was the opinion of everyone. When she was a small child people had stopped in the street asking why this little girl with the blonde, almost white, curls had never been chosen for the Pears soap advertisement . . . the one where it said, 'Growing up to be a beautiful lady'. In truth Emily did have dreams that one day in a park or on the street a talent scout would stop and see the perfect features and flawless skin of this child and come to the house begging on bended knees to transform her life.

Because if there was anything that Emily Mahon wanted for her little princess, it was a transformed life.

Emily wanted Nan to have everything that she had never had. She didn't want the girl to marry a bullying drunk like her mother had done. She didn't want a life of isolation stuck out here in a housing estate, only allowed to go out to work as a favour. Emily had read a lot of magazines, she knew that it was perfectly possible for a girl with Nan's looks to rise to be the highest in the land. You saw the very beautiful wives of rich businessmen, and the really good-looking women photographed at the races on the arms of well-known people from important families. It was obvious that not all these people could have come from the upper classes. *Their* women were often plain and horsey. Nan was in the running for that kind of life, and Emily would do everything in her power to get it for her.

It had not been hard to persuade Brian to come up with the fees for university. In his sober moods he was inordinately proud of his beautiful daughter. Nothing was too good for her. But that was when he was sober.

And then, during this last summer, Nan had said, 'You know, one day he'll break your jaw and then it'll be too late.'

'I don't know what you mean.'

'He hit you last night, while I was out, when the boys weren't here. I know he did.'

'Now you know nothing of the sort.'

'Your face, Em. What will you tell them today?'

'The truth. That I got up in the night and walked into an open press.'

'Is it going to be like that always? Will he get away with it for the rest of his life?'

'You know how sorry he is, Nan. You must know how he'd give any of us the moon after he's been – not himself.'

'It's too high a price to pay for the moon,' Nan had said.

And now today she was going to start out as a student, this lovely girl that Emily still looked on with awe. Brian had been handsome before alcohol had thickened his face, and she herself had good features, high cheekbones and deep-set eyes. Their daughter seemed to have taken the best features and left the bad ones. Nan had no trace of the coarseness that was in her father's face. Nor did she have any of the pale and slightly apologetic stance of her mother.

As Emily Mahon stood in the kitchen she hoped that Nan would be warm and pleasant to her father this morning. Brian had been drunk last night, certainly, but there had been no dog's abuse out of him.

Emily turned the rashers expertly. There were three for Paul, three for Nasey and four for Brian. Neither she nor Nan ate a cooked breakfast. Just a cup of tea and a slice of toast each. Emily filled the washing-up bowl with hot soapy water. She would collect their plates to steep when they had finished. Usually everyone left the house around the same time; she liked to have the table cleared before she closed the door behind her, so the place looked respectable when they came in again in the evenings. That way nobody would raise too many objections about Emily going out to work. It had been a battle hard fought.

Nan had been so supportive during the long war waged with Brian. She had listened wordlessly to her father saying, 'No wife of mine is going to work. I want a meal on the table. I want a clean shirt . . .' She had heard her mother say that she could provide these things, but that the days were long and lonely on her own and she would like to meet people and to earn her own money, no matter how small.

The boys, Paul and Nasey, had not been interested, but played the game to win and stuck with their father in the need to have a nice warm house and meals.

Nan had been twelve then, and it was she who had tipped the balance.

'I don't know what you're all talking about,' she had said suddenly. 'None of you are ever in before six, winter or summer, and so there *will* be a meal. And if Em wants more money and will do all your washing and clearing as well, then I can't see what the fuss is about.'

Nobody else could either.

So Emily had worked in a hotel shop since then; her own little world surrounded by nice things: glass and linen and high-class souvenirs for tourists. At first the hotel had been unwilling to employ someone with a young daughter. She would constantly need time off, they told her. Emily had been able to look them straight in the eye even then and say that Nan would cause no trouble. And she had been right. It was only Brian who had ever interrupted the even style of her working life by phoning or calling, to ask idiotic questions about things that had already been agreed or arranged, but forgotten through drink.

She called them, as she did every morning. 'Breakfast going on the table.'

Down they came, her two big sons, dark like their father, square and looking as if they had been manufactured by a toy firm to look like younger version's of a father in a game. Then came Brian, who had cut himself shaving, and was dabbing the blood on his chin. He looked at his wife without pleasure.

'Do you have to wear that bloody garment in the house? Isn't it bad enough going out to work as a skivvy in someone's shop without dressing as a skivvy at home.'

'It's to keep my blouse clean,' Emily said mildly.

'And you have your clothes draped around so that the place looks like a hand-me-down shop,' he grumbled.

Nan came in at that moment. Her blonde curls looked as if she had just come from a hairdresser rather than from the hand basin in her own bedroom which was where she had washed her hair this morning. Brian Mahon might have skimped on comfort for the rest of the house, but his daughter's bedroom had the best of everything. A wash basin neatly boxed in, a big fitted wardrobe with even a rail for her shoes in it. Nothing had been spared on Nan's room. Each item was an apology for a drunken bout. She wore a smart blue skirt, and her new navy three-quarter-length coat over her shoulders; a white lacy blouse with a navy-blue trimming. She looked like the cover of a magazine.

'That's right, attack Em for leaving her blouse there, but if it's seven of your shirts and seven each of the boys', that's twenty-one shirts ironed for you and there's no word of it being a hand-me-down shop then, is there?'

Her father looked at her in open admiration. 'They're going to look twice when you walk in the door of University College,' he said.

Nan showed no pleasure at the compliment – in fact Emily seemed to think it irritated her.

'Yes, that's all very well, but we never discussed the matter of pocket money.'

Emily wondered why Nan brought it up now. If she were to ask her father on her own he would give her anything.

'There's never been any shortage of pocket money in this house.' His face was red and angry already.

'Well, there hasn't been any question of it up till now. Paul and Nasey went in to work for you, so they got a wage from the start.'

'A *sort* of wage,' Paul said.

'More than any other human would give a lout like you,' his father retorted.

Nan continued, 'I wanted it to be clear from the start rather than having to ask every week.'

'What's wrong with asking every week?' he wanted to know.

'It's undignified,' she said shortly.

That was exactly what Emily had felt each week asking for her housekeeping; now she could work out a budget to suit herself.

'What do you want?' He was annoyed.

'I don't know. I'm not really entitled to anything. I'm going to be dependent on you for three or four years. What do *you* suggest?'

He was at a loss. 'We'll see.'

'I'd prefer if we could decide today. It would get things off to a good start. I'd know what I could buy, how long it would take me to save for something . . . a new dress or whatever.'

'I bought you that coat there! It cost an arm and a leg – it's an ordinary navy coat to me, and it cost as much as a fur.'

'It's very well cut, that's why. It will last for years.'

'I should hope so,' he muttered.

'So you see in order not to have discussions like this all the time, don't you think . . .'

Emily held her breath.

'A pound a week for . . .'

'Fares and lunches, yes, that's fair . . .' She stood looking at him expectantly.

'And what else is there . . . ?'

'Well, I suppose there's cinema, newspapers, books, coffee, going to a dance.'

'Another two pounds a week for that?' He looked anxiously at her.

'Oh, that's very generous, thank you. That would be marvellous.'

'And what about clothes then . . . ?' He nodded over at the coat that had cost him an arm and a leg.

'I could manage stockings out of what you've given me.'

'I want you as well dressed as the next man's daughter.'

Nan said nothing.

'What would it cost?' He was like a child now.

Nan looked at him thoughtfully, as if she knew he was in her power now.

'Some people's fathers give them an allowance by the month for clothes. A sum like . . . I don't know . . . twenty . . . but I don't know . . .'

'You'll have thirty pounds a month, nothing is shortchanged in this house.' He almost roared it.

Emily Mahon watched Nan start to smile.

'Thank you very much, Daddy, that's more than generous,' she said.

'Well,' he was gruff, 'I won't have you saying I'm not generous.'

'I never said that, never once,' she answered him.

'Well, all this business putting me on the carpet . . . implying that I might leave you short.'

'In your right mind, Daddy, you'd never leave me short, but I don't want to rely on your always being in your right mind.'

Emily caught her breath.

'What do you mean?' He was like a turkeycock now.

'You know exactly what I mean. You're two people, Daddy.'

'You're in no position to be giving me lectures.'

'I'm not. I'm explaining why I wanted it on a regular arrangement so that I wouldn't have to be annoying you when you're . . . well, when you've had a drink I suppose.'

There was a moment's silence. Even the boys wondered what would happen now. The usual way of coping with their father had been to make no reference to anything untoward that might have happened, for fear of bringing it all upon them again. But Nan had chosen her time and place well.

The silence was broken by Emily.

'Well, that's a very good allowance, there can't be many girls setting off today who'd get that.'

'No indeed.' Nan was undisturbed by the tension around her. 'I mean it, Daddy. And I honestly think that if you are going to give me that much, it's probably easier for you to do it once a month.'

'Yes, that's agreed,' he said.

'So will I ask you for forty-two pounds today and then not come near you for a month?'

Paul and Nasey looked at each other with widened eyes.

'Forty-two pounds?' Her father seemed astounded.

'You said three pounds a week, and thirty pounds for clothes.' She seemed apologetic. 'It is a lot, I know.'

'I'm not going back on my word.' He reached into his back pockets and took out a wad of old notes. He peeled them off.

Emily willed her daughter to show the right amount of gratitude, she prayed that the girl wouldn't take it for granted.

But as usual Nan seemed to know better than everyone what to do.

'I'm not going to go down on my knees and thank you,

72

Daddy, because that would just be words. I'll try to make you proud of me. Make you feel glad you've spent so much to put a daughter through college.'

Brian Mahon's eyes misted slightly. He swallowed but could say nothing. 'That's it. Now could a man have a cup of tea in this place does anyone think?'

In a big terraced house in Dunlaoghaire, another household was getting ready for the opening of the university term. Almost a town in itself, Dunlaoghaire was some miles from the centre of Dublin, a big harbour where the mail boat came in and left every day for Holyhead bringing the holiday visitors. Full also on the outgoing journeys with emigrants about to seek their fortune in London.

Ever since the days it had been called Kingstown, it had been a lovely place to live; tropical palm trees along the coast line made it seem like somewhere much more exotic than it really was. The sturdy Victorian houses spoke of a time when this was a place of substance and quality. It was healthy too; the two great arms of piers reached out into the sea and were a regular walking spot for anyone in need of a breath of air or some exercise.

It was a curious mixture of staid respectability with overtones of holiday fun. Every year there was a big noisy carnival with its ghost trains and chairoplanes, and yet matrons with shallow baskets did sociable shopping excursions usually ending with coffee in Marine Road and tut-tutting over the state of the borough.

Kit Hegarty moved swiftly around her large house in a quiet road that led down to the sea. She had a lot to do. The first day was always important, it set the tone for the whole year. She would cook them all a good breakfast and make it clear that she expected them to be at the table on time.

She had kept students for seven years now, and was known as one of the university's favoured landladies. Normally they didn't like to sanction a digs so far away from the city and the university buildings, but Mrs Hegarty had been quick to explain how near her house was to the railway station, how short was the train journey into town, how good the bracing sea air.

She didn't need to plead for long; soon the authorities realised that this determined woman could look after students better than anyone. She had turned her big dining room into a study; there each boy had his own place at the big felt-covered table, books could be left undisturbed. It was expected in Kit's house that there would be some period of study after supper, most nights at any rate. And her only son Frank studied with them too. It made him feel grown up sitting at the same table as real university students; engineers and agricultural science students, law or medicine, they had all sat and studied around the Hegarty dining table while young Frank was working for his Intermediate and his Leaving Certificate.

Today he would join them as a fully fledged student himself.

Kit hugged herself with pleasure at the thought that she

had raised a son who would be an engineer. And raised him all on her own. Joseph Hegarty had been long gone now, his life in England was no concern of hers any more. He had sent money for a little while, and dates when he was going to be back; and then excuses, and little money. And then nothing.

She had tried not to bring up Frank with any bitterness against his father. She had even left a photograph of Joseph Hegarty in the boy's room lest he should think that his father was being banished from his memory on top of everything else. It had been a heady day when she noticed the photograph no longer in a place of honour, on the chest of drawers, but moved to a shelf where it could hardly be seen, and then face down, and then in the bottom of a drawer.

Tall, gangly Frank Hegarty didn't need any mythical father's picture any more.

Kit wondered whether Joseph, if he had stayed around, would have had any views on Frank's motorbike. It was a black 250cc BSA – his pride and joy.

Probably not. He had never been a man to face up to anything unpleasant. And Frank's bike was unpleasant. And dangerous, and it was the only black cloud in her life on this morning when her son started university.

In vain she had pleaded and begged him to use the train. They were only minutes from the railway station, the service was frequent. She would pay for his weekly ticket. He could make as many journeys as he liked. It was the only thing he had ever stood out for.

He had gone to Peterborough and worked long hours in a canning factory only so that he could own this bike. Why did she want to take away the one possession that was truly valuable to him? Just because she didn't know how to ride a motorbike or even want to, it was unfair that she should try to stop him.

He was eighteen years and six months. Kit looked at the statue of the Infant of Prague that she kept in the house to impress the mothers of the students who boarded with her. She wished she had a stronger conviction that the Infant of Prague might be any earthly use in keeping her son safe on this terrible machine. It would be nice to have been able to offload your worries on to someone or something like that.

Patsy asked Mrs Hogan if she'd like her to wet another pot of tea.

'Ah, go on, Mam, you'd need tea on a bad day like this,' Patsy said encouragingly.

'That would be nice, Patsy.' She sank back into her chair, relieved.

It hadn't been so wet earlier, when Benny had left for her first day at college. Benny in her navy jumper and white blouse with the navy and grey check skirt.

'You'll be the belle of the ball,' Eddie had said to her, bursting with pride.

'Oh, Father, I won't. I'm so big and drab-looking,' Benny had said suddenly. 'I'm like some kind of hearse. I caught sight of myself in the mirror.'

Eddie's eyes had filled with tears. 'Child, you're

76

beautiful,' he had said. 'Don't talk about yourself like that. *Please*. Don't upset your mother and me.'

Annabel had wanted to hug her and tell her that she looked lovely. Big, certainly, but with that lovely glowing skin and all that chestnut hair tied back in a navy and white ribbon, she looked what she was: a girl from a nice family, from a house in the country, whose father ran an established business.

But it wasn't a morning for hugging. Instead she had reached out her hand.

'You are a handsome, lovely girl, and they'll all see that,' she said softly.

'Thank you, Mother,' Benny said dutifully.

'And what's more, you'll be very, very happy there. You won't be going back to dreary little bedsitters like a lot of girls have to do, or being half starved in some digs . . .' Annabel sighed with pleasure. '*You'll* be coming home to your own good home every night.'

Benny had smiled at her but again it had seemed a little as if it were expected.

The girl was nervous, as any girl would be starting out in a new place, with strangers.

'It'll be a quiet house from now on, Mam.' Patsy arrived with the teapot and put it on the stand. She placed the quilted cosy on it and patted it approvingly.

'I expect she'll make friends.' Annabel was doubtful. There had always been Eve and only Eve; it was going to be a big wrench.

'And will she be bringing them down here to stay do

you think?' Patsy's eyes shone at the excitement. She loved speculating.

'I hadn't thought of that. But I'm sure she will. After all she can't possibly stay up in Dublin with people we don't know or have never heard of. She knows that.'

Mother Francis was thinking about Eve as she watched the rain fall steadily on the convent grounds. She would miss her. Obviously she had to go to Dublin and stay in the convent there; this was the only way she could train for a career. Mother Francis hoped that the Community in Dublin would understand the need to make Eve feel important and part of the place as they had always done here in Knockglen. Eve had never felt remotely like a charity child, nor had there been any pressure on her to join the Order.

Her father had worked long hours for the convent in his time, he had paid many times over in advance for his child to be housed and educated, had he but known it. Mother Francis sighed and prayed silently that the Lord would look after the soul of Jack Malone.

At times there had been other options. Mother Francis and her old school friend of years ago, Peggy Pine, discussed it long and often.

'I could let her serve her time to me, and make her fit for a job in any shop in Ireland, but we want more than that for her, don't we?'

'Not that it isn't a very worthwhile career, Peggy,' Mother Francis had said diplomatically.

'You'd love the few letters after her name though, wouldn't you now, Bunty?' Few people on earth called Mother Francis that and got away with it.

And what Peggy said was true. Mother Francis *did* want everything that might help to push Eve up some kind of ladder. She had been such an innocent victim from the start it seemed only fair to help her all they could now.

There had never been enough money to dress the child properly and even if there had been they didn't have the style or the know-how. Peggy had advised from the wings, but Eve didn't want outside charity. Anything that came from the convent she regarded as her right. St Mary's was her home.

It was certainly the only place she thought of as home. The three-room cottage where she had been born had lost its interest for Eve as her dislike of the Westwards had grown. When she was a youngster she was forever going up the long path through the convent kitchen gardens, past the briars and brambles and peering in its windows.

When she was about ten she had even started to plant flowers outside it. Mother Francis had nurtured them behind the scenes, just as she had taken cuttings from the various bushes and plants in the convent garden and made a garden around the stony waste ground, the ugly edge of the cliff where Jack Malone had ended his life.

It was hard to know when this hatred of her mother's family had begun. But Mother Francis supposed it was only natural. A girl brought up in a convent with the whole town knowing her circumstances could not be expected to feel any warmth towards the people who lived in splendour over in Westlands. The man who used to ride around Knockglen as if it were all part of his estate; that was Eve's grandfather, Major Charles Westward. A man who had shown no wish to know his daughter's child. He had not been seen much in recent years, and Peggy Pine – who was Mother Francis's line of communication with the outer world – said that he was now in a wheelchair as a result of a stroke. And that small, dark young man Simon Westward, who was seen from time to time around Knockglen, he was Eve's first cousin. He looked very like her, Mother Francis thought, or maybe she was being fanciful. There was another child, too, a girl, but at some fancy Protestant school up in Dublin, hardly ever seen around the place here.

As Eve's resentment of the family had grown, so had her interest in the cottage dwindled. It stood empty. Mother Francis had never given up hope that Eve would live there one day, with a family maybe, and bring back some happiness to the little house that had known only confusion and tragedy.

And it was such a comforting little place. Mother Francis often sat there herself when she came up to tidy the place. It had always been the custom in St Mary's for the nuns to go anywhere in the grounds to read their daily Office. You were as close to God in the gardens, under the big beech tree, or in the walled garden with its smell of rosemary and lemon balm, as you were in the chapel.

Nobody thought it odd that Mother Francis often went

up the path past the blackberries to read her Office up by the cottage. She kept a watchful eye on any leaks that might have sprung. If there was anything she couldn't cope with herself she would ask Mossy Rooney, a man of such silence and discretion that he found it hard to reveal his own name in case it might incriminate someone.

If anyone were to ask whether the cottage was for sale or rent, Mother Francis was always ready with a helpless shrug of the shoulders to say that things hadn't been fully sorted out yet, but that it was in Eve's name and nothing could be done until she was twenty-one. Nobody ever brought the matter up with Eve; and as for Mossy Rooney, who had replaced some of the window frames and the guttering, it would have been pointless asking him for information. The whole town knew he was silent as the tomb, a man of deep thoughts, none of them revealed; or possibly a man of no thoughts at all.

Mother Francis would have loved that old cottage to be Eve's home; she could see in her mind's eye a kind of life where Eve would bring her student friends home from university to stay there for weekends, and they would call at the convent and have tea in the parlour.

It was such a waste of a little stone house with a wooden porch and a view across the county as well as down the craggy rocks of the stone quarry. The cottage had no name. And the way things were it might never have a name or a life of its own.

Perhaps she should have approached the Westwards directly. But the reply to her letter had been so cold.

Mother Francis had deliberately written on plain paper, not on the heavily embossed convent paper with Our Lady's name all over it. She had spent sleepless nights composing the right words, words that would sound neither sleeveen nor grasping. Evidently she hadn't found them. The letter from Simon Westward had been courteous, but firm and dismissive. His aunt's family had raised no objections to her daughter being brought up in a Roman Catholic convent, and that was where their interest in the matter ended.

Mother Francis had not told Eve about the letter. The girl had hardened her heart so much; there was no point in giving her further cause.

The nun sighed heavily as she looked back at her sixth-year class, heads bent over their composition books all intent on their essay, 'The Evils of Emigration'. She wished she could believe that Mother Clare in Dublin would welcome Eve and tell her that the Dublin convent would be her new home for the next year.

It wasn't Mother Clare's style, but God was good, and perhaps she had, for once, been open-hearted and generous.

She might have been generous; but on the other hand she probably hadn't been. There had been no word from Eve for a week, which was not a good sign.

Eve's room in the Dublin convent had no bedside table with a small radio on it. There was no candlewick bed-spread. A small neat iron bed with a shabby well-washed coverlet had one lumpy pillow and sheets which were hard to the touch. There was a narrow, poky cupboard and a jug and basin from early times but possibly necessary still today since the bathroom was a long way away.

It wasn't like a prison cell, it was like a maid's room, Eve told herself firmly. And in a sense that was how they must view her, a difficult prickly maid up from the country. Worst of all, a maid with airs and graces.

Eve sat on her bed and looked around the room. She could hear the regretful, gentle voice of Mother Francis telling her that life was never meant to be easy and that her best course was to work very hard now and get out of this place in record time. Study her grammalogues in the shorthand, take a sharp interest in the book-keeping, flex her fingers for the typing, practising over and over. Listen and take notes on office procedure. In a year's time or less she would land herself a good job, and a place to live.

Never again would anyone offer her an iron bed in a dark poky little room.

The Wise Woman would grit her teeth and get on with it, Eve told herself. That was a phrase she and Benny used all the time. What would the Wise Woman do about Sean Walsh? The Wise Woman would pretend that he did not exist. The Wise Woman wouldn't buy another half pound of toffees in Birdie Mac's because she'd get spots. The Wise Woman would do her homework because Mother Francis was on the warpath.

After a week Eve realised that the Wise Woman would

also need to be a canonised saint to adapt to the new surroundings.

Mother Clare had suggested a regime of light house-work, 'to cover all your obligations, my dear'.

And Eve would admit that she did have obligations. She was getting a free residential course for which others paid handsomely. There was no history of association with this convent as there was with St Mary's in Knockglen. She would have been eager to help from a sense of justice and also to do Mother Francis credit. But this was different.

Mother Clare's idea of covering obligations centred around the kitchen. She thought perhaps that Eve might like to serve the breakfast in the refectory and clear away, and that she should also leave classes ten minutes before lunch and be back in the refectory to serve soup to the other students when they came in.

In all her years in St Mary's Eve Malone had never been seen by the other girls to perform one menial task. She had been asked to help behind the scenes as would any girl in her own home. But in front of the other pupils Mother Francis had made an iron-hard rule that Eve must never be seen to do anything which would give her a different status.

Mother Clare had no such qualms. 'But my dear girl, you don't know these other pupils,' she had said when Eve had politely requested that she should not be put in a public position of a non-fee-paying student.

'And I hardly *will* get to know them if they think I'm there on some different basis to themselves,' she had said.

Mother Clare's eyes had narrowed. She sensed trouble in this girl, who seemed to have taken in the entire community below in Knockglen.

'But isn't that the case, Eve? You are here on a different basis,' she had said, smiling very sweetly all the while.

Eve knew the battle had to be fought and won there and then before the other students arrived.

'I am happy to cover my obligations in whatever way you suggest, Mother, but not in view of my fellow students. Can I ask you to rethink your plans for me?'

Two spots of red appeared on Mother Clare's cheeks. This was pure insolence. But Mother Clare had fought many battles since she had taken her vows and she always realised when she was on poor ground. Like now. The Community in Knockglen would defend Eve vociferously. Even some of the Sisters here in Dublin might see that the girl had a point.

'I'll tell you tomorrow,' she had said and turned to swish her long black skirts and veil down the polished corridor.

Eve had spent the day wandering around Dublin with a heavy heart. She knew she had visited heavy housework upon herself because of her attitude.

She looked in shop windows and willed herself to think of the days when she would be able to afford clothes like she saw there.

Imagine if you could go in and buy maybe four of the pencil-slim skirts in different colours. They were only twelve shillings and eleven pence each. It didn't matter that they were not great quality, you could have all these colours. And there was cotton gingham at two shillings a yard, you'd have a smashing blouse out of that at six shillings, maybe four of them to go with each of the skirts.

Eve dismissed the swagger coats. She was too short, they were too sweeping, they'd envelop her, but she'd love six pairs of the fully fashioned very sheer nylons just under five shillings each. And tapered slacks in wine or navy; she saw those everywhere. They varied in price, but usually around a pound a pair.

If she had a wallet of money she'd go and buy them now. This minute.

But it wasn't money for clothes that she wanted. Eve knew that only too well. She wanted a different kind of life entirely. She wanted to study, to spend three, even five, years at university. She was prepared to make sacrifices for it, but there seemed to be no way she could even begin.

There were stories of people putting themselves through college by working during the day and studying at night. But that would still mean the year with the terrible Mother Clare to qualify herself for any kind of work. Eve noticed that almost without realising it her journey had taken her up through St Stephen's Green towards the big grey buildings of University College. It was still empty and she wandered at will around the main hall, seeing only those involved in administration moving about.

The term would start next week. Lucky Benny would arrive as would hundreds of first-year students from all over Ireland.

Eve realised that there were thousands like herself who would never get there. But their expectations hadn't been raised. They hadn't been encouraged and treated well and led to believe that they had brains and insights like she had. That's what made it so hard.

Eve knew that through these doors next week would come girls who only intended to use university as part of their social life. There would be unwilling students, who didn't want to be here at all, who had other plans and other dreams, but came to satisfy the wishes of parents. There would be those who drifted in and would use the time to make up their minds. She felt a boiling rage about the Westwards, the family who cut off their own flesh and blood, who let her be raised by the charity of the nuns and never bothered themselves to think that she was now of university age.

There was no fairness on earth if someone who would appreciate it and work hard was kept out just because of a greedy, uncaring family who would prefer to forget the child of an unsuitable union rather than make a generous gesture and ensure that some right was done at the end of the day.

She looked in the glass-fronted noticeboards and read of the societies that would be re-forming when term started, and the new committees and the sports arrangements and the practice times, and the appeals for people to join this group and that club.

And she saw the big staircases leading up to the libraries and the lecture halls. She saw the red plush benches which would be filled with students next week, and she ached to be amongst them. To spend her days reading and writing and finding out more and talking to people, and to spend no time at all trying to outwit awful people like Mother Clare.

The Wise Woman would get on with her life and stop dreaming. Then she thought how tiring it was going to be for the rest of her life trying to be the Wise Woman all the time. It would be great to be the very Unwise Woman on occasions.

Benny took the bus to Dublin on the first day of term with more trepidation than she would ever have expected. At home they had behaved as if she were a toddler going to a first party in a party frock rather than a huge ungainly student eighteen years of age going to university dressed from head to toe in dark clothes.

She could still see the tableau this morning: her father with tears of pride in his eyes – she knew he would go to the business and bore everyone to death with tales about how his wonderful daughter was going to university. Benny could see her mother sitting there stretching her hand out full of what she had been full of for months now: the huge advantages of being able to come home every night by bus. Patsy, looking like the faithful old black mammy slave in a film except that she was white and she was only twenty-five. It had made Benny want to scream and scream.

And she had other worries too, as she sat on the bus

and started her university career. Mother Francis had told her that the bold Eve hadn't written or telephoned, and that all the Sisters were dying to hear from her. Yet Eve had phoned Benny twice in the last week to say that life in the Dublin convent was intolerable and she would have to meet her in Dublin because otherwise she would go mad.

'But how can we meet? Don't you have to stay in that place for lunch?' Benny had asked.

'I've told them I have to go to hospital for tests.'

As long as she had known her, Eve had hardly ever told a lie. Benny had to tell a lot of little lies in order to be allowed out late or indeed at all. But Eve had been resolute about never lying to the nuns. Things must be bad in Dublin if she had gone this far.

And then there was Sean Walsh. Naturally she had not wanted to go out with him, but both her mother and father stressed how nice it was of him to take such an interest in the fact that she was going off to university and wanted to take her to the pictures as a treat. She had decided to take what might be the easiest way out and accept. After all, if it were to be something to mark the beginning of a new stage in her life, then she could make it clear that this new life wouldn't involve any further outings with him.

Last night they had gone to the film *Genevieve*. Almost everyone else in the world must have loved it, Benny thought grimly, all over the place people left cinemas humming the tune and wishing they looked like either Kay

Kendall or Kenneth More. But not Benny. She had left in a black fury.

All through the film Sean Walsh had put his thin bony arm around her shoulder or on her knee and even on one particularly unpleasant occasion managed to get his hand sort of around her back, under her arm and around her breast. All of these she had wriggled out of, and as they were leaving the cinema he had had the nerve to say, 'You know, I really respect you for saying no, Benny. It makes you even more special, if you know what I mean.'

*Respected* her! For saying no to *him*? That was the easiest thing she had ever done, but Sean was the type who thought that she enjoyed it.

'I'll go home now, Sean,' she had said.

'No, I told your father we'd have a cup of coffee in Mario's. They won't be expecting you.'

She was trapped again. If she *did* go home they would ask why the coffee hadn't materialised.

Next to the cinema, Peggy Pine's shop had some new autumn stock. Benny had looked at the cream-coloured blouses and soft pink angora sweaters. In order to talk about something that did not have to do with fondling and stroking she spoke of the garments.

'They're pretty, aren't they, Sean?' she had said, her mind barely on them. She was thinking instead that once she got to university she would never need to see him again.

'Well, they are, but not on *you*. You're much wiser not to draw attention to yourself. Wear dark colours. Nothing flashy.'

There had been tears in her eyes as she crossed the road with him to Mario's and he brought two cups of coffee and two club milk chocolate biscuits to the plastic-topped table where she waited for him.

'It's an ill wind,' he had said.

'What do you mean exactly?'

'Well, that brought Eve off to Dublin and out of your life.'

'Not out of my life. I'm going to be in Dublin.'

'But not in her world. Anyway, you're grown up now, it's not for you to be as thick as thieves with the likes of *her*.'

'I like being as thick as thieves with her. She's my friend.' Why do I have to explain this to him? Benny had thought.

'Yes, but it's not seemly. Not any more.'

'I don't like talking about Eve behind her back.'

'No, I'm just saying, it's an ill wind. Now that she's gone you won't always be saying that you're off to the pictures with her. I can take you.'

'I won't have much time for the pictures any more. Not with study.'

'You won't be studying every night.' He had smiled at her complacently. 'And don't forget, there's always weekends.'

She had felt a terrible weariness.

'There's always weekends,' she repeated. It seemed easier somehow.

But Sean had felt like making a statement. 'Don't think

that it's going to come between us, you having a university education,' he had said.

'Not come between us?'

'Exactly. Why should it? There are some men that might let it but I'm not one. I tell you something, Benny, I've always modelled myself a lot on your father. I don't know whether you know this or not.'

'I know you work with him, so I'm sure you must learn from him.'

'Much more than that. I could learn from any outfitters in the country. I could learn tailoring by sitting at a bench. No, I watch the way Mr Hogan has faced the world, and I try to learn from that.'

'What have you learned in particular?'

'Well, not to be proud, for one thing. Your father married an older woman, a woman with money. He wasn't ashamed to put that money into his business, it's what she wanted and he wanted. It would have been a foolish, bull-necked man who would have looked a gift horse in the mouth . . . so I like to see myself in a small way as following in his footsteps.'

Benny had stared at him as if she had never seen him before.

'What exactly are you trying to say, Sean?' she had asked.

'I'm trying to say that none of it means anything to me. I'm above all that sort of thing,' he had said loftily.

There was a silence.

'Just to make my point clear,' he had ended.

That had been last night.

Mother and Father had seemed pleased that she had spent time having coffee with Sean.

If that's what they want for me, Benny asked herself, why on God's earth are they allowing me to go to university? If they want to take it all away in the end and match me up with that slimy halfwit, why then take me up to the mountain and show me the world? It was too hard to answer, as was Eve's problem. Eve had said not only was she going to be free for lunch, she would meet Benny off the bus and walk her up to University College. Hanged for a sheep was what Eve had said on the phone.

Jack Foley woke with a start. He had been dreaming that he and his friend Aidan Lynch were on Death Row in some American prison and they were about to die in the electric chair. Their crime seemed to be that they had sung the song 'Hernando's Hideaway' too loudly.

It was a huge relief to find himself in the big bedroom with its heavy mahogany furniture. Jack said you could hide a small army in the various wardrobes around the house. His mother had said that it was all very well to mock but she had stood many long hours at auctions all over the city finding the right pieces.

The Foleys lived in a large Victorian house with a garden in Donnybrook, a couple of miles from the centre of Dublin. It was a leafy place; professional people, merchants, senior civil servants had lived around here for a long time.

The houses on the road didn't have numbers; they all had names, and the postman knew where everyone lived. People didn't move much once they got to a road like this one. Jack was the eldest of the family and he had been born in a smaller house, but he didn't remember it. By the time he was a toddler his parents had arrived here.

He noticed that in the photographs of his childhood the rooms looked a lot less furnished.

'We were building up our home,' his mother had told him. 'No point in rushing and getting the wrong type of thing entirely.'

Not that Jack or any of his brothers really noticed the house much. It was there for them as it had always been. Like Doreen had always been putting the food on the table, like the old dog Oswald had been there for as long as they could recall.

Jack shook off his dream about Death Row and remembered that all over Dublin today there would be people waking to the first day of term.

The first day of term in the Foley household meant that Jack would put on a college scarf and head into UCD for the first time. In the dining room of the big Donnybrook house there was a sense of excitement. Dr John Foley sat at the head of the table, and looked at his five sons. He had assumed they would all enter medicine as he had, so it had been a shock when Jack had chosen law. Perhaps the same thing would happen with the others. Dr Foley looked at Kevin and Gerry. He had always seen them somewhere in the medical field as well as on a rugby pitch.

His eye fell on Ronan. Already he seemed to have the reassuring kind of manner one associated with being a doctor. That boy Ronan could convince even his own mother that the wounds he got in a playground were superficial, that the dirt on his clothes would easily wash out. That was the personality you needed in a good family doctor. Then there was Aengus, the youngest: his owlish glasses made him look studious and he was the only Foley boy not to be chosen for some kind of team in the school. Dr Foley had always seen his son Aengus as going into medical research when the time came. A bit too frail and woolly for the rough and tumble of ordinary practice.

But then he had been wrong about his eldest son. Jack said he had no wish to study physics and chemistry. The term he had spent at school trying to understand the first thing about physics had been wasted. Nor did he want botany and zoology, he'd be no good at them.

In vain Dr Foley had pleaded that the pre-med year was a necessary term of purgatory before you started the real business of medicine.

Jack had been adamant. He would prefer law.

Not the Bar either, but being apprenticed as a solicitor. What he would really and truly like was to do this new degree course for Bachelor of Civil Law. It was like doing a BA but all in law subjects. He had discussed it with his father seriously and with all the information to hand. He could be apprenticed to his mother's brother, surely. Uncle Kevin was in a big solicitors' practice: they'd find a place for him. He timed his request well. Jack knew that his father's head was buried as deeply in the world of rugby as the world of medicine. Jack was a shining schoolboy player. He was on the pitch for his school in the Senior Cup final. He scored two tries and converted one of them. His father was in no position to fight him. Anyway it would have been foolish to force someone into a life so demanding. Dr Foley shrugged. There were plenty of other boys to follow him down the good physician's route to Fitzwilliam Square.

Jack's mother Lilly sat at the far end of the table opposite her husband. Jack could never remember a breakfast when she had not presided over the cups of tea, the bowls of cornflakes, the slices of grilled bacon and half tomato which was the start to the day every morning except Fridays and in Lent.

His mother always looked as if she had dressed up for the occasion, which indeed she had. She wore a smart Gor-Ray skirt, always with either a twinset or a wool blouse. Her hair was always perfectly done, and there was a dusting of powder on her face as well as a slight touch of lipstick. When Jack had spent the night in friends' houses after a match he realised that their mothers were not like this. Often women in dressing gowns with cigarettes put food on kitchen tables for them. The formal breakfast at eight o'clock in a high-ceilinged dining room with heavy mahogany sideboards and floor-to-ceiling windows wasn't everyone else's way of life.

But the Foley boys weren't pampered either; their mother had seen to that. Each of them had a job to do in the mornings before they left for school. Jack had to fill the coal scuttles, Kevin to bring in the logs, Aengus had to roll yesterday's papers into sausage-like shapes which would be used for lighting the fires later, Gerry, who was meant to be the animal lover, had to take Oswald for a run in the park, and see that there was something on the bird table in the garden, and Ronan had to open the big heavy curtains in the front rooms, take the milk in from the steps and place it in the big fridge and brush whatever had to be brushed from the big granite steps leading up to the house. It could be cherry blossom petals or autumn leaves or slush and snow.

When breakfast was finished the Foley boys placed their plates and cutlery neatly on the hatch into the kitchen before going to the big room where all their coats, boots, shoes, school bags and often rugby gear had to be left.

People marvelled at the way Lilly Foley ran such an elegant home when she had five rugby-playing lads to deal with, and marvelled even more that she had kept the handsome John Foley at her side. A man not thought to be easy to handle. Dr Foley had a wandering eye as a young man. Lilly had not been more beautiful than the other women who sought him, just more clever. She realised that he would want an easy uncomplicated life where everything ran smoothly and he was not troubled with domestic difficulties.

She had found Doreen at an early stage, and paid her over the odds to keep the house running smoothly. Lilly Foley never missed her weekly hair-do and manicure.

She seemed to regard her life with the handsome doctor as a game with rules. She kept an elegant attractive home. She put on not an ounce of fat, and always appeared well groomed at golf club or restaurant, as well as at home. This way he didn't wander.

Today when the four younger boys left for school, Jack helped himself to another cup of tea.

'I'll know what you two talk about when you're alone now,' he grinned. He looked very handsome when he smiled, his mother thought fondly. Despite reddish-brown hair which wouldn't stay flat, those freckles on his nose, he really was classically good looking, and when Jack Foley smiled he would break any heart. Lilly Foley wondered would he fall in love easily, or did the rugby take so much time that he would just be satisfied with the distant adulation of the girls who watched and cheered the games.

She wondered would he be as hard to catch as his father had been. What would some wily girl see in him that he would respond to? She had captured his father by promising an elegant uncluttered lifestyle very different from the neglected unhappy home he had come from. But this would not be the way to lure away her Jack. He was happy and well looked after in this home. He wouldn't want to flee the nest for a long time yet.

'Are you sure you won't take a lift?' Dr John Foley would have been proud to drive his eldest son up to Earlsfort Terrace and wave him into his first day at university.

'No, Dad, I told a few of the lads . . .'

His mother seemed to understand. 'It's not like school, it's sort of more gradual, isn't it? There's no bell saying you all have to be there at such a time.'

'I know, I know. I've been there, remember.' Dr Foley was testy.

'It's just that I said . . .'

'No, your mother is right, you want to be with your friends on a day like this, and the best of luck to you, son, may it turn out for you just as well as you ever hoped. Even if you're not doing medicine.'

'Ah, go on, you're relieved. Think of all the malpractice suits.'

'You can get those in law just as well as medicine. Anyway, there's no reason why they shouldn't pick a law student for the first fifteen.'

'Give me a bit of time, Dad.'

'After the way you played in the Schools Cup? They're not blind in there. You'll be playing in the Colours match in December.'

'They never have Freshers for that.'

'They'll have you, Jack.'

Jack stood up. 'I'll be on it next year. Will that do you?'

'All right, if you play for UCD in 1958 that'll do me. I'm a very reasonable, undemanding man,' said Dr Foley.

When Benny got off the bus on the Quays, she saw Eve waiting, with her raincoat collar turned up against the rain. She looked cold and pale.

'God, you really will end up in hospital this way,' Benny said. She was alarmed by the look in Eve's eyes and the uncertainty of the future.

'Oh, shut up will you? Do you have an umbrella?'

'Do I have an umbrella? We're lucky that I don't have a plastic bubble encasing me, the weather was tested all night, I think. I have a folding mac that makes me look like a haystack in the rain, I have an umbrella that would fit most of Dublin under it.'

'Well, put it up then,' Eve said, shivering. They crossed O'Connell Bridge together.

'What are you going to do?' Benny asked.

'Anything. I can't stay there. I tried.'

'You didn't try very hard, less than a week.'

'If you saw it, if you *saw* Mother Clare!'

'You're the one who's always telling me that things will pass, and to make the best of them. You're the one who says we can stick anything if we know where we're going.'

'That was before I met Mother Clare, and anyway I don't know where I am going.'

'This is Trinity. We just keep following the railings, and up one of the streets to the Green . . .' Benny explained.

'No, I don't mean here. I mean, where I'm going really.'

'You're going to get a job and get shot of them as quick as possible. Wasn't that the plan?'

Eve made no reply. Benny had never seen her friend so low.

'Isn't there anyone nice there? I'd have thought you'd have made lots of friends.'

'There's a nice lay Sister in the kitchen. Sister Joan, she's got chapped hands and a streaming cold, but she's very kind. She makes me cocoa in a jug while I'm washing up. It has to be in a jug in case Mother Clare comes in and thinks I'm being treated like someone normal. I just drink it straight from the jug, you see, no cup.'

'I meant among the others, the other girls.'

'No, no friends.'

'You're not trying, Eve.'

'You're damn right I'm not trying. I'm not staying either, that's for good and certain.'

'But what will you *do*? Eve, you can't do this to Mother Francis and everyone.'

'In a few days I'll have some plan. I won't live in that place. I won't do it.' Her voice had a slightly hysterical ring about it.

'All right, all right.' Benny was different now. 'Will you come home on the bus tonight, back to Knockglen, back to the convent?'

'I can't do that. It would be letting them down.'

'Well, what would it be standing shivering around the streets here, telling lies about being in hospital? What'll they say when they hear that? Will we walk through the Green? It's nice, even though it's wet.' Benny's face looked glum.

Eve felt guilty. 'I'm sorry, I'm really making a mess of your first day of term. This is not what you need.'

They had reached the corner of St Stephen's Green. The traffic lights were green and they started to cross the road.

'Look at the style,' Benny said wistfully. Already they could see students in duffle coats, laughing and talking. They could see girls with pony tails and college scarves walking in easy friendship with boys along the damp slippery footpaths up towards Earlsfort Terrace. Some did walk on their own, but they had great confidence. Just beside them Benny noticed a blonde girl in a smart navy coat; despite the rain, she still looked elegant.

They were all crossing together when they saw the skid, the boy on the motorbike, out of control and ploughing towards the sedate black Morris Minor. It all seemed like slow motion, the way the boy fell and the bike swerved and skidded. How the car tried to avoid it and how both motorbike and car came sideways into the group of pedestrians crossing the wet street.

Eve heard Benny cry out, and then she saw the faces frozen as the car came towards her. She didn't hear the screams because there was a roaring in her ears and she lost consciousness, pinned by the car to the lamp post. Beside her lay the body of the boy Francis Joseph Hegarty, who was already dead.

## 4

Everyone said afterwards it was a miracle that more people hadn't been killed or injured. It was another miracle that it was so near the hospital, and that the driver of the car, who had been able to step out of it without any aid, had in fact been a Fitzwilliam Square doctor himself, who had known exactly what to do. Clutching a handkerchief to his own face, he felt blood over his eye but he assured them it was superficial, and gave instructions which were followed to the letter. Someone was to hold up the traffic, another to get the guards, but first someone was sent down the side lane towards St Vincent's Hospital to alert casualty and summon help. Dr Foley knelt beside the body of the boy whose motorbike had lost control. He closed his own eyes to give a silent prayer of relief that his own son had never wanted to ride a machine like this.

Then he closed the eyes of the boy with the broken neck, and placed a coat over him to keep him from the eyes of the students he would never get to know. The small girl with the wound in her temple had a slightly slow pulse and could well be concussed. But he did not think her condition critical. Two other girls had been grazed and bruised, and were obviously suffering from shock. He himself had bitten his tongue from what he could feel in his mouth, probably loosened a couple of teeth and had a flesh wound over his eye. His task now was to get things into the hands of the professionals before he asked anyone to take his blood pressure for him.

One of the injured girls, a big, soft-faced girl with chestnut-coloured hair and dark, sensible clothes, seemed very agitated about the one lying unconscious on the ground.

'She's not dead is she?' The eyes were round in horror.

'No, no, I've felt her pulse. She's going to be fine,' he soothed her.

'It's just that she didn't have any life.' The girl's eyes were full of tears.

'None of you have yet, child.' He averted his glance from the dead boy.

'No. Eve in particular. It would be terrible if she weren't all right.' She bit her lip.

'I've told you. You must believe me, and here they are . . .' The stretchers had been brought the couple of hundred yards from the hospital. There wasn't even a need for an ambulance.

Then the guards were there, and people directing the traffic properly, and the little procession moved towards the hospital. Benny was limping slightly and she paused to lean on the girl with the blonde curly hair who she had noticed seconds before the accident.

'Sorry,' said Benny, 'I didn't know if I could walk or not.'

'That's all right. Did you hurt your leg?'

She tested it, leaning on it. 'No, it's not much. What about you?'

'I don't know. I feel all right, really. Maybe too all right. Perhaps we'll keel over in a moment.'

Ahead of them on the stretcher was Eve, her face white. Benny had picked up Eve's handbag, a small cheap plastic one which Mother Francis had bought for her in Peggy Pine's shop as a going-to-Dublin present a few weeks ago.

'She's going to be fine, I think,' Benny explained in a shaky voice. 'The man with all the blood on him, the man driving the car, he says she's breathing and her pulse is all right.'

Benny looked so worried that anyone would have wanted to take her in their arms and stroke her, even though she was bigger than most people around.

The girl with the beautiful face, now grazed and muddy, the girl in the well-cut navy coat, now streaked with blood and wet mud, looked at Benny kindly.

'That man's a doctor. He *knows* these things. My name is Nan Mahon, what's yours?'


It was the longest day they had ever known.

The hospital machinery moved into action, but slowly. The guards took charge of the dead boy as regards telling his family. They had been through his things. His address was on a lot of his belongings. They had deputed two young guards to go out to Dunlaoghaire.

'Can you tell her it was instantaneous?' John Foley said.

'I don't know,' said the young officer. 'Can we tell her that?'

'It's true, and it might be some comfort to her,' John Foley said mildly.

The older Garda sergeant had a different view.

'You never know, Doctor, many a mother might like to think their son had time to whisper an Act of Contrition.'

John Foley turned his head away lest his annoyance be seen.

'And it wasn't his fault, be sure to tell her that,' he tried.

'I'm afraid my men can't . . .' the sergeant began.

'I know, I know.' The doctor sounded weary.

The nurse said of course they could use the phone, but they should have themselves looked at first. Then they'd be in a position to tell their parents what had happened. It made a lot of sense.

The news was good: minor cuts, nothing deep, anti-tetanus injections just in case, mild sedative for shock.

Eve was a different matter. Cracked ribs and mild concussion. Several stitches at the edge of her eye, and a broken wrist. She would be in hospital for some days, possibly a week. They wanted to know who to inform.

'Give me a minute,' Benny said.

'Well, you must know who it is, you're her friend.' The almoner was puzzled.

'Yes, but it's not that easy.'

'Well, what about her wallet?'

'There's nothing in it, no next of kin or anything. Please let me think, I just want to work out what's best.'

Benny was also putting off telling her own parents about the accident, but she had to decide which of the two nuns to talk to on Eve's behalf. Would Eve be furious if Mother Francis heard the whole story of the lies, the unhappiness and the circumstances that had brought her to the other side of the city and now into a hospital bed?

Would Mother Clare be as bad as Eve had said?

The woman was a nun after all, she must have some redeeming qualities if she were to keep her vows all her life.

Benny's head ached as she tried to work it all out.

'Would it be any help to tell me?' Nan Mahon asked. They had cups of sweet milky tea and they sat at a table.

'It's like a Grimms' fairy tale,' Benny said.

'Tell it,' Nan said.

So Benny told it, feeling slightly disloyal.

Nan listened and asked questions.

'Ring Mother Francis,' she said at the end. 'Tell her that Eve was about to ring her today.'

'But she wasn't.'

'It'll make the nun feel better, and what does it matter what day she was going to ring?'

It made sense. It made a lot of sense.

'But what about Mother Clare?'

'The baddy?'

'Yes, she sounds really awful and she'll crow over Mother Francis, the good one. It's awful to let her in for all this.'

'It's much better than ringing the bad one and bringing all the torments of Hell down on yourself for nothing.'

'I think you're right.'

'Good. Will you go and tell that Sister there, she's beginning to think you have delayed concussion or something. And by the way, put someone medical on to tell her about Eve's injuries. You'll only frighten her to death.'

'Why do you not want to tell your parents?'

'Because my mother works in a hotel shop where they don't really go a bundle on employing married women in the first place, so I don't want to get her all into a fluster for nothing. And my father . . .' Nan paused.

Benny waited.

'My father, that's different.'

'You mean he wouldn't care?'

'No, I mean the very opposite, he'd care too much. He'd come in here ranting and raving and making an exhibition of himself, saying that his poor little girl was injured, scarred for life and who was to blame.'

Benny smiled.

'I mean it. He's always been like that. It's good and bad. Good mainly because it means I can get what I want.'

'And bad?'

'Oh, I don't know. Bad too.' Nan shrugged. The confidences were over.

'Go on and ring the Good Sister before we have the starched apron in on us again.'

Kit Hegarty was in the big front bedroom, the one she had let to the two brothers from Galway. Nice sensible boys, she thought, well brought up by their mother, hung their clothes up neatly, which made a nice change. They wouldn't be much trouble during the year, one doing agriculture, one studying for a B.Comm. No matter what they said, it was the farmers who had the money. There were a good many farmers' sons going in the doors of University College today for the first time.

She thought of her own son amongst the crowd today. He would walk up those steps with a confidence he didn't feel, she knew that. She had seen so many of the students set out from her door, awkward and anxious, and after a few weeks it was as if they had been studying there all their lives.

It would be easier for Frank because he knew Dublin already. He didn't have to get to know a new city like the boys from the country did.

She heard the front gate squeak open, and as she saw the two young Garda officers look up at the window and come slowly up her path, Kit Hegarty suddenly knew without any doubt what they were coming to tell her.

Jack Foley had met several fellows from school. Not necessarily close friends, but it was amazing how welcome they were in that sea of faces. And they too seemed glad to see him.

There was an introductory lecture at twelve, but until then there wasn't much to do except get their bearings.

'It's like school without the teachers,' said Aidan Lynch, who had paid very little attention to any teacher during his days at school with Jack Foley.

'This is what's meant to be forming our character, remember? Jack said. 'It's like being on your honour to work all the time.'

'Which means we don't have to work at all,' Aidan said cheerfully. 'Will we go round the corner to Lesson Street? I saw armies of beautiful women all heading in that direction.'

Aidan was a better authority on women than any of the rest of them so they followed him willingly.

At the corner they saw that there had been an accident. People still stood around talking about it. It was a student, they said, very badly hurt, possibly dead. The blanket was over his face when they carried him away.

He had been on that motorbike, which was in bits over beside the wall. Someone said he was going to be doing engineering.

Aidan looked at the twisted wreck of steel and metal.

'Jesus, I hope it wasn't that fellow who was canning peas in Peterborough with me during the summer. That's the bike he was getting. Frank Hegarty. He was going to do engineering.'

'There could have been hundreds of people . . .' Jack

Foley began, but then he saw the car that had been pulled away from the corner where it had crashed. There was blood and glass all over the road. The car had been moved in order to let the traffic get through.

It was his father's car.

'Was anyone else hurt?'

'A girl. A young girl. She looked very bad,' said the man. The kind of man you always find at an accident, full of information and pessimism.

'And the man, the man driving the car?'

'Oh, he was all right. Big fancy coat on him, with a bit of fur on the collar. You know the type. Walked out of the car, giving orders left, right and centre, just like a general.'

'He's a doctor, he's meant to do that,' Jack said defensively.

'How do you know that?' Aidan Lynch was astonished.

'It's our car. You go on and have coffee. I'm going into the hospital to see if he is all right.'

He ran across the wet road and over to the hospital entrance before any of them could answer him.

'Come on,' Aidan said. 'The main thing with women is to be the first person they meet. They love that. It gives you a huge advantage.'

It was much easier to tell Mother Francis than Benny had feared. She had been calm and not at all put out about Eve having abandoned all the plans that had been so carefully thought out for her. She had also been very practical.

'Tell me as simply and quickly as you can, Bernadette, where does Mother Clare think that Eve is today?'

'Well, Mother . . .' Benny felt as if she were eight years of age again, instead of almost eighteen. 'It's a bit awkward . . .' It was partly to do with Mother Francis calling her 'Bernadette'. It put her straight back in the classroom, in her gym slip again.

'Yes, I'm sure, but the best thing is if I know everything, then I can judge how much has to be said to Mother Clare.' The nun's voice was smooth. Surely she couldn't be planning to go along with the lies.

Benny risked it. 'I think she thinks that Eve is sort of in hospital already. I think that's what Eve would have been telling you had she been able to give you a ring . . .'

'Yes, of course, she would. Please stop fretting, Bernadette. I am much more concerned that Eve gets well and is aware that we have all made things easier. Can you give me more details . . . ?'

Biting the corner of her lip Benny haltingly told a tale of mythical blood tests. It was noted crisply.

'Thank you, Bernadette. Now can you put me on to someone qualified to tell me about Eve's injuries?'

'Yes, Mother.'

'Bernadette?'

'Yes, Mother?'

'Ring your father at work first. Say you couldn't get through to your mother. It's easier to talk to men. They fuss a lot less.'

'But look at you, Mother, you don't fuss at all.'

'Ah, child, I'm different altogether. I'm a nun,' she said.

Benny gave the phone to the Sister, and sat down with her head in her hands.

'Was it awful?' Nan was sympathetic.

'No, like you said, it was easy.'

'It always is, if you do it right.'

'Now, I have to ring my parents. How do I do that right?'

'Well, what are you hiding from *them*?' Nan seemed amused.

'Nothing. It's just that they'll make such a fuss. They think of me as in nappies.'

'It all depends on how you begin. Don't say "Something terrible happened".'

'What do I start with, then?'

Nan was impatient. 'Maybe you *should* be in nappies,' she snapped. Benny felt her heart sink. It was probably true. She was a big baby, soft in the head.

'Hallo, Father,' she said into the phone. 'It's Benny. I'm absolutely fine, Father, I was trying to ring Mother but there was something wrong with the number. Wouldn't it be great to have the automatic exchange?' She looked across at Nan, who was giving the thumbs-up sign.

'No, I'm not actually *in* the college, but I'm just beside it. These people here are very over-careful you know, they just like to cover every eventuality so they asked us all to ring our families even though there isn't a thing wrong . . .'

*

Sean Walsh ran through Knockglen to tell the news to Annabel Hogan. Mrs Healy saw him running as she looked from her bow window and knew that something must be amiss. That young man always moved very correctly. He didn't pause as Dessie Burns called out to him from the hardware shop, he didn't notice Mr Kennedy looking over his glasses at all the bottles and apothecary jars in the window display of the chemist's shop. He ran past the chip shop where he had had coffee with Benny only last night, past the newsagents', the sweet shop, the pub and Paccy Moore's cobbler's shop. Up the short avenue to the Hogans' house; the ground was wet and covered with leaves. If *he* owned his house, he thought to himself, he would give it a good coat of paint, put a smart gate on it. Something more imposing than the way the Hogans had it.

Patsy answered the door. 'Sean,' she said, without much enthusiasm.

Sean felt his cheeks redden slightly. If he were master of the house, no maid would address a senior employee of the master's by his Christian name. It would be Mr Walsh, thank you very much, or sir. And she would wear something to show that she was a maid, a uniform, or a white collar and apron anyway.

'Is Mrs Hogan at home?' he asked haughtily.

'Come in, she's on the phone,' Patsy said casually.

'The phone? It's working again?'

'It never wasn't.' Patsy shrugged.

She led him into the sitting room. He could hear Mrs Hogan in the distance talking to someone. They had the phone in the breakfast room off the kitchen. He wouldn't have had it that way. A telephone should be on a half-moon table in the hall. A highly polished table under a mirror, perhaps a bowl of flowers beside it reflecting in the table. Sean had always looked around him when he went into people's houses. He wanted to know how things should be done. For when the time came.

The sitting room had shabby chintz furniture, and faded curtains in the long window alcove. It could have been a very smart room, Sean thought, mentally ticking off the changes he would make. He hardly noticed Patsy, who had come back in.

'She says you're to come out to her.'

'Mrs Hogan isn't coming in here?' He didn't want to be telling the news in the territory where the maid could be involved, but followed obediently to the shabby breakfast room.

'Ah, Sean.' Annabel Hogan was polite to him even if her maid wasn't.

'I'm very sorry to be the bearer of bad news, but there's been an accident,' he said in the sepulchral tones of an undertaker.

'I know, poor Eve, Mother Francis was on to me about it.'

'But Mrs Hogan . . . Benny was involved in it . . .'

'Yes, but she's not hurt at all, she was talking to Mother Francis and to her father. There was some fault on the phone here or else I was on the phone myself talking to Father Rooney about the Station.'

'She got scratches and a sprained ankle.' Sean couldn't believe this calm acceptance. He had expected to be the deliverer of the news and then the great consoler, but Mrs Hogan was making light of it. It was incomprehensible.

'Yes, but she's perfectly all right. She's going to sit there in the hospital, and they'll keep an eye on her and someone will put her on the evening bus, just as she planned. It's only the shock, Mother Francis says. Better to let her sit calmly there with people who know all about it.'

Sean felt all his thunder being stolen from him.

'I had thought I would drive to Dublin to collect her,' he said.

'Ah, Sean, we couldn't ask you to do that.'

'She might not like hanging around hospital, you know, sick people, smells of disinfectant . . . it's early closing and I was going to ask Mr Hogan for a loan of the car.'

Annabel Hogan looked at Sean Walsh's concerned face and at a stroke all the careful, calming work of Mother Francis was destroyed.

'You're very kind, Sean, but maybe if it's as bad as that my husband would want to go himself . . .'

'But Mrs Hogan, if I might presume, it's very hard to find a place to park the car in the centre of Dublin. Mr Hogan hasn't been used to driving in the city traffic of recent years, and I had planned to go to Dublin to collect the samples of material. You could ask them till kingdom come to put them on the bus, but they never do . . .'

'Will I come with you, do you think?'

Sean Walsh's mind did a slow careful calculation, then he came to a decision.

'I'll go on my own, Mrs Hogan, if that's all right. Then you can make all the preparations here.'

It had been the right thing to say. Annabel saw herself in the role of getting ready to welcome the invalid home.

Sean smiled as he left the house. This time he didn't run up the main street of Knockglen. He walked on the other side of the road. He nodded to Dr Johnson, who was coming out of his surgery. He glanced in the window of Peggy Pine's women's outfitters and saw with distaste the pastel colours that Benny had admired last night. Benny was such a big girl, she could hardly have wanted them for herself. Still, it was good that she sought his advice.

He saw that *Monsieur Hulot's Holiday* was coming to the cinema this weekend. That was good. Benny wouldn't be well enough, and Sean didn't like foreign-language films. They put him at a disadvantage.

He held his shoulders back. There was no reason for him to feel at a disadvantage. Things were working out fine.

All he had to do now was to let Mr Hogan know how distressed Mrs Hogan was and how he had saved the day.

Dr Foley said he'd just go in and see how that child was in casualty before he left.

'They've cancelled my appointments for this morning . . . Maybe you'd walk me down to the Shelbourne for a taxi?' he asked Jack.

'I could get one here, and come home with you.'

'No, no, you know I don't want that. Stay here in the waiting room, will you, Jack?'

Jack moved into the over-bright room with the yellow walls. Two girls sat at a table. One of them was a spectacularly pretty blonde; the other, a big girl with long chestnut hair tied back in a bow, had a bandage on her foot. He realised they must have been in the accident.

'Was it terrible?' he asked, looking questioningly at the empty chair, as if asking their permission to sit down. They pulled the chair forward and told him about it. They told him they had heard that the doctor had managed to avoid them all by driving into the lamp post. Only Eve, who had been hit by the moving car, was seriously hurt and even Eve would be out of hospital in a week.

They talked easily. Benny stumbled from time to time, and became tongue-tied when she looked at the handsome boy sitting beside them. Never before had she held a conversation with anyone like this, and she would begin a sentence and not know how to finish it.

Jack Foley's eyes rarely left Nan's face, but she seemed to be unaware of this and talked as if all three of them were equal partners in the conversation. Jack explained that it had been his father driving the car. Nan said that both she and Benny were busy trying to play down their bruises and scratches because it would cause such almighty upheavals in both their homes.

'I don't feel like going to college now. Do you?' She

looked from one to the other. It was if she knew a solution would be proposed.

'Why don't I take the pair of you for a plate of chips?' Jack asked.

Benny clapped her hands like a child. 'I didn't know that's what my soul cried out for, well possibly not my soul, but there was a cry there definitely,' she said. They both smiled at her.

'I'll just see my father to a taxi and come back for you.' He was looking straight into Nan's eyes.

'Where would we go? It's the best offer we've had all day,' Nan said.

'He's very nice,' Benny said, when Jack had gone.

'He's the college hero before he even gets there,' said Nan.

'How do you know?'

'I saw him play in the Schools Cup.'

'Play what?'

'He was on the wing.' Nan saw Benny's mystification and explained. 'Rugby. He really is very good.'

'How did you go to a rugby match?'

'Everyone does. It's a kind of social event.'

Benny realised that there were going to be a great many areas where she would be at a loss. Rugby matches would only be a very small part of them, and none of these gaps in her knowledge would be helped by continuing to live in Knockglen all her life.

She wished suddenly that she were someone totally different, that she were much smaller and had a small face and tiny feet like Nan had. That she could look up at men rather than over or down at them. She wished her parents lived in the Aran Islands and that there could be no question of her having to go home every night. She felt a sudden desire to dye her hair blonde and keep dyeing it every day so that the roots would never show. There was nothing she could do about her size. Even if she were thinner she would still have huge shoulders and great big feet. No operation had been invented to give you small feet.

She looked at them with distaste in their sensible shoes and thick bandage. Her mother had normal feet, her father had, why did Benny's have to be the way they were? At school they had once heard of some animal which had become extinct because of its huge flat feet. Benny hadn't known whether to envy it or be sorry for it.

'Is it hurting much?' Nan had seen Benny studying her foot and thought it must be paining her.

Jack came back at that moment.

'Well,' he said to Nan.

She stood up. 'I think Benny's foot is hurting her.'

'Oh, I'm sorry.' He looked at her briefly with a sympathetic smile.

'No, it's fine,' she said.

'If you're sure?' He was polite. Perhaps he wanted to go off with Nan on his own. She didn't know. But it would always be like this anyway so there was no point in getting upset about it.

'You were looking at it and frowning,' Nan said.

'No, I was only thinking about all those prayers we say for the conversion of China. Do you put three Hail Marys on to the Rosary for it?'

'I think it was the conversion of Russia in ours,' Jack said. 'But I'm not sure. Just shows you how well I'm able to escape it.'

'Well, I can't think why we should be praying for them,' Benny said with mock indignation. 'They have lovely habits out there. They bind everyone's feet.'

'What?'

'Oh yes, as soon as they're born, so there's no problem about people falling over them. Everyone has tiny feet and nice squashed-up bones. So elegant-looking.'

Jack seemed to realise she was there for the first time.

'And now chips,' he said, looking straight at her. 'Four plates, one plate each and one to pick off. And lashings of tomato ketchup.'

Then she heard the nurse tell someone that Miss Hogan was out in the waiting room, and there was Sean Walsh coming towards them. Her face fell.

'I've come to drive you home, Benny,' he said.

'I told Father I was coming home on the bus,' she said coldly.

'But he gave me the car . . .'

Jack looked politely from the thin-faced boy to the big girl with the red-brown hair.

No introductions were made.

Benny spoke with an authority she didn't know that anyone could have, let alone herself.

'Well, I hope you had some other work to do in Dublin, Sean. That you didn't come up specially, because I have to leave now. And I will be home on the bus as arranged.'

'What do you have to do? You're to come home. Now. With me.' Sean sounded petulant.

'She has to go for some more treatment,' Jack Foley said. 'I'm just taking her there. You wouldn't want her to miss that.'

## 5

Benny knew they would come to meet her off the bus. But she hadn't expected all three of them, not Patsy as well, and not the car. Sean must have driven home with dire tales to have brought such a gathering to the bus stop. Before Mikey had swung the bus around and brought it to a stop she had seen their pale faces in the wet night, the two umbrellas. She felt the familiar surge of irritation mixed with guilt. No one on earth had such a loving family, no one on earth felt so cooped up and smothered.

She walked with a heavy heart to the front of the bus.

'Goodnight, Mikey.'

'Good girl, Benny. Something wrong with your foot?'

'I hurt it,' she said, realising his wife would probably have the tale already.

'It's all this drunken life as a student. That's what it is,' he said, roaring with laughter at his wit.

'That's what it is.' She repeated it in a dull, polite way.

'There she is!' cried her father, as if there had ever been any doubt about her arrival.

'Oh, Benny, are you all right?' Her mother's eyes were wide with anxiety.

'Mother, I *told* Father on the phone. I'm fine. Fine.'

'Then why did you have to go back for treatment?' Annabel Hogan had the face of someone who thought that very bad news was being kept from her. 'We were very alarmed when Sean told us that they needed to look at you again, and you didn't ring a second time . . . so we were afraid . . .'

Her father's face had lines of worry.

'Sean had no business coming up there for me, interfering and giving orders and upsetting everyone here and there.' Benny's voice was calm, but a little louder than normal.

She saw Mrs Kennedy from the chemist turn and look at her. That would be a subject for discussion in *their* house tonight, a scene, no less, at the bus stop with the Hogan family of all people. Well, well, well. Hadn't it been a mistake to let that Benny go to Dublin on her own after all?

'He went to set our minds at ease,' Benny's father said. 'We were very worried.'

'No, Father, you weren't. You were quite happy for me to come home on the bus. I talked to you and you were grand, and you said Mother would be grand and then suddenly Sean manages to spoil everything.'

'The boy drove the whole way to Dublin on his half day to bring you home and then drove straight back and said you had to see another doctor. Do you blame us for being worried?' Eddie Hogan's face was working with distress: beside him Annabel raked her face for more information. Even Patsy didn't seem convinced that all was well.

'I didn't *want* him to come for me. You never said he was coming. There was nothing wrong with *me*, for God's sake. You *must* see that. I was perfectly all right, but a boy was killed. He was killed in front of my eyes. He was alive one minute and then he was dead with his neck broken. And Eve's in a hospital ward with broken ribs and concussion and all kinds of things. And all Sean Walsh can do is stand like a stuffed dummy in that hospital and talk about me!'

To her horror Benny realised that there were tears pouring down her face, and that a small circle of people were watching her in concern. Two schoolgirls from the convent who had been in Dublin to buy books with one of the young nuns turned to see what was happening. It would be all around the convent before bed time.

Benny's father decided to act. 'I'll get her into the car,' he said. 'Patsy, will you run down to Dr Johnson's like a good girl and ask him to come over as soon as he can. Now, Benny, it's all right. It's all right. It's natural, just shock.'

Benny wondered was there a condition which might be known as Rage. Because that was definitely what she felt her condition to be. Helpless rage.

Everyone in Knockglen heard about it in record time, but what they heard bore little relation to the facts. Mrs Healy said that she heard the girls were running and laughing like they had done in Knockglen and they were hit by a car. As a precaution they had both been admitted to hospital, but Sean Walsh had driven up and got Benny discharged. It was a lesson on how to conduct yourself in huge menacing Dublin traffic if you came from a small place like Knockglen.

Mr Flood was silent and blessed himself a great deal when he heard the news. He said that it was obviously meant as some kind of warning. What kind of a warning he couldn't say, but his family noticed with alarm that he had gone out to consult the tree again. They had hoped that this little habit had died down.

Mrs Carroll said it was a waste of good money sending girls to university. Not if the grocery was three times the size of Findlater's in Dublin would they send Maire and her sisters there. You might as well take money and shovel it down the drain. What did they do on the very first day except walk under the first vehicle they saw? Maire Carroll, serving in the shop and hating it, felt a firm and vicious sense of satisfaction over the fate of Eve and Benny, but of course she pretended great care and concern.

Bee Moore, who worked in Westlands and was a sister of Paccy Moore the shoemaker, had heard that Eve was dead from horrible injuries and that Benny was in such shock she couldn't be told. The nuns would all be going up to Dublin to collect her body shortly.

Birdie Mac in the sweet shop told people that it took a great amount of faith these days to realise that God was fair-minded. Wasn't it hard enough on that poor child to know no parents, to be totally disowned by her relations up in Westlands, to be brought up an orphan in the convent in second-hand clothes, and sent to a secretarial course when she had her heart set on going to university without being mown down by a car on her first week. Birdie sometimes questioned the fairness of life, having spent overlong looking after an ailing mother and missing her chances with a very suitable man from Ballylee who married another, who wasn't bound to an ailing parent.

Dessie Burns said that there was a lot of truth in the theory that if you fell down drunk, you never hurt yourself, a theory he had tested only too often. It was a girl like Eve Malone, a little pikasheen who wouldn't have had a drink on her at all, that would end up in hospital.

Father Ross said that Mother Francis would take it badly. She felt as much for that girl as if she had been her own flesh and blood. No mother could ever have done more for the girl. He hoped Mother Francis wouldn't get too great a shock.

Mother Francis had acted swiftly when she heard about

Eve. She had gone straight to Peggy Pine and waited demurely until the shop was free of customers.

'Do me a great favour, Peg.'

'Whatever you want.'

'Could you close the shop and drive me to Dublin?'

'When?'

'As soon as you can, really, Peg.'

Peggy pulled down the orange sheets of plastic intended to keep the glare off her goods in the window, both in summer when there might have been sunshine and in winter when it was unnecessary.

'Off we go,' she said.

'But the business?'

'One thing about you, Bunty, you have the good sense to ask a favour at the right time. You decide to leap over the convent wall and hightail it to England to a new life, and you have the wit to do it on early closing day.' She picked up her handbag, rooted for her keys and then put on her tweed coat and closed the door behind her. There were advantages about the single state. You didn't need to tell anyone what you were doing. Or why.

You didn't even need to ask why.

'Mother Francis!' Eve's voice was weak.

'You're going to be fine.'

'What happened to me? Please, Mother. The other people just say "Hush" and "Rest".'

'Not much point in saying either of those words to you.' The nun was holding Eve's thin hand. 'Broken ribs, but they'll knit together. A wrist that's going to be painful for a while, but it will heal. A few stitches. Truly I never lied to you in my life. You're going to be fine.'

'Oh, Mother, I'm so sorry.'

'Child, you couldn't have stopped it.'

'No. About you. Having to find out about me this way.'

'I know you were *going* to ring me. Benny told me that. She said you were about to phone.'

'I never lied to you, either, Mother. I wasn't going to phone.'

'Not immediately, perhaps, but you would have some time.'

'Do you still think any question must be answered?'

'Of course.'

'What'll I do, Mother, what on earth will I do when I get out of here?'

'You'll come home to get well and then we'll think of something else for you.'

'And Mother Clare?'

'Leave her to me.'


Jack came in the side door and found Aengus sitting in the cloakroom studying his glasses.

'Oh, Jesus, not *again*.'

'It's not my fault, Jack, I don't do anything, I swear I don't. I just went past these fellows and one of them shouted, "Hey, speccy four-eyes," and I ignored them like you told me and then they came and took them off and stamped on them.'

'So, it's my fault.' Jack looked at the glasses; they were beyond repair. Sometimes he had been able to fit the frames back and push in the lenses; not this time.

'Listen, Aengus, don't make a big thing out of it. They've had enough here today.'

'Well, what will I say?' Aengus looked naked and defenceless without his spectacles. 'I mean I can't say I stamped on them myself.'

'No, I know. Listen, I'll go in tomorrow and kick the shit out of the fellows who did it.'

'No, no, Jack, please. That would make it worse.'

'Not if I beat them to a pulp it won't. They won't try anything again. They'd be afraid they'd have to deal with me again.'

'But they'll know you won't be there all the time.'

'I can be there at odd times. You know, just happen to be passing when they're going out of school.'

'Wouldn't they think I was a telltale?'

'Nope.' Jack was casual. 'You're smaller. You have to wear glasses to see, if they don't respect that then you have to bring in reinforcements . . . that's the system.'

There was no need for a gong in their household, Lilly Foley said that Holy Mother Church looked after all that for them. As soon as they heard the angelus ring they gathered from all over the big house to the supper table. Jack's father had asked him not to mention the accident in front of the younger children. He didn't want to go into the fact that someone had died. His father looked pale, Jack thought, his eye slightly swollen but maybe he wouldn't have noticed it if he hadn't been involved. Certainly none of his brothers saw anything amiss. Ronan was entertaining them; he was a good mimic and this time he was doing a fussy Brother in the school trying to get everyone to sit still in the big hall for a lecture. Then he went on to a merciless performance as an inarticulate Garda, who had been called to the school to deliver the annual lecture on road safety.

Ronan had picked the wrong day for this story.

Another time his father might have laughed or mildly remonstrated about the cruelty of the imitation. But today Dr Foley's face was grey and set.

'And whatever his accent or his defects, I don't suppose one of those blockheads making a jeer of him listened to a word he was saying.' The voice was harsh.

'But, Daddy . . .' Ronan was bewildered.

'Oh, you can "But, Daddy" at me all you like – it's not going to bring you, or any of those amadans mocking the poor guard, back to life when they walk out under a ten-ton truck.'

There was a silence, Jack watched his brothers look at each other in alarm, and saw his mother frown slightly down the table at his father.

For no reason Jack remembered something that girl Benny had said earlier in the day. It was something about wishing she had the power to control conversations. If you could do that you could rule the world, she had laughed.

'You mean like Hitler?' he had teased her.

'I mean the reverse of Hitler. I mean sort of patting things down, not stirring them up.'

That was the moment when the fabulous Nan Mahon had flashed her eyes. Anyone could pat things down, she had said with a toss of all that blonde curly hair. The point was to liven things up. She had looked straight at Jack when she said it.

Nan Mahon turned the key in Number 23 Maple Gardens. She had no idea whether there would be anyone home yet. It was six fifteen. Whoever came in first turned on the electric heater in the hall to take the chill off the house, and then lit the gas fire in the kitchen. They had all their meals at a big kitchen table; there was never any company, so it didn't matter.

The hall was already slightly warm so somebody was home.

'Hallo,' Nan shouted.

Her father came out of the kitchen.

'That was a fine message you left. That was a great day's work, frightening the bloody lives out of us.'

'What is it?'

'What is it? What is it? Meek as milk! God Almighty, Nan, I've been here for the past two hours without knowing hair nor hide of you.'

'I left a message. I said there had been an accident. I wouldn't have, but the hospital said we had to. I left a message at the yard. I told Paul to tell you I was all right. Isn't that what he said?'

'Who'd believe the daylight out of that fool, reading magazines with one hand, stuffing his face with another . . .'

'Well, you were out.' Nan had taken her coat off and was examining the mud stains. She hung it up carefully on a big wooden coat hanger and began to brush hard at the dried mud.

'Someone was killed, Nan. A boy died.'

'I know.' She spoke slowly. 'We saw it.'

'And why didn't you come straight home?'

'To an empty house?'

'It wouldn't have *been* empty. I'd have come back. We'd have got your mother back out of that place.'

'I didn't want to get her back, disturbing her when there was nothing she could do.'

'She's worried sick too. You'd better ring her. She said she'd stay put in case you came by the hotel.'

'No, *you'd* better ring her. I didn't get her worried.'

'I can't understand why you're being so callous . . .' He looked at her bewildered.

Nan's eyes were blazing. 'You haven't even begun to *try* to understand . . . you haven't a notion what it was like, all the cars and the blood and the glass and the boy with the blanket over him, and a girl breaking her ribs, and all the hanging around and waiting . . . it was . . . it was . . . just awful.' He came towards her, arms outstretched, but she avoided him.

'Oh, Nan, my poor baby,' he was saying.

'That is precisely why I didn't want you to come to the

hospital. I'm not anyone's poor baby. I only had scratches. I didn't want you making an exhibition of yourself. And of me.'

He flinched.

Nan continued. '*And* I didn't ring Em because it's hard enough to get a job in any place as a married woman without having hysterical daughters ringing up crying for Mamma. Em's been working in that kip for six years, since I was twelve. And there *have* been days I'd have liked her at home when I had a headache or one of the nuns had roared at me at school. But I thought of her. You, you never give anyone a thought but yourself. You'd ring her if you couldn't find your socks where you thought they should be.'

Brian Mahon's hand was in a fist. He moved closer to where his daughter was starting again to brush the mud from the coat that hung on the side of the kitchen dresser.

'By God, you won't speak to me like that. You may well be upset, but you're not going to get away with treating me like dirt. Your own father out slaving day and night so that you'd have a college education. By God, you're going to take that back or you're going to get out of this house.'

Not a muscle of Nan's face moved, her stroke never faltered as she brushed and watched the flakes fall down on the newspaper she had spread beneath. She said nothing.

'Then you'll not stay under my roof.'

'Oh, but I will,' said Nan. 'For the moment anyway.'

*

Mother Francis had been putting off her visit to Mother Clare as long as possible. There had been a deliberately vague telephone call. But it became clear that she would soon have to go out in the rain and get a bus to their sister convent. She had sent Peggy home. It was not a visit she relished making.

Still, she thought, bracing her shoulders, if she had been a real mother she would have had to endure many such problems with a teenage daughter. As a schoolteacher she knew only too well the dance they led their parents. Natural mothers had to put up with a great deal. This was the very thought in her head as she turned the corner of the corridor and back into the waiting room and saw the weeping figure of a woman hunched over and hugging herself with grief.

Beside her stood a pleasant-looking, round, grey-haired woman, unsure of what to do, hesitating about whether to hush the weeping figure or let her cry.

'Frank,' the woman sobbed. 'Frank, tell me it's not true. Tell me it's someone else, tell me it was just someone that looked like you.'

'They're going to get the nurse again,' said her companion. 'She was fine a minute ago. We have a taxi ordered. I was taking her home with me . . .'

'Was it her son . . . ?' Mother Francis asked.

'Her only child.' The woman's eyes were eager but anxious. 'I'm her neighbour. She's going to spend the night with me. I've sent my sister in to look after the other lads.'

'Lads?'

'She keeps students, you see. This was her boy's first day at college.'

The nun's face was sad. Beside them, the anguished figure of Kit Hegarty rocked to and fro.

'You see, Sister, Mother, I'm the worst one for her. I have everything. A husband, and a family, and Kit has nothing now. She doesn't want to be with the likes of us. She doesn't want anything nice and normal and safe. It's only reminding her of what she hasn't got.'

Mother Francis looked at the women with appreciative eyes. 'You're obviously a very good friend, Mrs . . . ?'

'Hayes, Ann Hayes.'

Mother Francis was kneeling down beside Frank Hegarty's mother. She reached out and held the woman's hand.

Kit looked up, startled.

'In a few days, when the funeral's over, I want you to come and stay with me,' she said softly.

The ravaged face looked at her. 'What do you mean? Who are you?'

'I'm someone like you. I've lost my child, in a sense. I could tell you about it, maybe you could advise me. You see, I'm not a real mother. You are.'

'I was.' Kit smiled a terrible twisted grimace.

'No, you are, you still are, you'll always be his mother, nobody can take that away from you. And all you gave him, all you did for him.'

'I didn't give him much. I didn't do much for him. I let

him have that bike.' She clawed at Mother Francis's hand as she spoke.

'But you had to. You had to give him freedom. That was the greatest gift, that was what he would have wanted most. You gave him the best he could want.'

Nobody had said anything like this to Kit all day. Somehow she managed to take a proper breath, not the little shallow gasps she had been giving up to now.

Mother Francis spoke again. 'I live in the convent in Knockglen. It's simple and peaceful. And you could spend a few days there. It's different, you see, that's the main thing. It wouldn't have memories.'

'I couldn't go. I can't leave the house.'

'Not immediately, of course, but whenever you're ready. Ann will look after things for a few days. Ann Hayes and her sister.'

Somehow her voice had a hypnotic effect. The woman had become less agitated.

'Why are you offering me this?'

'Because my heart goes out to you. And because my girl was hurt in the same crash . . . she's going to be all right, but it's a shock seeing her so pale in a hospital bed . . .'

'She's going to be all right.' Kit's voice was flat.

'Yes, I know. I know you would accept your son to have any injury if you thought he was going to come out.'

'Your girl, what do you mean . . . ?'

'She was brought up in our convent. I love her every bit

as much as if she were my natural daughter. But I'm no use as a mother. I'm not out in the world.'

Through her tears Kit managed something like a real smile.

'I will come, Mother. The convent in Knockglen. But how will I know you? Who will I ask for?'

'I'm afraid you won't have any difficulty in remembering the name. Like your son, I was called after St Francis.'

Mario looked at Fonsie's yellow tie with disapproval.

'You're going to frighten them away.'

'Don't be an eejit, Mario. This is the way people dress nowadays.'

'You no call me eejit. I know what eejit means.'

'It's about the only word of English you *do* know.'

'You no speak to your uncle that way.'

'Listen, Mario, pass me those biscuit tins. If we put the player on top of something tinny it'll sound a bit more like real music'

'Eet soun horrible, Fonsie. Who will come to hear things so very, very loud?' Mario put his hands on his ears.

'The kids will.'

'The kids have no money.'

'The old ones wouldn't come in here in a fit anyway.'

The door opened and Sean Walsh walked in.

'Now do you see!' Fonsie cried.

At the very same moment Mario said, 'Now, what did I tell you!'

Sean looked from one to the other with distaste. It was a place he rarely went, and now he had been twice in twenty-four hours; last night with Benny, and tonight because he was so late and fussed getting back from his useless journey to Dublin. He had not been able to buy himself provisions, both grocery shops were closed. Normally Sean Walsh divided his custom. One day he might patronise Hickey's, beside Mr Flood; other days he would go to Carroll's, immediately next door to Hogan's. It was as if he were preparing for the day he would be a big man himself in this town and wanted everyone on his side, wanted them all to think of him as a customer. If he had been a drinking man he would have had a half pint in every establishment. It was the way to get on. But tonight there had been no time to get the cheese or sardines or cold ham that made his evening meal; Sean never liked to cook in his bedsit above the premises of Hogan's lest the smell of food linger and be deemed offensive. He had thought that he might slip in for a quick snack that would keep body and soul together before he went back to his room to brood about the situation that he had handled so badly.

Now it appeared that Mario and his halfwit nephew were making fun of him.

'He's old and he's come in here two times,' Mario was saying.

'He's not old, and the word is twice, you gobdaw,' the unappealing Fonsie said.

Sean wished that he had gone down to Birdie Mac's and

knocked on the door for a bar of Kit-Kat, anything rather than face these two.

'Are you serving me food, or am I interrupting some kind of talent contest?'

'How old are you, Sean?' Fonsie said. Sean looked at him in disbelief: the huge spongy soles making him four or five inches taller than he really was, the hair slicked into waves with some filthy oil, his narrow tie and huge, mauve-coloured jacket.

'Are you mad?'

'You tell how old you are.' Mario looked unexpectedly ferocious.

Sean felt the whole world had tilted. First Benny had turned her back on him in public and told him to go home without her after he had driven up especially to collect her. Now both men in the chipper. It was one of the rare occasions in his life when Sean Walsh spoke without calculation.

'I'm twenty-five,' he said. 'Since September.'

'There!' Fonsie was triumphant.

'No!' Mario was equally sure he was right.

'What *is* this?' Sean looked angrily from one to the other.

'Mario thinks the place is for old people. I say it's for young fellows like yourself and myself,' Fonsie said.

'Sean is not a fellow, he is a businessman.'

'Oh, Jaysus, does it matter? He's not on two sticks like most people in the town. What do you want, Sean? Rock salmon or cod?'

*

140

Patsy had gone for a walk with Mossy Rooney.

He had waited wordlessly in the kitchen until the daughter of the house had been soothed and put to bed. Mossy, a little like Sean Walsh, would have wished that the kitchen and living quarters of the Hogan household were more separate. Then he would have been able to sit down at the table, loosen his shirt collar, his shoelaces, and read the evening paper until Patsy was ready. But the Hogans lived on top of you when you went to that house. There was the master, a man of importance in the town that you'd think would want a house properly run for himself. And the mistress, much older by all appearances than her husband, who fussed too much over that great big daughter.

There had been a great deal of fussing tonight. The doctor had come and given her two tablets to take, he had said there wasn't a thing wrong with her that wouldn't be wrong with any red-blooded girl who had seen a fatal accident. She was shocked and upset and what she needed most was to be allowed to rest, alone.

Mossy Rooney, a man who, though he spoke little, noticed a lot, saw the look of relief pass over Benny Hogan's face, as she was sent to bed with a hot-water bottle and a cup of hot milk. He saw also the way the Hogans looked after her as she left the kitchen. He had seen that look on the faces of mother ducks when they took their little flock down to the river for the first time.

If he had been walking out with any other girl in service

in the town they could have stayed in on a wet night and talked by the kitchen range, but with the Hogans hovering around he had to bring Patsy out into the rain.

'Would you not like to take your ease indoors on a bad night like this?' Mrs Hogan had said kindly.

'Not at all, Mam, a nice fresh walk would be grand,' Patsy said with little enthusiasm.

For a long time Annabel and Eddie Hogan sat in silence.

'Maurice said that we're not to worry about a thing,' Eddie said eventually.

Maurice Johnson obviously realised who were the real patients in the house. He had uttered more words of advice to them than to the girl he was meant to be treating.

'It's easy for Maurice to say that. We don't worry about his children,' Annabel said.

'True, but to be fair he and Grainne don't worry much about them either.'

Kit Hegarty lay in her own narrow bed and heard the fog horn and the town hall clock, heard the occasional sound of a car going past. The sleeping tablets hadn't worked. Her eyes were wide open.

Everyone had been so kind. Nobody had counted the time or the trouble. The boys in the house, ashen-faced at the shock, had offered to leave. Their parents had telephoned from the country. And that little Mrs Hayes next door, who she hardly knew, had been a tower of strength, sending her sister in to cook and keep the place going. And the priests in Dunlaoghaire had been great, in and out all evening, three or maybe four of them saying nice things and talking to other people, making it seem somehow more normal, drinking cups of tea. But she had so wanted to be left alone for a while.

The only thing that stuck out in a day that seemed to have been a hundred hours of confusion was that nun. The aunt, possibly, of a girl who had been injured in the accident. *She* had understood that Frank had to have the bike. Nobody else appreciated that. Fancy a nun being able to realise it. And she had been insistent in her invitation. Kit thought that she would go and see her in that convent. Later, when she was able to think.


Judging from all the chatter, everyone in UCD must have got to know each other pretty quickly, Benny thought as she went up the steps the following morning. The main hall was thronged with people standing in groups, there were shouts of laughter and people greeting each other.

Everyone had a friend of some sort.

On another day it might have worried Benny, but not today.

She walked down a stone staircase to a basement where you could hang your coat. It smelled faintly carbolic, like school. Then up to the ground floor again and into the Ladies' Reading Room. This was not at all like school. For one thing nobody seemed to think that a reading room was a place where you were meant to read. There were girls fixing their make-up at a mirror over the mantelpiece, or scanning notices on the board – items for sale, extra tuition offered, rooms to share, sodalities to join.

A very confident group laughed and reminisced about their summers abroad. They had been in Spain, or Italy, or France . . . the only thing in common was how little of the language they had learned, how monstrous the children they had had to mind had been, and how late everyone ate their meals in the evening.

They were happy to be back.

Benny soaked it all up for Eve. She would visit her again at lunch time. This morning she had been pale, still, but cheerful as anything. Mother Francis was going to sort it out. There would be no recriminations.

'I'm going to try to get to college, Benny,' she had said, her face blazing with the intensity of it. 'I'll only be a few weeks late. I'll get a job, really I will. So you just watch out for everything for me, and take notice, so that I'll catch up.'

'Are you going to ask the Westwards?'

'I'm not going to rule it out.'

There were always a great many students who took English as a subject in First Arts. The lectures were held in a big hall, confusingly called the Physics Theatre. Benny streamed in with the others. It was so different to the classrooms at school. More like an amphitheatre, with rows of seats in semicircles high up at the back. There were some young student nuns already in place, they were in the front rows, eager and anxious to miss nothing. Benny walked slowly up towards the high seats at the back where she thought she might be more inconspicuous.

From her vantage point she watched them come in: serious-looking lads in duffle coats, earnest women in glasses and hand-knitted cardigans, the clerical students from the religious seminaries in their black suits all looking remarkably cleaner and neater than the other males not bound for religious life. And the girls, the confident, laughing girls. Could they really just be First Years, these troupers in brightly coloured skirts, flouncing their hair, aware of the impression they were creating? Perhaps they had spent a year abroad after they left school, Benny thought wistfully. Or even had a holiday job during the summer. Whatever it was, it didn't bear the hallmark of life in Knockglen.

Suddenly she saw Nan Mahon. Nan wore the smart navy coat she had worn yesterday, but this time over a pale yellow wool dress. Tied loosely around the strap of her shoulder bag was a navy and yellow scarf. Her curly hair was back from her face more than yesterday, and she had yellow earrings. As she walked in, flanked by a boy on each side, each competing for her attention, Nan was the object of all eyes. Her eyes roamed the banks of seats, deciding where to sit. Suddenly she saw Benny.

'Hallo, *there* you are!' she cried.

People turned round to see who she was waving at. Benny reddened at the stares, but Nan had left the two admirers and was bounding up to the back row. Benny was taken aback. She felt sure that Nan would know everyone in UCD in days. It was surprising to be singled out. And so warmly.

'Well, how did it go?' she asked companionably.

'What?'

'You know, you sent the young man packing and he more or less said you'd rue the day. I haven't seen anything so dramatic for years.'

Benny was dismissive. 'You couldn't get a message through to him. Mercifully he didn't turn up at home. I thought he'd be there, with big cow's eyes.'

'He's probably more madly in love with you than ever, now.' Nan was cheerful, as if this was good news.

'I don't think he has a notion of what love is. He's like a fish. A fish with an eye to the main chance. A gold-digging goldfish.'

They giggled at the thought.

'Eve's fine,' Benny said. 'I'm going to see her at lunch time.'

'Can I come too?'

Benny paused. Eve was often so prickly even when she was in the whole of her health. Would she like seeing this golden college belle at her bedside?

'I don't know,' she said at last.

'Well, we were all in it together. And I know all about her, and the business of Mother Clare and Mother Francis.'

For a moment Benny wished she hadn't told the story in

such detail. Eve certainly wouldn't like her business being discussed as she lay unconscious.

'That got sorted out,' Benny said.

'I knew it would.'

'Do you think you could come tomorrow instead?'

## 6

The body of Frank Hegarty was brought to the church in Dunlaoghaire.

Dr Foley attended the prayers and the Removal service with his eldest son.

Also in the church was Mother Francis, who had found it necessary to spend a little longer in Dublin than she had hoped, sorting things out with Mother Clare. Peggy had offered to collect her later. She knew there was some kind of trouble, but didn't ask what it was. She had given her own kind of encouragement to Mother Francis.

'Whatever that one says to you, Bunty, remember that her people were tinkers.'

'They weren't.'

'Well, dealers, anyway. That should give you the upper hand dealing with her.'

It hadn't, of course, any more than it should have. Mother Francis had a grim face as she waited in the big church for the funeral party to arrive. She didn't know why she was there; it was as if she wanted to represent Eve.

Nan Mahon went out on the bus to Dunlaoghaire and stood among the group at the back of the church. She was instantly spotted by Jack Foley who went to join her.

'That's nice of you, to come all the way out,' he said.

'You did too.'

'I came with my father. But do you see that group there, those are fellows who worked with him in the summer. That's Aidan Lynch – he was at school with me, and a whole lot more. They were all canning peas together.'

'How did they know?'

'His picture was in the paper, and there was some kind of announcement at the engineering lectures today,' he said. 'Where's Benny? Did you see her today?'

'Yes, but she couldn't come tonight. She has to go home, you see, every evening on this one bus.'

'That's hard on her,' Jack said.

'It's very foolish of her,' Nan said.

'What can she do about it?'

'She should make a stand at the outset.'

Jack looked at the attractive girl beside him. She would have made a stand, he knew that. He remembered the big soft-featured Benny.

'She stood up to that awful fellow with the white face who tried to take her off with him yesterday.'

'If you couldn't stand up to *him* you shouldn't be allowed out,' Nan said.

'This is Eve Malone,' Benny said, as Nan sat on the end of the hospital bed.

She wanted Eve to like Nan, to recognise that Nan could have been anywhere but had chosen to come and see Benny's friend. Benny had heard this fellow Aidan Lynch almost begging Nan to come and have lunch with him.

Nan had not brought flowers or grapes or a magazine; instead she had brought the one thing that Eve truly wanted, a college handbook. All the details of registration, late registration, degree courses, diplomas. She didn't even greet the girl in the bed. Instead she spoke about the matter which was uppermost in Eve's mind.

'I gather you're trying to get into college. This might be of some use to you,' she said.

Eve seized it and let her thumb rifle through the pages. 'This is just what I need, thank you very much indeed,' she said.

Then her brow darkened slightly.

'How did you think of bringing me this?' she asked suspiciously.

Nan shrugged. 'It's all in there,' she said.

'No, what made you think I'd need it?'

Benny wished Eve wouldn't be so prickly. What did it matter that Nan Mahon knew her hopes? There was no need to be secretive.

'I asked, that's all. I asked what you were doing and Benny said you hadn't enrolled yet.'

Eve nodded. The tension was over. She fingered the book again with gratitude and Benny felt a pang of regret that *she* hadn't thought of something so practical.

Little by little Eve was losing her look of wariness. And

as Benny watched the girls talk easily she realised they were kindred spirits.

'Will you have it sorted out fairly soon do you think?' Nan was asking.

'I have to go and ask a man for money. It's not easy but it won't get any easier by delaying,' Eve said.

Benny was astounded. Eve never talked of her business to anyone and the matter of approaching the Westwards for money was one she had only barely acknowledged to Benny herself. Nan was unaware of this.

'Will you play up the being injured bit?' she enquired.

Eve was on the same wavelength. 'I might. I've been considering it, but he's the kind of fellow who might regard that as weakness and snivelling. I'll have to work out how to play it.'

'What's it all about?' Nan asked with interest.

And as Eve began to tell her the story of the Westwards, the story never spoken aloud to anyone, Benny realised with a shock that Nan was in fact pretending to Eve that she hadn't heard any of this already. She had asked Nan to be discreet, and she certainly had followed the instructions to the letter. And judging by the way Eve was confiding, the instructions had been unnecessary.

It had been harder to deal with Mother Clare than Mother Francis would ever have believed possible. Sometimes Mother Francis talked directly to Our Lady about it and asked for immediate and positive advice.

'I've *said* I was sorry, I've *said* that we will look after

Eve from now on, but she goes on and on and says it's her duty to know what plans are being made for the girl. Why can't she just stay out of it? Why, Holy Mother, tell me?'

As it happened, Mother Francis got an answer which she presumed had come from the Mother of God, even though it was spoken by Peggy Pine.

'What that auld rip wants is to be able to prance around like the cock of the walk saying "I told you so, I told you so". She wants you to humble yourself, then she'll give up on it and start torturing someone else.'

Mother Francis agreed to use the tactics of humbling herself. 'You were right all along, Mother Clare,' she wrote in the most hypocritical letter she had ever penned. 'We were wrong to ask you to take on someone like Eve who had been given a wholly exaggerated set of expectations by our small Community here. I can only say that I bow to your wisdom on this as in so many other matters and hope that the Sisters were not unduly inconvenienced by the experiment which you knew was destined to be full of pitfalls.'

It had been the right approach. The regular bewildered and hurt interrogations from Mother Clare ceased.

And just in time too. Eve was pronounced fit to leave hospital a week to the day after she had been admitted.

'I'll come on the bus, with Benny,' Eve had said on the telephone.

'No, you won't, there's half a dozen people who'll go and collect you. I don't like to ask Peggy again but Mrs Healy will be going up.'

'*Please*, Mother.'

'All right, Sean Walsh? No, don't even tell me . . . !'

'I've caused you enough trouble. I'll go with anyone you say, though I *would* rather go on the bus.'

'Mario?'

'Marvellous. I love Mario.'

'All right, we'll see you tomorrow. I'm so glad you're coming home, Eve. I missed you.'

'And I missed you, Mother. We'll have to talk.'

'Of course we will. Wrap up warmly, won't you.'

When Eve hung up Mother Francis sat for a moment. It was true they would have to talk. Talk seriously.

As she sat there the telephone rang again.

'Mother Francis please?'

'Speaking.'

There was a pause.

'Mother, in a fit of generosity you said to me . . . I mean you wondered if I'd like . . . and isn't it odd, in the middle of everything I kept remembering it. I wonder would you think it strange if I *did* come to see you . . .?'

The woman's voice stopped again hesitantly.

A great smile lit up Mother Francis's face.

'Mrs Hegarty, I'm delighted to hear from you. This weekend would be lovely. You tell me which bus and I'll walk over and meet you. It's only a couple of minutes from the convent gate. I'm very pleased you're going to come and see us.'

She wondered where she would put the woman to sleep. She had thought of her as staying in Eve's room. But there was the extra parlour that they had always been meaning to do up as a guest room. All it needed was curtains. She'd get some material from Peggy and ask Sister Imelda to ask the senior girls to run them up at domestic science class. She'd get a bedside light from Dessie Burns and a nice cake of soap in Kennedy's chemist.

'Eve's going home today,' Benny reported when she met Nan for coffee in the Annexe as she did every morning.

'I know. She told me last night.'

'What?'

'Well, it's at night she really wants people to go in and see her, and you've long gone so I took a couple of fellows in to cheer her up.'

Benny felt a jolt. She knew that Nan and Eve got on well . . . but taking fellows in to a hospital bed!

'What fellows?' she asked lamely.

'Oh, you know, Aidan Lynch and some of that gang. Bill Dunne – do you know him?'

'No.'

'He's very nice, does Commerce. I bet you know him to see, he's always outside the History Library with a group.'

'Did Eve like them coming in?'

'Yeah, she loved it. Did you think she wouldn't?'

'It's just that she's a bit edgy sometimes . . . you know, on the defensive a bit.'

'I never noticed that.'

It was true. Eve had seemed much less chippy whenever Nan came in. Nan had a gift of making things simple, everyone went along with her way. Just then four boys approached the table. They were all looking at Nan.

'Would you girls like to come down Grafton Street and get some real coffee? Decent coffee for a change,' said the spokesman, a thin boy in an Aran Island sweater.

Nan smiled up at them warmly.

'Thanks a lot, but no, we have a lecture at twelve. Thanks anyway.'

'Come on, that's only a big lecture, no one'll miss you." He was encouraged by her smile to think it was only a matter of saying it often enough.

'No, honestly.' Nan stopped suddenly as if she had been thoughtless. 'I mean I'm only speaking for myself. Benny, do you want to go?'

Benny reddened. She knew the boys didn't want her. It was Nan who had attracted them. But they had nice faces and seemed a little bit lost, like everyone else.

'Why don't you sit down with us?' she suggested with a big smile.

That was exactly what they wanted to do. Chairs and benches were pulled up, names exchanged. School names given. Did they know this person or that? What were they studying? Where were they staying? It was much easier than Benny had thought to be in the middle of a group like this. She had completely forgotten that she was big and that they were boys. She asked eagerly about the societies, and which ones were good, and where were the best dances.

Nan didn't make as much effort, but she was very

pleased to hear all the information. Her smile was so bright that Benny could see the boys almost loosening their collars as she turned it towards them.

The boys said that the Debating Society on a Saturday night was great. And then when it was over you could go to the Solicitor's Apprentice or down to the Four Courts. They looked from one girl to the other.

Benny said that unfortunately she had to stay in the country at weekends. As she said it she realised what a death knell it sounded, so she cheered up at once and said that this was only for this term. Maybe things would change then. She looked around brightly and the boys seemed pleased with her. She knew they were all mad keen for Nan to go with them this Saturday, and Nan wasn't a bit flirtatious.

If she could, she would. She hadn't wanted to go because she didn't know anyone, she said.

'You know us,' said the thin boy in the grubby white sweater.

'I do, of course.' Nan's smile nearly broke his heart.

Benny knew that it would be a great night. She could see it. Of course, she would be in Knockglen. But her smile was bright. After all, one of the things she had been afraid of was that she wouldn't know how to talk to fellows when she got to college. She didn't have much practice at home. But it seemed to be easy enough, like talking to ordinary people. That was what she must think about. The good side. Not always dwelling on the bad side like having to go home before the fun began.

When Mario collected Eve in his ice-cream van it was Fonsie who ran lightly up the steps of the hospital to escort the patient to her transport.

'You're to take it easy, you'll remember that.' The Sister looked doubtfully at Fonsie as a companion.

'Nothing faster than slow jive.' Fonsie leaned back and clicked his fingers slowly. Sister was not amused.

'And you *are* staying in a convent?'

'Don't be prejudiced now,' Fonsie warned. 'Just because I don't look like your idea of a nun doesn't mean . . .'

'Oh shut up, Fonsie, Mario's nearly having a fit down there in the van.'

It was the first time she had seen the outside world for over a week. Eve shuddered when she saw the corner where the crash had taken place. They tucked her up in the van and drove back to Knockglen arguing all the while.

Some arguments she was able to take part in – like having brighter lights and music in the chip shop, like calling the chip shop a café, like having 'Island in the Sun' so that you could hear it from the street and it would make you want to come in.

'Make you want to call the guards, more likely,' Mario said.

There were other arguments she couldn't contribute to – like whether Mario's brother had been mad to marry an Irish girl, Fonsie's mother, or whether Fonsie's mother had been mad to marry an Italian, Mario's brother. She drifted off to sleep during that particular saga which she felt would never be solved anyway.

Eve sat up in bed and drank her beef tea.

'Sister Imelda made it. Have a taste?'

Benny sipped some from the cup.

'Patsy told me she heard her in Flood's talking about shin beef, and pointing to her ankle in case she wasn't making herself clear. Mr Flood was saying, "I know where the shin is, Sister, God forgive me I may not know much but I know where the shin is."'

'Is Patsy still going out with that dumbo, Mossy?'

'Yes, Mother's terrified she'll marry him.'

'Is he that bad?'

'No, we just don't want Patsy to marry anyone, because she'll leave.'

'A bit hard on Patsy,' Eve said. 'I feel like the prodigal son. I never had any time for him in the gospel, but still it's a nice feeling. The accident saved me, everyone's so sorry for me they forget I told all those lies and was so rude to awful Mother Clare. Listen, I meant to tell you, the most extraordinary thing. The boy that got killed, Frank Hegarty . . . Mother Francis met his mother that day. I don't remember it clearly, but anyway they got talking and she's coming here to stay for a few days. Here to Knockglen.'

'Will she stay in Healy's?'

'No, here in the convent would you believe? They've done up one of the parlours as a bedroom.'

'Go on!'

'She's coming on the bus today. It's going to be very hard to know what to say to her.'

'I know,' Benny agreed. 'I mean anything could be the wrong thing. She mightn't want to talk about it at all, but then it could be considered callous to start up chats about other things.'

'Nan would know what to say,' Eve said suddenly.

Benny felt a cold lurch in her heart. It was an unworthy thought, considering how kind Nan was to her and how she included her in everything. But Benny did feel that Nan got *too* much credit for things. Was it right that she would know what to do in every circumstance?

A little wave of pure jealousy came over her. She said nothing. She was afraid it might show in her voice.

Eve hadn't noticed. She was still musing what Nan would do or say.

'I think it's because she doesn't dither, like we do. She always sounds as if she knows what she's doing, whether she does or not. That's the secret.'

'I suppose it is,' Benny said, hoping the glum, mean note didn't sound in her voice.

'Nan could make anyone do anything,' Eve said. 'She got them to let us smoke in the ward!'

'But you don't smoke!' Benny was startled.

Eve giggled. 'Oh, I did for the fun of it, the others all did. It was the principle of the thing.'

'What will she do all day? Mrs Hegarty?' Benny asked.

'I don't know. Walk around. She's going to feel lonely and odd here.'

'She would at home too, I suppose,' Benny said.

'Have you talked to Sean since?'

'Not really. He was on his high horse last weekend, you know, head turned the other way when he saw me at Mass, a fit of the sulks. Unfortunately, that didn't last and he came round last night to discuss the pictures. I'm afraid I used you shamelessly. I said I couldn't make any plans until I knew what you'd be doing.'

'*That* didn't please him.'

'Well, he said that from what he heard you'd most likely be in Mario's, clicking your fingers with Fonsie . . . He was full of disapproval.'

Eve pealed with laughter.

'I wonder what Fonsie said. He's very funny, really he is. He thinks he's going to be Mr Big of Knockglen.'

'Lord, that wouldn't be hard.'

'I know, I told him. But he said I'd missed the point. He said that by becoming a Mr Big he would make Knockglen big too, he would drag it up with him.'

'It can't happen soon enough,' Benny said gloomily.

'God, you sound like a cross between Father Rooney and Mrs Healy with your dire voice,' Eve warned her.

'Maybe that's who I am. Maybe my parents were given the wrong baby.'

'Boy, would *that* be the wrong baby,' Eve said and that started them off all over again.

Kit Hegarty said she never saw such a lovely room. It was exactly what she wanted. It was small and low-ceilinged and there were no shadows or corners in it to keep her awake at night. She knew she would sleep here as she had not slept since it happened. She would love to do something to help, she said. She hadn't many skills, but she was used to running a house.

Mother Francis was soothing. Not now, later maybe, now she must rest. She showed her the chapel. It was quiet and dark. Two nuns knelt in front of the altar where Mother Francis explained that the Blessed Sacrament was exposed. There would be Compline later, if she liked to come and listen to the nuns singing their office.

'I'm not sure . . .'

'Neither am I,' Mother Francis said firmly. 'It might make you too sad, on the other hand it might be just what you need, to sit in a church with people you don't know and weep for your son. And there are the glasshouses. I'll show you those. They're not in very good condition. We don't have the money or the people to look after them. Ah, if only you'd known them when Eve's father was alive . . .'

She told the woman the story that was rarely told, the workman and the restless daughter of the big house, the unsuitable relationship, the pregnancy, the marriage and the birth of Eve and the two deaths.

There were tears in Kit Hegarty's eyes.

'Why are you telling me this?' she said.

'I suppose it's a clumsy attempt to let you know other awful things happen in the world,' said Mother Francis.

*

'Are you not going out tonight?' Annabel Hogan asked as Benny pulled up a chair with them in the breakfast room after supper. 'Out' meant out with Sean Walsh. Benny pretended not to realise this.

'No, Eve has to take it easy. She's up and everything and coming down for supper tonight with the nuns and Mrs Hegarty.' Her face was bland.

'I meant, nothing on at the pictures?' her mother asked equally innocently.

'Ah, of course there's something on, Mother. It's meant to be very exciting – about the sound barrier.'

'And wouldn't you like to be at that?' her father asked.

'I don't really like going by myself, Father. If we were *all* going now . . .' The Hogans hardly ever went to the cinema.

She knew that they liked to see her stepping out with Sean from time to time. Somewhere in their confused minds they must think it was company for her, entertainment, a date even. And from Sean's point of view, they knew he considered it an honour to take the daughter of the house out for all to see. Somehow it made things nice and orderly. Safe.

Sean wouldn't leave them, go to a better shop in a bigger town if he was happy, and this must be their view, however short term and foolish.

'You know we don't go to the pictures,' her mother said. 'We wondered were you going to go with Sean?'

'Sean! Sean Walsh?' asked Benny as if the town were full of Seans, all of them craving to take her to the cinema.

'You know I mean Sean Walsh.' Annabel's voice was sharp.

'Oh no, I don't think it's a good idea to go with him all the time.'

'You don't go all the time.'

'No, but with Eve not being here, there'd be a danger I could slip into the way of it.'

'And what would be the harm of that?'

'Not a bit of harm, Mother, but you know.'

'Did he not ask you? He told *me* he was going to ask you.' Eddie Hogan looked puzzled. He didn't like things that weren't clear.

'I said no to Sean because I didn't want Sean to think and me to think, and the whole of Knockglen to think, we were a twosome.'

It was the first time such a notion had ever been mentioned in their household.

Benny's parents looked at one another at a loss.

'I wouldn't say going to the pictures occasionally is making you into a twosome,' Annabel Hogan said.

Benny's face lit up. 'That's exactly my point too. I think it's fine to go to the pictures with Sean *occasionally*, but not every week. Occasionally was the very word I said, I think.'

Actually the words she had said were 'Sometimes, perhaps, but not in the immediate future', and he had looked at her with his cold small eyes, and she had shivered. But there would be little point in trying to explain this to her parents. It was quite enough to have told them as much as she had already told them.

Jack Foley and Aidan Lynch decided to go to the debate on Saturday night. It was held in the big Physics Theatre, and was fairly rowdy, despite the dinner jackets worn by the Committee and the Visiting Speakers.

As they stood at the doorway watching from the sidelines Aidan saw the blonde head of Nan Mahon in the centre of a sea of male duffle coats. She was laughing, her head thrown back and her eyes sparkling. She wore a white frilly blouse with a rose pinned to the top button, and a black skirt. She was the most attractive girl in the room.

'Look at the lovely Nan,' Aidan said, whistling a low envious sound through his teeth. 'I asked her to come with me to this and she said she'd rather be free.'

'So, she'd rather be free,' Jack said, looking at her closely.

'I thought she liked me.' Aidan sounded mock desolate.

'No, you didn't. You thought she liked Bill Dunne. In fact I thought she liked *me*,' said Jack.

'There's enough of them liking you,' Aidan grumbled. 'No, I thought I was special with Nan. She took me to see her friend in hospital.'

'You're a natural hospital visitor,' Jack laughed. 'Look at Nan over there. She likes everyone.'

He looked with a pang of regret at the girl in the centre of the crowd.

'What was the friend like in hospital?' he asked Aidan in order to take their minds off lost opportunities with Nan.

'Okay,' Aidan said unenthusiastically. 'A bit skinny and ready to bite your head off about everything, but all right, I suppose.' Even as he said it, Aidan realised that it might not sound all that gallant. 'Not that I'm exactly an Adonis myself,' he added.

'But you are, you are!' Jack Foley said. 'Listen, I've had enough of this caper looking at our girl in the middle of that crowd. Will we go for a pint?'

'You're on,' Aidan said.

Jack looked long and hard at Nan as they went out of the hall, but if she saw them come in and go out her eyes gave not a flicker of recognition. Jack could have sworn she was looking straight at them, but then perhaps there were so many in the crowd at the door she just didn't see them.

Eve was disappointed in the way that Mother Francis had invited Frank Hegarty's mother to stay. It would mean that their talk had to be put off for one thing, and she was restless and eager to know the nun's view on how she should approach the Westwards. She intended only to ask for her university fees. She would find a place to live where she could mind children. It must be possible. Not every single student who went in the doors of University College could have parents with money to pay for everything. There had to be some of them working their way through a degree. Eve had refused to consider a daytime job and night studying. She had heard of course of those who had done it, but the atmosphere was different. The students were older and greyer. They scurried in for lectures and scurried out again. It wasn't just the letters after her name that Eve Malone wanted. It was the life of a student. The life she could have had if things had been different.

She hoped that the Hegarty woman wouldn't stay long in Knockglen, because Eve needed to act soon. She must not malinger in the convent and prove Mother Clare's point about how she was a liability. Also if she were going to aim to be enrolled in UCD this year then she must do so within the next few days. And if there were to be an unpleasant interview with Simon Westward, the sooner it was over the better. She wished she had Mother Francis's attention to herself.

After supper Eve sat in the warm kitchen. Sister Imelda had clucked around for a while getting her some warm milk with a little pepper shaken on top, which was known to cure any condition. The tea towels had been washed and laid out on the Aga. The smell was familiar, it was home; but Eve didn't feel the sense of comfort that the place usually brought her.

Moving quietly as she always did, Mother Francis came in and sat down opposite her. 'Don't drink that if it's horrible. We'll pour it away and rinse the mug.'

Eve smiled. It had always been the two of them against the world.

'It's all right . . . not something you'd choose, though, if you had a choice.'

'You *do* have a choice, Eve, a series of them.'

'It means going up to Westlands, doesn't it?'

'If your heart is set on it . . . then yes.'

'And what will I say?'

'We can't write a script, Eve.'

'I know, but we could try to work out what would be the best way to approach them.' There was a silence. 'I expect you *have* approached them for me already?' It was the first time Eve had ever mentioned this.

'Not for a long time, not since you were twelve, and I felt that we should ask them in case they might want to send you to a posher boarding school in Dublin.'

'And no response?'

'That was different. That was six years ago and there was I, a nun wearing black, covered in beads and crucifixes . . . that's the way they might see it.'

'And was that the last time? You didn't ask them about university fees did you?'

Mother Francis looked down. 'Not in person, no.'

'But you wrote?'

The nun passed over the letter from Simon Westward. Eve read it, her face set in hard lines.

'That's fairly final, isn't it?'

'You could say that, or you could look at it differently. You could say that then was then and now is now. It's you, you can ask them for yourself.'

'They might say I never went near them except to ask for money.'

'They'd be right.'

Eve looked up startled.

'That's not fair, Mother. You knew how I felt all these years. I wouldn't lower myself to go to them cap in hand when you had all done so much for me and they had done nothing. It would have been letting the convent down.' She bristled at the injustice of the nun's remark.

Mother Francis was mild. '*I* know that. Obviously I do. I'm trying to look at it from their point of view. There's no point otherwise.'

'I'm *not* going to say I'm sorry. I'm *not* going to pretend . . .'

'True, but is there any point in going at all if you go with that attitude?'

'What other attitude is there?'

'There are many, Eve, but none of them will work unless . . .'

'Unless . . .?'

'Unless you mean it. You don't have to cringe and pretend a love you don't feel, you don't have to go up there with a heart filled with hate either.'

'What would your heart be full of, going up there?'

'I told you. It's *your* visit.'

'Help me, Mother.'

'I haven't been much help to you so far. Do this one on your own.'

'Have you lost interest in me? And what happens to me?' Eve's chin jutted up as it always did when she was warding off a hurt.

'If you believe that . . .' Mother Francis began.

'I don't. It's just that it's like a series of dead ends. Even if I *do* get the fees I'll have to find somewhere to live, some work.'

'One step at a time,' Mother Francis said.

Eve looked at her. The nun's face had that look she used to have years ago when there was some surprise in store.

'Do you have any ideas?' Eve asked eagerly.

'My last idea wasn't very successful, now was it? Go to bed, Eve. You'll need all your strength to deal with the Westwards. Go up there in the late morning. They'll be going to church at eleven.'

The avenue was full of pot holes, and there were clumps of weeds rising in the middle of what must once have been a well-kept drive. Eve wondered if her father had worked on this very road. Mother Francis had always been vague about Jack Malone when pressed. He had been a good man, a kind man and very loving of his little daughter. That was really the sum total of it. And it was what you *would* tell a child, Eve realised.

And about her mother there was even less information. She had looked very beautiful when she was young. She had always been very gracious, Mother Francis had said. But what else could she say about a gardener and the disturbed daughter of the Big House? Eve was determined that she would not lose her clear-sighted way of looking at her background. She had long realised that there was no mileage in romanticising her history. She squared her shoulders and approached the house. It was shabbier close up than it looked from the road. The paint on the conservatory was all peeling. The place looked untidy and uncared for. Croquet mallets and hoops were all thrown in a heap as if someone had played a game many months ago, but no one had ever bothered to tidy the set away or to have another game since. There were wellington boots in the hall, old golf clubs splintering, with their bindings coming undone. Tennis racquets slightly warped stood in a big bronze container.

Through the glass doors Eve could see a hall table weighed down with catalogues and brochures and brown envelopes. It was all so different from the highly polished convent where she lived. A stray piece of paper would never find its way on to the hall table under the picture of Our Lady Queen of Peace. If it did it would soon be rescued and brought to the appropriate place. How extraordinary to live in a house where you could hardly *see* the hall table for all that was covering it.

She rang the bell, knowing that it would be answered by one of three people. Bee, the sister of Paccy Moore, the shoemaker. Bee was the housemaid in Westlands. Or possibly the cook might come to the door if it was Bee's Sunday off. Mrs Walsh had been in the family for as long as anyone could remember. She hadn't come from Knockglen in the first place and didn't fraternise with the people of the town, even though she was a Catholic and seen at early Mass. She was a large woman who looked rather ominous on her bicycle. Or perhaps Simon Westward himself would come to the door. His father was in a wheelchair and reported to be increasingly frail, so he would not appear.

Ever since she could remember Eve had played a game. It was like not stepping on the cracks in a footpath. It was what mother Francis would have called superstition, probably. But she had always done it. 'If the next bird to hop up on the window sill is a thrush then I'll get my exam. If it is a blackbird, I'll fail. If I have to wait until I count twenty-five at the door of the convent in Dublin, I'm going to hate it.' For some reason she always felt like doing it at doors.

As she stood outside the unfamiliar door of the place that was once her mother's home, Eve Malone told herself firmly that if Bee Moore came to the door it would be a good omen, she would get the money. If Simon Westward himself came it would be bad. If it was Mrs Walsh the thing could go either way. Her eyes were bright as she waited and heard the sound of running feet.

She saw the figure of a schoolgirl, about ten or eleven years old, running towards the door. She reached up to open it and stood looking at Eve with interest. She was wearing the very short tunic that girls in Protestant schools always wore. In the convent everything had to be a bit more droopy and modest. She had her hair tied in two bunches, one sticking out over each ear almost like handles, as if someone were going to pick her up and carry her by them. She wasn't fat, but she was square and stocky. She had freckles on her nose and her eyes were the same dark blue as her school uniform.

'Hallo,' she said to Eve. 'Who are you?'

'Who are *you*?' Eve asked. She wasn't afraid of anyone in the Big House if they were this size.

'I'm Heather,' the child replied.

'And I'm Eve.'

There was a pause while Heather tried to work something out.

'Who did you come to see?' she said, after some consideration.

Eve looked at her with admiration. The child was trying to work out whether Eve was for the master or for the staff. She had phrased the question perfectly.

'I came to see Simon Westward,' she said.

'Oh, sure, well come in.'

Eve walked behind the little figure through the hall, full of dark pictures, hunting prints maybe. It was impossible to see. Heather? Heather? She didn't know of any Heather in the household, but then she didn't really keep up with who was who in this family. If people in Knockglen spoke of them she didn't join in the conversation. Sometimes the nuns mentioned them, but Eve would toss her head and turn away. Once she came upon an article about them in the *Social and Personal* magazine and she had turned the pages on angrily in case she would find out any more about them and their goings-on. Benny had always said that if the Westwards had been *her* family she would have wanted to know everything about them and would probably have made a scrapbook as well. But that was Benny all over. She'd probably have been doing their errands for them by now, and thanking them for everything instead of guarding the cold indifference that Eve had nurtured for so long.

'Are you one of Simon's girlfriends?' the child asked conversationally.

'No, indeed,' Eve said with no emotion.

They had reached the drawing room. The Sunday papers were spread out on a low coffee table, a sherry decanter and glasses stood on a silver tray. Over by the window in his wheelchair sat Major Charles Westward, his shoulders sloped down, and it was obvious even from a distance that he was not really aware of his surroundings. A rug over his knees had partly slipped to the floor.

This man was Eve's grandfather. Most people hugged their grandfather, they called them Grandad, and sat on their knee. Grandfathers gave you two-shilling pieces and took pictures of you on First Communion and Confirmation days. They were proud of you and introduced you to people. This man had never wanted to see Eve, and if he was in the whole of his sense he might have ordered her out of his house, as he had done her mother.

Once upon a time she had thought he might see her from his horse or his car and ask who was that lovely child. She had a look of the family about her. But that was long ago. She felt no sense of loss looking at him, no wish that things had been different. She was not embarrassed by his infirmity nor upset by looking at him closely after the years of rejection.

Heather looked at her curiously. 'I'll go and find Simon for you now. You'll be all right here?' she said.

The child's face was open. Eve found it hard to be stiff with her.

'Thanks. Thanks a lot,' she said gruffly.

Heather smiled at her. 'You don't look like his girl-friends usually look.'

'No?'

'No, you look more normal.'

'Oh good.' Despite herself Eve smiled.

The child was still curious. 'Is it about the mare?'

'It's not about the mare. I wouldn't know a mare from a five-bar gate.'

Heather laughed good-naturedly and headed for the door. Eve surprised herself by giving the information the child had been looking for.

'I'm not one of his girlfriends,' she called. 'I'm one of his cousins.'

Heather seemed pleased. 'Oh, then you're a cousin of mine too. I'm Simon's sister.'

Eve said nothing because of a slight lump in her throat. Whatever she had thought would happen when she went to Westlands it was not this. She would never have believed that any Westward would have been pleased to see her.

Mother Francis told Kit Hegarty that there was no need for her to hurry back to Dublin. She could stay as long as she liked, a week maybe.

'Don't go back too soon. The peace of this place could wear off you if you went back to the city too quickly.'

'Ah, that's country people for you. You think Dublin is all like O'Connell Street. We're out in *County* Dublin you see, by the seaside. It's a grand place full of fresh air.'

Mother Francis knew that the peace of Knockglen had nothing to do with it being in the country or the city. The advantage was, the place was far from the home where Frank Hegarty would return no more.

'Still, stay here a while and take our air.'

'I'm in the way.' Kit had sensed Eve's eagerness to have Mother Francis to herself.

'On the contrary. You are very helpful in that Eve needs time to talk to other people before she commits herself to *any* plan. There's no point in she and I going round in circles. Much as I hate it, I realise that she *has* to make up her own mind.'

'You would have made a marvellous mother,' Kit said.

'I don't know. It's easier one step removed.'

'You're not removed. You just manage not to do what all the rest of us wish we didn't do. You don't nag.'

'I don't think you were a nagger either,' Mother Francis smiled.

'Did you not want to marry and have children?' Kit asked.

'I wanted a wild unsuitable farmer's son that I couldn't have.'

'Why couldn't you have him?'

'Because we hadn't a farm of land to go with me. Or so

I thought. If he had really wanted me he'd have taken me, farm or no farm.'

'What happened to him?'

'He married a girl who had legs much better than Bunty Brown, and who *did* have a farm to go with her. They had four children in five years, then he found another, as they say.'

'And what did the wife do?'

'She made a fool of herself the length and breadth of the county. That's not what Bunty Brown would have done. *She* would have thrown him out, started a guest house, and held her head high.'

Kit Hegarty laughed. 'Are you telling me *you* are Bunty Brown?'

'Not any longer. Not for a long time.'

'He was a fool not to take you.'

'Ah, that's what I said too. I said it for three years. They didn't want to take me in the convent at first. They thought I was just running away, trying to hide from the world.'

'And do you regret it, not waiting for a different farmer's son?'

'No, not a bit.'

Her eyes were far away.

'And you've had everything, in a way,' Kit said. 'You've had all the joy of children in a school.'

'It's true,' Mother Francis said. 'Every year, new children, every year new young faces coming in.' She still looked sad.

'It will work out for Eve.'

'Of course it will. She's probably talking to him now.'

'Who is she talking to?'

'Her cousin, Simon Westward. Asking him for fees. I hope she doesn't lose her temper. I hope she won't throw it all away!'

Heather had left the room as soon as her brother came in. Simon went over first to the figure in the wheelchair, picked up the rug, and knelt to tuck it in around the old man. He stood up and came back to the fireplace. He was small and dark, with a thin handsome face, dark-eyed, and his brown hair fell into his eyes. He had had to shake it away so often it was now a mannerism. He wore riding breeches and a tweed jacket with leather cuffs and elbows.

'What can I do for you?' His voice was cold and polite.

'Do you know who I am?' Eve's voice was equally cold.

He hesitated. 'Not really,' he said.

Her eyes blazed. 'Either you do or you don't,' she said.

'I *think* I do. I asked Mrs Walsh. She said you were the daughter of my Aunt Sarah. Is that right?'

'But you know of me, surely?'

'Yes, of course. I didn't recognise you coming up the drive, so I asked.'

'What else did Mrs Walsh say?'

'I don't think that's relevant. Now can I ask you what it's about?'

He was so much in command of the situation that Eve wanted to cry. If only he could have looked ill at ease, guilty about his family's treatment of her, confused and wondering what lay ahead. But Simon Westward would always know how to handle things like this.

She was silent as she looked at him. Unconsciously imitating his stance, hands behind her back, eyes unflinching, mouth set in a hard thin line. She had dressed carefully, deciding not to wear her best outfit in case he would think she had put it on specially, or had come from Mass. Instead she had worn a tartan skirt and grey cardigan. She had a blue scarf tied around her throat in what she had thought was a jaunty look.

Her glance didn't fall from his stare.

'Would you like a glass of sherry?' he asked, and she knew she had won the first round.

'Thank you.'

'Sweet or dry?'

'I don't know the difference. I've never had either.' She spoke proudly. There was going to be no aping the manners of her betters from Eve Malone. She thought she saw him raise his eyebrows in surprise that bordered on admiration.

'Then try the sweet. I'll have that too.'

He poured two glasses. 'Will you sit down?'

'I'd rather stand. It won't take long.'

'Fine.' He said nothing more, he just waited.

'I would like to go to university this term,' she began.

'In Dublin?'

'Yes. And there are a few things standing in the way.'

'Oh yes?'

'Like that I cannot afford it.'

'How much does it cost in Trinity now?'

'It's not Trinity and you know that well. It's UCD.'

'Sorry, I didn't know, actually.'

'For years Trinity wouldn't let Catholics in, and now when it does, the Archbishop has said it's a sin to go there, so you know it's UCD.'

He put his hands out as if warding her off. 'Peace, peace,' he said.

Eve continued. 'And since you ask, the fees are sixty-five pounds a year for three years for a BA, and after that I would like to do a Diploma in Librarianship so that would be another sixty-five pounds. There would be books to buy. I am talking about one hundred pounds a year.'

'And?'

'And I was hoping you would give it to me,' she said.

'Give? Not lend?'

'No, give. Because I wouldn't be able to pay it back. It would be a lie to ask for a loan.'

'And how will you live there? You'll have to pay for rooms and everything.'

'I told you. It's not Trinity. There are no rooms. I'll get a job in a family, earn my keep. I'd be able to do that. It's just the fees I don't have.'

'And you think we should pay them?'

'I'd be very glad if you did.' Not grateful, Eve told herself firmly, she had sworn she would not use that word. No matter how much Mother Francis had warned her. Glad was the nearest she could get.

Simon was thinking. 'A hundred pounds a year,' he repeated.

'It would be for four years,' Eve said. 'I couldn't really start unless I knew I wouldn't have to come and beg for it every year.'

'You're not begging for it now,' said Simon.

'That's right, I'm not,' Eve said. She felt a great pounding in her head. She hadn't known it was going to be remotely like this.

He smiled at her, a genuine smile. 'I never beg either, it must be a family trait.'

Eve felt a hot flush of anger. Not only was he going to refuse her, he was going to make fun of her as well.

She had known that she might be refused, she thought it would be with apologies cold and distant, closing the door firmly, and this time for ever. She had steeled herself against it. There would be no tears. No pleading. Neither would there be recriminations. She had heard enough in the gossip of the town to know that her father had sworn and cursed this family long years ago. She wasn't going to let history repeat itself.

She had rehearsed staying calm. 'So what do we do now?' she asked in a level voice. There was nothing arrogant or pleading about it.

'That seems perfectly reasonable,' Simon said.

'What?'

'What you ask for. I don't see any reason why not.' His smile was very charming.

She felt that to smile back would put her in some kind of danger.

'Why now?' she asked. 'Why not before?'

'You never asked me before,' he said simply.

'Not personally,' she agreed.

'Yes. It's quite different to be asked indirectly, by a religious order who never made any other approach to me.'

'What approach might they have made?'

'Oh, I don't know. Hard to say. I can't say I'd have liked them to ask me to tea or to pretend a friendship I didn't feel. But it was rather bald just to ask for money on your behalf as if you hadn't a mind or a voice of your own.'

She considered it. It was true. Of course it was also true that she should never have had to ask him or any of the Westwards for what was rightfully hers. And Mother Francis had been sent away twice with a flea in her ear.

But these were not the subjects at issue. And the need was for calm, not for raking up the past.

'I see,' she said.

Simon had almost lost interest in it. He was prepared to talk about other things.

'When does term start, or has it started?'

'Last week. But there's late registration.'

'Why didn't you register in time?'

'I tried another kind of life. I couldn't bear it.'

He must have been used to short answers. It seemed to satisfy him.

'Well, I'm sure you won't have missed very much in a few days. All I ever see in Dublin when I go there is students from both universities drinking coffee and talking about changing the world.'

'They might, one day.'

'Of course.' He was courteous.

She was silent. She couldn't ask him to get the money now, she didn't want to launch into any thanks. The word grateful might slip out. She sipped her sherry thoughtfully.

Their eyes met. 'I'll get a cheque book,' he said, and went out to the hall. Eve heard him rooting around amongst the papers and documents stacked on the table.

By the window the old man sat silently staring with unseeing eyes at the unkempt garden. Out on the lawn the sister who must have been nearly twenty years younger than her elder brother played with a couple of large dogs, throwing them sticks. It was like a foreign land to Eve.

She stood there like the visitor she was, until Simon came back in.

'You'll have to forgive me, I am not saying this in any way to be offensive, but I don't know if your name is Maloney or O'Malone, or what?'

'Eve Malone.' She spoke without expression.

'Thank you. I didn't want to go out and check with Mrs Walsh. It was one or the other, ask you or ask her.' He smiled.

Eve did not return the smile. She nodded her head slightly. He wrote the cheque slowly and deliberately, then folded it in half and handed it to her.

Common politeness must make her thank him. The words stuck in her throat. What had she said before, what had been the word which had pleased her? Glad.

She used it again. 'I'm glad you were able to do this,' she said.

'I'm glad too,' he said.

They did not use each other's names, and they knew there was no more to say. Eve put the cheque in the pocket of her cardigan and stretched out her hand.

'Goodbye,' she said.

Simon Westward said exactly the same thing at the same time.

She waved cheerfully at the child who seemed disappointed to see her go, and walked down the avenue of the house that had been her mother's home with her back straight, because she knew that she was being watched from the house. From the kitchens, from the garden where the dogs were playing, from the drawing room and from a wheelchair.

She didn't let the skip come into her step until she was outside.

In the convent Mother Francis and Kit Hegarty were having lunch in the window of the Community dining room, and a place had been set for Eve.

'We didn't wait for you,' Mother Francis said, her eyes anxiously raking Eve's face for the answer.

Eve nodded twice. The nun's face lit up.

'I'll go now. I have a lot of things to do. Eve, your

meal's in the kitchen. Bring it out and sit here with Mrs Hegarty like a good girl.'

'Perhaps . . .' Kit looked uncertain. 'Can't I go and let you two talk?'

'No, no, no you've not finished yet, I have. And this is Eve's home and mine. We have years to talk. You'll be going away soon.'

Eve brought out her heaped plate of bacon and floury potatoes with a white sauce. She placed it on the table and saw the sad tired face of the older woman watching her.

'Sister Imelda's always trying to fatten me up, but it's no use. When you've got my kind of way of going on it just burns up food.'

Mrs Hegarty nodded.

'I expect you're the same,' Eve said. She felt almost lightheaded with relief. She was only making small talk until the lunch was over, until she could run up the road to tell Benny the news, until she could talk to Mother Francis alone when this sad woman went away.

'Yes, I am the same,' Kit Hegarty said. 'I never rest, I hardly ever sleep. I think about everything too much.'

'You've had a lot to think about,' Eve said sympathetically.

'Not always. Frank used to say to me that I couldn't sit down, that my eyes were never still.'

'People say that to me, too,' Eve said, surprised.

They looked at each other with a new interest, the two who had been competing for Mother Francis's time and attention. They didn't think it odd that she hadn't come back to them. They didn't notice that Sister Imelda never came in to take away their plates. As the grey clouds that raced along behind the big banks of convent trees turned black, as the short winter afternoon turned into evening, they talked on.

Their stories fell into place, like pieces of a jigsaw. Eve Malone needed somewhere to live, a place where she could earn her keep. Kit Hegarty needed someone to help her with her guest house. She had no heart to stay in it all day now that Frank, the reason for all the work, had gone. They both could see the solution and yet were afraid to voice it.

It was Eve who spoke first. In the convent which had been her home, Eve softened her voice to ask. Eve, who could never ask for a favour, who hadn't been able to form words of thanks for the £400 in her cardigan pocket, was able to ask Kit Hegarty could she come and live with her.

And Kit Hegarty leaned across the table and took Eve's hands in hers.

'We'll make some kind of a life out of it,' she promised.

'We'll make a great life out of it,' Eve assured her.

Then they went to tell Mother Francis, who seemed very surprised and thought it must be the direct intervention of God.

## 7

Brian Mahon had been drinking now for several days. Not a real batter, nothing that had involved any violence or a brawl as it sometimes did, but steady drinking. Emily knew that things were shaping up for a fight. And this time it was going to be about Nan's bedroom.

Nan had decided that from now on she would study there in the evenings. She had said it was not possible to study downstairs with the radio on and the family coming and going all the time. Nasey had fixed her up a simple desk and Paul had put a plug on an electric fire. This is where she would work from now on. Emily sighed. She knew that Brian would object as soon as it was brought to his notice. Why had he not been consulted? Who was going to pay for the electricity? Who did Nan think she was?

The answer to the last part was that Nan thought she was a lot too good for Brian Mahon and Maple Gardens. Her mother had ensured that over the years. As she brushed her daughter's golden hair, Emily had always made the girl believe that there would be a better and a different life. Nan had never doubted it. She felt no need to conform to the lifestyle of a house ruled by an often drunken father.

Nan Mahon was not afraid of her father because she knew with a certainty which her mother had helped to create that her future didn't lie in her father's kind of world. She knew without arrogance that her beauty would be her means of escape.

Emily wished that there was some way that she could take Brian aside and talk to him in a way that he would listen. Really listen and understand. She could say to him that life was short and there was no point in crossing Nan. Let her work up in the bedroom if that's what she wanted. Be nice – be pleasant about it, then she'd come down and sit with them afterwards.

But Brian didn't listen to Emily these days. If he had ever listened to her. She sighed to herself as she opened up the new delivery of Belleek china, and put the packing neatly into a big container under the counter. She arranged the little jugs and plates on a shelf so that they would best catch the eye and began to write out price tags in her meticulous handwriting. Emily Mahon sighed again. It was so easy to run a hotel shop, and so hard to run a family. People didn't realise how often she'd like to make her bed in the corner of this little world, amongst those nice car rugs and cushions with Celtic designs on them. It would be simpler by far than going back to Maple Gardens.

She had been quite right of course. The row had well begun when Emily Mahon let herself into the family home.

'Do you know anything about all this?' Brian roared.

Emily had decided to try and play it lightly.

'Well, I must say that's a great greeting to one of the workers of the world,' she said, looking from her husband's hot, red face to Nan's cool and unruffled expression.

'Aw, shut up with that workers of the world crap, will you? We all know there isn't a reason in the world for you to be going out to work. Only because you took some figario. If you'd stayed at home and minded your business we wouldn't have all this trouble now.'

'What trouble?' Emily was weary.

'Well might you ask what trouble. Sure you don't know what's going on in your own house.'

'Why are you picking on Em?' Nan asked. 'She's only in the door, she hasn't her coat off, or her shopping put down.'

Her father's face was working. 'Don't call your mother by her Christian name, you young pup.'

'I'm not.' Nan was bored with this argument. 'I'm calling her M, short for Mother, Mama, Mater.'

'You're dismantling that contraption you have upstairs, and coming back down here to where we have the house heated. You'll study your books in this room like a normal human being.'

'Excuse me,' Nan asked. 'Excuse my mentioning it, but what kind of study could anyone get in a room like this with people bellowing and shouting.'

'Listen to me, you impertinent young rossie . . . you'll feel the weight of my hand on you if there's any more of this.'

'Ah, Dad, don't hit her . . .' Nasey had stood up.

'Get out of my way . . .'

Nan didn't move. Not an inch did she stir from where she stood, proud, young, confident in her fresh green and white blouse and her dark green skirt. She had her books under her arm, and she could have been a model picture for student fashion.

'Am I breaking my back for you to speak to me like that in front of the family? Am I working to make you into a bad-mannered tinker?'

'I haven't said anything bad-mannered at all, Dad, only that I'm going up to work, to get a bit of peace. So that I'll get my degree eventually, so that you'll be prouder of me than ever.'

The words were inoffensive, but Brian Mahon found the tone of his daughter almost more than he could bear.

'Get up there out of my sight then, we don't want to see hair or hide of you this evening.'

Nan smiled. 'If you want me to give you a hand, Em, just call me,' she said, and they heard her light step going up the stairs.

The three students in Mrs Hegarty's digs were delighted to hear of Eve's arrival. They had felt awkward and unsure of themselves in a place where the son of the house had been killed so tragically. Now at least an attempt was being made to return to normality.

They liked Eve too, when she appeared. Small, attractive in a wiry kind of way and prepared to put up with no nonsense from the very start.

'I'll be getting your breakfast from now on. Mrs Hegarty is feeding you like fighting cocks so you get bacon and egg and sausage every day and scrambled eggs on a Friday. But I have a nine o'clock lecture three days a week so I was wondering if you could help me clear and wash those days, and the other days I'll run round after you like a slave . . . pouring you more cups of tea and buttering you more toast.'

They went along with her good-naturedly, and they did more than she asked. Big lads who wouldn't have known where the hoover was kept in their own homes were able to lift it out for Eve on a Tuesday before they went to catch the train to college. They wiped their feet carefully on the hall mat. They said they never again wanted to risk anything like the reception that they got when they had accidentally walked some mud in on top of a carpet that Eve had cleaned. They kept the bathroom far cleaner than they had ever done before Eve had come on the scene. Kit Hegarty told her privately that if she had known how much the presence of a girl would smarten the lads up, she might have had a female student years ago.

'Why didn't you? They'd have been easier.'

'Don't you believe it, always washing their hair, wanting the lavatory seat put down, drying their stockings over chairs, falling in love with no-hopers . . .' Kit had laughed.

'Aren't you afraid of any of those things happening with

me?' Eve asked. They got on so well now they could talk easily on any subject.

'Not a chance of it. You'll never fall for a no-hoper. Hard-hearted little hannah that you are.'

'I thought you said I was like you?' Eve was making bread as she spoke. Sister Imelda had taught her to make soda bread when she was six. She had no idea of the recipe, she just did it automatically.

'Ah, you *are* like me, and I didn't fall for a no-hoper, there was lots of hope in Joseph Hegarty. It's just that as time went on it didn't seem to include me.' She sounded bitter and sad.

'Did you make any attempt to find him, you know, to tell him about Frank?'

'He didn't want to know about Frank when there was something to tell like when he learned to swim, or when he lost his first tooth, or when he passed his Inter. Why tell him anything now?'

Eve could see a lot of reasons, but she didn't think it was the time or the place.

'Suppose he came back,' Eve asked. 'If Joe walked in the door one day . . .'

'Funny, I never called him Joe, always Joseph. I'm sure that tells us something about him or me. Suppose he came back? It would be like the man coming to read the meter. I gave up looking at that gate years ago.'

'And yet you loved him? Or else thought you did?'

'Oh, I did love him. There's no use denying it just because it wasn't returned and didn't last.'

'You're very calm about it.'

'You didn't know me years ago. Let me see. Around the time you were one or two, if you'd known me then you wouldn't have said I was calm!'

'I've never loved anybody,' Eve said suddenly.

'That's because you were afraid to.'

'No, the nuns were much more liberal than people think. They didn't fill me with terror of men.'

'No, I meant afraid to let yourself go . . .'

'I think that's right. I feel things very strongly, like resentment. I resent those bloody Westwards. I hate asking them for money. I can't tell you how much it took to make me walk up there that Sunday. And I feel very protective too, if anyone said a word against Mother Francis or Sister Imelda I'd kill them.'

'You look very fierce with that knife. Put it down, for God's sake.'

'Oh.' Eve laughed, realising she was brandishing the carving knife, which she had used to put a cross on the top of the soda bread. 'I didn't notice. Anyway it wouldn't harm anyone. It's as blunt as anything. It wouldn't cut butter. Let's get one of those budding engineers inside there to take it into the lab and sharpen it up for us.'

'You *will* love somebody one day,' Kit Hegarty said.

'I can't imagine who.' Eve was thoughtful. 'For one thing he'd have to be a saint to put up with my moods, for another I don't see many good examples, where love seems to have worked out well.'

\*

'Have you anything planned on Sunday?' Dr Foley asked his eldest son.

'What am I letting myself in for if I haven't?' Jack laughed.

'Just a simple answer. If you're busy I'll not bother you.'

'But then I might miss something great.'

'Ah, that's what life is all about, taking risks.'

'What is it, Dad?'

'You *are* free then.'

'Come on, tell me.'

'You know Joe Kennedy, he's a chemist in the country. He wants to see me. He's not well, I think. We go back a long way. He wondered if I'd come and call on him.'

'Where does he live?'

'Knockglen.'

'That's miles away. Don't they have doctors there?'

'They do, but he wants a friend more than a doctor.'

'And you want me to come, is it?'

'I want you to drive me, Jack. I've lost my nerve a bit.'

'You can't have.'

'Not altogether, but just for a long wet drive, slippy roads. I'd be very grateful.'

'All right,' Jack said. 'What'll I do while you're talking to him?'

'That's the problem. I wouldn't say there's all that much *to* do there, but maybe you could go on a drive or sit in the car to read the Sunday papers.'

Jack's face brightened. 'I know. There's a girl that lives there. I'll give her a ring.'

'That's my boy. Only a couple of months at university and already there's a girl in every town.'

'She's not a girl in that sense. She's just a nice girl,' Jack explained. 'Have you the phone book? There can't be that many Hogans in Knockglen.'

Nan was very excited when Benny said that Jack Foley had rung her.

'Half the girls in college would give anything to have *him* coming to call on them, let me tell you. What'll you wear?'

'I don't think he's coming to call, not in that sense. I mean it's not something to get dressed up for. I won't wear anything,' Benny said, flustered.

'That should be a nice surprise for him when you open the door,' Nan said.

'You know what I mean.'

'I still think you should get dressed up, wear that nice pink blouse, and the black skirt. It *is* a party when a fellow like Jack Foley comes to call. If he was coming out to Maple Gardens I'd dress up. I'll get you a length of pink ribbon and a black one and you can tie them both round your hair to hold it back. It'll look great. You've got gorgeous hair.'

'Nan, it won't look great on a rainy Sunday in Knockglen. Nothing looks great there. It'll just look pathetic.'

Nan looked at her thoughtfully. 'You know those big thick brown bags, the ones they sell sugar in. Why don't you put one of those over your head and cut two slits for eyes? That might look right.'

Annabel Hogan and Patsy planned to make scones, and queen cakes and an apple tart. There would be bridge rolls first with chopped egg on one plate and sardines on the other.

'Maybe we shouldn't overdo it,' Benny suggested.

'There's nothing overdone about a perfectly straight-forward afternoon tea for your friend.' Benny's mother was affronted at the notion that this might not have been their normal Sunday afternoon fare.

They were going to light a fire each day in the drawing room to heat it up for the occasion and after tea had been cleared away Benny's parents would withdraw to the breakfast room, leaving the young people the run of the good room on their own.

'There's not any question of having the run of the place,' Benny had begged, but to no avail. 'He's only coming here because he has to kill the time,' she pleaded. They wouldn't hear of it, a nice young man telephoning courteously several days in advance to know if he could call. It wasn't a matter of killing time. There was a rake of things he could do in Knockglen.

Personally Benny could think of very few. Window shopping didn't bear thinking about. The cinema wasn't open in the afternoon. Healy's Hotel would pall after half an hour, and Jack Foley wasn't likely to put away an afternoon in Mario's, however entertaining Fonsie might be. The Hogans were the only game in town. Still, it was nice that he remembered her. Benny rehearsed the pink and black ribbon. It looked well. She started wearing it on Friday evening so that the household wouldn't think it was part of the dressing-up.

When Sean asked her to the pictures she said no, that since she was having a friend from Dublin she had to stay at home on Saturday and get things ready.

'A friend from Dublin!' Sean sniffed. 'And might we know her name?'

'It's a him, not a her,' Benny said mulishly.

'Pardon me,' Sean said.

'So that's why I can't go, you see,' she added lamely.

'Naturally.' Sean was lofty and knowing.

For some reason that she couldn't explain Benny heard herself saying, 'It's just a friend, not anything else.'

Sean's smile was slow and cold. 'I'm sure that's true, Benny. I wouldn't have expected anything less of you. But it's good of you to say it straight out.'

He nodded like a self-satisfied bird. As if he were being generous and allowing her to have her own friends until the time came. And a pat on the head for defining that there was nothing but friendship involved.

'I hope it's a very pleasant visit. For all of you,' Sean Walsh said, and bowed in what he must have thought was an elegant or a gracious manner. Something he had seen Errol Flynn or Montgomery Clift do, and stored up for a suitable occasion.

\*

Jack Foley was the easiest guest they had ever known at the Hogans'. He ate some of everything put in front of him. He praised it all. He had three cups of tea. He admired the teapot and asked was it Birmingham 1930s silver. It was. Wasn't that amazing? they said; no, Jack said, that's what his parents' silver was. He just wondered was it the same. He punched Benny playfully like a brother when they talked about university. He said how marvellous it was to have boys and girls in the same classes. He had felt so gauche when he had come there from a single-sex school. Benny saw her mother and father nodding sagely, agreeing with him. He spoke of his parents and his brothers, and the boy Aengus with the glasses, which were always getting broken at school.

He said that the debates were great on a Saturday night, you learned a lot from them as well as having fun. Had Benny been? No, Benny hadn't. You see there was this problem about getting back to Knockglen, she said in a flat voice. Oh, that was a pity he thought, they really were part of college life. Perhaps Benny could stay with her friend Nan, he sometimes saw her there. They all nodded. Perhaps. Some Saturday.

He was discreet about why his father wanted to meet Mr Kennedy. It could be anything, he said, rugby club business, or new drugs on the market, or old school reunions. You never knew with his father, he had so many irons in the fire.

Benny looked at him with admiration. Jack Foley didn't even look as if he were putting on an act.

The only other person she knew who could do that was Nan. In many ways they would be ideally suited.

'It's nice and fine. Do you think you could show me the town?' he asked Benny.

'We were just going to leave the two of you to . . . er, chat,' Benny's mother began.

'I've eaten so much . . . I think I do need a walk.'

'I'll get proper shoes.' Benny had been wearing flat pumps, like party shoes.

'Get boots, Benny,' he called after her. 'We're really going to walk off this fabulous tea.'

They walked companionably together. Benny in her winter coat, with the pink collar of her smart blouse showing over it. She had put on wellingtons, and she felt that the cold wind was making her cheeks red, but it didn't matter. Jack wore his purple and green Law Society scarf wound round his neck.

Several people were out walking in the wintry sunshine which would soon turn into a sunset.

'Where will we go?' he asked at the Hogans' gate.

'Through the town, out the other side, and up to Westlands. That'll undo the harm of all the apple tart.'

'Poor Mr Kennedy's dying. He wanted to talk to my father about it. He doesn't get much joy out of the local man, apparently.'

'That's very sad. He's not old,' Benny said. 'That's where the local man, as you call him, lives.' She waved across the road to Dr Johnson's house, where the children were throwing sticks for a dog.

'I didn't mention that to your parents . . .' Jack began.

'Nor will I, don't worry,' Benny said.

They knew the story would travel the length of the one-street town.

Benny pointed out places, and gave a little commentary. Bee Moore called out from the doorway of Paccy Moore's cobbler's shop that there were lovely new skirts arrived into Peggy Pine's.

'They're just right for you, Benny,' Bee said, and added, with no sense of offence, 'they'd fit an elephant, and there's a great stretch in them.'

'Beautiful!' Jack commented, with a grin.

'Ah, she doesn't mean any harm,' Benny said.

In Mario's, both Fonsie and his uncle blew extravagant kisses out to Benny. And in Dessie Burns's hardware shop they wondered who could have written 'Useful Gift' over a saw. They passed Kennedy's chemist swiftly without saying anything about the man inside talking to Jack's father. Benny took him across to point out some of the finer points of Hogan's Gentleman's Outfitters.

Jack admired the shop courteously, and said it was very discreet. You'd never know from the outside what it was like on the inside. Benny wondered was that a good thing, but decided it probably was. Country people were different. They didn't like anyone knowing their business.

She asked Jack to keep staring in the window and to notice the reflection of Mrs Healy across the road watching them beadily from her hotel. Jack heard about Mrs Healy's corsets, and what amazing structural feats they were. There was a rumour that Mrs Healy was quite a plump, soft person, but nobody except the late Mr Healy would have had any proof of this. New and ever more taxing underpinnings were bought every time she went to Dublin, and there was a rumour that she had once gone to London on a corset-buying spree, but this might only be a rumour.

When she had gone back into her hotel Benny felt it safe to move on. She showed Jack the clean white slabs of Mr Flood's the butcher's. She said that Teddy Flood, his son, didn't really want to work there, but what else could he do? It was hard to be born into the business if you were a boy. Mr Flood was becoming very odd these days.

Jack said he could see that without being told. It was surely highly questionable to have so many cows and pigs and lambs around the wall in a highly coloured gambolling state. It must make people feel sensitive about buying them in their very dead condition, and eating them. Benny said that this was nothing. Mr Flood had always had piteous-looking animals peeping at you from the walls. The real thing was that he now had a fairly permanent vision of something up a tree. A saint possibly, but definitely a nun. It was a source of worry to the family and a cause of great fits of giggling among the customers when he would suddenly pause in sawing or chopping and go out of doors for a brief consultation upwards.

They passed the church and paused to study the details

of the Men's Mission, which would be coming to the church shortly. Benny said that during the two weeks of the mission's little wooden stalls selling prayer books and beads and holy objects and Catholic Truth Society pamphlets did huge business outside the church. Was it the same in Dublin? Jack was apologetic. He didn't really know. He had gone to the mission of course, but like everyone he and Aidan had always wanted to try and find out which had the lecture on sex. That was the one that was usually packed out, but the missioners were becoming more and more cunning. They sort of hinted each night that the big sex sermon would be tomorrow and they had crowds coming in every night, in case they missed it.

Benny said that men were much more honest than women, really. Girls felt exactly the same but didn't admit it.

She showed him the square where the bus came in. Mikey was just drawing up.

'How's Benny?' he called out.

'Great altogether,' Benny said, with her big smile.

They paused in front of the gates of St Mary's and she pointed out the landmarks to him. The big long lawns, the camogie field, the glasshouse, the windy path through the kitchen gardens that went uphill to the quarry path, where Eve had her cottage.

She knew everything and everyone, he told her, and there was a story attached to whatever they saw.

This pleased her. At least he wasn't bored.

Neither of them saw Sean Walsh looking at them from

inside Birdie Mac's sweet shop. Birdie often made tea and toast of a Sunday afternoon and Sean Walsh had taken to dropping in. His eyes were cold as he watched Benny Hogan and the arrogant young pup that she had gone off with that very first day, trick acting and showing off right outside the convent gates in full view of the town. It didn't please him one little bit.

They stood on the five-bar gate that had a good view down over the Westwards' land. Benny pointed out places to him. The graveyard where all the Westwards lay. The small war memorial in it that had wreaths of poppies in November, because so many of them had died in wars.

'Wasn't it odd to think of them all fighting in those wars when they lived here?' she said.

'But that would be their whole culture and tradition and everything,' Jack said.

'I know, but when the others would be talking about homeland and fatherland and king or queen and country . . . they'd only be talking about Knockglen.'

'Don't knock Knockglen,' he said, laughing.

'Don't let Fonsie in the chipper bar hear you say that, he'll be trying to turn it into a hit single. Move over Bill Hayley . . . that's Fonsie . . .'

'Where did he get the name?'

'Alphonsus.'

'God.'

'I know. Didn't you escape lightly, Jack Foley, with your nice normal name?'

'And what about you . . . Benedicta was it?'

'No, nothing as exotic. Mary Bernadette, I'm afraid.'

'Benny's nice. It suits you.'

It was dark as they walked back. The lights were on up in the convent. Benny told Jack of Eve's life there, and the lovely bedroom where you could sit and look down the town.

'Now I have you home safely in good time,' she said, delivering him to the door of Kennedy's chemist.

'Will you come in?'

'No, he might be upset.'

'Thanks, Benny. It was a lovely visit.'

'I enjoyed your being here. Wasn't it lovely for me too?'

'Will you come out one night in Dublin?' He spoke suddenly, almost surprising himself.

'Not at night. I'm Cinderella, remember. But I'll see you around.'

'Maybe a lunch?'

'Wouldn't that be grand?' she said, and walked off down the dark street.


'Poor Joe,' his father said after a long silence in the car.

'Has he got cancer?'

'Riddled with it. He's only a couple of months, I'd say, from the sound of things.'

'What did you tell him?'

'He wanted me to listen.'

'Has he no one here who'll do that?'

'No. According to him there's an arrogant, bad-tempered GP, a wife who thinks it's all safe and in the hands of the Little Flower or the Infant of Prague, or some such helpful authority, and won't brook any discussion on the matter . . . However, enough's enough. How was your friend? Joe said she was a nice girl, big horse of a girl he called her.'

'Isn't it a pity he couldn't have found a better way to describe people?'

'Let me get this straight again,' Nan said, her eyes wide with disbelief. 'He asked you out. I mean he said the words "I would like you to come out with me one night", and you said no?'

'No, I didn't say no, and he didn't ask me out like that.'

Nan looked to Eve for guidance. They were all three together waiting for the lecturer to arrive. They sat away from the main body of the students in order to get this matter sorted.

'Well, did he or didn't he?' Eve asked.

'It was like you'd ask a friend. Casual. It wasn't like a date.'

'It certainly wasn't if you said no,' Eve said dryly.

'Don't go on like that.' Benny looked from one to the other. 'I swear, if he *does* ask me out I'll go. Now are you satisfied?'

'And where will you stay the night in Dublin?' Eve asked.

'I could stay with you, couldn't I, Nan?'

'Oh yes, sure.' The reply was half a second late.

Benny looked to Eve. 'Or if there was any problem with that I could stay with you, Eve, out in Dunlaoghaire.'

'Easily.' That was said quickly, but of course Mother and Father would never let her stay in a guest house full of boys with a woman they didn't know, even if Eve did live there in a semi-work capacity. Benny was philosophical. It wouldn't happen anyway. What were all the plans for?

In the Ladies' Reading Room stuck into the criss-cross tapes on the noticeboard was a folded piece of paper. 'Benny Hogan, First Arts.' She opened it casually. It must be from that pale-faced clerical student who had missed the history lecture and she had promised to give him the notes. Benny had remembered to take carbon paper with her. He could keep the copy for himself. She didn't know his name. He was a worried young man, definitely not strong, his white face made even whiter by the black clothes. She got an odd feeling when she saw that the letter was from Jack Foley. It was like the sudden jolt you get if you touch something too hot or too cold.

Dear Benny,
    I remember you said evenings were difficult at the moment, so what do you say to lunch in the Dolphin? I've never been there but I'm always hearing about it. Would a Thursday be good? I remember you saying you didn't have a tutorial or anything on Thursdays. I'll probably see you before then, but if you can't make it or don't want to, can you leave a note in the porter's office? I hope I won't hear from you because

that means I'll see you in the Dolphin at one fifteen on Thursday week.

And thank you for the lovely afternoon in Knockglen. Love, Jack

Love, Jack. Love, Jack, she said it to herself over and over. She closed her eyes and said it again. It was possible, wasn't it? Just possible that he did like her. He didn't *need* to ask her out, or to remember that she had a free afternoon on Thursdays, or be so kind as to think of lunch. He could have sent a postcard if he wanted to be mannerly, as her father would call it. Jack Foley didn't need to ask her to lunch in a big posh hotel where the high of the land went. He must have done it because he liked being with her, and that he liked her.

She didn't dare to believe it.

Benny heard Nan's infectious laugh in the corridor outside. Hastily she pushed the note deep into her shoulder bag. It seemed a bit shabby considering how enthusiastic Nan and Eve always were on her behalf, but she couldn't bear them giving her advice on what to wear and what to say. And worst of all she couldn't bear them to think that Jack Foley might in fact fancy her, when she so desperately hoped it was true.

## 8

Benny decided she would be thin on Thursday week. She would have hollows in her cheeks and a long narrow neck. It would, of course, involve eating nothing. Not easy to do at home where Patsy would put a bowl of porridge, a jug of cream and the silver sugar basin in front of her to start the day. Then there was the brown bread and marmalade. And on either side of her, a parent determined she should have a good start to the day.

Benny realised that you'd need great ingenuity if you were to lose an ounce of weight as a resident of Lisbeg in Knockglen. So she first pretended that she had gone off porridge. In fact she loved it, swimming in cream and dusted with brown sugar. Then she would leave her departure until as late as possible and cry is that the time? I'll take my bread and butter with me.' When no one was looking she would tip it into Dr Johnson's hen run or drop it into the bin outside Carroll's or Shea's.

Then there was lunch time. She found it beyond human endurance to go into the cafés where the smell of sausage and chips in one kind of place or almond buns in another would drive her taste buds wild.

She told Nan and Eve that she had to work and stayed resolutely in the library all the time.

The stuffiness of the library and no food made her feel headachy and weak all afternoon. It was another test of will to pass the sweet shops when she knew a packet of Rollos would give her the energy to struggle down to the Quays and get the bus. Then back in Knockglen she had to cope with the meat tea as well.

'I had a huge feed-up in town today,' she'd say apologetically.

'What did you do that for when there's good food waiting for you here?' her mother would reply, puzzled.

Or else she'd try the angle that she didn't feel like it because she was tired. They didn't like that either. Should they have a word with Dr Johnson about her? What could be making a normal healthy girl tired? Benny knew that it would be useless to tell them the truth, that she wanted to lose some weight. They would tell her she was fine. They would worry and discuss it endlessly. Meals would become a battleground. It was quite hard enough already to resist slices of Patsy's treacle tart, and to toy with one piece of potato cake when she craved half a dozen. Benny knew that the road to beauty was not meant to be an easy one, but she wondered grimly whether it was such hard going for everyone else.

She wondered should she wear a corset like Mrs Healy, or better still not like Mrs Healy's very obvious whalebone. There was the one she had seen advertised. 'Nu Back corset . . . expands as you bend, stoop or twist . . . returns to position easily and cannot ride up when sitting.' It cost 19/11d, almost a pound, and it did seem to promise everything you could dream of. Except of course it didn't hold out any hope for the cheeks and the neck.

Benny sighed a lot. Wouldn't it have been great going to lunch in a smart Dublin place if she were small and neat like Eve was? Or better still if she looked like Nan. If she looked so gorgeous that everyone would look and Jack Foley would be so proud and pleased that he had asked her.

Because Benny was never available for lunch any more, Nan and Eve often found themselves walking together to one of the cafés near the university. Eve watched with a wry amusement as the boys came to join them wherever they went.

Nan put on an amazing performance, Eve thought to herself. She had a practised charm, but no gush whatsoever. Eve had never known anyone play such a role. But then she asked herself, *was* it a performance? She seemed totally natural and was invariably warm and pleasant to those who approached. Almost regal, Eve thought. It was as if she knew that there would be admiration everywhere and was quite accustomed to coping with it.

Eve was always included in the conversations and, as she told Kit Hegarty in their easy companionship out in

Dunlaoghaire, it was the best introduction you could have to every single male in UCD.

'Of course they do see me as a pale shadow,' Eve said sagely. 'Like the moon not having any light of its own, it reflects the light of the sun.'

'Nonsense,' Kit said loyally. 'That's not a bit like you to be so humble.'

'I'm being practical,' Eve said. 'I don't mind it at all. There's only one Nan in every generation.'

'Is she the sort of College Belle?'

'I suppose so, though she doesn't act it. Not like that Rosemary, who thinks she's at a party all day every day. Rosemary has a foot of make-up on, and she has eyelashes about ten inches long, you wouldn't believe it. She keeps looking up and down so that no one will miss them. I wonder that doesn't make herself dizzy or blind herself.' Eve sounded very ferocious.

'But Nan's not like that?' Kit Hegarty had yet to meet this paragon.

'No, and she's just as nice to awful fellows as she is to real hunks. She spends ages talking to ones that are covered in pimples and can hardly string two words together. Which drives the hunks out of their minds.'

'And does she not have her eye on anyone for herself?' Kit asked. She thought that Eve was seeing far too much of the dazzling Nan and not nearly enough of her old friend Benny Hogan.

'Apparently not.' Eve was surprised too. 'Because she could have anyone she liked, even Jack Foley, but she doesn't seem to want them. It's as if there's something else out there that we don't know about.'

'Martians?' Kit suggested.

'Nothing would surprise me.'

'How's Benny, by the way?' Kit's voice was deliberately casual.

'Funny you should ask. I haven't seen her all week, except at lectures, and then only to wave across to.'

Kit Hegarty knew better than to probe or criticise, but her heart went out to that big untidy girl with the bright smile, the girl who had been Eve's friend through thick and thin and now seemed to be left out in the cold. It was tough on ordinary moths and insects when a gorgeous butterfly like Nan came on to the scene.


'Eve, are you going to the Annexe?' Aidan Lynch seemed to be everywhere. He had a fawn duffle coat which had seen much better days, long curly hair which fell into his eyes, and dark horn-rimmed spectacles that he always said were plain glass but made him look highly intellectual.

'I wasn't thinking of it, no.'

'Could the thought of my company there and back and the distinct possibility that I would buy you a coffee and a fly cemetery make you change your mind?'

'I'd love a fly cemetery,' Eve said, referring to the pastries with the black, squashy filling. 'I cook breakfast for huge greedy men and I forgot to have any myself today.'

'Huge greedy men?' Aidan was interested. 'Do you live in a male harem?'

'No, a digs. I help with the housework to earn my keep.' She spoke without self-pity or bravado. For once the joky Aidan was without words. But not for long.

'Then it's my duty, not just my pleasure, to feed you up,' he said.

'Nan won't be there. She has a tutorial.'

A flicker of annoyance passed over his face. 'I didn't want Nan to be there. I wanted you.'

'Well recovered, Mr Lynch.' She smiled at him.

'Is there anything more harsh in this life than to be misjudged, and have one's motives entirely misunderstood?' he asked.

'I don't know. Is there?' Eve liked the lanky law student. She had always thought of him as part of Jack Foley's gang. Full of nonsense of course and all that lofty talk. But basically all right.

They walked companionably down the corridor towards the stone stairs that led to the Annexe, the college coffee shop. They passed the Ladies' Reading Room on the way. Through the door Eve caught a glimpse of Benny sitting in a chair on her own.

'Aidan, just a minute. I'll ask Benny to come with us.'

'No! I asked *you*,' he said petulantly.

'Well, God Almighty, the Annexe is open to everyone in the whole place. It's not as if you'd asked me to candlelit dinner for two,' Eve blazed at him.

'I would have, but I don't know where they serve them at this time of the morning,' he said.

'Don't be a clown. Wait here a second.'

Benny's mind seemed far away. Eve touched her shoulder.

'Oh, hallo,' she said, looking up.

'Good, you admit you know me. Let me introduce myself. My name is Eve Malone. We met some years ago in . . . where was it . . . Knockglen . . . yes that's where it was!'

'Don't, Eve.'

'What is it? Why don't you play with me any more?'

'I can't tell you.'

'You can tell me anything,' Eve said, kneeling down beside the chair.

Out in the corridor Aidan Lynch cleared his throat.

'No, go on, there's a fellow waiting for you.'

'Tell me.'

'I'm on a diet,' Benny whispered.

Eve threw back her head and pealed with laughter. Everyone in the room looked over at them. Benny's face got red.

'Now look what you've done,' she hissed furiously.

Eve looked into her friend's eyes. 'I'm only laughing with relief, you great fool. Is that all? Well, I don't think there's any point in it. You're grand as you are, but if you want to, be on one, but don't run away from everybody. I thought I'd done something awful to you.'

'Of course not.'

'Well, come on, come and have a coffee with Aidan and myself.'

'No, I can't bear the smell of food,' Benny said

piteously. 'My only hope is to keep away from where it is.'

'Will we have a walk in the Green at lunch then? There's no food there,' Eve suggested.

'We might see someone feeding the ducks and I could snatch the bread and run off stuffing it down my throat,' Benny said with a hint of a smile.

'That's better. I'll pick you up in the main hall at one.'

'Don't tell anyone.'

'Oh, Benny, honestly!'

'What was all that about?' Aidan said, pleased to see that Eve had returned alone.

'I was letting Benny know where I was going and explaining that if I wasn't back by a stated time she was to ring the guards,' Eve said to him.

'Aren't you very droll.'

'Well, you're not a great one at taking life too seriously yourself,' she said with spirit.

'I knew we were suited, I knew from the very first minute I saw you. In bed.'

Eve just raised her eyes, not to encourage him. But Aidan was warming to the theme.

'It will be a nice thing to tell our grandchildren in years to come.'

'What?'

Aidan spoke in a child's voice. ' "Tell me, Grandad, how did you and Grandma meet?" and then I'll say, "Ho, ho, ho, little boy, we met when she was in bed. I was introduced to her in bed. It was like that way back in the fifties. It was a racy time, ho, ho, ho." '

'You are an idiot,' Eve laughed at him.

'I know. I said we were well suited,' he said, tucking her arm into his as they joined the crowds on the stairs down to coffee.

Benny took out a small mirror from her handbag. She put it inside a copy of *Tudor England* and examined her face carefully. Five days with no food to speak of and her face was still round, her jaw was still solid and there was no sign of a long swan-like neck. It would almost make you give up believing in God.

'Are there women after you in college?' Aengus asked Jack Foley.

'I never looked.' Jack wasn't concentrating.

'You'd know. They'd be breathing heavily,' Aengus explained.

Jack looked up from his notes. 'They would?'

'So I hear.'

'Where do you hear this?'

'Well, mainly from Ronan. He was doing a very funny imitation of people in a car, huffing and puffing. He says that girls get like that when they're passionate.'

'And where did he see all this that he could be imitating it?' Jack asked, a trifle anxiously.

Aengus was innocent. 'I don't know. You know Ronan.'

Jack did know his brother Ronan, and had an uneasy feeling that there had been someone in the vicinity when he was saying goodbye to Shirley the other night. Shirley was quite unlike most of the other girls in UCD. She had been in America for a year, which made her very experienced. She had offered Jack a lift home from the Solicitors' Apprentice Dance last Saturday night at the Four Courts. She had her own car and her own code. She had parked right outside his house under a street light.

When he had murmured that they might have more shade, Shirley had said, 'I like to see what I'm kissing.'

Now it looked as if his brother had also seen whatever kissing had been going on.

Jack Foley made a note to leave Shirley alone. Next time it would be Rosemary or even the ice-cool Nan Mahon. No more crazy ladies, thank you very much.

Benny ate an apple walking around St Stephen's Green at lunch time and felt a little bit better. Eve never spoke of the diet again. Benny knew she didn't even need to warn her not to tell Nan. It wasn't that Nan wouldn't be helpful, she'd be very helpful. It was just that Nan didn't ever need to try. She just was perfect already, and it put her in a different world.

Instead they talked about Aidan Lynch and how he was going to come out to Dunlaoghaire tonight and take Eve to the pictures. He understood that she had to wash up after supper. He'd come out on the train.

'I've missed you a lot, Eve,' Benny said suddenly.

'Me too. Why can't you stay in town some evening?'

'You know.'

Eve did know. The arguments about the evenings drawing in, the dark nights, it would be such hard work they decided they should wait until Benny had a real date, a real reason to stay in town. It almost seemed like frittering it away to use a night off just for the two of them to be together like the old days.

'I'd love it if you'd come home to Knockglen,' Benny said. 'And not that I'm twisting your arm, but I know Mother Francis would too.'

'I will,' Eve promised. 'It's just that I've got obligations too. It's then that I'm the most help to Kit. I get the Saturday tea over so quickly it would make your head swim. I keep telling the lads they have to be on the six thirty train into town to see the action. They don't know what I mean but it gets a bit of urgency into them. Otherwise they'd be dawdling there all night.'

Benny giggled. 'You're a terrible tyrant.'

'Nonsense. I was raised by an army general in St Mary's, that's all. Mother Francis would get her way over anything. Then on Sundays we have this rule. They get a big Sunday lunch, and there's a plate of salad left under a tea towel for each of them in the evening, no serving or anything.'

'I'm sure she's delighted with you,' Benny said.

'I'm a bit of company. That's all.'

'Does she ever talk about her son?'

'Not much. But she cries over him at night. I know that.'

'Isn't it extraordinary that people can love their children so much that they kind of live for them?'

'Your parents do. That's part of the problem. Still, it's nice to know they do,' Eve said.

'Yours would have, if they'd stayed around long enough.'

'And if they'd been sane,' Eve said dryly.

Benny sat beside Rosemary at the history lecture. She had never really spoken to her before. She wanted to look at Rosemary's make-up and wondered was there anything she could learn.

As they waited for the lecturer to arrive they talked idly.

'Knockglen?' Rosemary said. 'That's the second time I heard of that today. Where is it?'

Benny told her, and added glumly that it was too far to be accessible and too near to let you live in Dublin. 'Who was talking about it?'

Rosemary puckered up her face, trying to think. She often applied a little Vaseline to her eyelashes in the privacy of the lecture hall. It was meant to make them grow. She did so openly in front of Benny, who was no rival that must be kept out of beauty secrets.

Benny watched with interest. Then Rosemary remembered.

'I know. It was Jack. Jack Foley. He was saying that a friend of his fancies someone from Knockglen. It's not you by any chance?'

'No, I don't think so.' Benny's heart was like lead. Rosemary was on such close terms with Jack, and Jack was making a joke out of Knockglen.

'His friend Aidan. You know, goofy Aidan Lynch. He's quite witty actually, it sort of makes up for everything else.'

Benny felt her cheeks burning. Is this the way people talked? People like Jack and Rosemary and maybe even Nan, for all she knew. Did handsome people have different rules?

'And did Jack approve of whoever Aidan fancied?' She wanted to keep Jack's name in the conversation, however painful it was.

'Oh yes. He said it was a great place. He's been there.'

'Really.' Benny remembered every moment of the day that Jack Foley had been in her town in her house in her company. She could probably give a transcript like they did in court cases of every word that had been said.

'He's really out of this world,' Rosemary confided. 'You know, not only is he a rugby star, but he's bright. He got six honours in his Leaving, and he's nice.'

So Rosemary had prised out of Jack how well he had done in his exams leaving school, just like she had.

'Are you going out with him?' Benny asked.

'Not yet, but I *will* be, that's my project,' Rosemary said.

All during the lecture on Ireland under the Tudors Benny sneaked little looks at her neighbour. It was so monstrously unfair that a girl like Rosemary should have a bar of Kit-Kat in her bag and have no spots and no double chin.

And when had she had all these conversations with Jack

Foley? In the evenings probably. Or even the early evenings, when poor Benny Hogan was sitting like a big piece of freight on the bus back to Knockglen.

Benny wished she hadn't eaten the apple. Perhaps what her system had wanted was a complete shock. No food at all after eighteen years of too much food. Maybe the apple had delayed the process.

She looked at Rosemary and wondered was there any hope that she would fail in her project.

'How's work, Nan?' Bill Dunne prided himself on getting on well with women. He thought that Aidan Lynch's reputation was quite unjustified. That was fine at school when everyone was joky. But in university, women were there because they were studious. Or because they wanted people to think they were studious. You couldn't go on trick acting and making schoolboy jokes to university women. You pretended to take their studies seriously.

Nan Mahon smiled one of her glorious smiles. 'I suppose it's like it is for everyone else,' she said. 'When you like the lectures, when you enjoy the subject, it's fine. When you don't, it's hell, and there's going to be hell to pay at the end.'

The words themselves were meaningless, but Bill liked the tone. It was warm and almost affectionate.

'I wonder could I take you to dinner one night?' he asked.

He had thought this out carefully. A girl like Nan must get asked to hops, and to pubs and to parties and to cinemas. He wanted to move it one grade up the ladder.

'Thank you, Bill.' The smile was still warm. 'I don't go out very much. I'm a real dull stick. I study a bit during the week, you see. In order to keep up.'

He was surprised and disappointed. He had thought dinner would work.

'Perhaps we could dine at a weekend, then. When you're not so tied up.'

'Saturdays, I usually go to the debate, and then down to the Four Courts. It's become a bit of a ritual.' She smiled apologetically.

Bill Dunne wasn't going to beg. He knew that would get him nowhere.

'I'll catch you at one of those rendezvous then,' he said loftily, refusing to let his pique be seen.

Nan's room became her living quarters. She had an electric kettle there and two mugs. She took her tea with lemon, so there was no need for milk and sugar.

Sometimes her mother came in and sat with her.

'It's peaceful in here,' Emily said.

'That's why I wanted it this way.'

'He's still annoyed.' Nan's mother sounded as if she were about to plead.

'He has no reason to be, Em, I am perfectly polite always. He's the one who uses the language and loses control of himself.'

'Ah, if only you understood.'

'I do. I understand that he can be two different people.

I don't have to be dependent on his moods. So I won't be. I won't sit down there wondering when he'll come home and what condition he'll be in.'

There was a silence.

'Neither should you, Em,' Nan said at last.

'It's easy for you. You're young and beautiful. You've the world ahead of you.'

'Em, you're only forty-two. You've a lot of the world ahead of you.'

'Not as a runaway wife, I wouldn't.'

'And anyway you don't want to run away,' Nan said.

'I want *you* to be away from it.'

'I will be, Em.'

'You don't go out with any young men. You never go out on dates.'

'I'm waiting.'

'What for?'

'For the Prince, the white knight, the Lord, or whatever it was you said would come.'

Emily looked at her daughter, alarmed.

'You know what I meant. Something much better than here. Something far above Maple Gardens. You meet people amongst your friends, these law students, these young engineers . . . these boys with fathers who have big positions.'

'That's only the same as Maple Gardens except a bit more garden and a downstairs cloakroom.'

'What do you mean?'

'I haven't held on to this dream just to end up in another

Maple Gardens, Em, with another nice fellow who'd turn out to be a drinker like Dad.'

'Hush, don't say that.'

'You asked me. I told you.'

'Yes, I know. But what do you hope to get?'

'What you told me I'd get, anything I wanted.'

She looked so proud and confident there at her desk, her mug of tea in her hand, her blonde hair back from her brow, her face unruffled by the kind of conversation they were having.

'You could too.' Emily felt the belief she had always held in her heart soar back again.

'So there's no point in going out with the people I don't want to live amongst. It's only a waste of time.'

Emily shivered. 'There could be some very, very nice people in all that number.'

'There could, but not what you and I want.'

Emily's glance fell on the desk and amongst Nan's books and files were magazines, *The Social and Personal*, *The Tatler*, *Harpers and Queen*. There were even books of etiquette borrowed from the library. Nan Mahon was studying a great deal more than First Arts.

Mrs Healy looked through the thick net curtains and saw Simon Westward getting out of his car. He had his small stocky sister with him. Perhaps he was going to take her into the hotel for a lemonade. Mrs Healy had long admired the young Squire, as she called him. Indeed she had half harboured some little notions about him. He was a man of around thirty, within a few years of her own age.

She was a fine substantial widow in the town, a person of impeccable reputation. Not exactly his social class of course, and not the right religion. But Mrs Healy was a practical woman. She knew that when people were as broke as the Westwards would appear to be a lot of the old standards might not be as firm as they used to be.

She knew that Simon Westward owed Shea's since last Christmas for the drink he had bought to cover the Hunt and what they called the Boxing Day party. Many a traveller came and had a drink in Healy's Hotel and spoke indiscreetly because he would have thought that the lofty and distant landlady had not the remotest interest in the tittle-tattle of the neighbourhood.

In most cases they would have been correct, but in terms of the Westwards, Mrs Healy had always been interested. She had grown up in England where the Big House had always been much more a part of the town. It had never ceased to amaze her, back home again in her native land, that nobody seemed to know or care about the doings up at Westlands.

To her disappointment the Westwards went into Hogan's Gentleman's Outfitters across the road.

What could they want there? Surely they would deal in Callaghan's up in Dublin, or Elvery's. But perhaps credit had run out in those places. Maybe they were going to try locally where a man as nice as Eddie Hogan would never ask to see the colour of their money before lifting the bale of material down from the shelf and starting to write the measurements into his book.

From the inside of his dark shop, peering through his dark window with its bales of materials and its shutters that never fully opened, Eddie Hogan saw with delight that Simon Westward and his small sister were coming into the premises. He wished he had time to smarten the place up.

'You'll never guess . . .' He began to whisper at Sean.

'I know,' Sean Walsh hissed back.

'It's very dark,' Heather complained, screwing up her eyes to get used to the change from the bright winter sunshine outside.

'Shush.' Her brother didn't want her to seem rude.

'This is an honour,' Eddie Hogan said.

'Ah good morning, Mr . . . Hogan, isn't it?'

'Of course it is,' Heather said. 'It's written outside.'

Simon looked annoyed; Heather immediately became repentant.

'Sorry,' she muttered, looking at the ground.

'It is indeed Edward Hogan at your service and this is my assistant, Sean Walsh.'

'How do you do, Mr Walsh.'

'Mr Westward.' Sean bowed slightly.

'I'm afraid after all that, it's only something rather small. Heather wants to buy a present for my grandfather. It's his birthday. Just a token.'

'Ah yes. Might I suggest some linen handkerchiefs.'

Eddie Hogan began to produce boxes of them, and opened a drawer where they were stocked singly.

'He's got more hankies than he knows what to do with,' Heather explained. 'And he's not great at blowing his nose anyway.'

'A scarf, maybe?' Eddie Hogan was desperate to please.

'He doesn't go out, you see. He's very, very old.'

'It's a puzzler all right.' Eddie scratched his head.

'I thought you might have some sort of gewgaws,' Simon said, smiling from one man to the other. 'It doesn't really matter what. Grandfather isn't really in a position to appreciate anything . . . but . . . you know.' With a flick of his head he indicated Heather, who was prowling earnestly around the shop.

Eddie Hogan had now ventured into the whole problem. 'Might I suggest, Miss Westward, if it's something just to give your grandfather a feeling of pleasure that you remembered him and marked his birthday, you might think in terms of sweets, rather than clothing.'

'Yes.' Heather was doubtful.

'I know I may appear to be turning business away, but we want to think of what's best for everyone. A little box of jellies possibly. Birdie Mac would wrap it up nicely and you could get a card.'

Simon looked at him with interest. 'Yes, that's probably much more sensible. Silly of us not to see it. Thanks.'

He must have seen the look of naked disappointment on Eddie Hogan's face. 'Sorry to have bothered you, Mr Hogan, wasting your time and everything.'

Eddie eagerly looked back at the small dark confident young man.

'It was an honour, as I said, Mr Westward,' he said foolishly. 'And maybe now that you've been in our place you'll come back again.'

'Oh, undoubtedly.' Simon held the door open for his sister and escaped.

'That was very clever of you, Mr Hogan,' Sean Walsh said approvingly. 'Putting him under an obligation to us.'

'I was only trying to think of a present for the little girl to give her grandfather,' Eddie Hogan said.

Thursday arrived. Benny looked at herself in the bathroom mirror. She stared long and hard. There was a possibility that she had lost some weight around her shoulders. Only a possibility, and even if it were true what a useless place to lose it.

She had washed her hair the night before and it looked nice and shiny. The skirt that Peggy Pine had said might crush did indeed crush. It looked awful. But it was a lovely blue colour, not like all the sensible navy and brown that she had worn like a school uniform. The kind of colours that wouldn't draw attention to you. The blouse looked a bit raggy too, not like the heavy ones she normally wore. But it was much more feminine. If she were sitting across a table from a gorgeous man like Jack Foley he would have nothing to look at except her top. She *had* to have something fancy, not look as if she were a governess or a school prefect.

Her heart soared and plummeted a dozen times as she dressed. He had been so easy and natural that day he was here in Knockglen. But in college it was different. You always heard people talking about him as if he were some kind of Greek god. Even real Holy Marys in her class spoke of him. These were girls with straight hair and glasses and shabby cardigans, who worked harder than the nuns and seemed to have no time for fellows or a social life; even those kind of girls knew of Jack Foley.

And he was asking her out today. She'd love to tell Rosemary. She would really adore to see her face. And lots of them, she'd love to go up to Carroll's shop now and kick on the door and tell horrible Maire Carroll who used to call her names at school how well things were turning out. Maire who didn't get called to the Training College like she had thought, and was sulking in her parents' grocery shop, while Benny would be having lunch in the Dolphin with Jack Foley.

Benny folded the flimsy blouse up and put it in her big shoulder bag. She also put in a small tube of toothpaste and a toothbrush, her mother's Blue Grass talcum powder, which she would say she had borrowed by mistake if it were noticed. It was seven thirty-five. In six hours' time she would be sitting opposite him. Please God may she not talk too much and say stupid things that she'd regret. And if she did say stupid things let her remember not to give a great laugh after them.

She felt a flicker of guilt that she hadn't told Eve about the outing. It was the first time she had kept anything from her friend. But there hadn't been time, and she was afraid that Eve would tell Nan – there was no reason not to after all. And Nan would have been great and lent her a nice handbag or a pair of earrings to match her skirt. But she didn't want it all planned and set up. She wanted to do it on her own, and be herself. Or sort of herself. Benny smiled wryly at her reflection. It wasn't exactly her own ordinary self that would walk into the Dolphin in six hours' time. It was a starved over-polished shiny Benny who hadn't given one minute's thought to her books for the last ten days.

'I wish you'd tell me what's wrong with the porridge, Benny.' Patsy was on her own in the kitchen when Benny came down.

'Nothing, Patsy, I swear.'

'It's just that if ever I married I'd want to be able to put a decent pot of porridge for a man and his mother on the stove.'

'His mother?'

'Well, I'd have to marry in somewhere, wouldn't I? I've nowhere for anyone to marry into.'

'Do you fancy anyone, Patsy?'

'Divil a point in yourself or myself fancying anyone. I haven't a penny to bless myself with, and you'd have to be sure he'd be a grand big ox of a fellow the size of yourself,' said Patsy cheerfully.

Somehow the morning passed. Benny skipped her twelve o'clock lecture. She didn't want to have to run through the

Green, down Grafton Street and round by the Bank of Ireland in order to be in the Dolphin at one fifteen. She would be able to do it, but she didn't want to arrive flushed and panting. She would walk down slowly and take her ease. Then at the last moment she would change somewhere nearby in the ladies' cloakroom of a pub or a coffee shop and put on more talcum powder and brush her teeth. She would look so relaxed and unfussed.

She pitied the people she saw as she walked slowly through the Dublin streets. They looked grey and harassed. They had their heads down against the wind that blew instead of holding themselves high and facing it as Benny did. They were all going to have dull ordinary things at lunch. Either they would go home on a bus to a house where the radio would be on and children were crying, or they would queue up for a meal in a city restaurant where it would be crowded and the smell of other people's dinners would be unattractive.

She checked herself finally, and decided she was as good as she could be. She should of course have started the diet much earlier. Like maybe three years ago. But there was no point in crying over that.

She had been big and fat when he had met her in Knockglen only a couple of weeks ago. It hadn't stopped him asking her out in a place like this. She looked up at the Dolphin unbelievingly. He hadn't said which part. She knew his letter off by heart. But he must mean the hall.

There were three men in the entrance. None of them

was Jack. They were much older. They were wealthy-looking, possibly people who went racing.

She saw with the shock that comes with recognition that one of them was Simon Westward.

'Oh, hallo,' said Benny, forgetting she didn't actually know him, just all about him from Eve.

'Hallo.' He was polite but mystified.

'Oh, Benny Hogan, from the shop in Knockglen.'

She spoke naturally, with no resentment at not being recognised. Simon's smile was warm now.

'I was in your father's shop yesterday.'

'He told me. With your little sister.'

'Yes, he's a very courteous man, your father. And his assistant . . . ?'

'Oh, yes.' Benny wasn't enthusiastic.

'Not the same type of person?'

'Not at all, but you couldn't tell my father that. He thinks he's fine.'

'No boys in the family to help him run it?'

'No, only me.'

'And do you live in Dublin?'

'Oh, I wish I did. No, I go up and down every day.'

'It must be exhausting. Do you drive?'

Simon lived in a different world, Benny decided.

'Only on the bus,' she said.

'Still it makes it a bit better if you can have nice lunches in a place like this . . .' He looked around him approvingly.

'This is the first time I've been here. I said I'd meet someone. Do you think I should wait in the hall?'

'The bar, I think,' he said, pointing.

Benny thanked him and went in. It was crowded but she saw him immediately over in a corner . . . He was waving.

'There she is!' Jack cried. 'Now we're all complete.'

He was standing up smiling at her, from the middle of a group of seven people. It wasn't a date. It was a party. There were to be eight people. And one of them was Rosemary Ryan.

Benny didn't really remember much about the party before they went into the dining room. She felt dizzy, partly with the shock and partly with the lack of food over the past few days. She looked wildly to see what the others were drinking. Some of them had glasses of club orange, but it could have been gin and orange. The boys had glasses of beer.

'I'd like one of those.' She pointed weakly to a beer glass.

'Good old Benny, one of the lads,' said Bill Dunne, a boy she had always liked before. Now she would have liked to pick up the heavy glass ashtray and beat him over the head with it until she was perfectly sure he was dead.

They were all chatting easily and happily. Benny's eyes raked the other girls. Rosemary was as usual looking as if she had come out from under the hair dryer and hours of ministration in the poshest place in Dublin. Her make-up was perfect. She smiled at everyone admiringly. Carmel was small and pretty. She had been going out with her boyfriend Sean since they were sixteen or maybe even fifteen. They were known as the college's Perfect Romance. Sean looked at Carmel with adoration and he listened to every word she said as if it were pronouncement. Carmel was no threat. She would have eyes for nobody, not even Jack Foley.

Aidan Lynch, the long lanky fellow who had taken Eve to the pictures, was there too. Benny breathed a prayer of relief that she had told nobody about what she had thought was her date. How foolish she would have felt had the story got around. But of course Aidan would tell Eve that Benny was there, and Eve might very reasonably wonder why nothing had been mentioned. Benny felt cross and hurt and confused.

The other girl was called Sheila. She was a law student. A pale sort of girl, Benny thought, looking at her savagely; pale and rather dull-featured. But she was small. God, she was small. She had to look up at Jack Foley, not over at him like Benny did. She remembered Patsy talking about her needing a big ox of a man. She willed the tears back into her eyes.

None of them had ever been there before. It was all Jack's great plan they said . . . a scheme that would make them well-known, highly respected personages here by the time they qualified. Lots of lawyers and a lot of racing people met here. The thing to do was to establish yourself as a regular.

The words of the menu swam in front of Benny. She was going to eat real food for the first time in ten days. She knew it would choke her.

233

She was sitting between Aidan Lynch and the wordless Sean when the final seating arrangements had been made. Jack Foley was between Rosemary and Sheila across the table from her. He looked boyish and pleased, delighted with his notion of getting the four boys to pay for a smart lunch like this.

The others were pleased with him too.

'I must say you went out and plucked the best of the bunch for us to be seen with,' Aidan Lynch said extravagantly.

Faithless pig, Benny thought to herself, remembering that he had sworn such undying devotion to Eve Malone earlier in the week.

'Only the best is good enough.' Jack's smile was warm and included everyone.

Benny's hand was reaching for the butter, but she pulled back. To her fury, Bill Dunne saw her.

'Ah, go on, Benny, hanged for a sheep as a lamb,' he said, pushing the butter dish towards her.

'You should see the marvellous teas that go on the table in Benny's house,' Jack said, trying to praise her. 'I was down there not long ago and you never saw the style. Scones and savouries and tarts and cakes, and that was just an ordinary day.'

'That's the country for you. They like to feed them up down there. Not like us poor starved Town Mice,' Aidan said.

Benny looked around them. The thin blouse with the frills had been no good, nor had the blue skirt. She could feel the waft of Blue Grass coming from under her arms and down the front of her bra. She wasn't the kind of girl that people would admire and want to protect like they felt about Rosemary Ryan and the little loving Carmel and the pale but interesting Sheila from the Law Faculty. Benny had been brought along only as a joky person. Someone that they'd all talk to about big feeds and being hanged for a sheep as well as a lamb.

She smiled a brave smile.

'That's it, Aidan. You come down to Knockglen and we'll fatten you all right. You'd be like one of those geese that they stuff so that they'll have nice livers.'

'Benny, please.' Rosemary fluttered her lashes and looked as if she were going to come over all faint.

But Bill Dunne was now interested. 'Yeah, we could be seeing Lynch's Liver on menus.'

Jack was entering into it, too. 'A Knockglen speciality. Fattened fifty miles from Dublin,' he said.

'I'd have to go into hiding. They'd want me dead, not alive. God, Benny, what have you got planned out for me?'

'But think of what a delicacy you'd be,' said Benny. Her cheeks were glowing. Fattened fifty miles from Dublin. Had Jack really said that? Had he meant it as a joke about her? The most important thing was not to seem hurt.

'It's a high price to pay.' Aidan was looking thoughtful as if he were considering it as a serious possibility.

'I think it's all rather awful to joke about raising poor defenceless animals to eat them,' Rosemary said, looking fragile.

Benny wished she could remember what Rosemary had ordered. But she didn't need to. Jack did.

'Come on, that's hypocritical,' he said. 'You've ordered veal chops . . . the calves didn't exactly enjoy getting ready to become that, now did they?'

He smiled at her across the table. The knight who had come to her rescue.

Rosemary sulked and pouted a little, but when nobody took any notice she recovered.

Rosemary and Sheila competed all during the meal for Jack's attention. Carmel only cared what her Sean thought of this or that item on the menu; they ate little pieces from each other's plates. Benny entertained Bill Dunne and Aidan Lynch as if she had been a hired cabaret. She worked at it until she could feel beads of sweat on her forehead. She was rewarded with their attention and their laughter. She could see Jack straining to join in at times, but he seemed pinioned by the warring women on each side.

The less she tried to seek his attention, the more he tried to engage her in chat. It was obvious that he liked her company, but only as someone who was a load of fun. With a smile that nearly cracked her face Benny knew inside that Jack Foley liked to be where there was laughter, and good times. He wouldn't in a million years have thought of asking someone like Benny out alone.

Simon Westward passed the table.

'See you back in Knockglen some time,' he said to Benny.

'Who's he? He's rather splendid?' Rosemary asked. She seemed to be losing slightly on points to Sheila who had the advantage of being able to compare notes about lecturers with Jack. Rosemary must have decided on the making-him-jealous routine.

'He's one of the ones we didn't manage to fatten up properly in Knockglen,' she said.

The others all laughed at this, but Jack didn't.

'Don't knock Knockglen,' he said softly.

He had said that before to her. This time he seemed to be saying something else.

Mossy Rooney worked on the roof of the cottage over the quarry. There had been a high wind and eleven slates had been lifted right off. They probably lay in smithereens now at the foot of the quarry.

He had been asked by Mother Francis to come urgently and repair the damage.

The nun came up and watched anxiously as he worked out what needed to be done.

'It won't be very dear, will it, Mossy?'

'Not to you, Mother Francis.' His face was expressionless as always.

'But you must be paid for your work.' She looked worried.

'It won't bankrupt you and the Order,' he said.

Never once did he hint that it was odd of the convent to maintain a small house up here that nobody used. By nothing in his tone was there any trace of surprise that a place which had seen two deaths nearly two decades ago was still kept as a kind of shrine for a young rossie who was above in Dublin getting a university education, if you don't mind, and never came next or near the place.

Mossy wasn't a person to speculate about things like that. And even if he were, his mind was too busy. He had another thought in it.

He might ask Patsy to meet his mother. He was collecting information about her first. He didn't want to get into anything he might have to extricate himself from later . . .

'Simon, will you come and see me at school?'

'What?' He was studying a ledger.

'You heard. You only say "What" to give yourself time to think,' Heather said.

'I can't, Heather. I have far too much to do here.'

'You haven't,' she grumbled. 'You're always going to Dublin. Even to England. Why can't you stop for a day and come and see me? It's awful. You've no idea. It's like a prison.'

'No it's not, it's perfectly all right. All school is boring. It gets better when you get older.'

'Did yours?'

'What?' He laughed. 'Yes, it did. Look, the holidays come quickly. You're having a lovely half-term now, and then you'll be back for Christmas before you know it.' His smile was very broad.

'Haven't we any other relations? They only let relations come.'

'Not here, you know that.'

They had cousins in England and in Northern Ireland. But Simon, Heather and their old grandfather were the only surviving members of the Westward family to live on the big estate in Westlands.

Nobody ever said it, but the crazed crying out of Jack Malone praying that none of the family should die in their beds seemed to have been heeded. There were very few Westwards about.


'I saw your friend Benny yesterday, I expect she told you,' Aidan Lynch said to Eve as he sat patiently in Kit Hegarty's kitchen waiting for the washing-up to be finished so that they could go out.

'Take a tea towel, Einstein, and we'll be finished quicker,' Eve said.

'She didn't tell you, then?'

'Amazingly no. You may find this hard to believe but a day passed by in the forest without a record of your movements being sent by the tomtoms.'

'I thought she might have dropped it, after all it isn't every day one goes to the Dolphin.'

'Benny was in the Dolphin?'

'And I was, I was there, don't forget about me.'

'It's not easy,' Eve admitted.

'Perhaps she was covering up for me.'

Eve had lost interest in Aidan's ramblings, she was much more curious as to what Benny had been doing in the Dolphin.

'Was she eating anything?' she enquired.

'Like a horse. She ate everything before her,' he said.

'I didn't know you knew Jack Foley,' Rosemary said next day to Benny.

'Not very well.'

'Well enough for him to go to tea with you in Knockglen.'

'Oh, he was just passing through. His father had to see someone.'

Rosemary wasn't satisfied. 'Are they family friends then?'

'No. It was a nice lunch, wasn't it?'

'Yes, it was. Aidan Lynch is an awful eejit, isn't he?'

'I think he's rather nice. He takes a friend of mine to the pictures now and then. She says he's great fun.'

Rosemary Ryan did not look convinced.

'Sean and Carmel would make you sick, wouldn't they, all that gooey stuff.'

'They seem very well settled certainly.' Benny's eyes were dancing with mischief.

She knew the next attack would be on Sheila.

'Did you know that one, Sheila, from the BCL course before?'

'No.' Benny's face was innocent. 'She seemed to be very well up in all her studies. I thought they all seemed very fond of her.'

Rosemary returned to her notes in disgust. Benny noticed that she had a bar of Fruit and Nut and nibbled at it from time to time. Comfort eating is what that was. Benny knew it well.

Brian Mahon was very drunk on Friday night. Nan heard only some of it. She locked her door and turned on her radio so that she couldn't hear what was being said. She knew her mother wasn't a whore, and so did Paul and so did Nasey. So did her father when he was sober. But when he was drunk he seemed to want to say at the top of his voice that not only was she a whore but a frigid one and that the sooner people realised this the better. Nan also knew that her mother would never leave the home where such humiliations were forced on her with ever greater frequency.

'It's for you, Eve.' One of Kit's students answered the phone on Saturday morning.

'Oh, good.' Eve hoped it was Benny. Maybe she would go down to Knockglen on the lunch-time bus. Kit had said that she was free to go whenever she wanted.

But it wasn't Benny. It was Nan.

'Can I tempt you out for a walk today?'

'Yes, that would be nice. Will I come in your way and learn a bit of that side of town? I could pick you up.'

'No.' Nan spoke sharply. Then her voice softened. 'Anyway it's much nicer out your side. We could go down the pier. I'll pick *you* up.'

'Sure.'

Eve felt a vague sense of disappointment. She would

have preferred it to be Benny saying she'd meet her off the bus.

Five minutes later Benny rang. But it was too late now.

'Can't you ring Nan and tell her you're coming home?'

'I can't. I don't have her number. Do you?'

'No.' Benny too had hoped that Eve would come back.

'You never told me you were at the Dolphin,' Eve challenged.

'I was going to tell you all about it.'

'Not only that, but threatening to pickle Aidan's liver.'

'I had to say something.'

'Why?'

'They expected me to.'

'They sure as hell didn't expect you to say that,' Eve said. 'But they seemed to enjoy it. And are you back on your food again?'

'Oh yes. Patsy's making currant bread here. You should smell it.'


Nan wore a white pleated skirt and a dark green jacket. The boys who were in the digs looked up with great interest when she came in.

Kit Hegarty too looked at her with interest. She was indeed a striking young woman. Most of all because she seemed so much in control of herself. She spoke in a low clear voice as if she expected that others would listen without her having to make any effort.

She went to Eve's bedroom with her and Kit could hear her exclaiming with admiration.

'A sea view as well. Lord, you are lucky, Eve.'

With the familiar feeling of loss she always felt, Kit heard Eve explain, 'It used to be Frank Hegarty's room. I wanted to keep some of his things around it, but Kit said no.'

'What are you going to wear?' Nan asked.

'Why? It's only a walk on the pier!' Eve protested.

'Everywhere's only a walk somewhere. So that you look nice. That's why.'

Kit Hegarty heard Eve sigh, and the door close as she changed into the red blazer and red tartan skirt which really did look nice on her, and went well with her dark colouring.

But Kit in her heart agreed with Eve. It was only a walk on the pier. Nan was making it seem like a public appearance. Maybe that's what she did everywhere.

They walked companionably along with the crowds from Dublin, among people who had come out from Dublin City to walk off the effects of lunch or who were trying to keep children and mothers-in-law entertained.

'Look at those kids,' Nan said suddenly, pointing out a crocodile of small schoolgirls walking purposefully with two well-wrapped-up women teachers.

'What about them?' Eve asked.

'Look, one of them's waving at you.'

Eve looked over. It was true, one of the small blue-clad figures was making great signs.

'Eve, hallo, Eve,' she called behind her hand so as not to alert the teachers.

'Who is she?' Nan asked.

'No idea.' Eve looked bewildered. The child was wearing a school beret and had a round face, snub nose and freckles. Then Eve saw the two bunches of hair, one on each side of the little head like two jug handles.

It was Heather Westward. Simon's little sister.

'Oh hallo,' Eve said lamely, and without much enthusiasm.

'Do you live near here?' the girl hissed at her.

'Why?' Eve was wary.

'I was wondering would you come and take me out some time? Just for a bit?'

Eve looked at her dumbstruck. 'Take you out? Where? What for?'

'Anywhere. I'd be no trouble.'

'Why me?'

'We can only go out with relations. You're my cousin. Please?'

'I can't. It's not possible.'

'Yes, it is. If you phoned the school and said you're my cousin.'

'But your brother?'

'He never comes up. He's too busy at home. Trying to organise things.'

'Your other relations?'

'I don't have any.'

The crocodile which had been pausing to look at the big mail boat moored at the jetty was now moving on. The teachers were shepherding them for the off.

'Please,' called Heather Westward.

Eve stood there wordlessly looking after them.

'Well?' Nan asked her.

'I suppose I'll have to,' Eve said.

'Of course you will.'

'She's only a child. You can't disappoint a child,' Eve said crossly.

'And it would be foolish. Look at all the housepoints you'd get.'

'Housepoints?'

'Well, they'll have to ask you to the Big House if you're a friend of Heather's. And they'll owe you. Don't forget that. You won't be going cap in hand any more.'

'I won't go there, anyway, cap or no cap.'

'Yes you will,' said Nan Mahon firmly. 'And what's more you'll take me with you.'

## 9

Peggy Pine regarded the arrival of her niece Clodagh as something of a mixed blessing. The girl wore very, very short skirts; she was loud and flamboyant. She had worked for two years in shops in Dublin and spent a summer in London. According to her aunt she felt herself a world authority on dress and the buying habits of the female population.

There was much about her aunt's shop she was going to change.

'She *might* be a nice friend for you,' Annabel Hogan told Benny, weighing it up. 'But we should wait and see. She might be altogether too flighty for Knockglen, from what Peggy says, and indeed from first impressions.'

'Oh, Sean up in the shop is full of disapproval of her,' Eddie Hogan observed.

'Then I like her already,' Benny chimed in.

'You need a friend now that you don't see Eve any more,' Annabel said.

Benny's eyes flashed. 'What do you mean, Mother? Don't I see Eve three or four times a week in college?'

'But it's not the same,' her mother said. 'She never comes home here any more, and she has her own friends out in Dunlaoghaire in that house she works in. And there's this Nan. You never say Eve any more, it's always Eve and Nan.'

Benny was silent.

'It was only to be expected,' her mother consoled. 'And you'll make lots of new contacts, where you need them. Round here.'

'Who have you asked to the dance?' Bill Dunne asked Jack as they walked out of their lecture together. One of the big college dress dances was coming up in a few weeks' time.

'I knew your mind wasn't on constitutional law,' Jack said.

'We have a written Constitution here. No need to upset ourselves about it,' Bill said.

'All the more reason, it would appear. I haven't done anything yet. What about you?'

'I was waiting to see who you were going to ask so that I could pick up the crumbs from the rich man's table.'

'You're a pain. You're beginning to talk as obscurely as Aidan.'

'I think he's all right. He's going to ask Eve Malone, I think, when he gets up enough courage. She's inclined to bite off his head. I'm more interested in knowing what *you're* going to do.'

'I wish I knew.'

'Well ask somebody,' Bill begged, 'and leave the field clear for the rest of us.'

That was the problem. Who should he ask? Jack had been vague any time Shirley phoned. He had been busy disentangling himself there, and Sheila who sat beside him at lectures had dropped fairly heavy hints. But the gorgeous Rosemary Ryan had rung him only last week saying she had two free tickets to a show which meant of course that she had gone out and bought two tickets for a show, but didn't want him to know that.

And Nan Mahon had smiled a lot at him across the Annexe and the main hall and places where she had been and he had been. He would like to ask her in many ways. She was so lovely and yet so unattainable.

Suddenly he had an inspiration.

'I know what we'll do,' he said to Bill Dunne, banging him on the arm enthusiastically. 'We'll ask them all. All the girls we fancy. Tell them to pay for themselves, and then we'll have our pick.'

'We couldn't do that!' Bill gasped at the audaciousness of the plan. 'It would be very mean. They wouldn't say yes. They'd go with fellows who'd pay for them.'

'We could have a little party first.' Jack was thinking on his feet.

'Where? You're not going to get girls in evening dress to go into Dwyer's or Hartigan's.'

'No, in a house.'

'Whose house?'

'Mine, I suppose,' Jack said.

'Why can't you just take a girl to a dance like every normal boy? Jack's father grumbled.

'I don't know who to take,' Jack said simply and truthfully.

'It's not committing you for life, there won't be a breach of promise action if you take the wrong girl to a dance in your first term.'

'I thought that you both might like to use the opportunity . . . ?' Jack looked hopefully from his mother to his father.

'Use it for what, might one ask?' Lilly Foley asked.

'Well, you know, the way you're always saying that you mean to have people in for drinks . . .'

'Yes . . . ?'

'And you know the way you're always grousing that you never meet any of my friends . . .'

'Yes . . . ?'

'I thought you could have a sherry party on the night of the dance, and sort of kill two birds . . . ?'

Jack's smile was very powerful. In minutes it was all agreed.


Rosemary Ryan offered Benny a peppermint. She must be about to divulge some information or do some detective work. Benny wondered which it was. It turned out to be both.

'Jack Foley's asked me to the big dance,' she said.

'Oh, that's nice.' Benny's heart was like lead.

'Yes, well I did tell you earlier in the term I was sort of making him my project.'

'You did indeed.'

'I think it's a large party.'

'Well, they usually are, I hear,' Benny said. She had heard little else in conversations in the Ladies' Reading Room and overheard in the cloakrooms and the cafés. People went to the dress dances in parties of ten or twelve. The boys decided on the groupings and the girls were their guests. The tickets were about twenty-one shillings, and there was dinner, and everyone danced with everyone else apparently, but with their own special date most of all and at the end.

She had a vain hope that Aidan Lynch might get up a party for it and include her. But then he couldn't really unless she had been asked by some other fellow. Those were the rules.

Rosemary was chewing her pencil as well as the peppermint.

'It's a bit odd, though. It's like a big group, and we're all meeting at Jack's house first. I was wondering were you going?'

'Not as far as I know.' Benny was cheery.

'You weren't asked?'

'No, not as yet. When were *you* asked?'

'About an hour ago,' Rosemary admitted grumpily.

'Oh well, then, there's every hope.' Benny wondered did your face break by putting these false smiles on?

After the lecture she met Jack Foley in the main hall by chance.

'Just the girl I was looking for. Will you join our group? It's a sort of Dutch party for the big dance.'

'Lovely,' Benny said. 'Will we dress in clogs?'

'No, I meant like we all sort of get our own tickets.' Jack looked embarrassed.

'That makes much more sense, then we can all be free as birds,' she said.

He looked at her, surprised. 'Birds?'

'Different kinds of birds. Sparrows, emus, but free,' she said, wondering was she actually going mad to be having this stupid conversation.

'You'll come then?'

'I'd love to.'

'And we'll have drinks in my house. I'll write down the address. My parents are having friends of their own age in. Would your parents like to come, do you think?'

'No.' Her voice was like a machine gun. 'No, what I mean is thank you, but they hardly ever come up to Dublin.'

'This might be the excuse they need.' He was politely courteous. He had no idea how much she would hate them there.

'It's very kind of you, but I think not. However, I certainly would love it.'

'That's great,' he said, pleased. 'We need someone to cheer us up in these dim and dismal days.'

'Ah, I'm the one for that,' Benny said. 'Never short of a word, that's me.'

The wind lifted his hair, and his shirt collar stood high around his neck over his navy sweater, coming out over his navy jacket. He looked so handsome she wanted to reach out and stroke him.

His smile seemed as if he had never smiled for anyone else in the world.

'I'm really glad you're going to be there,' he said.

'Stop looking as if you're going to your execution,' Kit said to Eve. 'She's only a child.'

'In a big posh Protestant school,' Eve grumbled.

'Not at all. It's shabbier than our own, I can tell you.'

'Still, full of airs and graces.'

'She can't have that many airs and graces. She wouldn't have begged an old misery boot like you to come and see her.'

Eve grinned. 'That's true. It's just we won't have anything to say to each other.'

'Why don't you bring a friend? It might be easier.'

'Oh God, Kit, who could I bring on an outing like this?'

'Aidan Lynch?'

'No, he'd frighten the wits out of her.'

'Nan?'

'Not Nan,' Eve said.

Kit looked up sharply.

There was something about Eve's tone that meant the matter was closed. Mother Francis had warned Kit about this. She said that Eve had areas where nobody followed her.

Eve was now miles away from the conversation. She was thinking about what Nan had said, using the child to get accepted into the life at Westlands.

It wasn't a joke either. She had meant it. She had said that she would go down to Knockglen and stay with Benny if there was a chance of meeting the Westward family socially.

'But they're a senile old man, a kid and Simon, an uppity fellow with an accent you could cut, who wears riding breeches,' Eve had exclaimed.

'They're a start,' Nan had said perfectly seriously.

It had made Eve shiver to think that someone could be so determined and so cool.

Also so graceful in defeat. When Eve had said that Nan would *never* visit Westlands through her introduction, Nan shrugged.

'Someone else, somewhere else then,' she had said, with her easy smile.

Heather had her coat and beret on when Eve arrived at the school. She was received by the headmistress, a woman with hair cut so short it might have been shaved at the back of her head. How could she have thought this looked attractive? Eve wondered. It was such an old style, so like pictures in school stories of the way schoolmistresses looked in the twenties and thirties.

'Miss Malone. How good of you to arrive so promptly. Heather has been ready since she got up, I do believe.'

'Good. Well, we said two o'clock.' Eve looked around

the parlour. It was so strange to be in a school without pictures of saints everywhere on the walls. No statues, no little Sacred Heart lamps. It didn't feel like a school at all.

'And Heather must return for supper at six, so we like the girls to be back at five forty-five.'

'Of course.' Eve's heart sank. How could she entertain this child for nearly four hours?

'As you suggested, we telephoned Mr Simon Westward, but he wasn't at home. We spoke to Mrs Walsh, the housekeeper, who confirmed that you are indeed a cousin.'

'I just wanted to make sure that they agreed. I haven't been in close contact with the family for a long time.'

'I see,' said the headmistress, who saw only too well. A slightly shabby girl with the surname Malone, that was *indeed* likely to be a relation not in close contact. Still, the housekeeper had said it was all in order.

'Enjoy yourself, Heather, and don't be too much trouble for Miss Malone.'

'Yes, Miss Martin. No, Miss Martin,' Heather said.

Together they walked down the avenue.

There were no words and yet the silence didn't seem uncompanionable.

Eve said, 'I don't know what you'd like to do. What do you normally do when you go out?'

'I've never been out,' Heather said simply.

'So what do you think you'd like to do?'

'I don't mind. Honestly. Anything. Just to be out, to be away from it all is smashing.'

She looked back at the school as an escaped prisoner might.

'Is it awful?'

'It's lonely.'

'Where would you rather be?'

'At home. At home in Knockglen.'

'Isn't that lonely too?'

'No, it's lovely. There's my pony Malcolm, and Clara the dog, and Mrs Walsh and Bee and of course Grandfather.'

She sounded enthusiastic when she talked about them all. That big empty house was home. The school full of chattering children her own age and class was prison.

'Would you like an ice cream in a glass?' Eve said suddenly.

'I'd love it. At the end of the afternoon if that would be all right. We have it to look forward to . . . as the crown of the day.'

Eve smiled a big wide smile. 'Right, the crown of the day it will be. In the meantime we'll have a good walk down to the sea to get up an appetite.'

'Can we go near it and feel the spray?'

'Yes, that's the best bit.'

Their legs were tired when they reached the Roman Café.

'They always stop us from going near the spray when we're out on school walks,' Heather said.

'I'll have to tidy you up a bit so that they'll not discover.'

'Are you going to have a Knickerbocker Glory?' Heather asked, studying the menu.

'No, I think I'll just have a coffee.'

'Is Knickerbocker Glory too dear?' Heather asked.

Eve took the menu. 'It's on the dear side, but it is the crown of the day so that's all right.'

'You're not just having coffee because of the cost?' Heather was anxious.

'No, truly. I want a cigarette. It goes better with coffee than ice cream.'

They sat contentedly. Heather chatted about the games at school, lacrosse and hockey.

'Which did you play?' she asked Eve.

'Neither. We played camogie.'

'What's that?'

'Well might you ask! It's a sort of gaelicised version of hockey in a way, or a feminine version of hurley.'

Heather digested this with some interest.

'Why didn't we know you before, Simon and I?' she asked.

'I'm sure you must have asked Simon that, the day I came to your house.'

'I did,' Heather said, truthfully. 'But he said it was a long story.'

'He's right.'

'But it's not a mystery or a crime or anything is it?'

'No,' Eve said thoughtfully. 'No. It's not either of those things. My mother was called Sarah Westward, and I think she may have been wild or a bit odd or something, but whatever caused it she fell in love with a man called Jack Malone. He was the gardener in the convent, and they were mad about each other.'

'Why was that odd?'

'Because she was a Westward and he was a gardener. And anyway they got married, and I was born. And when I was being born my mother died. My father carried me down from the cottage to the convent. The nuns went rushing up to the cottage, but it was too late. They sent for Dr Johnson and there was a terrible commotion.'

'And what happened then?'

'Well, apparently there was some kind of row and a lot of shouting at my mother's funeral.'

'Who shouted?'

'My father, I believe.'

'What did he shout?'

'Oh, a lot of old rameis . . . rubbishy stuff about some of the Westwards dying in their beds . . . because they hadn't behaved better to Sarah.'

'And where was the funeral?'

'In the Protestant church. Your church. She's buried in your family grave. Under the name Westward, not Malone.'

'And what happened to the cottage?'

'It's still there. It's mine, I suppose. I never use it though.'

'Oh, I know I wouldn't either.'

'And was Sarah my aunt?' Heather asked.

'Yes . . . your father was her older brother . . . there were five in the family, I believe.'

'And they're all dead now,' Heather said factually. 'Whatever your father was shouting at that funeral seems to have worked.'

'What happened to your parents?'

'They were killed in India, in a car accident. I don't remember them. Simon does of course, because he's so old.'

'How old is he?'

'He's nearly thirty. I wonder. Did he know all about the shouting and everything at your mother's funeral? I suppose he was there.'

'He might have been. He'd have been about eleven.'

'I'm sure he was.' Heather was scraping the bottom of her glass.

'I wouldn't necessarily . . .' Eve began.

Heather looked up and their eyes met. 'Oh, I wouldn't tell him all about our conversation,' she said. And changing to something that interested her much more, she leaned across the table eagerly. 'Tell me, is it true that nuns put on shrouds and sleep in their coffins at night like vampires?'

Eddie and Annabel Hogan were pleased that their daughter had been asked to dance.

'It's nice that it will be just a group of friends going to it, isn't it?' Annabel sought reassurance. 'It's not as if she had a special boy yet that she was keen on or anything.'

'In my day the men took the women to dances, paid for

them and went to their houses to pick them up,' Eddie complained.

'Yes, yes, yes, but who's going to come the whole way down to Knockglen to the door and pick Benny up and then deliver her back again? Don't go saying that now, and making trouble where there isn't any.'

'And you're happy enough to let her stay in this boarding house in Dunlaoghaire?' Eddie looked at his wife anxiously.

'It's not a boarding house. There you go again, getting it all wrong. You remember the woman who was down staying with Mother Francis in St Mary's, whose son was killed. That's where Benny will stay. They'll put another bed in Eve's room.'

'Well, as long as you're happy.' He patted her on the hand.

Shep sat between them at the fire, and looked up from one to the other as if pleased to see this touching.

Benny was out at the pictures with Sean Walsh.

'I'm happy enough about her going to the dance and staying with Eve, of course I am. I want her to have a great night, something she'll always remember.'

'What are you not happy about then?'

'I don't know what's going to happen to her. Afterwards.'

'You said she'd go back to this house that isn't a real boarding house.' Eddie was bewildered.

'Not after the dance. After . . . after everything.'

'None of us knows what will happen in the future.'

'Maybe we're wrong sending her up there. Maybe she should have done a book-keeping course and gone into the shop with you. Forget all these notions of getting a degree.'

Annabel was chewing her lip now.

'Haven't we been talking about this since she was born?'

'I know.'

They sat in silence for a while. The wind whistled around Lisbeg, and even Shep moved closer to the grate. They told each other they were glad to be indoors on a night like this, in and settled, not out in Knockglen where people were still sorting out their lives. Sean and Benny would be leaving the cinema shortly and going for a cup of coffee at Mario's. Patsy was up with Mrs Rooney being inspected as a suitable candidate for Mossy. Peggy Pine's niece Clodagh was going through the order books with her aunt. People said that it was a fallacy nowadays that the young didn't work. In fact, some young people couldn't stop working. Look at Clodagh, and Fonsie and Sean Walsh. Between them they would change the face of Knockglen in the next ten years.

'I hope they'll change it into a place we'll like to live in,' Eddie said doubtfully.

'Yes, but we won't have all that much longer to live in it. It's Benny we should be thinking about.'

They nodded. It was nearly always Benny that they were thinking about anyway, and what the future had in store. They had lived their whole adult lives in a thirty-mile radius of this place. A huge city like Dublin on their doorstep had never affected them.

They simply couldn't envisage a life for their daughter that didn't revolve around Knockglen, and the main street business of Hogan's Gentleman's Outfitters. And, though they hardly dared speak of the matter to each other, they thought too that it might best revolve around Sean Walsh.

Benny looked across the table in Mario's at Sean Walsh. In the very bright light his face looked thin and pale as always, but she could see the dark circles under his eyes.

'Is it hard work in the shop?' she asked him.

'Not hard, exactly, not in terms of physical work . . . or hours . . . just trying to know what's best, really.'

'How do you mean?'

For the first time ever, Benny was finding it easy to talk to Sean. And it was all thanks to Nan Mahon. Nan, who knew what to do in every situation.

Nan said that Benny should always be perfectly pleasant to Sean. There was nothing to be gained by scoring points off him. She should let him know in a variety of ways that there was no question of ever sharing any kind of life or plans with him, but that he was highly thought of as her father's employee. That way he couldn't fault her, and it would also keep her parents happy.

'I'm sure I'll do it wrong,' Benny had said. 'You know me. I'll think I'm being pleasant and distant, and I'll end up walking up to Father Ross arranging for the banns to be read out.'

But Nan had said it was easy. 'Ask him all about himself, sound interested but don't get involved. Tell him things about yourself that you'd like him to know and never answer any question directly, that's the secret.'

So far it seemed to be working quite well. Sean sat there in Mario's and, raising his voice to compete with Guy Mitchell on the new record player, he told a tale of how the clothing industry was changing and how men were going to Dublin and buying ready-made suits off the peg, and how the bus from Knockglen stopped so near McBirney's on the Quays in Dublin it was as bad as if McBirney's had opened a branch next to Mr Flood's.

Sean said that it was sometimes hard to convince Mr Hogan of the need for change. And perhaps not his place to do so.

Benny listened sympathetically with her face and about a quarter of her mind. The rest of her thoughts were on the dance and what she should wear. She was back on her diet again, drinking bitter black coffee instead of the frothy, sugary cups that everyone else in the café was having. She moved the chocolate biscuits on the plate around, making patterns of them with the yellow ones underneath and the green ones on top. She willed her hands not to rip one open and stuff it into her mouth.

There were no dresses big enough for her, in any of the shops in Dublin. Well, there *were*, but not the kind of shops she'd go to. Only places that catered for rich, older women. Dresses with black jet beading on them, or dove grey with cross-over fronts. Suitable for someone in their sixties at a state banquet. Not for Benny's first dance.

Still, there was plenty of time, and there were dressmakers, and there were friends to help. Nan could probably come up with a solution for this as well as everything else. Benny had asked Nan if she could stay the night in her house after the dance.

Nan hadn't said yes or no. She asked why Benny didn't stay with Eve.

'I don't know. It *is* the place she's working, after all.'

'Nonsense. It's her home. You two are old friends, you'd enjoy staying there.'

Perhaps this is what Nan meant by not answering any question directly. Certainly Benny hadn't felt even slightly offended. It would be wonderful to know how to deal with people like Nan did.

Sean was still droning on about the need to have a sale. And the dangers of having a sale. Mr Hogan felt that if a place like Hogan's had a sale it might look to customers as if they were getting rid of shoddy goods. Also what would people who had paid the full price for similar items a few weeks previously think if they saw them reduced now?

Sean saw the reason in this, but he also wondered how you could attract local people to buy their socks and shoes in Hogan's instead of going up to O'Connell Street in Dublin on a daytrip and coming home sliding past the door trying to hide the name Clery's on the package?

Benny looked at him and wondered who would marry him and listen for the rest of her life. She hoped that this new policy of being polite but uninvolved would work.

'What about next week?' Sean said, as he walked her down the town and round the bend of the road to Lisbeg.

'What about it, Sean?' she asked courteously.

'*Jamaica Inn*,' he said triumphantly, having read the posters.

The old Benny would have made a joke and said that Jamaica was a bit far to go on an outing. The new Benny smiled at him.

'Oh, Charles Laughton, isn't it, and Maureen O'Hara?'

'Yes,' Sean said, a trifle impatiently. 'You haven't seen it, I don't remember it being here before.'

Never answer a question directly. 'I loved the book. But I think I preferred *Rebecca*. Did you read *Rebecca*?'

'No, I don't do much reading. The light's not very good up there.'

'You should have a lamp,' Benny said eagerly. 'I'm sure there's one in the spare room we never use. I'll mention it to Father.'

She beamed such enthusiasm for this helpful idea, and put out her hand so firmly to shake his, that he couldn't press her for a yes or a no about the pictures next week. Nor could he press his cold, thin lips on hers with any dignity at all.

Mother Francis moved around the small cottage. She had been very heartened by Kit Hegarty's report on the meeting between Eve and Heather. Perhaps the way to a reconciliation was opening up after all. The agreement to pay the fees had done nothing to soften Eve's heart to the cold distant family who had treated her mother, her father and herself so shabbily.

In some ways it had almost strengthened her resolve not to give in to them in any way.

If only Mother Francis could get her to stay a night in this cottage, to sleep here, to feel the place was her own. If Eve Malone were to wake in this place and look out over the quarry she might feel she belonged somewhere rather than perching here and there, which was what she felt now. Mother Francis had high hopes that she might be able to install Eve by Christmas. But it was work of high sensitivity.

It would be no use pretending that she needed Eve's room in the convent. That would be the worst thing to do. The girl would feel she had been evicted from the only home she knew. Perhaps Mother Francis could say that the older members of the Community would like a little outing and that since they couldn't leave the convent grounds perhaps Eve might arrange a tea party for them in her cottage. But Eve would see through that at once.

When Mother Francis and Peggy Pine were young together, Peggy used to say, 'It will all come clear in the end.'

Mainly it had. This cottage was an area where it had taken a long time for things to come clear.

She was always careful to lock the door with the big key, and put it under the third stone in the little wall near the iron gate. There was a big padlock that Mossy had suggested she put on the gate as well, but it looked ugly and forbidding. Mother Francis decided to risk doing without it.

Not many came up this way unless they had business here. Either you came through the briar- and bramble-covered paths of the convent or else if anyone wanted a view of the big stone escarpments they chose a much better and broader way which went up at a gradual incline from the square where the bus turned every day.

To her shock, when she turned around she saw a figure standing only a few feet away.

It was Simon Westward. He had his back to her and was looking out over the dark, misty view. She rattled the gate so that he would hear her and not be startled.

'Oh . . . um, good afternoon,' he said.

'Good afternoon, Mr Westward.'

In religious life a part of the day was known as the Great Silence. It meant that nuns did not feel uneasy when there was no conversation. Mother Francis waited easily for the small dark man to speak again.

'Rotten weather,' he said.

'Never very good, November.' She could have been at a garden party instead of on top of a quarry in the mist and rain with a man she had crossed swords with several times.

'Mrs Walsh said you come up here a lot,' he said. 'I told her I didn't feel I'd be quite in place in the convent. I wondered where I might run into you casually, as it were.'

'You'd be very welcome in the convent, Mr Westward, you always would have been.'

'I know. Yes, I know.'

'But anyway you've found me now.'

It would have been more sensible for them to go back into the cottage but there was no way that she would take him over Eve's doorstep. It would have been the final betrayal. He looked at the house expectantly. She said nothing.

'It's about Eve,' he said eventually.

'Oh yes.'

'It's just that she very kindly went and took my sister out from school. I'm afraid Heather very probably asked her to do so, in fact I know she did. But anyway Eve took her on a nice day out and is going to again . . .'

'Yes.' Mother Francis had cold eyes and a heavy heart. Was he going to ask Eve to stay clear of the family? If so, she would have a heart as hard as Eve's.

'I was wondering if you could tell her . . .'

The nun's glance didn't waver.

'If you could tell her how grateful I am. I mean truly.'

'Why don't you tell her yourself?' Mother Francis felt the words come out of her mouth in a quick breath of relief.

'Well, I would, of course. But I don't know where she lives.'

'Let me write it down for you.' She began to seek deep in the pockets of her long black skirt.

'Let me. Farmers always have backs of envelopes to scribble things on.'

She smiled at him. 'No, let *me*. Nuns always have little notebooks and silver-topped pencils.'

She produced both from the depths of her pockets and wrote with a shaking hand what she thought might be the outline plans for an olive branch.

Clodagh Pine came into Hogan's shop.

'How are you, Mr Hogan? Do you have a loan of a couple of hat stands?'

'Of course, of course.' Eddie Hogan went fussing off to the back of the shop to look for them.

'Opening a millinery section are we?' Sean Walsh said to her in a lofty tone.

'Watch your tone with me, Sean. You don't know what you're dealing with here,' she said, with a loud laugh.

Sean looked at her without pleasure. She was pretty, certainly, in a flashy sort of way. But she had her long legs exposed for all to view, in a ridiculously short skirt. She wore a lime-green dress with a black jacket over it, a pink scarf, and her earrings, which were long and dangly, were precisely the same green as her dress, and her very obviously tinted blonde hair was held up with two black combs.

'No, I probably don't.'

'Well, you will,' she said.

There were just the two of them standing in the shop. Old Mike was at his tailoring and Mr Hogan was out of earshot.

'I'll hardly miss you, that's for sure.'

'You'd be wise not to.' She deliberately misunderstood him. 'We can be rivals or friends. It's probably more sensible to be friends.'

'I'd say everyone's your friend, Clodagh.' He laughed a scornful little laugh.

'You'd be wrong there. A lot of people aren't my friends at all. However, my aunt is. I'm doing a major reorganisation of her window. Every notice saying "A Fashion Snip" has already been burned. Wait till you see the new display.'

'On Monday, is it?' He was still superior.

'No, genius. This afternoon, early closing day, the only day anyone really looks in your window. And tomorrow we'll let it rip.'

'I should congratulate you.'

'Yes, you should. It's harder for me coming in than it is for you. I haven't any plans to marry my aunt.'

Sean looked nervously at the back storeroom where Eddie Hogan had found some hat stands and was returning with them triumphantly.

'I'm sure your new windows will be a great success,' he said hastily.

'Yes, they'll be fabulous,' she said. She gave the surprised Eddie Hogan a kiss on the forehead, and was gone in a flash of colour, like a bird of paradise.


'I'm not spending hard-earned money on a dress,' Eve said with a ferocious scowl when Nan started talking about what they should wear.

She expected Nan to tell her that you are how you look, and that you must expect people to take you or leave you on the way you present yourself. It was one of Nan's theories.

'You're right,' Nan said unexpectedly. 'Whatever you buy it shouldn't be an evening dress.'

'So?' Eve was wrong-footed now. She had expected an argument.

'So what will you do?' Nan asked.

'Kit said I can look through her things, just in case. She's taller than I am, but then so's everyone. I could take the hem up, if I found something.'

'Or you could have my red wool skirt,' Nan said.

'I don't think so . . .' Eve began, the prickles beginning to show.

'Well, nobody's seen it in college. Red looks great on you. You could get a fancy blouse or maybe Kit Hegarty has one. Why not?'

'I know it sounds ungrateful, but I suppose it's because I don't want to wear your cast-offs,' Eve said straight out.

'But you wouldn't mind wearing Kit Hegarty's, is that it?' Nan was quick as a flash.

'She offers them because . . . because she knows I wouldn't mind taking them.'

'And what about me? Haven't I got the same motive?'

'I don't know, to be honest.' Eve fiddled with her coffee spoon.

Nan didn't plead with her, and she didn't shrug. Very simply she said, 'It's there, it's nice, it would look well on you.'

'Why are you lending it to me, I mean what's in your mind?' Eve knew she sounded like a five-year-old but she wanted to know.

'Because we're a group of friends going to this dance. I want us to look knock-out. I want us to wipe the eyes of people like that stupid Rosemary and that dull Sheila. That's why!'

'I'd love it,' Eve said, with a grin.

'Mother, would it be awful if I was to ask you for a loan of money, like to get some material for a dress?'

'We'll buy you a dress, Benny. Your first big dance. Every girl should have a new dress from a shop.'

'There isn't one to fit me in the shops.'

'Don't be full of misery like that. I'm sure there is. You haven't looked.'

'I'm not even remotely full of misery. People don't come in my size until they're old. I don't mind now that I *know*. I used to think people were born with big bones and large frames, but apparently these grow when you're about sixty-eight. You'd better watch it, Mother, it could happen to you.'

'And where did you develop this nonsensical theory, may I ask?'

'After slogging round every shop in Dublin. Lunch times, Mother, I didn't miss my lectures!'

She looked not remotely put out about it, Annabel was relieved to see. Or perhaps she was, inside. With Benny it was hard to tell.

There was nothing to be gained by probing. Benny's mother decided to be practical.

'What material had you in mind?'

'I don't know. Something rich . . . I don't know if this is ridiculous, but I saw something in a magazine. She was a biggish woman and it was like tapestry . . .'

Benny's smile was broad, but not totally sure.

'Tapestry?' Her mother sounded doubtful.

'Maybe not. It might make me look like a couch or an armchair.'

Annabel wanted to take her daughter in her arms, but she knew she must do nothing of the sort.

'Do you mean brocade?' she asked.

'The very thing.'

'I have a lovely brocade skirt.'

'It wouldn't fit me, Mother.'

'We could get a bit of black velvet let into it, maybe, as panels, and then a top of black velvet and some of the brocade to trim it. What do you think?'

'We couldn't cut up your good skirt.'

'When will I ever wear it again? I'd love you to be the belle of the ball.'

'Are you sure?'

'Of *course* I am. And it's better than anything you'd buy in the shops.'

It was. Benny knew that. Her heart sank though at the thought of what her mother might envisage as a design.

A sudden picture of her tenth birthday flashed before Benny. The day she thought she was going to get a party dress and had been given that sensible navy-blue outfit. The pain of it was as real now as then. But there seemed few alternatives.

'Who'd make it, do you think?'

'Peggy's niece is a great hand with the needle, we hear.'

Benny brightened. Clodagh Pine looked anything but frumpish. The project might not be doomed after all.

Dear Eve,

Just a very brief note to thank you most sincerely for your visit to my sister at her boarding school. Heather has written glowingly of your kindness. I wanted to express my appreciation, but to tell you not to feel in any way obligated to this in consideration of any assistance with fees that this family may have given you. I need hardly add that you are very welcome to call at Westlands during the Christmas vacation should you wish to do so.

Yours in gratitude,

Simon Westward

Dear Simon,

I visit Heather because I want to and she wants me to. It has nothing to do with considerations, as you call them. During the Christmas vacation I shall be in residence at St Mary's Convent, Knockglen. You are very welcome to call there, should you wish to do so.

Yours in explanation,

Eve Malone

Dear Mr and Mrs Hogan,

As Benny may have told you, a group of us are

going to the end of term dress dance next Friday week. My parents are having a small sherry party in our house in Donnybrook, where we will all gather before setting off for the dance. They asked me to suggest to some of the parents that they might like to drop in for the drinks party should they be in the area. I realise it is rather far away, but just in case there was a chance, I thought I would mention it.

Thank you again for that wonderful afternoon at your home weeks ago during my visit to Knockglen.

Kind regards,

Jack Foley

Dear Fonsie,

I'm going to have to ask you very firmly to cease writing these notes to me. My aunt thinks there is only one Miss Pine in the world and that she is it. She has read aloud to me your letters about being groovy, and inviting me to where the action is. She has begun to ask me what 'turning someone on' is about, and why do people say, 'It's been real'.

I have a healthy respect for my aunt. I have come here to help her modernise her shop and improve her business. I do not intend to spend every morning listening to her reading 'See you later Alligator' at me.

I am perfectly happy to meet you and talk to you, but the correspondence must now cease.

Cordially,

Clodagh

Dear Mother Francis,

I intend to spend Christmas at St Mary's in Knockglen for a variety of reasons. I hope this will not duly disturb the Community. I shall be in touch later with full details.

Your Sister In Christ,
Mother Clare

Lilly Foley was pleased about the party. John would enjoy it. He would like seeing their big house filled with lights and flowers and the rustle of evening dresses, beautiful girls.

Her husband would enjoy playing host to a roomful of handsome young people. It would make him feel their age.

She was determined it would be just right, and that she herself would look her very best. There was no way he could be allowed to look across at her and think she was drab and grey compared to all the glitter around them.

She would think of her own outfit later. In the meantime she must plan it properly. She could not let Jack know how welcome the excuse was. She would let him and his father know what a wonderful wife and mother she was to cope with his demands.

'Will they want sausages and savouries, do you think?' Lilly asked.

'They'll want whatever we give them.' Jack had no interest in details.

'Who'll serve it? Doreen will need help.'

Jack looked round the table. 'Aengus,' he said.

'Can I wear a napkin on my arm?' Aengus asked.

'You'd probably better wear one on your bottom as well,' Ronan said.

His mother frowned.

'It's for *your* friends, Jack. I wish you'd pay some attention.'

'And for yours and Dad's. Look, aren't the pair of you delighted? You've got those new curtains you've been talking about and you had the gate painted.'

'It'd be like you to tell everyone that.'

'Of course I won't. I keep telling you that I think it's great all your friends are coming round.'

'And all yours!'

'Mine will only be here for an hour or two. Yours will stay all night and disgrace themselves. I'm as well off not to be a witness to it.'

'And what about the oldies, as you call them? The parents of your friends.'

'I asked Aidan Lynch's parents. You know them already.'

'I do.' Mrs Foley raised her eyes to heaven.

'And Benny Hogan's parents, the people from Knockglen. But they can't come. They wrote to you, remember? It's only going to be people like Uncle Kevin and the neighbours, and all your own crowd. You'll hardly notice my few.'

'I wish I knew why you've inflicted this on us,' his mother said.

'Because I couldn't decide which girl to ask, so I asked them all.' Jack beamed at her in total honesty.

The weekend before the dance, Eve came home to Knockglen.

'I've left it far too long,' she confessed to Benny on the bus on the Friday evening. 'But it really was that I didn't want to run out on Kit. Do you think Mother Francis knows that?'

'Tell her,' Benny said.

'I will. She said she had a favour to ask of me. What do you think it could be?'

'Let's guess. Help her set up a poteen still in the kitchen garden?'

'I'd be good at that. Or maybe, based on my huge experience beating off the advances of Aidan Lynch, she wants me to give Sixth Year a course of lessons in sex education.'

'Or take the older nuns to Belfast on a day excursion to see a banned film.'

'Or bring Sean Walsh into the art room and drape a duster over his vital parts and have him for a life class.'

They laughed so much that Mikey the driver said they put him off concentrating.

'The pair of you remind me of those cartoons of Mutt and Jeff, do you know the ones I mean?' Mikey shouted at them.

They did. Mutt was the big one, Jeff was the tiny one. Mikey was always pretty subtle.

'I can't turn her away,' Mother Francis pleaded with Eve in the kitchen.

'Yes you can, Mother, yes you bloody can.'

'Eve! Please!'

'No, honestly, you can do anything. You've always been able to do anything you wanted. Always.'

'I don't know where you got this idea.'

'From living with you, from watching you. You can tell Mother Clare that it damn well won't suit the Community to have her here just because her own lot above in Dublin want to be shot of her for Christmas.'

'It's hardly a charitable thing to say, or do.'

'Since when has that had anything to do with it?'

'Well, we must have raised you under some mis-apprehension here. Charity is meant to have quite a lot to do with the religious life, actually.'

They both laughed at that.

'Mother, I couldn't be in the same house as her.'

'You don't *have* to, Eve. The rest of us do.'

'What do you mean?'

'You have your own house, if you want to use it.'

'Another of your ploys!'

'On my word of honour. If you think that I went to all the trouble to arrange that Mother Clare came here just so that I could manoeuvre you into that cottage, then you really don't understand anything at all.'

'It would be going a bit far, certainly,' Eve agreed.

'Well, then.'

'No.'

'Why? Just one good reason.'

'I won't take their charity. I won't live in their bloody grace and favour home like some old groom who broke his back looking after horses for the squires and gets some kind of bothan and tugs his remaining bit of hair out in gratitude for the rest of his life.'

'It's not like that.'

'It *is,* Mother, it is. She was thrown out, not good enough to walk through their doors, never let back in again. But they didn't want her to die on the side of the road so they gave her that cottage that no one wanted because it was miles from anywhere and in addition, horror of horrors, beside the Roman Catholic convent.'

'They liked it, Eve. It was where they wanted to live.'

'It's not where I want to live.'

'Not even look at it? I go to so much trouble minding it for you, always hoping, I thought you'd be delighted.'

Mother Francis looked tired, weary almost.

'I'm sorry.'

'I was so sure you'd be so relieved to have a place to escape . . . but I suppose I got it wrong.'

'I wouldn't mind having a look, Mother. To please you. Nothing to do with them.'

'Tomorrow morning, then. We'll go up, the pair of us.'

'And my room here . . .'

'Will be your room here until the day you die.'

'What do you think?' Benny looked anxiously at Clodagh.

'It's a gorgeous bit of stuff. A pity to cut it up.'

'You've seen people going to these places. Will it look all right?'

'When I'm through with it and you, it will be a sensation.'

Benny looked doubtfully at Clodagh's own outfit, which was a white smock over a mauve polo-necked jumper and what looked like mauve tights. It was very far ahead for anywhere, let alone Knockglen.

'We'll cut the bodice well . . . well down like this.'

Benny stood in her slip. Eve sat companionably on a radiator smoking and giving her comments.

Clodagh made a gesture with the black velvet top which implied a startlingly low neckline.

'Cut it where?' Benny screamed. Clodagh gestured again.

'That's what I thought you said. I'd fall into my dinner, for God's sake.'

'Presumably you'll be wearing some kind of undergarment to prevent this.'

'I'll be wearing a bra made of surgical steel . . .'

'Yes, and we must push your bosom right up and in like this.'

Clodagh made a grab at her and Benny gave a yell.

'I haven't had as much fun in years,' Eve said.

'Tell her, Eve. Tell her my mother's paying for this. She won't let me out like the whore of Babylon.'

'It's a dance, isn't it?' asked Clodagh. 'It's not a function to put forward the cause of your canonisation or anything, is it?'

'Clodagh, you're off your head. I can't. Even if I had the courage.'

'Right. We'll give you a modesty vest.'

'A what?'

'We'll cut the thing the way it should be cut and mould you into it. Then I'll make a bit of pleated linen or something and a couple of fasteners and we can tell your mother that this is what you'll be wearing. You can take it out as soon as you are outside the city limits of Knockglen.'

Clodagh fiddled and draped and pinned.

'Put your shoulders back, Benny,' she ordered. 'Stick your chest out.'

'Jesus, Mary and Joseph, I look like the prow of a ship,' said Benny in alarm.

'I know. Isn't it great?'

'Fellows love the prows of ships,' Eve said. 'They're always saying it.'

'Shut up, Eve Malone. I'll stick the scissors in you.'

'You will not. Those are my expensive pinking shears. Now isn't that something?' Clodagh looked pleased.

Even in its rough and ready state they could see what she had in mind for Benny. And it looked very good indeed.

'The Wise Woman wouldn't let her mother near the fittings for this dress,' Eve said sagely.

'They'll be climbing all over you in this,' Clodagh said happily as she began to unpin it.

'Wouldn't that be fantastic?' Benny said, smiling delightedly at her reflection in the mirror.

## 10

'It's great that you'll be working late tonight,' Nan said to her mother. They poured another cup of coffee at the kitchen table. The dance was in the same hotel as Emily's shop. Nan planned to bring her friends in to introduce them and parade their finery.

'You don't have to, you know, I can always peep out and see you going into the ballroom.'

'But you know that I'd love to, Em. I want you to meet them and them to meet you.'

Between them, unspoken, lay the certainty that Nan would never bring them home to Maple Gardens.

'Only if it seems right at the time. There might be people there that you don't want to bring into a shop . . . you know.'

Nan laid her hand on her mother's.

'No, I don't know, as it happens. What do you mean?'

'Well, we've had such hopes for you . . . you and I, that you'll get out of all this.' Emily looked round the small, awkward house. 'You mightn't want to be bringing grand people in on top of me in a shop.' She smiled apologetically.

'It's a gorgeous shop. And you run it like a dream. I'd be proud to have them see you there,' Nan said.

She didn't say that she was not relying on the Aidan Lynches, the Bill Dunnes or the Jack Foleys to take her out of Maple Gardens. She had set her sights much higher than that.

'I wish you'd come in tonight for the drinks bit,' Eve said to Kit.

'No, I'd be no good at a thing like that, all falling over my words. I was never any good at social occasions.'

'Aidan Lynch's parents are going to be there. You could talk about him!'

'God, Eve, leave me alone. I'd a million times prefer to be here. Ann Hayes and I are going to the pictures. That's much more our style than having cocktails with doctors in Ailesbury Road.'

'It's not Ailesbury Road,' Eve said defensively.

'It's not far off it.' Her face softened. 'To be asked is enough. Have you the bed made up for Benny?'

'I have. We won't make a noise and wake you.'

'It's easy to wake me. I sleep very lightly. Maybe you'll tell me about it. That outfit is gorgeous on you. I never saw anything like it.'

They had a dress rehearsal the night before, with an evening bag borrowed from Mrs Hayes next door, and the good white lacy blouse from Kit's wardrobe starched and pressed until it was like new. Now Kit's surprise gift was produced. Scarlet earrings exactly the same colour as the skirt.

'No, no. You can't be buying me things,' Eve stammered.

Something in Kit's face reminded Eve that Frank Hegarty might have been dressing up in a dinner jacket this night to go to the dance if things had been different.

'Thank you very, very much,' she said.

'You really are very beautiful. Very striking.'

'I think I look a bit like a bird,' Eve said seriously. 'A sort of crazed blackbird with its head on the side before it goes picking for things.'

Kit pealed with laughter. 'I mean it. I really do,' she said. 'You *are* very attractive, mad as a brush of course, but with any luck people might not notice that.'

Benny's outfit had been packed in a box in tissue paper. It had been much admired at home. There had been a dangerous moment when Patsy had giggled and said she hoped nobody would snatch Benny's modesty vest away. The Hogans looked at each other, alarmed.

'Why would a thing like that happen?'

Benny had glared at Patsy, who went back to the range in confusion.

'I'd love to see you all dressed up setting out tonight,' Benny's mother said. 'You and Eve and all your friends.'

'Yes, well you could have come up of course to Dr Foley's. You *were* invited.'

Benny felt hypocritical. She would have hated them to have been there.

'Yes, it was very civil of them certainly,' Eddie Hogan said. 'Repaying the hospitality we gave to that boy.'

Benny felt herself wince with embarrassment. How provincial and old-fashioned they were compared with people in Dublin. Then a wave of guilt came over her and she felt protective about them. Why *should* they have the same style and way of going on as people who went to cocktail parties?

'And you'll be home on the morning bus?' her mother said hopefully.

'Maybe the later one. It would be nice to get value out of the visit, and meet the girls for coffee . . . or lunch.'

'But you'll ring?' her father asked.

'Of course I will.' She was dying to be gone. 'Tomorrow morning.'

'You'll be fine, up in Dublin,' her father said, sounding as doubtful as if she were going to the far side of the moon.

'Don't I go there every day, Father?'

'But not every night.'

'Still I'm safe with Mrs Hegarty, you know that.' Oh, please let them let her go.

'And enjoy every minute of it,' her mother said.

'I'd better go for the bus, Mother. I don't want to be rushing, not carrying this parcel.'

They stood at the door of Lisbeg – Mother, Father, Patsy and Shep. If Shep had known he would have raised his paw to wave. He would have.

'Enjoy the dance, Benny,' Dr Johnson called to her.

Clodagh, already rearranging her now much talked-of windows in Pine's shop made marvellous gestures, miming Benny ripping off a modesty vest and exposing enormous amounts of bosom.

Fonsie watched this from across the street with interest.

'Fabulous bird, isn't she?' he said.

'There's great talent here in Knockglen,' Benny agreed.

'Keep on rocking,' Fonsie encouraged her.

Outside Hogan's, Sean Walsh was polishing the brasses.

'Tonight's the big night,' he said with a slow smile.

Remember Nan's advice. It doesn't hurt to be nice. It often helps.

Benny smiled back. 'That's it, Sean,' she said.

'I was trying to persuade your father to let me drive them up to that reception he was invited to.'

'It wasn't a reception. It was more a few drinks in Dr Foley's house.'

'The very thing. He showed me the letter inviting them. I said it would be a matter of nothing for me to drive them.'

'But they refused.' She knew her voice was high-pitched now.

'Ah, sure what would that be except to lift the phone and say they were able to come after all? I told them they owed it to themselves to go out once in a while.'

'Did you?'

'Yes. And I said, when better than on the night of Benny's big dance?'

'What a pity they weren't able to take you up on it.'

'The day's young yet,' Sean Walsh said, and went back into the shop.

He was only saying it to annoy her. He must have known how much she would hate her parents to be at something like this. She felt slightly faint and leaned against the wall of Birdie Mac's.

Birdie knocked on the window, mouthing at her.

God, Benny thought, this is all I need. She's going to give me some broken chocolate or something now to build me up.

'Hallo, Miss Mac' She tried to make her voice steady. She must try to be sane. Her parents had just said goodbye to her. They had no intention of coming to Dublin. There would have been preparations for a week.

Birdie was at the door. 'Benny, I just had a phone call from your mother. She wants me to give her a home perm this morning. I forgot to ask her, does she have a hair dryer at home?'

Birdie Mac looked at Benny anxiously.

'Are you all right, child? You're very pale.'

'A home perm you say.'

'Yes. It's easy for me, I can run down now and wind it on, and then come back later and do the neutralising. It's the dryer I was wondering about . . .'

'There is a dryer.' Benny spoke like a robot.

She moved up to the square without realising it. She was startled by the hooting of the bus.

'Well, Benny, are you going to get on? Do you need a special invitation?'

'Sorry, Mikey. Are you leaving? I didn't notice.'

'No, not at all. We've all day, and all night. Leisure is the keynote in our bus service, never hurry a passenger, that's our motto.'

She sat down and looked unseeingly out.

They couldn't have decided to come up to Dublin. Not to the Foleys. Not tonight.


Rosemary wasn't at her history lecture.

'She's gone to the hairdresser,' said Deirdre, a busy, fussy girl who knew everything. 'Apparently she's going to the big dance tonight in a party. They're all going to drinks in Jack Foley's house first. Imagine. In his house.'

'I know,' Benny said absently. 'I'm going too.'

'You're what?'

'Yes.' Benny looked up at the girl's highly unflattering surprise.

'Well, well, well,' Deirdre said.

'Nobody's taking anyone. We're all paying for ourselves.' She was determined to bring Rosemary down, in some respects anyway.

'Yes, but to be included. Heavens.' Deirdre looked Benny up and down.

'I'm looking forward to it.' Benny knew she had a grim, despairing look on her face.

In addition to all her anxieties she now feared that her parents would be there, fumbling and apologising and mainly horrified by the amount of bosom she would be revealing. It was not beyond the possible that they might actually order her out of the room to cover herself. The thought made Benny go hot and cold.

'I suppose it's being friendly with that Nan Mahon that does it,' Deirdre said eventually.

'Does what?'

'Gets you invited to lots of places. It's a great thing to have a friend like that.'

Deirdre had shrewd, piggy eyes.

Benny looked at her for a moment or two with dislike.

'Yes. I usually choose my friends for that reason,' she said.

Too late she remembered how Mother Francis had warned them to beware of sarcasm.

'It's a way to go, certainly,' Deirdre said, nodding her head sagely.

The day seemed very long. She met Eve and they went out to Dunlaoghaire on the five o'clock train. There were a lot of office workers going home. And at some of the stations schoolchildren in uniform got on. Eve and Benny nudged each other in pleasure to be part of a different world. A world of going to a big dress dance, as part of a big, glittering circle.

Kit had sandwiches for them.

'I'm too excited,' Eve protested.

'I've been on a diet. I'd better not fall at the last fence,' Benny explained.

Kit was adamant. She wasn't going to have them fainting at the dance, and anyway the food had to be digested and turned into fat, and there wouldn't be time for that to happen. There was no fear that Benny would burst through her outfit. Kit had declared the bathroom a no-go area for her lodgers, though she said that was not strictly necessary. Most of them didn't see the need to spend hours in it.

The coffee and sandwiches were on a tray in their room. Kit seemed to understand their need to giggle and reassure each other.

The meal that night was her responsibility, she said. Eve wasn't to think of either preparing it or serving it.

They zipped and hooked each other. They held the light at a better angle for the application of eyeliner and eyeshadow. They advised on the amount of lipstick blotting, and they dusted a lot of powder over Benny's bosom, which was whiter than her neck and arms.

'Probably everyone's is. It's just we don't get a chance to see them.'

Benny's hand flew to her cleavage.

'Don't *do* that. Remember Clodagh says it looks as if you're drawing attention to it.'

'It's easy to say that. Specially wearing a smock like she does.'

'Come on, now. Didn't she make you look marvellous?'

'Did she, Eve? Or did she and I make me look a fool?' Benny looked so troubled and upset, Eve was startled.

'Come on. We're all a bit nervous. I think I look like a horrible bird of prey, but when I try to be objective I think that's probably not so.'

'Of course it's not so. You look terrific. You must *know* that. Look at yourself in the mirror, for heaven's sake. You're so petite, and colourful.' Benny's words were stumbling over each other in their eagerness to convince her small worried friend.

'And so must *you* know you look great. What's wrong? What don't you like?'

'My chest.'

'Not again!'

'I'm afraid of what people will think.'

'They'll think it's terrific . . .'

'No, not fellows. Ordinary people.'

'What kind of ordinary people?'

'Whoever's there first. You know, at the drinks bit. They might think I'm fast.'

'Don't be stupid.'

Kit called up the stairs. 'Can I come and see you? Mr Hayes will be here to drive you in in about ten minutes.'

'Come on up and talk sense into my friend.'

Kit came in and sat on the bed. She was full of praise.

'Benny's worried about her cleavage,' Eve explained.

'She shouldn't be. Let the other girls worry about it, and envy it.' Kit said it as one who knew there was no argument.

'But . . .'

'It's not Knockglen. Your parents aren't going to be here.' Eve stopped suddenly. 'What's wrong?'

'Nothing.' Benny's eyes were too bright.

Eve and Kit exchanged glances.

'Mrs Hegarty, could I use your phone do you think?'

'Certainly,' Kit said. 'It's a coin-operated one, I'm afraid.'

Benny snatched up her handbag and ran downstairs.

They looked at each other in bewilderment.

'What's that about?'

'I've no idea,' Eve said. 'Something to do with Knockglen. She's ringing home. You can bet on it.'

'Hallo, Patsy. It's Benny.'

'Oh, are you at the dance yet?'

'Just setting out. Is Mother there, or Father?'

'No, Benny. They're out.'

'They're what?'

'They're out. They went out about six o'clock.'

'Where did they go?'

'They didn't tell me,' Patsy said.

'Patsy, they must have. They always say where they're going.'

'Well, they didn't. What did you want them for?'

'Listen, were they dressed up?'

'What do you mean?'

'What were they wearing, Patsy? *Please.*'

'God, Benny, I never notice what people are wearing. They had their outdoor clothes on.' Patsy was doing her best.

'Are they in Dublin do you think?'

'Surely not. Surely they'd have said?'

'Did Sean Walsh collect them?'

'I don't know. I was out in the scullery.'

'You must have noticed something.' Benny's voice was very impatient. Patsy got into a huff.

'I'd have noticed plenty had I been told there was going to be a Garda enquiry on the phone,' she said, offended.

'I'm sorry.'

'It's all right,' said Patsy, but it wasn't.

'I'll see you tomorrow and tell you all about it.'

'Oh, very nice.'

'And if they do come back . . .'

'Well, Mother of God, Benny, I hope they will come back.'

'If they do come back, just say I rang to thank them for everything, and the lovely dress and all.'

'Sure, Benny. I'll say you rang all sweetness and light.'

Benny stood in the hall for a few moments to catch her breath.

She would not burden Eve with the whole thing. She would put her shoulders back and her chest forward. She would go to this party. If her parents turned up she would tell them she had lost the modesty vest. That it had blown away when she took it out of the parcel. She would be fun and make jokes and be jolly.

Even if her parents said mortifying things to people like Rosemary, if they made crass remarks about hospitality being repaid, she would hold her head up high.

Nobody would know that in these hoops of steel which were meant to be called an uplift brassière there was a heart of lead surrounded by a lot of wavy, nervous, fluttery feelings.

The doorbell rang and she answered it. A man in a hat and overcoat stood there.

'I'm Johnny Hayes, to drive two ladies into Donnybrook,' he said and, looking at the expanse of bosom approvingly, he added, 'though it wouldn't take much to make me drag a grand armful like yourself into the car and head off for the Dublin mountains.'

Now that it had started Lilly Foley was beginning to enjoy herself. Jack had been right. It was indeed well time they gave a party, and this was an ideal occasion. Their neighbours could admire the young people heading off to the dance. The house could be filled with young men in dinner jackets and girls in long, sweeping dresses without it looking pretentious. That was the style these big houses were meant for, Lilly Foley told herself. But she didn't tell her husband or sons. They had a habit of sending her up over what they called her notions. If Lilly Foley liked to see cars draw up in their tree-lined road and hear the sound of long dresses swishing up the steps to the hall door then she kept that little pleasure to herself.

An early arrival was Sheila, one of Jack's fellow students. To Lilly Foley she had been a fairly constant voice on the telephone, wanting to go over some notes with Jack. Now here in the house she was an attractive girl, in a yellow and black dress, over-eager to impress, Lilly thought, busy explaining that she had an uncle a

Judge and a cousin a Senior Counsel so that she was practically born to be a barrister. Soon, a young couple, Sean and Carmel, arrived, who talked animatedly to each other and no one else. Lilly was pleased to see Bill Dunne . . . a personable and easygoing young man. He made a nice antidote to that Aidan Lynch, whose antics she had never understood and whose parents both had voices like fog horns.

She looked proudly at Jack who was extraordinarily handsome in his rented dinner jacket, welcoming people in and laughing his easy laugh. He had an arm around first this girl and then another. You'd need to be a better detective than Lilly Foley considered herself to know which of them he liked most. The very pretty but rather over-made-up girl, Rosemary, had allowed her glance to fall only briefly on Lilly before turning the full-voltage charm on Dr Foley.

Aengus was extremely solemn in his duty as waiter. He stood at the foot of the stairs with his glasses steaming, his new spotted bow tie resplendent. He felt the centre of attention, the figure that everyone would be aware of as they came in and left their coats in the dining room.

So far it had all been strangers. He was relieved to recognise Aidan Lynch, Jack's friend from school.

'Good evening,' Aidan said to him formally. 'Are you from a catering agency? I don't remember seeing you much on the social scene around Dublin.'

'I'm Aengus,' Aengus said, overjoyed not to have been recognised.

'You're very kind to let me use your first name. I'm Aidan Lynch. My parents have gone ahead into the drawing room and I think are having their drink requirements met by Dr Foley. Do I give you my order . . . er, Aengus, is it?'

'Aidan, I'm Aengus, Jack's brother.' The smile of triumph was wide on his face.

'*Aengus*. So you are. I didn't realise!' Aidan said, smiting his forehead.

'You can have a dry sherry, or sweet sherry or a beer or a club orange,' Acngus said.

'My goodness.' Aidan was lost in indecision.

'But only one at a time.'

'Ah, that's disappointing. I was just about to ask for them all together in a glass with a dollop of whipped cream on top.' He looked saddened.

'Seeing that you're a friend of Jack's I'll ask if you can . . .' Aengus was about to set out for the kitchen where the drink was.

'Come back, you fool. Listen, did a beautiful, small dark girl come in?'

'Yes, she's in there. She's with some fellow. She keeps licking his ear and drinking out of his glass.'

Aidan pushed past him into the drawing room. How could Eve be behaving like this? Maybe she too had mixed all her drinks. But she was nowhere to be seen. His eyes went round the big room with its warm lights, its huge Christmas tree in the window. He saw a lot of familiar faces, but no Eve.

He came back to Aengus.

'Where is she? Quick.'

'Who?' Aengus was alarmed.

'The beautiful dark girl.'

'The one licking the fellow's ear?'

'Yes, yes.' Aidan was testy.

Aengus had come to the door. 'There!' He pointed at Carmel and Sean, who were, as usual, standing very close to each other.

Relief flooded over Aidan.

Carmel and Sean saw him and waved.

'What was all the pointing about?' Carmel asked.

'You look utterly beautiful, Carmel,' Aidan said. 'Leave this man instantly. I'll give you a better life. You have disturbed my dreams so much . . . Come and disturb my waking hours as well!'

Carmel smiled a wise, mature, women-of-the-world smile and patted Aidan's hand.

At the same moment, Aidan heard Eve's voice behind him.

'Well, hallo, Aidan. Here you are tongue-tied and wordless as ever.'

He turned and looked at her. She looked so good that he got a lump in his throat and for a few seconds he was literally unable to find words.

'You're gorgeous,' he said. Very honestly and unaffectedly.

Nan had warned Eve not to say that the red skirt was on loan. If it was praised then thank for the praise, Nan had said. Why throw people's compliments back in their faces?

Eve had never spoken to Aidan in anything other than joky terms. But his admiration had been unqualified.

'Thank you,' she said simply.

Then it was as if the mist had cleared and they went back to their old way of going on.

'I'm glad you arrived just when you did, because Carmel was propositioning me here. It's been deeply embarrassing in front of Sean, but what can I do?' Aidan looked at her helplessly.

'It's something you're going to have to cope with all your life. I'd say it's a physical thing, you know the way animals give off scents. It couldn't be intellectual or anything.'

Eve laughed happily and spun around to the admiring glance of Bill Dunne.

'You look *terrific*,' Bill Dunne said to her. 'Why don't you dress like that all the time?'

'I was just going to ask you exactly the same question,' she laughed up at him.

Bill fixed his tie and smiled foolishly. Aidan looked put out. He spoke hastily to Jack, who was at his elbow.

'I don't know whether this was such a good idea.'

'What?' Jack looked at the glass of beer in Aidan's hand. 'Is it flat?'

'No. I mean asking all the girls. We thought we'd have them under our control. Maybe we'll lose them all.'

'Jack?' Aengus had arrived, looking anxious.

'Aha, Mr Fixit is here,' Aidan said, looking malevolently at the small boy he would never forgive for confusing him so at the outset of the evening.

'Jack, will I bring out the sausages yet? Mummy wants to know is everyone here.'

'Nan's not here yet. Wait another few minutes.'

'Everyone else is here, are they?' Aidan looked round the room. He didn't like the way Bill Dunne was making Eve laugh. He didn't like the way everyone in the older set seemed to be making his parents laugh too loudly.

'I think so. Look, here's Nan now.'

Standing at the door utterly naturally, as if she had entered a crowded room like this every evening of her life, was Nan Mahon. She had a beautiful lemon dress, the skirt in flowing silk, the top a strapless bodice of thousands of tiny seed pearls on a lemon taffeta base. Her shoulders were graceful, rising from the dress; her hair, a mass of golden curls, was scooped up into a clasp, also decorated with tiny pearl ornaments. Her skin looked as if she had never known a spot or a blemish.

Jack went over to greet her, and take her to meet his parents.

'Is that Jack's lover, do you think?' Aengus asked Aidan Lynch hopefully. Aidan was the kind of person who sometimes told you unexpected things.

He was disappointed this time.

'You are a remarkably foolish and unwise young man to talk about lovers to boys who have been through a Catholic education and know that such things must be confined to the Holy Sacrament of Matrimony.'

'I meant like in the pictures . . .' Aengus pleaded.

'You don't know what you mean, your mind is a snake pit of confusion. Go and get the sausages while you still have a few brain cells left alive,' Aidan ordered him.

'They're not all there,' Aengus was mutinous.

'Yes, they are.'

'No, there's someone in the cloakroom. She's been there since she came in.'

'She probably got out the window and left,' said Aidan. 'Get the sausages or I'll tear the face off you.'

Aengus knew it had all been going too well. The bow tie, the attention and people thanking him. Now Aidan Lynch was speaking to him just like he had at school.

He went gloomily out towards the kitchen in search of the party food.

In the hall a big girl was looking at herself in the mirror without very much pleasure.

'Hallo,' he said.

'Hallo,' she replied. 'Am I the last?'

'I think so. Are you Nan?'

'No. She just went in, I heard her.'

'They said I couldn't serve the sausages until Nan arrived. She was the only one missing.'

'Well, I expect they forgot me,' she said.

'They must have,' he said comfortingly.

'Are you Jack's brother?'

'Yes, I'm Aengus Foley.'

'How do you do. I'm Benny Hogan.'

'Do you like sausages?'

'Yes, why?'

'I'm getting some now. I thought you could have a few before you went in, to stock up like.'

'Thanks, but I'd better not. I'm afraid of bursting out of my dress.'

'You've burst out of most of it already,' said Aengus indicating her bosom.

'Oh God,' said Benny.

'So you might as well have the sausages anyway,' he said cheerfully.

'I'd better go in,' she said.

She straightened her shoulders and trying not to look at the small boy who had thought her dress was ripped open, she held back her shoulders as she had promised Clodagh Pine she would and moved into the drawing room feeling like an ocean liner.

Bill Dunne and John O'Brien saw her first.

'God, is that Big Benn? Doesn't she look fantastic?' Bill said, behind his hand.

'Now, that's what I call a pair of Killarneys,' John O'Brien said.

'Why Killarneys?' Bill was always interested in explanations of things.

'It's an expression.' John O'Brien was still looking at Benny. 'She's not bad-looking at all, is she?'

Benny saw none of them. Her eyes were roaming the room to see if in the middle of this happy and confident throng her parents were standing, awkward and ill at ease.

Worse, would she find them holding forth on subjects of interest only in Knockglen? Worst of all, would they make a scene when they saw her dress?

But as far as she could see there was no sign of them. She peered and twisted, looking at the backs of people's heads, trying to see if they were hidden in that group of older people, where a man with a very loud laugh stood holding court.

No, they definitely weren't there.

She had seen a Morris Cowley pull away from the footpath just as they arrived. It was driven by one person. It was dark and hard to see either the face or the registration number. It *could* have been their car. That was what had unhinged her. She had fled straight into the cloakroom hissing at Eve to go in without her.

'I'll wait for you,' Eve had said, thinking that she was just going to the lavatory.

'If you do, I'll kill you, here and now in front of everyone. There'll be so much blood your blouse will be the same colour as your skirt.'

'You've made your point. I'll go in without you,' Eve had said.

For fifteen minutes Benny had sat in the Foleys' downstairs cloakroom.

Several times she felt the door handle rattle when a girl wanted to go in and check her appearance. But there was a mirror in the dining room and they made do with that.

Finally, she realised that there were no more sounds of people arriving and she emerged.

She felt foolish now, and a dull flash of anger with Sean Walsh for having tricked her into thinking that her night would be spoiled spread over her face. She felt a sense of rage with the unfortunate Patsy that she hadn't found out where the master and mistress had gone on a rare evening out. But most of all she felt an overpowering sense of annoyance with herself.

Now that she was sure they were not in the room she could ask herself what would have been so very terrible if they had turned up.

Slowly normality came back and she realised she was the centre of a lot of very interested attention.

'That's a very classy-looking outfit.' Rosemary didn't even bother to disguise her surprise.

'Thanks, Rosemary.'

'So where did you get it?'

'Knockglen.' Benny's answer was brief. She wanted to catch Eve's eye and tell her that she was all right again. But Eve had her back turned.

Before she could get to her there were several more compliments. As far as she could see they were genuine. And mainly unflattering in their astonishment.

Still, it was heady stuff.

She touched Eve on the shoulder.

'I'm back,' she said, grinning.

Eve turned away from the group. 'Am I allowed to talk to you or do you still have some kind of plan to carve me up?'

'That's over.'

Eve lowered her voice. 'Well then.'

'What is it?'

'Every single person in the room is looking at the pair of us. We're a Cinderella story come true.'

Benny didn't dare to look.

'I mean it,' Eve said. 'The glamour pusses like Rosemary and Sheila and even Nan are expected to look great at a dance. You and I are the surprise element. We're going to be danced off our feet. Mark my words.'

'Eve, what would the Wise Woman do now?'

'In your case the Wise Woman would get a drink, and hold it in one hand and your evening bag in the other. That way you physically can't start covering up your bosom.'

'Don't call it bosom,' Benny begged.

'Sister Imelda used to call it the craw. You know, like in a bird. "Make sure you cover your craw, Eve," she'd say. As if I had one to cover.'

'As if any of us took any notice of her.'

Nan came up and put her arm into each of theirs. It was no treat for Nan to be admired, and she seemed to see nothing staggering about her two friends having emerged from the chrysalis. She behaved as if she had expected them to look magnificent.

She spoke almost as a cat would purr.

'Now, haven't we knocked those awful Rosemarys and Sheilas into a cocked hat?'

They all laughed happily, but Benny would have been happier if there had been any sign that Jack Foley, the handsome young host who was handing round plates with his little brother, had even by a flicker of his eye acknowledged that she was in the room, with most of her bosom bare, and if you were to judge by everyone else's glances, looking very well indeed.

The last car door banged as the young people left. John and Lilly Foley stood on the top step and waved goodbye. Inside there was still a lively drinks party with their own friends, and Aidan Lynch's parents. Lilly knew she looked well. It had taken a lot of time, but she had found exactly the right cocktail dress, glittery without being overdone, dressy without it looking as if she should be going to the dance with the youngsters. It was a heavy lilac silk and she had earrings to match it. Her feet hurt in her new shoes, but no one would know that, certainly not the tall handsome man beside her.

'That was lovely, wasn't it? You were a great host.' She smiled at her husband, full of congratulations as if it were he rather than she who had organised everything.

'You're wonderful, Lilly,' he said, giving her a kiss on the forehead, and he put his arm around her as they closed the door and rejoined the guests.

All the work had been worth it, just for that.

The ladies' cloakroom was full of excited girls combing and lacquering their hair and flattening their lips out into grotesque shapes in order to apply lipstick. Two women behind a counter took their coats and gave them pink cloakroom tickets which the girls tucked into their bags.

There was a smell of perfume and face powder and a little nervous sweat.

Nan was ready before anyone else, unaware of the slightly jealous glances from others in the room. Suddenly their own strapless dresses looked a bit like something from the metal industry. They became aware of how the firm supports cut into their flesh. How could Nan's hair look so perfect without having to be licked into shape with cans of hair spray? Why didn't she need to dab at her chin and hide spots with tubes of covering paste?

'I'm just going to have a wander round until you're ready,' she said to Benny and Eve. 'Then I'll take you into the shop to meet my mother.'

She left gracefully in a sea of other girls who were bouncing or bobbing or running up and down the carpeted stairs. She looked serene.

Nan walked in one side of the hotel bar smiling politely around her as if she were waiting to meet someone.

It was a place with dark oak panelling and red plush seats. By the bar a lot of men stood talking. Drinks here were very much more expensive than in an ordinary Dublin pub. This was a bar where the wealthy met.

You would find county people, up in Dublin for the bloodstock sales, or some kind of land business. There might be stockbrokers, bankers, visitors from England, people with titles. It was not the kind of bar where you could ever come in on your own.

But on the night of a dance in the hotel ballroom, a lone

girl looking for her partner would be quite acceptable. Nan stood where the light fell on her and looked around her. It wasn't long before everyone in the place saw her. She was aware without having to look at individual groups that everyone had seen her, and that they were admiring the cool young woman in the exquisite dress with the golden hair who stood confidently at the door.

Just when they had all had sufficient time to look at her, she turned around and with a wave of delight moved off to the foyer, where Eve and Benny were waiting.

'What were you up to?' Eve asked.

'Surveying the talent in the bar,' Nan replied.

'Won't there be enough of it at the dance? My God, you're insatiable, Nan Mahon.'

'Yes, well less of that to my mother.'

Nan led them into the hotel shop where an attractive, rather tired-looking woman sat by the till. She had fair hair too, like her daughter, but it was faded. She had a nice smile, but it was wary. Nan must have got her really striking good looks from her father, Eve decided. Her father who was hardly ever mentioned at all in Nan's conversation.

Nan did the introductions and they paraded their dresses for her. Emily Mahon said all the right things. She told Eve that the scarlet skirt looked much better on a dark person. It had drained the colour from Nan's face. She told Benny that anyone could see at ten miles that this was beautiful expensive brocade, and that the girl who had remodelled it for her must be a genius. She never mentioned the huge cleavage which cheered Benny greatly. If anyone else mentioned it she was going to dig out that modesty vest and reinstate it.

'And do any of you have any particular boyfriends tonight?' Emily asked eagerly.

'There's a fellow called Aidan Lynch who fancies Eve a lot,' Benny said proudly, and then in order to define things properly for Mrs Mahon she added, 'And everyone fancies Nan.'

'I think you're going to have a deal with Johnny O'Brien yourself,' Nan said to Benny. 'He's been following you around as if you had a magnet somewhere about your person.'

Benny knew only too well what part of her person John O'Brien was following around.

Emily was pleased that her daughter had such nice friends. She had rarely met anyone that Nan knew. They had never been invited to the school plays or concerts like other parents. Nan had never wanted her father to know anything about school activities. It had always been her dread as a child that he would turn up the worse for wear at her convent school. To meet Eve and Benny was a big occasion for Emily Mahon.

'I'd offer you a spray of perfume from the tester, but you all smell so lovely already,' she said.

They said they didn't smell nearly nice enough. They'd love a splash of something.

They leaned over to Emily, who doused them liberally with Joy.

'The only problem is that you'll all smell the same,' she laughed. 'The men won't know one of you from the other.'

'That's good then,' Nan said approvingly. 'As a group we'll have made an impact on them. They'll never forget us.'

They were aware that a customer had come into the shop and might want to be served.

'We'd better move on, Em, we don't want you sacked,' Nan said.

'It's a treat to see you. Have a wonderful evening.' Her eyes hated to see them go.

'Don't hurry on my account,' the man said. 'I'm just browsing.'

His voice made Eve turn sharply.

It was Simon Westward. He hadn't seen her. He had eyes only for Nan.

As usual Nan seemed unaware that anyone was looking at her. She had probably grown up with those looks of admiration, Eve thought, like she herself had grown up with the sound of the convent bell. It became part of the scenery. You didn't notice it any more.

Simon did indeed start to browse among the shelves of ornaments and souvenirs, picking some up and examining them, looking at the prices on the box.

Emily smiled at him. 'Tell me if you want any help. I'm just having a chat here . . .'

She saw Nan frown at her slightly.

'No, honestly . . .' He looked straight at Nan.

'Hallo,' he said warmly. 'Did I see you in the bar a moment ago?'

'Yes, I was looking for my friends.' Her smile was radiant. 'And now I found them.' She spread her hands out to indicate Eve and Benny.

Out of politeness he moved his eyes from Nan to acknowledge them.

'Hallo,' Benny grinned. Simon looked at her startled. He knew her from somewhere certainly, but where? A big, striking girl, very familiar.

He looked at the smaller dark girl. It was his cousin Eve.

'Well, good evening, Simon,' she said slightly mocking. It was as if she had the advantage of him. She had already recognised him and had been watching while he ogled her friend.

'Eve!' There was warmth in his smile. Swift warmth.

Now he remembered who Benny was also. She was the Hogan girl.

'Small world, all right,' Eve said.

'Are you all going to a dance?'

'No, heavens no. This is just our casual Friday night out. We dress up a lot in UCD, you know. Not scruffy Trinity students shuffling round in duffle coats.' Her eyes danced, taking the sharpness out of her response.

'I was just going to compliment you and say you all looked splendid, but if it's like this every Friday, then I *have* been missing out on the social scene.'

'Of course it's a dance, Simon,' Benny said.

'Thank you, Miss Hogan.' He couldn't remember her

name. He waited expectantly to be introduced to Nan, but it didn't happen.

'Will you be going to see Heather this weekend?' Eve asked.

'Alas no. I'm going to England, actually. You really have been frightfully good to her.'

'I enjoy meeting her. She has a lot of spirit,' Eve said. 'And she'd need it in that mausoleum.'

'It's meant to be the best . . .'

'Oh, it's about the only place for you lot to send her, certainly,' Eve reassured him. But she did not imply that if Simon and his lot were less blinkered there would have been many more places to send the child.

Simon let another tiny pause develop, enough for him to be presented to the blonde girl if he was going to be. But no move was made.

She didn't stretch out her hand and introduce herself, and he wasn't going to ask.

'I must get on with my purchases and leave you all to enjoy the dance,' he said.

'Was it anything in particular?' Emily was professional now in her manner.

'I wanted a gift, a small gift for a lady in Hampshire.' His eyes were resting on Nan as he spoke.

'Something particularly Irish?' Emily asked.

'Yes, not too shamrocky though.'

Nan had been fiddling with a small paperweight made of Connemara marble. She left it back rather pointedly on the shelf.

Simon picked it up.

'I think you're right.' He looked straight into her eyes. 'I think this is a very good idea. Thank you so much.' He ended the sentence on a rising note, where if anyone was going to give a name it would be given now.

'It's very attractive,' Emily said. 'And if you like I could put it in a little box for you.' His eyes were still on Nan.

'That would be lovely,' he said.

Aidan Lynch appeared at the door.

'I know I'm always the spectre at the feast, but was there any question of you ladies joining us? It's not important or anything. It's just that the people at the door want to know where the rest of our party is and it's a question that's becoming increasingly hard to answer.'

He looked from one to the other.

Nan made the decision.

'We got sidetracked,' she explained. 'Come on, Aidan, lead us to the ball.'

She gathered the other two with her like a hen clucking at chickens.

Benny and Eve said their goodbyes, and Nan smiled from the door.

'Goodbye, Em, I'll be seeing you.'

She didn't say she'd be seeing her tonight, or at home. Simon watched them as they walked with Aidan Lynch towards the ballroom.

'What a very beautiful girl that is,' Simon said.

Emily looked after the three girls and boy walking through the crowded hotel.

'Isn't she?' said Emily Mahon.

They had a table for sixteen on the balcony. Dancing was well under way when they trooped in. Girls at other tables looked up when they saw Jack Foley, and people craned to see who he was with.

They had no luck in guessing. He went in talking to Sean and Carmel.

Boys at the other tables saw with envy that Jack Foley's table had Rosemary *and* Nan Mahon. That seemed too much for one party. College beauties should be spread about a bit. Some of them wondered how that goofy Aidan Lynch always seemed to be in the thick of everything, and one or two asked each other who was the very tall girl with the wonderful cleavage.

At their table the plan of campaign was under way. Everyone was drinking a glass of water from the large jug on the table. Then as soon as it was empty the eight boys would each pour the quarter bottle of gin which they had in their pockets into the jug. For the rest of the evening, only minerals would be ordered. They would ask for more and more club oranges, and the gin could be added from the jug.

Nobody could afford hotel prices for spirits. This was the clever solution. But the trick was not to let them remove the jug of so-called water, or worse still, fill it up, thus watering the gin. The table was never to be left empty and at the mercy of waiters.

The bandleader called out that they were to take the floor for a selection of calypsos.

Bill Dunne was first on his feet with his hand out to Rosemary. She had positioned herself near Jack, but that had been the wrong place. She should have sat opposite him, she realised too late. That way he could have caught her eye. With a hard, forced smile she stood up and went down to join the dancers.

Johnny O'Brien asked Benny. She stood up eagerly. Dancing was something she was good at. Mother Francis had employed a dancing teacher who came once a week and they learned the waltz and the quickstep first, but she had also taught them Latin American dancing. Benny smiled at the thought that girls from Knockglen would probably beat any Dublin girls when it came to doing the samba, the mambo or the cha cha cha.

They were playing 'This Is My Island in the Sun'. Johnny looked with open admiration at Benny.

'I never knew you had such a nice . . .' He stopped.

'Nice what?' Benny asked him directly.

Johnny O'Brien chickened out. 'Nice perfume,' he said.

It *was* nice, too, the perfume. It was heady, like a cloud around her. Of course he hadn't meant perfume at all, but he was right. That was nice also.

Aidan was dancing with Eve.

'This is the first time I've been able to hold you in my arms without your beating at me with your bony little fists,' he said.

'Make the most of it,' Eve said. 'The bony little fists will be out again if you start trying to dance with me in your father's car.'

'Were you talking to my father?' Aidan asked.

'You know I was. You introduced me to him three times.'

'He's all right really. So's my mother – a bit loud but basically all right.'

'They're no louder than you are,' Eve said.

'Oh they are. They boom. I just talk forcefully.'

'They talk more directly, normally. Sentences and everything,' Eve said, thinking about them.

'You're very beautiful.'

'Thank you, Aidan. And you look great in a dinner jacket.'

'When are you going to stop fighting this hopeless physical passion you have for me and succumb? Allow yourself to have your way with me.'

'Wouldn't you drop dead if I said I would?'

'I'd recover pretty quickly, I tell you.'

'Well, it mightn't happen for a while. The succumbing bit, I mean. A good while.'

'That's the trouble about being brought up by nuns. I might have to wait for ever.'

'They weren't nearly as bad as everyone says.'

'When are you going to take me to meet them?'

'Don't be ridiculous.'

'Why not? I took you to meet *my* family.'

'You didn't arrange for your nuns to rent motorbikes

and roar up to the party. I think that was socially rather inept of you,' Aidan said.

'They couldn't make it,' Eve explained. 'Friday's their poker night and they just won't change for anyone.'


Sean and Carmel danced entwined. The music played 'Brown Skin Girl Stay Home and Mind Bay-bee'.

'Imagine, that won't be long now,' Carmel said.

'Another four years,' Sean said happily.

'And we've been together four years already if you count the year before Intermediate Cert.'

'Oh, I do count that. I couldn't get you out of my mind that year.'

'Aren't we lucky?' Carmel said, holding him tighter.

'Very lucky. Everyone in the room envies us,' said Sean.


'Wouldn't Sean and Carmel sicken you?' Eve said to Benny as they all went back up the stairs.

'Not much value out of asking them anywhere, certainly,' Benny agreed.

'They remind me of those animals in the zoo that keep picking at each other, looking for fleas,' Eve said.

'Don't, Eve,' Benny laughed. 'Someone will hear.'

'No, you know, monkeys obsessed with each other. Social grooming I think it's called.'

Back at the table Jack Foley and Sheila were sitting. Jack had elected to mind the jug of gin for the first watch. Sheila was pleased to have been chosen to sit with him, but she would have preferred to have been on the dance floor.

Nan came back to the table with Patrick Shea, an Architectural student, a friend of Jack's and Aidan's from school. Patrick Shea was hot and sweating. Nan looked as if she had been dancing on an ice rink in a cool breeze. There wasn't a sign of exertion on her face.

Benny looked across the table at her admiringly. She was so much in command of every situation and yet her mother was quite shy, and not a confident person at all. Perhaps Nan got it all from her father. Whom she never mentioned.

Benny wondered why Eve hadn't introduced her to Simon. It was rather gauche not to. If it had been anyone else Benny would have made the introduction herself, but Eve was always so chippy about those Westwards.

Still Nan had said nothing, and knowing Nan, if she had wanted an introduction she would have asked for one.

Johnny O'Brien was offering her a glass of orange. Benny took a great gulp of it thankfully and it was only when she had swallowed it she remembered it was full of gin.

She choked it back and saw Johnny O'Brien looking at her admiringly.

'You're certainly a woman who can hold her drink,' he said.

It wasn't the characteristic she would most like to be praised for, but at least it was better than having gagged or got sick.

Rosemary had been looking at her.

'I envy you being able to do that,' she said. 'I get dizzy after even a little drink.'

She looked around her, knowing that there would be silent praise and admiration for this feminine trait.

'I'm sure,' Benny said gloomily.

'It must be coming from the country,' Rosemary said, still with the look of mock admiration. 'I expect they drink a lot there, don't they?'

'Oh, they do,' Benny said. 'But differently. I mean when I drink gin in the country it's usually by the neck out of a bottle. It's a rare treat to get it in a glass and mixed with club orange.'

They laughed as she had known they would.

It was never hard to make them laugh. It was hard to make them look at you with different eyes, though.

Benny looked at Jack, relaxed and happy, leaning back in his chair surveying the scene both around him and down on the tables near the dance floor. He would be the perfect host. He would ask every girl at the table to dance.

She felt an extraordinary urge to reach across and stroke his face, just touch his cheek gently. She wondered was she going mad? She had never known an urge like that before.

He would ask her to dance soon. Maybe now, perhaps the very next dance, he would lean across the table and smile. He would put out his hand towards her and smile with a slight questioning look. She could see it happening so clearly she almost believed it had happened already.

'Benny?' he might say, just like that, and she'd get up

319

and walk down the stairs with him, hands touching lightly. And then they would just move towards each other.

The bandleader had said that their vocalist would knock strips off Tab Hunter in any singing contest and he would now sing 'Young Love' to prove it.

Benny willed Jack to catch her eye and dance three soft slow numbers with her, beginning with 'Young Love'.

But Rosemary caught his eye first. Benny didn't know how she did it, it might have been something to do with some awful beating of her eyelashes, but she managed to drag his glance over to her.

'Rosemary?' he said in that voice which he should have used to say 'Benny?'

Her heart was like a lump of lead.

'Will you risk it, Benny?' Aidan Lynch was at her elbow.

'Lovely, Aidan, thank you.'

She stood up and went downstairs to the floor where Jack Foley and Rosemary were dancing and Rosemary had put both her arms around Jack's neck and was leaning back a bit away from him as if to study him better.

The dance was a success every year. This year the organisers seemed to think it was better than ever. They measured these things by enthusiasm. The spot prizes went very well.

'First gentleman up with a hole in his sock.'

Aidan Lynch won that easily. He pointed out that the

part you put your foot in was a hole. They had to give it to him. He got a huge cheer.

'How did you know that?' Benny was impressed.

'A friend of mine was a waiter here once. He told me all the spots.'

'What are the other questions?' Benny asked.

'There's one which says "The first lady up with a picture of a rabbit". That's easy too.'

'It is? Who'd have a picture of a rabbit?'

'Anyone with a threepence. There's a rabbit on the thruppenny piece.'

'So there is. Aren't you a genius, Aidan?'

'I am, Benny, I am, but not everyone apart from yourself and myself recognises this.'

They were welcomed as heroes back to the table and the wine they had won was opened.

'More drink. Aren't you marvellous, Benny?' Rosemary said. She had somehow managed to nestle her body into Jack's by leaning against him. Benny wanted to get up and smack her face hard. But fortunately Jack had moved away and the need that she felt to separate them passed.

Some waltzes were announced. Benny didn't want to dance this set with Jack. Waltzes were too twirly, too active. No time to lean against him, to touch his face even accidentally.

The others were starting to go downstairs as the music soared up at them. 'Che Sera, Sera, whatever will be, will be.'

A tall, handsome boy came over to the table and asked

courteously, 'May I ask Nan for just one dance please, you have her all evening . . . is that all right? Nan, will you?'

Nan looked up, everyone else seemed to be occupied.

'Of course,' she said, and went smiling to the dance floor.

Benny remembered at school when you were picked for teams the awful bit about being the last one to be chosen. Or worse when there was an uneven number and Mother Francis would say 'All right, Benny, you go with that team' at the very end. She remembered the musical chairs and being the first one out. She had an uneasy feeling that it was all going to happen again.

Jack was with Rosemary again! She saw Bill Dunne and another boy, Nick Hayes, talking at the end of the table, miles from where she was. If they had noticed her and come to sit with her or asked them to join her that would have been all right.

Benny sat with a fixed smile on her face, fiddling with the menu which said they would have melon, soup, chicken and trifle. She wondered absently had they forgotten it was a Friday? She poured out a fizzy orange drink into her glass and drank it. From the corner of her eye she saw a waiter approaching with a large metal jug about to refill the water jugs on the table.

Benny stood up. 'No,' she said. 'No, they don't want any.'

The waiter looked an old man. He looked tired. He had seen too many of these student dances, and danced at none of them.

'Excuse me, miss, let me fill it.'

'No.' Benny was adamant.

'Even if you don't want any, the ones that did get to dance might want it when they come back,' he said.

There was something in the mixed pity and scorn of his speech that brought a sharp sting of tears to her eyes. 'They said they didn't *like* any more water. Before they went off to dance. Truly.'

She must not make him suspicious either. Suppose he reported something odd about their table.

A great weariness came over her. 'Listen,' she said to him. 'I don't give a damn. They told me they didn't want any more but I don't care. Fill it up if you're set on it. What the hell.'

He looked at her uneasily. He obviously thought she was slightly mad, and that it was kind of somebody to have given her an outing.

'I'll go on to the next table,' he said hastily.

'Great,' Benny said.

She felt awkward sitting on her own. She would go to the ladies'. There was no one to excuse herself to. Nick and Bill were having an animated discussion at the far end of the table; they didn't see her go.

In the lavatory she sat and planned. The next dance would probably be rock and roll. That wasn't what she wanted for her dance with Jack either. She wouldn't catch his eye for this one. She'd wait until it was something lovely and slow again. Maybe they'd have 'Unchained Melody'. She loved that. Or 'Stranger in Paradise'. That was nice too. 'Softly, Softly' was a bit too sentimental. But it would do.

To her surprise she heard Rosemary's voice at the hand basins outside.

The waltzes couldn't be over yet, surely. They normally had three of them.

'He is utterly gorgeous, isn't he?' Rosemary was saying to someone. 'And he's nice too, not full of himself like a lot of those sporty fellows are if they're any way good-looking.'

Benny didn't recognise the other girl's voice. Whoever she was, she thought that Jack and Rosemary were together.

'Have you been going with him long?' she asked wistfully.

'No, I'm not going out with him at all. *Yet,* that is,' she added menacingly.

'He looked pretty keen out there.'

Benny's heart lurched.

'He's a good dancer as well as everything else. The waltz isn't my strong point. I pretended I had turned my ankle. I just wanted to come in here for a rest.'

'That was clever.'

'Well, you have to use every trick in the book. I said to him that I'd grab him for another dance later because we didn't finish this one.'

'You've got no competition.'

'I don't like the look of Nan Mahon. Did you see her dress?'

'It's out of this world. But you look just as good.'

'Thanks.' Rosemary was pleased.

'Where is he now?'

'He said he'd finish off the waltzes with Benny.'

Benny's face burned. He had *known* she was a wall-flower. He had bloody known. He hadn't deigned to ask her for a full dance, but when ravishing Rosemary walked out on him, he'd get good old Benny for the rest of it.

'Who's Benny?'

'She's that huge girl – from way down the country. He knows her through her family or something. She's always turning up at these things.'

'No competition there then?'

Rosemary laughed. 'No, I don't think so. Whoever she is, her people must have money. They know the Foleys somehow and she's wearing a very expensive dress. I don't know where she got it, but it's fabulous, brocade and beautifully cut. It takes stones off her. She says she got it in Knockflash or wherever she lives.'

'Knockflash?'

'Somewhere, real hick town. She no more got it there than she got it in the Bog of Allen.'

Their voices faded. They had freshened themselves up, resprayed their hair, put on more perfume. They were ready to go out again, full of confidence, and face it all.

Benny sat on the lavatory. Ice cold. She was huge. She was no competition for anyone. She was the kind of person someone would come and finish off a dance with but not choose in the first place.

She looked at the small wristwatch her mother and father had given her for her seventeenth birthday. It was five to ten.

More than anywhere in the world she wanted to be sitting by the fire in Lisbeg. Her mother in one chair, her father in another and Shep looking at pictures in the flames and wondering what it was all about.

She would like to be hearing the kitchen door latch go and Patsy come in from her walk with Mossy and make them all a cup of drinking chocolate. She didn't want to be in a place where people said she was huge and no competition and must have lots of money and be a family friend of the Foleys to be invited anywhere. She didn't want to be fighting to save jugs of gin on tables for people who wouldn't dance with her.

But wishing wouldn't get her home out of this humiliating place. Benny decided that she would take the good out of what she had overheard. It was good that her dress looked expensive and well cut. It was good though sad that it was necessary to hear that it took stones off her. It was good that Rosemary wasn't any way sure of Jack. And it was good that he hadn't found her sitting at the table, lonely and abandoned, and now he couldn't feel he had fulfilled his obligation to dance with her. There were lots of good things, Benny Hogan told herself as she took the little piece of cotton wool that Nan's mother had soaked in Joy perfume for them and rubbed it behind her ears.

She would go back and Rosemary would never know

that her cruel dismissive remarks had only served to make Benny feel more positive and confident than ever.

They were making an announcement from the stage that the meal would be served shortly, and thanks to a special dispensation from the Archbishop's House the Friday abstinence need not be observed. There was a huge cheer.

'How did they get that?' Eve asked.

'The Archbishop knows we've all been so good he wants to reward us,' Jack suggested.

'No, it's just that chicken's the easiest to serve. You know everyone gets a wing. They breed special chickens for functions, with ten wings,' Aidan said.

'But why would the Archbishop want us to have chicken, seriously?' Benny asked.

'It's a deal,' Aidan explained. 'The dance organisers promise not to have dances on Saturday night that might run into the Sabbath day and the Church lets them eat chicken on Fridays.'

'You ran away on me.' Jack leaned over to Benny just as the soup was being served.

'I what?'

'You ran off. I was looking for you to waltz with me.'

'No, I didn't,' Benny said smiling. 'That was Rosemary that ran off on you. She hurt her ankle. I expect you mix us all up, we all look the same to you.'

The people around laughed, Rosemary didn't. She looked at Benny suspiciously. How did she know about the ankle?

Jack used the chance to make a flowery compliment. 'You don't all look the same. But you all look marvellous. I mean it.' And he was looking straight at Benny when he said it. She smiled back and managed not to make a joke or a smart remark.

There was a raffle during the meal, and the organisers came around to invite Rosemary and Nan to go and sell tickets.

'Why us?' Rosemary said. She didn't want to leave her post. The committee didn't want to explain that it was easier to force people to buy tickets if beautiful women were doing the asking. Nan had stood up already.

'It's for charity,' she said. 'I certainly don't mind.'

Rosemary Ryan looked very annoyed. Nothing had been going her way this evening. Nan had won all the honours in this little incident and that big Benny across the table seemed to be smiling at her in some awful smug knowing way.

'Of course I'll come too,' she said, jumping to her feet.

'Mind your ankle,' Jack said, and she looked at him sharply. He was probably just being concerned, but there was something about Benny's eyes she didn't like.

The man who thought he was streets ahead of Tab Hunter but just hadn't got the breaks also thought he was a pretty good Tennessee Ernie Ford and went down to great depths in his version of 'Sixteen Tons', a song Benny had detested since it had been popular when they were studying for the Leaving Certificate and Maire Carroll had always managed to be singing it when she was near Benny.

Benny was dancing with Nick Hayes.

'You're very light to dance with. It's like holding a feather,' he said in some surprise.

'It's easy to dance if someone leads well.' She was polite.

He was all right, Nick Hayes, but only all right.

Jack was dancing with Nan.

Somehow it was more disturbing than watching him dance with Rosemary.

Nan didn't make those very obvious little efforts. She really made no play for him at all and that must be maddening to someone like Jack Foley who was used to everyone adoring him. In fact they were very much alike, those two. She hadn't really noticed it before.

Both so sure of themselves because they didn't need to fight for anyone's attention like everyone else seemed to have to do. But just because they were sure, they could afford to be nice and easygoing. Those kind of good looks freed you to be whatever kind of person you wanted to be.

'I never see you round anywhere in the evenings,' Nick was saying.

'Nobody does much,' Benny said. 'What kind of places do you go?'

She didn't care where he went. She just wanted to get him talking so that she could take her mind off the awful tune they were dancing to, and think more of Jack.

'I have a car,' he was saying right across her happy thoughts of the next dance when surely Jack must choose her.

'I could come and see you in Knockglen some time. Jack said he had a very nice day when he went to your house.'

'He did? Good, I'm glad he enjoyed it.' This was hopeful. This was very good indeed. 'Maybe you'll come back together one time and I'll try and entertain you both.'

'Oh no, that's not the idea. The idea would be to keep you to myself,' Nick said with a leer. 'One doesn't want Jack Foley getting in on all one's discoveries, does one?'

He was putting on an accent deliberately trying to pretend he was being posh. Somehow it was flat and silly and didn't work. He couldn't make people laugh like Aidan Lynch could, like she herself could.

She tried to dull the pain she felt watching Nan and Jack dance together.

Nick Hayes was looking at her, waiting for a response.

'I always hate this song,' she said to him suddenly.

'Why? It's quite nice I think.'

'The words.'

'I owe my soul to the company store,' he sang along with the vocalist. 'What on earth's wrong with those words?' he asked, mystified.

She looked at him. He genuinely didn't remember the first line – you load sixteen tons and what do you get?

He had made no connection.

It was there only in her mind. Nobody else in the room heard the song title and swivelled their eyes to Benny Hogan. She must remember this. And she must remember that both Johnny O'Brien and Nick Hayes were asking her for a date.

These were the things she would remember from the night. As well as the dance with Jack when he asked her.

He asked her at twenty-five to twelve. When they had dimmed the lights and the vocalist had told them that since Frankie Laine hadn't been able to show he would sing Frankie's song, 'Your Eyes are the Eyes of a Woman in Love', Jack Foley leaned across the table and said, 'Benny?'

They danced together easily, as if they had been partners for a long time.

She forced herself not to prattle and chatter and make fifteen jokes.

He seemed to be happy to dance without conversation.

Sometimes, looking over his shoulder she saw people looking at them. She was as tall as he was, so she couldn't have looked up at him to speak anyway, even if she had wanted to.

He drew her a little closer which was great except that she feared the place he had his hand on her back was just the part where the heavy-duty bra ended and there was a small roll of flesh.

God, suppose he held that bit of her – it would be like a lifebelt. How could she get him to move his hand up her back? How? These were the things you needed to know in life, rather than what was set out in a syllabus for you.

Mercifully the number ended. They stood beside each other companionably waiting for the next one to start. He leaned over and touched a lock of her hair.

'Is it all falling down?' Benny asked, alarmed.

'No, it's lovely. I just pretended it was out of place so that I could touch your face.'

How extraordinary that he had wanted to feel her face as she had yearned to touch his all night.

'I'm afraid . . .' she began.

She was going to say 'I'm afraid it's a very sweaty face, your finger might get stuck to it.'

But she stopped herself.

'What are you afraid of?' he asked.

'I'm afraid other Fridays are going to seem very dull after tonight.'

'Don't knock Knockglen.' He always said that. It was like a special phrase between them.

'You're right. We have no idea what plans Mario and Fonsie have for the place.'

The singer was sorry that Dino couldn't make it so he was going to give his own rendition of the Dean Martin number 'Memories Are Made of This'.

Benny and Jack drew towards each other, and this time his hand was higher on her back. The devil roll of flesh like a lifebelt was not in evidence.

'You're a marvellous person to have in a party anywhere,' he said.

'Why do you say that?' Her face showed nothing of what she felt. None of the despair that he only thought of her as some kind of cabaret.

'Because you are,' he said. 'I'm only an ignorant old rugby player. What do I know of words?'

'You're not an ignorant old rugby player. You're a great

host. We're all having a great night because you got us all together and invited us to your home.' She smiled and he gave her a little hug. And when he had held her tight he didn't release her again.

Into her ear he whispered, 'You smell absolutely lovely.'

She said nothing. She didn't close her eyes. It looked too confident. She didn't look around and see the envious glances as she was held by the most sought-after man in the room. She just looked down. She could see the back of his dinner jacket, and the way his hair curled at the back of his neck. Pressed close to her she could feel his heart beating, or maybe it was her heart. She hoped it was his, because if it was hers it seemed a bit over-strong.

Even when the third song, 'The Man from Laramie', was over Jack didn't suggest going back to the table. He wanted the next dance.

Benny blessed that dancing teacher who used to drive around in a battered old car teaching the tunic-clad girls of Ireland to dance. She blessed her with all her heart as she and Jack did stirring versions of 'Mambo Italiano' and 'Hernando's Hideaway'. Laughing and flushed they came back to the table. Sheila wasn't even pretending to listen to Johnny O'Brien and Rosemary looked distinctly put out. Nan caught Benny's eye and gave her a discreet thumbs-up sign. Eve sitting across the table with Aidan Lynch's arm loosely round her shoulder gave her a huge grin of solidarity. They were on her side.

'We thought we'd lost you for the night,' Nick Hayes said waspishly.

Neither Benny nor Jack took any notice. Aidan Lynch had won yet another spot prize – this time a huge box of chocolates which were opened. Carmel was busy feeding Sean with the soft-centred coffee ones he liked. Rosemary foolishly grabbed the box to offer it to Jack. 'You must have one before they're all gone,' she said. But her movement was too swift and she spilled them all.

Benny looked on. It was the kind of thing she would normally have done. How perfect that it should be Rosemary who did it tonight.

'You owe me another dance for the one we didn't finish,' Rosemary said, as people tried to retrieve the chocolates.

'I do indeed. I wasn't going to let you forget it,' Jack said gallantly.

His fingers were still touching Benny's slightly. She was sure he had been going to dance with her again. Then suddenly and unbelievably the last dance was announced. They wanted to see everyone on the floor for 'California Here I Come'.

Benny could have cried.

Somehow, yet again, she had lost the high ground to Rosemary Ryan. She was going to have the last dance with Jack. Nick had his hand out to her, and so had Johnny O'Brien. She thought she saw a look of regret on Jack's face. But she must have imagined it, because when she and Johnny O'Brien took to the floor Jack and Rosemary were whirling around both laughing. Though she couldn't be sure, she thought she saw him push some of the hair out of Rosemary's eyes as he had done to her.

She kept a happy smile on her face for Johnny O'Brien as she clicked through her brain the possibilities that Jack Foley was just a fellow who liked everyone, and said nice things to every single woman he met. Not out of devious cunning, but because he genuinely did feel that every woman had some attraction for him.

This *must* be the case, Benny thought, because the way he had held her when they were dancing together was suspiciously like the way he held Rosemary when everyone was dancing to 'Goodnight Sweetheart, See You in the Morning'.

There was a lot of excitement at the door where the photographers gathered to take snaps. They gave out little pink cards with the address of the places where the small prints could be inspected next day.

Benny was leaving just as Jack called.

'Here,' he called. 'Benny, come here and let's pose for posterity.'

Hardly able to believe that he had called her, she leaped to his side.

Just then Nan came down the steps.

'Nan too,' he said.

'No, no.' She moved away.

'Come on,' he said, 'the more the merrier.'

The three of them smiled at the flash. And then with a lot of calling goodnight, and see you, and wasn't it great, they were all in the cars that Jack had organized. Nick Hayes was to drive Benny, Eve and Sheila home because they all lived on the south side. The others were within a couple of miles of the city centre.

Nan was going with Sean and Carmel.

Rosemary, to her great rage, had a lift with Johnny O'Brien, who lived in the same road.

Kit had left sandwiches for them and a note saying that she had been out late playing cards so not to wake her until morning.

They crept up to bed.

'He's really nice, Aidan Lynch,' Benny said as they got undressed. 'I mean really nice. Not just all jokes and playing the fool.'

'Yes, but he talks like the Goons, nine tenths of the time. It's like having to learn a new language understanding him,' Eve complained.

'He seems very fond of you.'

'I ask myself what can be wrong with him then. Hereditary insanity maybe. His parents are like town criers. Did you hear them?'

Benny giggled.

'And what about you and Jack? You were doing great.'

'I thought I was.' Her voice was heavy and sad. 'But I wasn't really. He's just a dreamboat who's nice to everyone. He likes to be surrounded by the whole world, and have the whole world in a good humour.'

'It's not a bad way to be,' Eve said. She lay in her bed with her arms folded behind her neck. She looked so much more cheerful and happy than she had a few short months ago.

'No, it's not a bad way to be. But it's not a good thing to hitch your star to. I must keep remembering that,' Benny said.

Next morning they were woken by Kit.

'There's a call for you, Benny.'

'Oh God, my parents.' She leapt out of bed in her nightie.

'No, not at all. A young man,' Kit said, raising her eyebrows in approval.

'Hallo, Benny. It's Jack. You said you were staying with Eve. I asked Aidan for the phone number.'

Her heart was beating so strangely now, she thought she might fall down.

'Hallo, Jack,' she said.

'I was wondering if you'd like to have lunch,' he said.

She knew what lunch was now. Thank God. Lunch was a lot of people gathered together in a crowd around a table, with Benny entertaining them.

He certainly was someone who liked all his friends around him all the time. Benny was glad that she had identified that last night to Eve. That she hadn't allowed herself to build up any hopes.

She paused for a couple of seconds before she accepted. Only because she was thinking it all out.

'I meant on our own,' he said. 'This time just the two of us.'

# 11

Eddie and Annabel Hogan had raised their eyebrows at each other in surprise as Patsy banged around the kitchen getting breakfast and muttering to herself. They had no idea what it was about.

They could decipher parts of her muttering . . . in all the years she had been in this house she had never been spoken to like that, shouted at, given dog's abuse. Mutter, mutter, crash, crash.

'Probably had words with Mossy,' Annabel whispered as Patsy went out to give some scraps to the four hens in their little wire-covered run.

'If so, she must be the first who ever had. I never knew such a silent man,' Eddie whispered back.

They had managed to get the information that Benny had telephoned from Dublin shortly before she went to the dance while they had gone for a walk.

Dr Johnson had said that Annabel should take more exercise and form the routine of a regular walk. Last night they had taken Shep on a long and invigorating journey half a mile out along the Dublin road. So they had missed the call.

'It was only to say thank you for the dress again, is that all, Patsy?' Annabel asked, yet again.

'That's what she said it was,' Patsy said darkly.

Benny's parents were mystified.

'She was probably overexcited,' Eddie said, after a lot of thought.

'She was that all right,' Patsy agreed.


Clodagh Pine told her aunt they should stay open at lunch time.

'Child, you'll have us all in the County Hospital if we work any more.'

Peggy couldn't believe that she had thought this niece of hers was going to be a lazy lump. Already she had increased the turnover of the shop significantly, and despite her own appearance, which was to say the least of it eccentric, she had managed not to alienate any of the old customers either.

'But look at it, Aunt Peg. When else would people like Birdie Mac be able to come down and look at cardigans? When would Mrs Kennedy come over and see the new blouses? Mrs Carroll closes the grocery for lunch. She doesn't spend the whole lunch hour eating, by the look of her, thin string of misery that she is. Wouldn't she walk down and see what the new skirts are like?'

'It might seem a bit unfair somehow. Unfair on the others.' Peggy knew her thinking was confused.

'Tell me, Aunt Peg, have I missed something in my walks up and down Knockglen? Are there several women's draperies, open and competing with us? Is there a whole circle of women running shops like ours thinking that we're a bit sharp opening at lunch time?'

'Don't be impertinent,' Peggy said.

'Seriously. Who would object?'

'They might think we were anxious to make money. That's all.' Peggy was defensive.

'Oh, gosh, wouldn't that be dreadful. And there you were all those years not trying to make a penny. Trying to lose it. How could I have been so stupid?' Clodagh put on a clowning face.

'We'll be dropping off our feet.'

'Not when we get another girl in we won't.'

'There'd never be the call for it.'

'Go over the books with me today and you'll see.'


Mrs Kennedy looked without pleasure on the picture of Fonsie who stood in her shop.

'How's the drugs business, Mrs K?' he asked. He always winked slightly at her as if she were engaged in something shady.

'What can I do for you?' she asked in a clipped voice.

'I'm looking for a nice fancy cake of soap.'

'Yes . . . well.' She managed to suggest that it was not a moment before time.

'For girls, like,' Fonsie said.

'A gift?' She seemed surprised.

'No, for the new ladies' room,' Fonsie said proudly.

He had spent a long time persuading Mario that they should do up the two outhouses as toilets. And make the female one look attractive. Girls liked to spend time painting themselves and doing their hair. Fonsie had driven out to an auction and bought a huge mirror. They put a shelf underneath it. All they needed now was a couple of nice towels on a roller and a bit of smart soap to start off with.

'Would Apple Blossom be a bit too good for what you had in mind?' Mrs Kennedy brought out what was called a gift pack of soap.

Fonsie made a mental note to tell Clodagh to stock soaps and talcs. Sneak them in before Peggy could protest that they were taking business from the chemist. Mrs Kennedy was an old bat, and a bad old bat at that. She didn't deserve to have the monopoly on the town's soap.

She wouldn't have, not for much longer.

But in the meantime . . .

'That's precisely what we need, Mrs Kennedy, thank you so much,' he said with a great beam and handed the money across the counter without even wincing at the cost.

Sean Walsh saw from the shop window that Mrs Healy across the road was polishing the brass sign for the hotel. She was looking at it critically. He wondered had it been defaced, she was frowning so much. There was nobody in Hogan's so he strolled across the road to see what was happening.

'It's hard to get in and out of the letters,' Mrs Healy said. 'Bits remain in there clogging them up.'

'You shouldn't be doing this, Mrs Healy, it's not fitting,' he said. 'A member of your staff should do the brasses.'

'You do the ones across the road. I've seen you,' she countered.

'Ah, that's different. It's not my place, across there.'

'Not yet,' said Mrs Healy.

Sean ignored this. 'You must have somebody, Mrs Healy, one of the kitchen maids.'

'They're so unreliable. Just standing chatting to people instead of getting on with it.' Mrs Healy seemed quite unaware that this is what she was doing herself.

'If you like, I'll do yours when I'm doing ours,' Sean offered. 'But early in the morning, before anyone would see.'

'That's extraordinarily kind of you.' Mrs Healy looked at him, surprised, as if wondering why he would do this. She prided herself on being able to understand human nature. Running a hotel you met all sorts and you had to make judgements about people. Sean Walsh was a difficult person to categorise. It was obvious that he had his eye on the daughter of the house. A big strong-willed girl with a mind of her own. Mrs Healy thought that Sean Walsh would be wise to make some contingency plans. Just because she was a large girl who might not get many offers, Benny Hogan, once she had her degree from Dublin, might well hightail it off somewhere else. Leaving Sean Walsh's plans in tatters.

*

Mother Francis was pleased that it was a nice bright Saturday morning and not drizzling with rain like it had been most mornings in the week.

She would go up to the cottage for an hour when school finished and see what else needed to be done. Sometimes she told herself that she was like a child with a doll's house. Perhaps all the aching that a woman out in the world might have for her own home was coming to the surface. She hoped that this wasn't going to threaten the whole basis of her vocation to the religious life. You were meant to put your own home and family behind you and think only of your calling. But there was nothing in any rules that said you couldn't help to build up a home for an orphan who had been sent by the intervention of God into your care.

Mother Francis wondered how her orphan had got on at the dance last night. Kit Hegarty had phoned to say that Eve looked splendid. Mother Francis wished it hadn't been in a borrowed skirt, no matter how elegant and how rich a red.

She wished that class would be over and she could release the girls who were dying to escape anyway and go to Mario's café and look in the very much changed windows of Peggy's shop. Wouldn't it be wonderful if she could just ring the bell now, at eleven thirty in the morning, and shout 'You're free'.

The children would remember it all their lives. But undoubtedly it would get to the ears of Mother Clare. Her heart sank as it always did at the thought of her sister in

343

religion. If Mother Clare hadn't been coming they might have invited Kit Hegarty for Christmas. They couldn't now. Mother Clare would say they were turning a religious house into some kind of boarding house.

In two and a half hours she would be taking the key from its place in the wall and going into the cottage, polishing the piano and covering the damp stain on the wall with a lovely gold-coloured wall hanging.

One of the missionary Sisters had brought it from Africa. They had all admired it, but it wasn't a holy picture. It didn't really seem suitable to put it up in the convent. Mother Francis had kept it carefully. She knew just where it would be useful. And maybe she might get some gold-coloured material somewhere and Sister Imelda could run up a couple of cushion covers too.

Eve was almost bouncing up and down on her bed when she heard about the invitation to lunch.

'I *told* you, I *told* you,' she kept saying.

'No, you didn't. You said he *looked* as if he was enjoying dancing with me. That's all.'

'Well, you thought he looked as if it was Purgatory on earth and that he was making eyes at people over your shoulder to rescue him.'

'I didn't quite think that,' Benny said. But she had almost thought it.

When she had played the whole thing over in her mind again and again, those six lovely dances they had together, she was torn between believing that they were as enjoyable for him as they were for her, and that they were a simple courteous duty. Now it looked as if he really had liked her. The only problem was what to wear to the lunch.

Only the old cast-off clothes of yesterday were available. You couldn't wear a ball gown and expose your bosom on a November Saturday. So much the pity!

'I have seventeen pounds. I could lend you some if you wanted to buy something,' Eve offered.

But buying was no use. Not for Benny. They simply didn't have the clothes in her size.

If it had been Eve they could have run up Marine Road in Dunlaoghaire to Lee's or McCullogh's and got something in two minutes. If it were Nan all she would have to do was open a cupboard and choose. But Benny's clothes, such as they were, were fifty miles away in Knockglen.

Knockglen.

She had better ring her parents. And find out where they had been. And tell them it would be the evening bus, and say something to Patsy.

She got the coins and went back down to the phone.

They were delighted to hear from her and pleased that the dance had gone well, and wanted to know what had been served for supper. They were very startled to hear about the dispensation to eat meat. They had been out for a walk when she had telephoned last night. It was very good of her. And had the party in the Foley's house been nice? And had she explained again how grateful they were to be asked?

Benny felt her eyes misting.

'Tell Patsy I have a pair of stockings for her as a present,' she said suddenly.

'You couldn't have chosen a better time to give her something,' Benny's mother said in a low, conspiratorial voice. 'She's been like a weasel all day. A weasel with a head cold if you ask me.'

Eve said that Kit would find a solution to the clothes problem. Kit had an answer for everything.

'Not about huge clothes.' Benny was gloomy.

But she was wrong. Kit said that one of the students who stayed in the house had a gorgeous emerald-green jumper. She'd borrow it off him. Say it needed a stitch or something. Boys never noticed that kind of thing. If he wanted to wear it today he bloody couldn't. That was all. Then Kit would sew a nice lacy collar of her own on it and lend Benny her green handbag. She'd be dressed to kill.

Fonsie wanted Clodagh to be the first to see the new ladies' cloakroom.

'God, it's lovely.' She was full of admiration. 'Pink towels, pink soap, and purple curtains. It's fabulous.'

He was anxious about the lighting. Was it too bright?

Clodagh thought not. If they were old people, who didn't want to see wrinkles, then yes, have it subdued. But they'd be young. Let them see the worst in their faces.

Clodagh wished she could get her aunt to install two fitting rooms. Peggy said that it wasn't needed in somewhere like Knockglen. People could take things on approval. If they didn't like them they could bring them back.

This was uneconomic and, with the increased volume of stock they carried, hard to organise. There was a storeroom that Clodagh had her eye on. All it needed was lights, mirrors, carpet and bright curtains. They sighed, Clodagh and Fonsie, at the uphill battles with their relations.

'Will we go and have a drink in Healy's?' Fonsie said suddenly.

'I don't know. I said I'd unpack a whole lot of stuff that came in this morning.'

'To celebrate my new bathrooms and to plan your new fitting rooms,' he pleaded.

They walked companionably up the street, Clodagh in her short white wool dress worn over a pair of baggy mauve trousers and mauve polo-necked jumper. Great white plastic hoops of earrings dangled under a man's tweed hat with a ribbon of mauve and white on it.

Fonsie's spongy shoes made no sound on the footpath. His red crushed velvet jacket was bound in a yellow braid, his shirt neck was open and a red thin string like a tie hung down on each side of the collar. His dark red trousers were so tight that it appeared that every step would cause him pain in most of his body.

On Saturdays at lunch time the bar in Healy's Hotel was like a little club. Eddie Hogan would call in for a drink and meet Dr Johnson coming back from his rounds. Sometimes Father Ross would appear, and if Dessie Burns was off the drink he would sip a club orange loudly and know he was welcome in their midst.

Mr Flood hadn't been in much recently. The visions he had been seeing were preoccupying him. He had been seen standing in front of his shop looking thoughtfully up at the tree. Mr Kennedy when he was alive had been a regular. His wife would not have dreamed of coming in his stead. Sometimes Peggy had gone in for a swift gin and vermouth with Birdie Mac.

Clodagh and Fonsie paused at the entrance to the bar; they didn't want to join the group of old people and yet it would have been rude to ignore them.

As it happened they didn't have to make the decision.

Suddenly between them and the room stood the well-corseted figure of Mrs Healy.

'Can I do anything for you?' She looked from one to the other without hiding her distaste.

'Very probably, but I think we'll confine it to just having a drink at the moment,' Fonsie laughed, and ran his hand through his mop of dark and well-greased hair.

Clodagh giggled and looked down.

'Yes, well, perhaps Shea's or somewhere might be nice for a drink,' Mrs Healy said.

They looked at her in disbelief. She could not be refusing them entrance to her hotel?

Their silence unsettled her. Mrs Healy had been expecting a protest.

'So maybe we could see you, here, when you are . . . um . . . more appropriately dressed,' she said, with an insincere smile on her lips, but nowhere near her eyes.

'Are you refusing to serve us a drink, Mrs Healy?' Fonsie said in a very loud voice, intended to make every head in the place look up.

'I'm suggesting that perhaps you might present yourself for a drink in garb that is more in tune with the standards of a town like this and a hotel of this calibre,' she said.

'Are you refusing us because we are the worse for drink?' Clodagh asked. She looked over to the corner where two farmers were celebrating a small field bought and sold and were distinctly the worse for wear.

'I think out of respect for your aunt, who is one of our most valued customers, you might mind your tongue,' Mrs Healy said.

'She's joking, Clodagh. Don't mind her,' Fonsie said, trying to push past.

Two spots of red on Mrs Healy's face warned everyone that she most certainly was not joking.

Fonsie said that there were four men in the bar without ties, and he was perfectly willing to close his tie if it meant he could get a half pint of Guinness.

Clodagh said that if any of her garments offended Mrs Healy she would be very happy to remove them one by one until she was in something acceptable like a vest and knickers.

Eventually they tired of the game. With exaggerated shrugs and bewildered expressions, they left the bar. They both turned at the door with the sad, bloodhound faces of condemned criminals, but their laughter could be heard all the way down the corridor and out into the street.

The group in the corner looked at each other in some alarm. The main problem was Peggy, one of the town's most respected citizens. How would she take to her niece being refused entrance to the hotel? The little group of people that Mrs Healy cherished in her hotel looked down furtively.

Mrs Healy spoke in a steady voice. 'One has to draw the line somewhere,' she said.

Lilly Foley said that Aidan Lynch's terrible parents never knew where to draw the line.

Jack asked why they hadn't stopped serving drink, then the Lynches would have gone home. That apparently had been done early on. The bottles had been physically taken away from Aengus, but they had still stayed on and boomed.

'It irritated your father,' Lilly told Jack.

'Why didn't he do something about it then, like saying "Good God, is that the time?"' Jack saw no problems in the tardy Lynch parents.

'It's a woman's place to organise these things. It was left to me. As things always are.' Lilly Foley seemed put out.

'But apart from that it was a great party. Thanks a lot.' Jack grinned at her.

It mollified her a bit. She noted that her son had been on the phone already asking some girl out to lunch. She couldn't hear which one, but she assumed it was the glamorous Rosemary, who kept boasting of her relations in the Law, or the very beautiful girl, Nan, in the dress with all the little pearls on it. The girl who had said hardly anything, but was still the centre of attention.

Lilly looked affectionately at her eldest son. His hair was tousled, he smelled of Knight's Castille soap, he had eaten a huge breakfast and read the sporting pages of two newspapers. He had given Aengus half a crown for all his help at the party.

Lilly knew that like his father before him Jack Foley was a heartbreaker, and would be one until the day he died.

He had said the name of the restaurant as if everyone knew it. Carlo's. Benny had heard of it. It was down near the Quays, her old stamping ground getting on and off the bus from Knockglen. It was small and Italian, and she had once heard Nan say that she had been there in the evening and they had candles in wine bottles like you saw in the pictures.

Much too early as usual, she went into a big store and examined the cosmetics. She found a green eyeshadow and smeared some on each lid.

It was exactly the same colour as the veterinary student's enormous jumper that she was wearing. The shop assistant urged her to buy it, insisting that it was often hard to find exactly the right shade when you were looking for it and you should seize the hour.

Benny explained that it wasn't her sweater. It was

borrowed from a fellow. She wondered why she needed to tell so much to strangers.

'Maybe he'll lend it to you again,' said the girl in the short pink nylon coat whose job was to sell cosmetics.

'I doubt it. I don't even know who he is. His landlady pinched it for me.'

Benny knew she was sounding very peculiar but conversation of any kind made her feel less anxious. It filled that great empty echo chamber of anxiety she felt about the lunch that lay ahead.

It had been so easy when she smelled of Joy and when she was able to be in his arms. It would be quite different now, in a green sweater across a table. How would she smile and attract him, and hold him? There must have been something about her that appealed to him last night. It couldn't have been all naked bosom, could it?

'Do you think I could have a spray of Joy perfume without buying any?' she begged the girl.

'We're not meant to.'

'Please.'

She got a small splash. Enough to remind him of last night.

Carlo's had a small door. That was a poor start. Benny hoped it wouldn't have those awful benches, the kind of church pew seats that were popular now. They were desperately hard to squeeze into. Even though it was bright out on the street, with a cold, wintry sun picking everything out sharply, it was dark and warm inside.

She gave her coat to the waiter.

'I'm to meet someone here,' she said.

'He is here already.'

That meant that Jack must be well known in this place, she thought with a wave of disappointment. Maybe he came every Saturday with a different girl.

'How do you know it's the right person?' she asked the waiter anxiously. It would be humiliating to be led to the wrong table in front of everyone and for Jack to have to rescue her.

'There is only one person here,' the waiter said.

He stood up to greet her.

'Don't you look lovely and well rested considering the night that was in it?' he said admiringly.

'That's the good bracing air of Dunlaoghaire,' she said.

*Why* had she said that? There were words like bracing you didn't say. They reminded people of big, jolly girls on hikes. Like the word strapping.

But he hadn't made any unfortunate word associations. He still seemed quite admiring.

'Whatever it is, it works. Our house is full of the day-after feeling, glasses and ashtrays piled up in the kitchen.'

'It was a lovely party, thank you very much.'

'It was fine. Aengus sends you his regards. He was very taken with you.'

'I think he thought I was mad.'

'No. Why should he think that?'

It had been the wrong thing to say. Why had she said it? Bringing herself down, why couldn't she have asked about Aengus?

The waiter came and fussed over them. He was a kindly man, like a thinner version of Mario. Benny wondered was he any relation? There couldn't be that many Italians working in Ireland.

Benny decided to ask him.

'Do you have a relative working in Knockglen?'

He pronounced the name of her home town over and over, rolling it around, but his eyes narrowing suspiciously.

'Why do you think I have relations in Knocka Glenna?'

'There's an Italian there, called Mario.'

Benny wished the purple and red sunburst carpet would open up at her feet and suck her into it, then close over her head.

Jack rescued her. 'It's probably a bit like, do you know my Uncle Mo in Chicago?' he said. 'I'm always doing that.'

She couldn't imagine him ever doing it. Was there any way at all of trying to get back some of the magic of last night?

They hadn't even begun the lunch and already he must have regretted asking her. She had talked about the bracing air of Dunlaoghaire, reminding him of fat ladies on postcards. She had engaged the waiter in an endless and confused dialogue about whether he knew another Italian living miles away. What a great fun person she was. And there wasn't even anybody in the restaurant to distract him, to make him feel that the outing had any excitement at all. Benny wished she were back in the Dolphin hotel with half of Dublin there and all the Rosemarys and

Sheilas and even Carmel and Sean picking at each other and feeding each other bread rolls.

Anything was better than this catastrophic setting.

'Isn't it super to have it to ourselves?' Jack said at that moment. 'I feel like a sultan, or some millionaire. They do – you know – ring up restaurants and say they want to book all the tables so that they won't be disturbed.'

'They do?' Benny asked eagerly.

At least it was conversation and he seemed to be making the best of the place being empty.

'Well, I did it today, of course! Carlo, we need the whole place to ourselves . . . a pianist possibly. No? Well, all right. Just a few violinists at the table later. Just don't let any hoi polloi in, no awful Dubliners having their lunch or anything sordid like that.'

They laughed and laughed just like last night.

'And what did Carlo say?'

'He said, "For you, Meester Foley, anything you like, but only eef the Signorina ees lovely." '

The words were bitten back. She was about to say, 'Well, we fell down on that one, didn't we?'

She was going to put herself down for fear of thinking that she might actually believe herself to be acceptable. But something warned her it wasn't the right thing to do. She put her head on one side and smiled at him.

'And then you arrived and he saw you were very beautiful, so he has now put a House Full sign on the door,' Jack said.

'Is that Carlo who's serving us, do you think?' Benny asked.

'No idea,' Jack said. 'He looks much more like a man who has a secret cousin in Knockglen, but doesn't want anyone to know.'

'I must remember every detail of this place to tell Mario about it,' Benny said, looking happily around.

'You're lovely, Benny,' Jack said, and laid his hand on hers.

Clodagh told her aunt that she had been barred from Healy's. It didn't matter all that much because it wasn't a place she planned on visiting much anyway, but she felt that Peggy should know from her before anyone else told her.

'What were you doing, the pair of you?' Peggy asked.

'I'd tell you if we *were* doing anything, you know that. But as it happened we just walked in. She decided she didn't like the look of us.'

'She can't do that under the Innkeeper's Act.'

'I think she can. Management reserves the right and all that. We thought you ought to know, you and Mario, but honestly Fonsie and I don't care. That's the truth.'

The truth also was that Peggy and Mario did care. Very much. Neither of them liked the way that the young people dressed, in fact it was a source of great common grumbling between them. But to be refused service in the town's only hotel. That was something else. That was war.

\*

356

It wasn't long before Mrs Healy discovered how the lines were being drawn. Mr Flood, who was having one of his clear spells where he neither saw nor mentioned the nun in the tree who had been visiting him with messages, said that it was time that someone had taken a stand. Those two were an abomination. He had read in the papers that there was an international movement to take over the civilised world, and that its members knew each other by these kind of garish clothes. It was no accident that Fonsie and Clodagh had gravitated to each other, he said, nodding his head sagely. Mrs Carroll was with Mrs Healy too. The sooner this very undesirable influence in the town was stamped on, the better. Neither of these two young people had parents to deal with them, relying only on a maiden aunt and a bachelor uncle. No wonder they had run wild. Her own daughter Maire, who was working in the shop and doing book-keeping by correspondence course, had often been drawn to the bright lights in the café, and to the garish clothes in what had once been a respectable window. Mrs Healy had been quite right to make her point.

Mrs Kennedy on the other hand took a different view. She was heard to say that Mrs Healy had a cheek. She hadn't even been born in Knockglen. Who did she think she was, making rules and regulations for the people of the town? Mrs Kennedy said that there were many unsavoury people seen in the corner of Healy's bar on a Fair Day and when commercial travellers had too much to drink and knew they could always get a drink in the hotel. Mrs

Kennedy, who had never liked the young widow and thought that her own husband used to spend too many evenings there, was outraged that she should think of refusing a drink to a niece of Peggy Pine, no matter how unwisely the poor girl garbed herself.

Birdie Mac wasn't sure. She was a timid woman who had lived all her life looking after an aged mother. She had neither wanted to do this or not wanted to. It was just that Birdie was unable to make a decision. She had never made her own mind up about anything. Even though she was a friend of Peggy's she also listened to what Mrs Carroll said. Even though Mario was a good customer and bought biscuits from her every day, she still agreed with poor Mr Flood that Mario's nephew was going too far altogether and how could it be stopped unless somebody shouted stop?

She didn't like Mrs Healy personally, but she admired her courage in running a business so well in a man's world, instead of retreating humbly behind the counter of a sweet shop, which was all that Birdie had been able to do in terms of independent living.

Dr Johnson said that Mrs Healy was free to serve or refuse whosoever she wanted. Father Ross wouldn't be drawn at all. Paccy Moore told his cousin Dekko that Mrs Healy had two bunions, one on each foot. That was his only comment. It was taken to be support for Clodagh and Fonsie.

Eddie and Annabel Hogan discussed it for a long time over their Saturday lunch. There were ways of course that

Clodagh and Fonsie had misunderstood Knockglen and gone too far. They both looked as if they were in fancy dress almost all of the time. But they were hard workers, it couldn't be denied, and that was their great saving grace. If they had been standing smoking on the corner there would have been no sympathy for them.

But nobody could accuse either of them of being idle. And in Knockglen that would cover a multitude of sins, like dressing so mutinously.

'If someone came into your shop, you'd serve them no matter how they were dressed, wouldn't you, Eddie?'

'Yes, but if they had manure on their boots I'd ask them not to walk it in,' he said.

'But they weren't walking anything in,' Annabel Hogan said. She had always thought that Mrs Healy had a special smile for the men and nothing nearly so warm for their wives. And also Clodagh had made such a lovely dress for Benny it would be hard not to be on her side. All that brocade had looked so well, there were little bits of chestnut colour in it, just like Benny's hair, and that beautiful dash of white at the front, that pleated insert over the bosom. It had given the whole thing such a classy touch. So elegant and ladylike, and not at all the kind of thing you'd ever have thought Clodagh would have dreamed up.

Mother Francis heard about the scene in the hotel as well. Peggy drove up to the convent that afternoon for tea and advice.

'Rise above it, Peggy. Rise right above it.'

'That's not easy to do if you're out in the world, Bunty.'

'It's not easy to do if you're inside a convent either. I have that Mother Clare descending on me for Christmas. Imagine trying to rise above that.'

'I'll never go in there for a drink again.'

'Think carefully, Peggy, think. If you do want a drink where will you go? The spit and sawdust in Shea's maybe? The poky little snugs of the other places? Don't do anything rash.'

'God, Bunty, for a nun you've a great knowledge of all the bars in town,' said Peggy Pine admiringly.

They talked about the dance, and how wonderful Aidan had been. No other table had won so many spot prizes. And there had been an incident Jack told her where a girl fainted at another table and when they had loosened her clothes and tried to revive her, two bread rolls had fallen out of her bra. Jack laughed good-naturedly at this. Benny thought of how the girl must be feeling today, and how she would never be able to remember the dance with anything but shame.

'Oh, go on, it *is* funny,' he said. She knew she must see the light-hearted side. 'Yes, and full of crumbs, very scratchy I'd say.' She felt like Judas to this girl she didn't even know, but she was rewarded with the smile.

'Not anything you'd ever need, Benny,' he said, smiling at her across the table.

'Everyone's different.' She looked down, very, very embarrassed.

'You're different in a good way,' he said.

At least the veterinary student, whoever he was, had a nice floppy jumper. You couldn't see the outline of her breasts. She looked at her front, relieved. What could she say now to change the subject?

The door opened and another couple came in. Jack shrugged.

'I said only people from Napoli could come, and then only if they stayed quiet.' He looked at them warningly.

They were a pair of middle-aged Dubliners. Cold and shivery.

'Probably civil servants having an affair,' Benny whispered.

'No, two school inspectors planning to make everyone fail the Leaving Certificate next year,' he countered.

Most of the time it was easy to talk to him. He was so normal and relaxed, and there really was nothing in his manner that made her feel anxious. It was just herself. Benny realised that she had spent years sending herself up and playing the fool. When it came to the time to play the romantic lead, she didn't have a clue. And worse, she wasn't at all sure that was the part she was actually being cast to play. She wished she could read his signals, and understand what he was saying.

If only she could know then she could respond.

The ice cream was offered. The waiter explained cassata, a beautiful Neopolitan ice cream, he said, lovely bits of fruit and nuts chopped up in it, some candied peel, some macaroons. *Bellissima.*

Something told Benny that the right thing was to have it, not to talk of diets or calories or waistlines.

She saw Jack's face light up. He'd have some too.

The waiter saw them smile at each other.

'It's a very dark afternoon. I light a little candle to give you light to see each other when you talk,' he said.

Jack's open shirt over his navy sweater was a pale pink. It looked beautiful in the candlelight. She felt again that urge to stroke him. Not to kiss his lips or press against him, just to reach out and rub her hand softly from his cheek to his chin.

She had drunk only one glass of wine. It couldn't be some drink-crazed feeling.

Benny watched as if it was happening to someone else as she leaned across and stroked his face softly three times.

The third time he caught her hand and held it to his lips.

He kissed it with his head bent over it so that she couldn't see his eyes.

Then he gave it back to her.

There was no way he was making fun of her, or making a silly extravagant gesture like Aidan might.

Nobody would hold your hand like that and kiss it for such a long time unless they wanted to.

Would they? Would they?

Dessie Burns said that Mrs Healy could be a bit uppity in herself, and there had indeed been times when she had spoken to him more sharply than was called for. But to be fair, there had been a question of drink involved and perhaps there were those who would say that the woman had been within her rights. There was nothing more scrupulously and boringly fair than Dessie Burns when he was on the dry.

And when all was said and done that young Fonsie had been told he couldn't walk around this town as if he owned it. Who was he? The nephew of an Eyetie, with no sign of the Eyetic mother and the Dub father since the day he'd set foot in the place. That was a young lad without a background, without a history, in Knockglen. Let him take things more slowly. And as for Peggy's niece, she was a sore trial with the get-up of her. Maybe this would make her settle down.

Mario said that he would go and stand on the step of Healy's Hotel and spit in the door and then spit out the door, and then he'd come home and spit at Fonsie.

Fonsie said that none of this would advance them, they should instead go to Liverpool and buy a beautiful second-hand Wurlitzer juke box that he had seen advertised there.

Mario developed a most unexpected loyalty to Fonsie. Having denounced him to everyone in the town individually and generally, he now said that his sister's child was the salt of the earth, the mainstay of Mario's old age and the shining hope for Knockglen.

He also said with a lot of pounding on whatever surface he was near that he would never drink in Healy's again. Which, considering he never drunk there anyway, was a threat more powerful in the utterance than the deed.

*

Simon Westward came into Healy's that afternoon to enquire if they did dinners.

'Every day, Mr Westward.' Mrs Healy was delighted to see him in the place at last. 'Might I offer you a little something on the house to celebrate your first visit to us?'

'Very kind of you . . . er . . . Mrs . . . er . . .'

'Healy.' She looked rather pointedly at the hotel sign.

'Ah yes, how stupid of me. No, I won't stay for a drink now. You do do dinners. That's wonderful. I wasn't sure.'

'Every day from noon until two thirty.'

'Oh.'

'Do those hours not suit you?'

'No, I mean they're perfectly fine hours. I was thinking of dinner in the evening.'

Mrs Healy always prided herself on being ready when opportunity came to call.

'Up to now, Mr Westward, we have merely served high teas, but coming up to the Christmas season and thereafter we will indeed be serving dinner,' she said.

'Starting?'

'Starting next weekend, Mr Westward,' she said, looking him straight in the eye.


The waiter thought they must have a sambucca. It was a little Italian liqueur. This was with the compliments of the house. He would put a coffee bean in it and set it alight. It was a wonderful drink to have at the end of a lunch on a winter's day.

They sat there and wondered would the disgruntled

couple get one too, or was it only for people who looked happy?

'Will we see you next weekend?' the waiter asked eagerly. Benny could have killed him. She was doing so well. Why must the waiter bring up the subject of another date?

'Certainly another time, I hope,' Jack said.

They walked along the Quays, which had often looked cold and wet to Benny, but this afternoon there was a glorious sunset, and everything had a rosy light.

The second-hand booksellers had wooden stands of books on display outside.

'It's like Paris,' Benny said happily.

'Were you ever there?'

'No, of course I wasn't,' she laughed good-naturedly. 'That's me, just showing off. I've seen the pictures and I've been to the films.'

'And you're studying French of course, you'd be able to take it in your stride.'

'I doubt that. Great chats about Racine and Corneille in English would be more my line.'

'Nonsense. I'll be depending on you to be my guide when I'm playing in the Parc des Princes,' he said.

'I bet you will,' she said.

'No, that's me showing off. I'll never play for anyone if I keep eating like I did last night and today. I'm meant to be in training. You'd never know it.'

'You're lucky you didn't have practice today. You often do on Saturdays, don't you?'

'We did. I skipped it,' he said.

She looked at him suddenly. The old Benny would have made a joke. The new Benny didn't.

'I'm glad you did. It was a lovely lunch.'

She had her overnight bag in a shop near the bus stop. The woman handed it over the counter to her and together they walked towards the bus.

'What will you do tonight?' he asked her.

'Go to Mario's café and tell people about the dance. What about you?'

'No idea. Hope there are some invitations when I get home.' He laughed lazily, the kind of man who didn't have to plan his own life.

He passed her zippered bag on to the bus. Benny willed Mikey not to make any smart-aleck remarks.

'There you are, Benny. I knew we didn't have you yesterday. The weight in the bus was lighter altogether,' he said.

Jack hadn't heard, or if he had heard he hadn't understood Mikey's mumblings. That's what she told herself as she sat and looked out at the darkening city and the beginnings of the countryside.

She had danced close to Jack Foley, who had then invited her out to lunch. She had said nothing too stupid. He had said he'd see her in the Annexe on Monday. He had kissed her hand. He had said she was lovely.

She was absolutely exhausted. She felt as if she had been carrying a heavy weight for miles and miles in some kind of contest. But whatever contest it was, and whatever the rules, it looked as if she had won.

## 12

Heather wanted to know all about the dance and mainly what they had for pudding. She was stunned that Eve couldn't remember. She found it beyond comprehension that there could be too much else happening to remember pudding.

She broke the news that Simon said he was going to join them on their outing.

'I didn't know anything about this,' Eve said, annoyed.

'I didn't tell you in case you wouldn't come.' Heather was so honest that it was hard to attack her.

'Well, if you have him . . .'

'I want you,' Heather said simply.

Simon arrived in the car.

'Think of me as the chauffeur,' he said. 'You ladies are in charge.'

Almost immediately he gave them his own plan for the afternoon. A drive through County Wicklow and afternoon tea in a rather nice hotel he knew.

Eve and Heather had been planning to take the train to

Bray, go on the bumpers and have ice creams with hot butterscotch sauce. Eve was pleased that Simon's outing sounded so dull and tame compared with her own. She knew which Heather would have preferred.

But Heather was a dutiful sister, and she saw far too little of Simon already. She gave a mild show of enthusiasm. Eve after a deliberate pause did the same.

Simon looked from one to the other. He knew that this was second best. He was very cheery and answered all Heather's questions about her pony, about Clara's puppies, about Woffles the rabbit.

He explained that Mrs Walsh was still as silent and as majestic on her bicycle as ever. That Bee Moore was upset over some young man she had wanted and he had turned his attentions to Another. Eve had to put her hand over her face when Heather's questioning revealed the man to be Mossy Rooney and Another to be Patsy.

'How's Grandfather?' Heather asked.

'The same. Come on, we're boring Eve.'

'But he's Eve's grandfather too.'

'Absolutely.'

The subject was closed. Eve knew he wanted something. She had no idea what it was.

At tea time he brought it up.

'That was a remarkably beautiful girl, your friend.'

'Which friend?'

'In the shop, at the dance. The blonde girl.'

'Oh yes?'

'I was wondering who she is?'

'Were you?'

'Yes, I was.' He was short now.

For ages afterwards Eve hugged herself with delight and congratulations that she had managed not to answer such a direct question with any kind of response that would please him. And yet she had remained perfectly polite. For the girl who used to speak so unguardedly, whose temper was a legend in St Mary's, it was a triumph.

'Who is she? Oh, she's a student at UCD, doing First Arts, like about six hundred of us.'

Her smile had told Simon Westward that this was all he was going to get.

The veterinary student was a nice boy called Kevin Hickey. He was very polite and he thanked Mrs Hegarty for having taken his new green sweater to sew a tape on the back of it in case he wanted to hang it up with a loop. He had thought you should fold them, or put them on a clothes hanger, but still, it was very nice of her. He might wear it tonight. It was a great colour. When he picked it up he thought there was a faint smell of perfume, but he must have imagined it. Or else it was Mrs Hegarty's perfume. Kevin Hickey's mother was dead. It was nice to live in a house where there was a kind woman looking after him. He had asked his father to send her a turkey for Christmas. It would come by train, wrapped in straw and tied well with string.

He smelled his green jumper again. There was definitely

some cosmetic. Maybe if he hung it up in the fresh air by the window it would go away.

He heard the gate opening and drew back. He wouldn't like Mrs Hegarty to see him airing the jumper. But it wasn't Mrs Hegarty back from her shopping. It was a dark-haired man he hadn't seen before.

The doorbell rang and rang, so Kevin ran down to answer it. Mrs Hegarty was out, he said. The man wanted to wait. He looked respectable. Kevin was at a loss.

'It really is all right.' The man smiled at him. 'I'm an old friend.'

'And what's your name?'

'It's Hegarty also, as it happens.'

As Kevin went back upstairs he turned and saw the man who was sitting in the hall pick up the picture of Mrs Hegarty's son who had died. Possibly he was a relation.

Sheila noticed that Jack ran off immediately after his law lectures these days. No hanging around and chatting. No little jokes, just off like an arrow. Once or twice she asked him why he needed to run so fast.

'Training.' He had smiled at her with that boyish kind of laugh which meant he knew he would be forgiven anything.

Sheila decided that he must be seeing that Rosemary Ryan in First Arts.

She enquired from Carmel if that was true. It was easy to talk to Carmel because she wasn't really playing in the same game, she was so preoccupied with Sean that other people were only a vague background to her.

'Rosemary and Jack? I don't think so,' Carmel said after a lot of thought. 'No, I haven't seen them together at all. I've seen Jack in the Annexe a couple of mornings, but only talking to Benny Hogan.'

'Ah, well, that's all right, so,' said Sheila with some relief.

Benny and Patsy were friends again. It had taken the promised stockings plus a tin of French Moss talcum powder and an explanation that her nerves were over-wrought because she was frightened of going to the dance. Once Patsy had come round she was as usual a strong champion of the daughter of the house.

'What did you have to be frightened of? Aren't you a fine big girl who shows all the signs of being well fed and well looked after all her life?'

That was one of the things that Benny feared was only too obvious. But it was hard to explain to small, stooped Patsy who had been brought up without enough to eat in an orphanage.

'How's your romance?' she asked instead.

'He's not much with the words,' Patsy complained.

'But the words he does say? Are they nice?'

'It's very hard to know with men what they mean,' Patsy said sagely. 'You'd need someone standing at your shoulder saying this means this, and this means the other.'

Benny agreed fervently. When Jack Foley said he had

missed her at a party did he mean that he had looked around and thought it would be lovely if only Benny had been there? Had he thought it all evening, or only once? And if he missed her that much why had he gone to it? At the party in Jack's house Aengus had asked Benny if she was one of the ones who was always phoning looking for Jack. She had decided that she would never be one of those. It had worked so well the way things were. Or had it? Patsy was right. With men it was impossible to know what they meant. Nan used to say they never meant anything, but that was too depressing to contemplate.

Mrs Healy had been disappointed not to see Sean Walsh arriving full of support for her predicament. She knew his distaste for Fonsie and Clodagh and the kind of lifestyle they represented. But then Sean was not a customer in Healy's Hotel. It had something to do with not presuming, she imagined. Not putting himself forward, styling himself as Mr Hogan's equal when he was in fact a hired hand.

It was nice to see that kind of respect but sometimes Sean carried it too far. Like polishing the brasses, like living in a cramped room over the shop. He seemed to be biding his time and maybe he might bide it too long.

'You should invite young Sean Walsh in for a drink with you some time,' she suggested to Eddie Hogan.

Eddie's honest face told her what she already knew. 'I've asked him a dozen times, but he won't come in with me. I don't think he's a drinking man. Weren't we blessed the day he arrived in Knockglen?'

Emily Mahon marvelled at the way her daughter kept her clothes and her room. Every garment was sponged and hung up when it was taken off. Her coats and jackets always looked as if they had come straight from the dry cleaners.

The shoes had newspapers stuffed in the toes and stood on a small rack by the window. She polished her belts and handbags until they gleamed. On the wash-hand basin in her room were samples of soaps that Emily had been able to get her through the hotel. There was a book on how to apply make-up. Nan Mahon didn't rely on weekly magazines or Sunday newspapers to teach her style. She did the thing thoroughly.

Emily smiled affectionately as she saw the books on etiquette that Nan studied as well as her university texts. Nan had once told her mother that anyone could talk to anyone if they knew the rules. It was a matter of learning them.

The book was open at a section telling you how introductions are made.

'Marquesses, Earls, Viscounts, Barons and their wives are introduced as Lord or Lady X, Honourables as plain Mr.' Imagine if Nan was in a world where such things would be of use to her. But then it wasn't all that far beyond the possible. Look at the way she had looked at that dance. People who weren't even part of the student crowd were admiring her. She might very well end up in twinset and pearls on the steps of a big house, with dogs beside her and servants to do her work.

It had always been Emily Mahon's dream for her daughter. The only problem was, what part would she play in it? And it didn't bear thinking about how little a part Nan's father might be expected to take in any such lifestyle.

If Nan were to get there it was easy to see that she would no longer be any part of Maple Gardens.

Rosemary Ryan wore far too much make-up for the daytime. Benny could see that quite clearly now. There was a ridge at the side of her jaw where it stopped.

She was also brighter than people gave her credit for. When she was with a crowd she always simpered and played the dumb blonde, but in tutorials she was sharp as a razor.

'What are you going to do when this is over?' she asked Benny.

'Go to the Annexe.' Benny was meeting Jack. She hoped Rosemary wouldn't come too. 'I have to meet a whole lot of different people,' she said hastily, to discourage her.

'No, I meant this. All of this.' Rosemary waved a vague hand around the university.

'Do a postgrad diploma and be a librarian, I think,' Benny said. 'What about you?'

'I think I'll be an air hostess,' Rosemary said.

'You don't need a degree for that.'

'No, but it helps.' Rosemary had it worked out. 'It's a great way to get a husband.'

Benny didn't know whether she meant doing a degree

374

was a good way or being an air hostess. She didn't like to ask. It was such a strange coincidence that Rosemary should say that, because only the day before Carmel had asked Nan would she think of joining Aer Lingus. She had the looks and the style. And she'd meet lots of men.

'Only businessmen,' Nan had said, as if that settled it.

Carmel's eyes had narrowed. Her Sean was doing a B.Comm. and was aiming hard to be a businessman.

'Carmel says Nan doesn't think it's a good job.' Rosemary was probing. 'Do you think Nan's going out with Jack Foley?'

'What makes you think that?'

'I don't know. He hasn't been sighted much. I wondered was he holed up with someone mysterious?'

'*I* see him from time to time,' Benny said.

'Oh, that's all right then.' Rosemary was pleased. 'He's around. He hasn't been snatched away from under our noses. What a relief!'

Kit Hegarty let herself in and found her husband Joseph sitting in the kitchen.

She put her shopping on the floor and steadied herself with a hand on the kitchen chair.

'Who let you in?' she asked.

'A boy with freckles and a Kerry accent. Don't say anything to him. He interrogated me and asked me to sit in the hall.'

'Which you didn't.'

'I was cold.'

'Did you tell him who you were?'

'Just that my name happened to be Hegarty. Sit down, Kit. I'll make you a cup of tea.'

'You'll make me nothing in my kitchen,' she said.

But she did sit down and looked at him across the table. He was fifteen years older than he was the day he had taken the mail boat out of their lives.

How long had she cried herself to sleep at night wanting him to return? How often had she played the scene where he would come back and she would forgive him? But always in that version Francis would be young and would run towards them both, arms outstretched, crying out that he had a daddy and a real home again.

He was still handsome. His hair had only little bits of grey, but he looked shabbier than she remembered, as if he were down on his luck. His shoes weren't well polished. They needed to be taken to a cobbler's. His cuffs were not frayed exactly, but thin.

'Did you hear about Francis?' she said.

'Yes.'

The silence hung long between them.

'I came to tell you how sorry I was,' he said.

'Not sorry enough to see him ever, to care to be involved in his life when he had a life.'

She looked at him without hate, the man who had abandoned them. She had been told that he had gone to live with a barmaid. At the time somehow that had made it worse, more humiliating that the woman was a barmaid. It was such an obvious kind of thing to do. Now she wondered why the woman's job had been remotely important.

She thought of all the questions she had parried and eventually answered while her son grew up asking about his father, and wondering why he didn't have what everyone else at the Christian Brothers school had in their homes.

She thought of the day Francis had got his Leaving Certificate and run home with the results, and how she had an urge to find her long-lost husband that day – only a few months ago – and tell him that the child they had produced together would go to university.

In those long nights when she had not been able to find any sleep and thoughts had run scampering around in her head, she remembered with relief that she hadn't raised the hopes of this philandering husband and led him to believe that he had fathered a university student.

She thought of all this as she looked at him sitting in her kitchen.

'I'll make you tea,' she said.

'Whatever you think.'

'Did she throw you out?' Kit asked. She asked because he hadn't the look of a man who was cared for by a woman, not even a woman who had been brassy and taken him, even though she must have known he had a wife and child in Ireland.

'Oh, that all ended a long time ago. Years and years ago.'

It had ended. But he had not come back. Once gone he

was truly gone. Somehow that was sadder than the other. For years she had seen him in some kind of domesticity with this woman. But in fact he might have been living alone, or in digs or bedsitters.

That was worse than leaving her for a grand passion, however ill advised. She looked at him with a look of great sadness.

'I was wondering . . .' he said.

She looked at him, kettle in one hand and teapot in the other.

He was going to ask, could he come back?

Nan wanted to know if Eve had taken Heather out at the weekend. She often enquired about Heather, Eve noticed, rarely about the digs and Kit or the convent and Mother Francis.

She said they went to Wicklow and it had been wet and misty, and they went to a hotel where tea and sandwiches cost twice what real food like ice cream and butterscotch sauce would cost.

'You must have gone in a car to a place like that,' Nan said.

'Yes.' Eve looked at her.

'Did Aidan drive you?'

'Lord, I couldn't let Aidan near her. He's quite frightening enough for our age. He'd give a child nightmares.'

Nan left the subject of Aidan Lynch.

'So who did?'

Eve knew it was ridiculous not to tell her. She'd get to

know some day. It was like being an eight-year-old, having secrets at school, anyway it was making too much of it all.

'Her brother Simon drove us,' she said.

'The one we saw in my mother's shop at the dance, and you didn't introduce me.'

'The very one.'

Nan pealed with laughter. 'You're marvellous, Eve,' she said. 'I'm so glad I'm your friend. I'd really hate to be your enemy.'

Most of the cottages on the road up by the quarry behind the convent were fairly dilapidated. It was never a place that anyone would really seek out to live. It had been different when the quarry was operating, in those days there had been plenty of people wanting to live there. Now there were very few lights in windows. Mossy Rooncy lived in a small house there with his mother. There had been rumours that Mossy had been seen with building materials and a consequent speculation that he might intend building an extra room at the back. Could this mean that he had plans to marry?

Mossy was not a man to do things in a hurry. People said that Patsy shouldn't count her chickens too soon.

Sean Walsh sometimes went for a walk up that way on a Sunday. Mother Francis would nod to him gravely and he always returned the greeting very formally.

If he ever wondered what the nun was doing pushing her way past the dark green leaves of the wild fuchsia and rolling up her sleeves to polish and clean he never gave any sign of his curiosity. Neither did she pause to think why he walked there. He was a lonely young man, not very attractive to speak to. She knew that Eve had always disliked him. But that might just have been a childish thing, a loyalty to Benny Hogan, who had some kind of antipathy towards her father's assistant.

She was surprised when he addressed her. With a long preamble of apology he asked if she knew who owned the cottages and whether they might perhaps belong to the convent. Mother Francis explained that they had once belonged to the Westlands estate, and had devolved somehow to various quarry workers and others. Politely with her head on one side in her enquiring manner she wondered why he wanted to know.

Equally courteously Sean told her that it had been an idle enquiry but the nature of small towns being what it was, perhaps an enquiry that might remain confidential between the two of them.

Mother Francis sighed. She supposed the poor fellow who had scant hope of making much of a living in Hogan's might be looking to the day when he could buy a house for himself and start a family, and that he was realistic enough to start looking up on this wild craggy road where nobody would really live by choice.

Benny hated going into the Coffee Inn. The tables were always so small. She was afraid that her skirt or her shoulder bag would swoop someone's frothy coffee off on to the floor.

Jack's face lit up when he saw her. He had been holding a seat with some difficulty.

'These awful country thicks wanted to take your stool,' he hissed at her.

'Less running down the country people,' Benny said. She glanced up and saw with a shock that the three students who had lost the battle for the seat were Kit Hegarty's students, the boys who lived where Eve worked. And one of them, a big fellow with freckles, was wearing his lovely emerald-green sweater.

Aidan Lynch asked Eve to come home and meet his parents.

'I've met them,' Eve said ungraciously, handing him another dinner plate to dry.

'Well, you could meet them again.'

Eve didn't want to meet them again; it was rushing things. It was saying things that weren't ready to be said like that Eve was Aidan's girlfriend, which she wasn't.

'How is this relationship going to progress any further?' Aidan asked the ceiling. 'She won't get to know my family. She won't let me near her body. She won't go on a date with me unless I come out to Dunlaoghaire and do the washing-up after all the culchies first.' He sounded very sorry for himself.

Eve's mind was on other things. Aidan could amuse himself for hours when he was in one of his rhetorical moods. She smiled at him absently.

Kit was out. For the very first time since Eve had been in the house; what was more, there was no message.

Kevin, the nice freckled vet student whose jumper had been purloined for Benny's date, had said that Mrs Hegarty had gone out with a man.

'Everyone goes out with men,' Aidan had interrupted. 'It's the law of nature. Female canaries go out with male canaries. Sheep go out with rams. Women tortoises go out with men tortoises. Only Eve seems to have reservations.'

Eve took no notice. She was also thinking about Benny. Almost every day for a week now Benny had met Jack Foley, either in the Annexe or the Coffee Inn or a bar. She said he was very easy to talk to. She hadn't put a foot wrong yet. Benny's face looked as if someone had turned on a light inside when she talked about Jack Foley.

'And of course this Eve that I have the misfortune to be besotted with . . . she won't even stay in Dublin for the Christmas parties. She's leaving me on my own for other women to have their way with, and do sinful things with my body.'

'I have to go to Knockglen, you idiot,' she said.

'Where there will be no parties, where people will go out and watch the grass grow and see the rain fall and moo-cows will walk down the main street swishing their foul tails.'

'You've got it wrong,' Eve cried. 'We'll be having a *great* time in Knockglen, down in Mario's every evening, and of course there'll be parties there.'

'Name me one,' Aidan countered.

'Well, I'll be having one for a start,' Eve said, stung.

382

Then she stood motionless with a dinner plate in her hands.

Oh God, she thought. Now I have to.

Nan rang the *Irish Times,* and asked for the sports department. When she was put through she asked them to tell her what race meetings would be held before Christmas.

Not many, she was told. Things slackened off coming up to the festival season. There'd be a meeting every Saturday, of course, Navan, Punchestown, run-of-the-mill things. But on St Stephen's Day it would all get going again. The day after Christmas there'd be Leopardstown and Limerick. She could take her pick of those. Nan asked them what did people who usually went racing do when the season slackened off. In a newspaper office people are accustomed to being asked odd questions on the phone. They gave it some consideration. It depended on what kind of people. Some might be saving their pennies, some might be out hunting. It depended.

Nan thanked them in the pleasant unaffected voice that had never tried to imitate the tones of another class she wanted to join. An elocution teacher at school had once told them that there was nothing more pathetic than people with perfectly good Irish accents trying to say 'Fratefully naice'. Nothing would mark you out as a social climber as much as adopting that kind of accent.

They sat in a café in Dunlaoghaire, Mr and Mrs Hegarty. Around them other people were doing ordinary things, like having a coffee before going to an evening class in typing, or waiting for the pictures to start.

Ordinary people with ordinary lives and nothing bigger to discuss than whether the electric fire would eat up electricity or if they could have two chickens instead of a turkey for Christmas Day.

Joseph Hegarty fiddled with his spoon. She noticed that he didn't take sugar in his coffee now. Perhaps the woman had put him off that. Perhaps his travels had taken him to places where there were no sugar bowls on the table. He had left one insurance company and gone to another. He had moved from that to working with a broker, to having a book himself, to working with another agent. Insurance wasn't the same, he told her.

She looked at him with eyes that were not hard, or cold. She saw him objectively. He was kindly and soft-spoken, as he had always been. In those first agonised months after he had left that was what she had missed above all.

'You wouldn't know anyone here anymore,' she said haltingly.

'I'd get to know them again.'

'It'd be harder to find insurance work here than there. Things are very tight in Ireland.'

'I wouldn't go back on that. I thought maybe I could help you . . . build up the business.'

She thought about it, sitting very still and with her eyes down so that she wouldn't meet the hope in his. She thought of the way he would preside over the table, make the place seem like it was run by a family. She could almost see him giving second helpings, making boys like Kevin Hickey laugh, being interested in their studies and their social lives.

But why had he not done that for his own son? For Francis Hegarty who might still be alive this day if he had had a firm father who would brook no nonsense about a motorbike.

'No, Joseph,' she said, without looking up. 'It wouldn't work.'

He sat there very silent. He thought about his son, the son who had written to him all these years. The son who had come to see him during the summer, on a weekend from canning peas. Frank, the boy who had drunk three pints with his father and told him all about the home in Dunlaoghaire and how maybe his mother's heart was softening. But he had never told his mother about the visit or the letters. Joseph Hegarty would keep faith with the dead boy. Frank must have had reasons, his father would not betray him now or change his mother's memory of him.

'Very well, Kit,' he said. 'It's your decision. I just thought I'd ask.'

The Westwards were in the telephone book. The phone was answered by an elderly woman.

'It's a personal call for Mr Simon Westward from Sir Victor Cavendish.' Nan spoke in the impersonal voice of a secretary. She had taken the name from *Social and Personal*.

'I'm sorry, Mr Westward isn't here.'

'Where can Sir Victor find him, please?'

Mrs Walsh responded immediately to the confident tone that expected an answer.

'He's going to have lunch in the Hibernian, I believe,' she said. 'Perhaps Sir Victor could telephone him there.'

'Thank you so much,' Nan said, and hung up.


'I want to give you your Christmas present today,' Nan said to Benny in the main hall.

'Lord, Nan, I didn't bring anything in for you.' Benny looked stricken.

'No, mine is a treat. I'm taking you to lunch.'

She would listen to no refusals. Everyone deserved to have lunch in the Hibernian at least once in their life. Nan and Benny were no exceptions. Benny wondered why Eve wasn't being included.


They met Bill Dunne and Johnny O'Brien as they were crossing St Stephen's Green.

The boys suggested a Christmas drink. When that was turned down, they came up with chicken croquette and chips in Bewley's with sticky almond buns to follow. Laughing, Benny said they were going to the Hibernian.

'You must have a pair of sugar daddies then,' Bill Dunne said crossly to hide his disappointment.

Benny wanted to tell them it was Nan's treat, but she didn't like to. Perhaps Nan mightn't want to admit that it was just the two of them. She looked hopefully at her friend for some signal. But Nan's face gave no hints of anything. She looked so beautiful Benny thought, again with a pang. It must be amazing to wake up in the morning and know your features were going to look like that all day, and that everyone who saw your face would like it.

Benny wished that Bill Dunne didn't look so put out. On an ordinary day it would have been lovely to have gone to Bewley's with him. Jack was up at the rugby club all afternoon. She would love to have been with Bill and Johnny in many ways. They were Jack's people. They were part of his life. She felt disloyal to Nan and her generous present. And wasn't it marvellous to go inside the Hibernian for something better than walking through its coffee lounge to the ladies' cloakroom at the back which was all she had ever done before.

Eve had no lectures in the afternoon. She couldn't find either Benny or Nan. Aidan Lynch had invited her to join his parents, who liked to combine an hour of Christmas shopping and four hours of lunch several times in the weeks leading up to the festive season. She had declined, saying it sounded like a minefield.

'When we're married we'll have to see them, you know, invite them over for roast lamb and mint sauce,' he had said.

'We'll face that when we come to it in about twenty years' time,' Eve had said to him grimly.

You couldn't put Aidan Lynch off. He was much too cheerful, and totally confident that she loved him. Which of course she didn't. Eve didn't love anybody, as she had tried to explain. Just very strong affections for Mother Francis and Benny and Kit. Nobody had ever shown her why love was such a great thing, she told him. Look what it had done for her mother and father. Look how boring it made Sean and Carmel. Look at the way it had wrecked Kit Hegarty's life.

Thinking about Kit made her think that that was where she would go, home to Dunlaoghaire. Kit had looked very strange in the last couple of days. Eve hoped that she wasn't sick, or that the man who had come back hadn't been who Eve feared it had.

She took the train out to Dunlaoghaire and let herself in. Kit was sitting in the kitchen with her head in her hands. Nothing had been touched since Eve had left that morning. Eve hung up her coat.

'Sister Imelda had a great saying. She used to believe that there was no problem on the face of the earth that couldn't be tackled better with a plate of potato cakes. And I must say I agree with her.'

As she spoke she took the cold mashed potato from the bowl, opened a bag of flour and dropped a lump of butter in the frying pan.

Kit still didn't look up.

'Not that it solved everything, mind you. Like I remember when nobody would tell me why my mother and father were buried in different churchyards. We had potato cakes then, Mother Francis and I. It didn't really explain it, or make me feel better about it. But it made us feel great eating them.'

Kit raised her head. The casual voice and the ritual actions of cooking had soothed her. Eve never paused in her movements as Kit Hegarty told her the story of the husband who had left and come back and been sent away again.

Nan had spotted Simon Westward the moment that she and Benny were led into the dining room. The waiter had been intending to put two such young-looking female students away in a corner, but Nan asked could they have a more central table. She spoke like someone who had been there regularly. There wasn't any reason why she shouldn't get a better table.

They studied the menu and Nan asked about the dishes they couldn't understand.

'Let's have something we never had before,' she suggested.

Benny had been heading for lamb because it looked nice and safe. But it was Nan's treat.

'Like what?' she asked fearfully.

'Brains,' Nan said. 'I never had those.'

'Wouldn't it be a bit of a waste? Suppose they were awful?'

'They wouldn't be awful in a place like this. Why don't you have sweetbreads or guinea fowl or snipe.'

'Snipe? What's that?'

'It's with game. It must be a bird.'

'It can't be. I never heard of it. It's a belt, taking a snipe at someone.'

Nan laughed. 'That's taking a swipe, you idiot.'

Simon Westward looked up just then. Nan could see him from the corner of her eye. She had been aware that he was at a table with a couple, a very tweedy, older man and a younger, horsey-looking woman.

Nan knew that she had been seen. She settled back into her seat. All she had to do now was wait.

Benny struggled with the things they didn't know on the menu.

'I could have scampi, I don't know that.'

'You know what it is. It's a big prawn in batter.'

'Yes, but I've never tasted it, so it would be new to me.'

At least she had got out of brains and sweetbreads and other strange-sounding things.

'Miss Hogan. Don't you dine in the best places?' Simon Westward was standing beside her.

'I hardly ever go anywhere posh, but any time I do you're there.' She smiled at him warmly.

He didn't even have to look enquiringly across the table before Benny introduced him. Very simply, very correctly.

In Nan's books of etiquette she would have broken no rule, not that she had ever read them.

'Nan, this is Simon Westward. Simon, this is my friend Nan Mahon.'

'Hallo, Nan,' said Simon, reaching for her hand.

'Hallo, Simon,' said Nan, with a smile.


'You were out with a sugar daddy. I heard,' Jack accused her laughingly next day.

'No, indeed I wasn't. Nan took me to the Hibernian for lunch, as a treat. A Christmas present.'

'Why did she do that?'

'I told you. A Christmas present.'

Jack shook his head. It didn't add up.

Benny bit her lip. She wished now that she hadn't gone. In fact she wished at the time that she hadn't gone. She had ordered potatoes with the scampi and hadn't known that you were meant to have rice until she saw surprise on the waiter's face. She had asked for a little of everything from the cheeseboard instead of just picking two cheeses, which is what other people did. She had asked for nice frothy cappuccino coffee and was told gravely that it wasn't served in the dining room.

And there was something about Simon and Nan that made her uneasy too. It was as if they were playing some game, a game that only they understood. Everyone else was outside.

And now here was Jack implying that Nan must have had some kind of ulterior motive to take her to lunch.

'What's wrong?' He saw her looking distressed.

'Nothing.' She put on her bright smile.

There was something very vulnerable about it. Jack could see Benny as what she must have been like when she was about four or five pretending that everything was all right even when it wasn't.

He put his arm around her shoulder as they walked across at the traffic lights between Stephen's Green and Grafton Street.

All the shops were done up with Christmas decorations. There were lights strung across the street. A group of carol singers shivering in the cold were starting 'Away in a Manger'. The collection boxes were rattling. Her face looked very innocent. He felt a need to protect her from all sorts of things. From Bill Dunne who said that a big girl like that with an enormous chest would turn out to be a great court. From drunks walking round with bottles in their hand, wild-eyed and with wild hair. He wanted to keep her on the footpath so that the busy Christmas traffic wouldn't touch her, and from the small children with dirty faces who would wheedle the last pennies from someone gentle like Benny Hogan. He didn't want her to go back to Knockglen on the bus this afternoon, and to be there for nearly three weeks of the holidays.

'Benny?' he said.

She turned her face to him to know what he wanted. He held her face in both his hands and kissed her very softly on the lips. Then he drew away and looked to see the surprise in her eyes.

He put his arms around her then, standing right at the top of the busiest street in Dublin, and held her to him with his arms. He felt her arms go round him and they clung to each other as if it were the most natural thing in the world.

## 13

Fonsie had a new black velvet jacket for Christmas. Clodagh had made him a set of lilac-coloured button covers, and a huge flouncy handkerchief to put in his breast pocket.

He startled most of Knockglen by moving very deliberately up the church to receive Communion in his outfit.

'He has added blasphemy to the list of his other crimes,' Mrs Healy hissed at the Hogans, who were sitting near her.

'He must be in a State of Grace, otherwise he wouldn't go,' Annabel said. She thought Mrs Healy was making too much of this vendetta. She envied Peggy and Mario for having such lively young blood in their businesses. If only Benny and Sean had made a go of it, then perhaps the dead look of failure might not hang around the door of Hogan's, while the other two establishments went from strength to strength. She looked at Eddie beside her. She wondered what he was praying about. He always seemed genuinely devout, as if he were talking to God when they were in the church, unlike herself. Annabel found that being at Mass seemed to concentrate her anxieties about daily life rather than raise her nearer to God. Benny wasn't praying. That was for sure. Nobody who was praying had such a strange faraway look on their face.

Annabel Hogan was fairly sure that her daughter was in love.

Clodagh Pine looked at her friend Fonsie with pleasure. He really did look smart. And he *was* a smart fellow. She had never thought she would meet anyone remotely like Fonsie when she was banished to Knockglen in a foolish effort to quieten her by sending her to a backwater. And her aunt had been very good to her also, much better than Clodagh had dared to hope. She had been generous with her praise for the developments, while at the same time resisting each new one that came along. Once she had accepted an idea, Peggy Pine would get the bit between her teeth and run with it. Like the smart home knits which were now attracting people to come from Dublin.

Like the idea of designer labels with the word Pine on them.

All had added greatly to the shop's turnover. And the place looked smart and lively. It had been a success for both of them.

Clodagh decided that she would not outrage the sensitivites of Knockglen, so for Christmas Day Mass she wore a short herringbone tweed coat with a black leather belt. She wore high black boots and a black leather beret pulled down the side of her head. It would have looked really good with big chunky flashy earrings. But for Christmas Mass Clodagh showed restraint. She was unaware that her aunt knelt with her head in her hands and asked the Mother of God why a girl so good and helpful as Clodagh should dress like a prostitute.

Sean Walsh knelt stiffly. He had the look of someone who was poised waiting for a blow. He looked rigidly in front of him, lest he be caught gazing around.

Sean had been invited to Christmas lunch at the Hogans' this year. Other Christmases he had gone home to his people, a world of which he spoke not at all, in a town which no one could remember because Sean Walsh had never referred to it. But this year he had persuaded Mr Hogan to stay open late on Christmas Eve and not close at lunch time, as they had done in other years.

Most people had a few presents still to buy on Christmas Eve, Sean reasoned. And if Hogan's wasn't open they could always buy men's handkerchiefs in Peggy Pine's, or boxes of cheroots in Birdie Mac's, or masculine-smelling soaps in Kennedy's. All those places would now be open to catch the trade. Knockglen was changing fast.

'But you can't do that,' Mr Hogan had pleaded. 'You'll miss your bus home.'

'There's not going to be much of a Christmas there anyway, Mr Hogan,' Sean had said apologetically, knowing that now an invitation would have to be forthcoming.

Sean was looking forward to sitting at Christmas lunch with the Hogans as if he were a person of status. He had bought a dried flower arrangement for Mrs Hogan, something that could stand on her table all year, he would say. And a talcum powder called Talc de Coty for Benny. It was 4/11d, a medium-range talcum powder that would please her, he thought, without embarrassing her by its grandness.

She had been pleasant this morning, smiled at him very affably and said she was glad he was coming to lunch and that they'd see him about one o'clock in Lisbeg.

He had been pleased to be told what time they expected him. He was wondering if he should have gone back with them after Mass. It was as well to have it pointed out to him.

Benny had realised that since Sean was inevitable, she might as well be polite about it. Patsy told her that her mother and father had been worried in case she'd make a fuss.

'It's only lunch. It's not a lifetime,' Benny had said philosophically.

'They'd be well pleased if it was a lifetime.'

'No, Patsy, you can't be serious. Not any more. Surely not any more. Once they may have thought about it.'

'I don't know. You can't lay down laws for what people think and hope.'

But Patsy was wrong. Benny knew that her parents couldn't have any hopes that she should consider Sean

Walsh. Business was poor. Money was tight. She knew this. And she knew that they couldn't have embarked on the whole costly business of letting her have a university education unless they had hopes of better things for her. If they believed she would marry Sean Walsh and that he would run Hogan's, they would have tried to force her into doing a secretarial course and book-keeping. They would have put her into the shop. They would never have let her near a world that had all it had in it. The world that had given her Jack Foley.

The Mass in the convent was always a delight. Father Ross loved the pure clear voices of the younger nuns in the choir. There was never coughing or spluttering or fidgeting when he said Mass in the Chapel of St Mary's. The nuns chanted responses and rang the bells perfectly. He didn't have to deal with sleepy or recalcitrant altar servers. And there was nothing like the amazing and highly disrespectful fashion show to which the parish church in Knockglen had been treated this morning. Here everybody was in the religious life except of course young Eve Malone, who had grown up here.

His eyes rested on the small dark girl as he turned to give the final blessing '*Ite Missa Est*'.

He saw her bow her head as reverently as any of the Sisters when she said '*Deo Gratias*'.

He had been worried to hear that she was going to live in that house where her mother had died, out of her senses in childbirth, and where her poor father too had lost his life. She was too young a child to have a place on her own, with all the dangers that this might involve. But Mother Francis, who was an admirably sensible woman, was in favour of it.

'It's only up the garden, Father,' she had reassured him. 'In a way it's part of the convent. It's as if she never left us at all.'

He looked forward now to his breakfast in the parlour. Sister Imelda's crisply fried rashers, with triangles of potato cakes which would make a man forget everything in the world and follow its smell and its taste wherever it led.

Mrs Walsh cycled back to Westlands from Knockglen. Mr Simon and Miss Heather would go out to church at eleven thirty. The old gentleman hadn't gone to any service for a long time. It was sad to see him so feeble in his chair and yet at times he would remember very clearly. Usually things best forgotten. Sad incidents, accidents, disasters. Never happy times, no weddings, christenings or festivities.

Mrs Walsh never spoke of her life in the Big House. She could have had a wide audience for tales of the child sitting talking to Clara about her puppies, to Mr Woffles about his Christmas lettuce and to the pony about how she was going to become a harness maker and invent something softer than the bit for his poor tender mouth.

Mrs Walsh had warned Bee Moore that she didn't want to hear any stories coming from her reporting either.

People were always quick to criticise a family which was different to the village. And the Westwards were a different religion, a different class and also a different nationality. The Anglo-Irish might consider themselves Irish, Mrs Walsh said very often, to make her point more firmly to Bee Moore. But of course they were nothing of the sort. They were as English as the people who lived across the sea. Their only problem was that they didn't realise it.

Mr Simon, now, he had his eye on a lady from England, from Hampshire. He was going to invite her to stay. But not in Westlands. He was going to put her up at Healy's Hotel, which was his way of saying that he hadn't made his mind up about her enough to have her at the house.

Mrs Walsh cycled back to cook the breakfast and thought that Mr Simon was ill advised. Healy's Hotel was no place to put a rich woman from Hampshire. It was a place with shabby fittings and cramped rooms. The lady would not look favourably on Mr Simon and on Westlands, and on the whole place. She would go back to Hampshire with her thousands and thousands of pounds. And the object of the invitation surely had been for her to stay and marry into the family, bringing more English blood and, even more important, bringing the finances the place needed so desperately.

Mother Clare looked at Eve with a dislike she barely attempted to conceal.

'I'm pleased to see that you have recovered from all your

various illnesses, such as they may have been,' she said.

Eve smiled at her. 'Thank you, Mother Clare. You were always very kind to me. I am so sorry that I didn't repay it properly at the time.'

'Or at all,' sniffed Mother Clare.

'I suppose I repaid it in some form by getting myself out of your way.' Eve was bland and innocent. 'You didn't have to think about me any more and try to fit me into your world, just out of kindness to Mother Francis.'

The nun looked at her suspiciously, but could find no mockery or double meaning in the words.

'*You* seem to have got everything you wanted,' she said.

'Not everything, Mother.' Eve wondered whether to quote St Augustine and say that our hearts were restless until they rested in the Lord. She decided against it. That was going over the top.

'Not every single thing, but a lot certainly,' she said. 'Would you like me to show you my cottage? It's a bit of a walk through the briars and everything, but it's not too slippy.'

'Later, child. Another day, perhaps.'

'Yes. It's just I didn't know how long you were staying . . .' Again her face was innocent.

Last night, as on so many Christmas Eves, she had sat and talked with Mother Francis. This time even telling the nun a little about Aidan Lynch and the funny quirky relationship they had.

Mother Francis had said the worst thing about Mother Clare's visit was that it seemed to be open-ended. She couldn't ask the other nun when she was going to leave. Eve had promised to do it in her stead.

Mother Clare did not like to be asked her plans so publicly.

'Oh . . . I mean . . . well,' she stammered.

'What day *are* you going, Mother Clare, because I want to be sure I can show it to you. You brought me into your home, the least I can do is bring you into mine.'

She forced Mother Clare to give a date. Then by an amazing surprise it turned out that Peggy Pine was driving to Dublin that day. The departure was fixed.

Mother Francis flashed a glance of gratitude at Eve.

A glance of gratitude and love.

Patsy had had a watch from Mossy for Christmas. That meant only one thing. The next present would be a ring.

'Eve says she thinks he's building on to the back of the house,' Benny said.

'Ah, it's hard to know with Mossy,' Patsy said.

They set the table with crackers, and criss-cross paper decorations as they had done every year as long as Benny could remember.

Around the house they had paper lanterns. The Christmas tree in the window had had the same ornaments on it for years. This year Benny had bought some new ones in Henry Street and Moore Street in Dublin.

She felt a lump in her throat when her father and mother examined them with pleasure as if they were anything except the most vulgar red and silver tatty objects you could come across.

They were so touched at anything she did for them, and yet she was the one who should be thanking them. You didn't need to be Einstein to see that the business was not doing well. That it was a struggle for them to keep going and to give her what they did. And yet there was no way to tell them that she would one million times prefer to do what Eve was doing, to work her own way through college, staying in a house helping with the work, or minding children.

Anything at all, including being down on her hands and knees cleaning public lavatories. If it meant that she didn't have to come back to Knockglen every single night, if it meant that she would live in the same town as Jack Foley.

'Poor Sean. He won't be any trouble?' Benny's mother spoke in a question.

'And I couldn't let him work all day yesterday and not ask him for a bite to eat today, seeing that he missed his bus home?' Benny's father's remark was a question too.

'Will he ever get a place to live himself, you know, a house here?' Benny asked.

'Funny you should say that. There's talk that he's above on the road over the quarry looking at this place and that. Maybe that's what's on his mind.'

'He'll have his job cut out for him saving enough for a house with what he's paid above in the shop.' Eddie Hogan was regretful.

He didn't need to say, because they all knew it, that

there wasn't a question of Sean being underpaid. It was just that the takings were so poor there wasn't much to pay anyone at all out of it.

Everything happened at the same time. Sean Walsh knocked on the front door which nobody ever used, but he thought that on Christmas Day things would be different. Dessie Burns arrived at the back door as drunk as a lord saying that he only wanted a stable to sleep in, just a stable. If it was good enough for Our Saviour, it would be good enough for Dessie Burns, and perhaps a plate of dinner brought out to him wouldn't go amiss. Dr Johnson came roaring out of his avenue to borrow Eddie Hogan's car. 'Of all the bloody times that thoughtless bastard up in Westlands has to go and have a turn it has to be bloody Christmas Day just as I was putting my fork in the bloody turkey,' he roared and drove off in the Hogans' Morris Cowley.

Birdie Mac arrived agitated saying that Mr Flood, who had normally seen one nun in the tree above his house, now saw three and was out with a stick trying to attract their attention and get them to come in for a cup of tea. Birdie had been down to Peggy Pine to ask her advice and Peggy had been something akin to intoxicated and told her to tell Mr Flood to get up in the tree with them.

And Jack Foley rang from Dublin, braving the post office which hated connecting calls on Christmas Day unless they were emergencies.

'It *is* an emergency,' he had explained.

And when Benny came on the line he said that it was the

greatest emergency in his whole life. He wanted her to know how much he missed her.

Patsy went for a walk with Mossy, when everything had been cleared away. This year for the first time, Benny suggested that they should all take part in the washing-up. They opened front and back doors to let out the smells of food. Benny said it was hardly tactful to the hens to let them smell the turkey dinner, but perhaps hens had closed-off sections of their minds on this subject. Sean didn't know how to react to this kind of chat. He debated several attitudes and decided to look stern.

The big grandfather clock in the corner ticked loudly as first Eddie Hogan and then Annabel fell asleep in the warm firelight. Shep slept too, his big eyes closing slowly and unwillingly as if anxious not to leave Benny and Sean to talk on their own.

Benny knew that she could sleep too, or pretend to. Sean would regard this not as the rudeness it was, but as some kind of sign that he was a welcome intimate in their home. Anyway she was too excited to sleep.

Jack had phoned from his own house where he had said they were all playing games and had sneaked away to tell her that he loved her.

Benny was as wide awake as she ever had been. She longed for better company than Sean Walsh, and yet she felt sorry for him. Tonight he would go back to that small room two floors above the shop. Nobody had telephoned to say they missed him. She could afford to be generous.

'Have another chocolate, Sean.' She offered the box.

'Thank you.' He even managed to look awkward eating a simple thing like a sweet. It went slowly down his neck. There was a lot of swallowing and clearing his throat.

'You look very . . . um . . . nice today, Benny,' he said, after some thought. Too much thought for the remark that resulted.

'Thank you, Sean. I suppose everyone feels well on Christmas Day.'

'I haven't particularly, not up to now,' he confessed.

'Well, today's lunch was nice, wasn't it?'

He leaned across from his chair. 'Not just the lunch. *You* were nice, Benny. That gives me a lot of hope.'

She looked at him with a great wave of sympathy. It was something she never thought would happen. Within an hour two men were declaring themselves to her. In films the women were able to cope with this, and even play one off against the other.

But this was no film. This was poor, sad Sean Walsh seriously thinking that he might marry into the business. She must make sure that he realised this was not going to happen. There had to be words somewhere that would leave him with a little dignity and make him realise that things would not be improved by his asking again. Sean was of the old school that thought women said 'No' when they meant 'Yes', and all you had to do was ignore the refusals until they became an acceptance.

She tried to think how she would like to hear it herself. Suppose Jack were to tell her that he loved someone else, what would be the best way for her to find out? She would like him to be honest, and tell her directly, no apologies, or regrets. Just the facts. And then she would like him to go away and let her digest it all on her own.

Would it be the same for Sean Walsh?

She looked into the changing pictures and leaping flames of the fire as she spoke. There was a background of her parents' heavy breathing. The clock ticked, and Shep whimpered a little.

She told Sean Walsh her plans and her hopes. That she would live in Dublin, and she had great hopes that it would all work out.

Sean listened to the news impassively. The part about the person she loved caused him to smile. A crooked little smile.

'Would you not agree that this might be just what they call a crush?' he asked loftily.

Benny shook her head.

'But it's not based on anything, any shared hopes or plans, like a real relationship is.'

She looked at him astounded. Sean Walsh talking about a real relationship as if he would have the remotest idea what it was.

She was still humouring him. 'Well, of course you're right. It might not work out, but it's my hope it will.'

The smile was even more bitter. 'And does he, this lucky man, know anything about your infatuation. Is he aware of all this . . . hope?'

'Of course he is. He hopes too,' she said, surprised. Sean

obviously thought that she just fancied someone from afar like a film star.

'Ah well, we'll see,' he said, and he sat looking into the fire with his sad pale eyes.

Patsy had been up in Mossy's house for the evening wearing her new watch and going through a further inspection by Mossy's mother. Mossy's married sister and her husband had come in to give the encounter even further significance.

'I think they thought I was all right,' she told Benny, with some relief.

'Did you think *they* were all right?'

'It isn't up to me to be having opinions, you know that, Benny.'

Not for the first time Benny wanted to find the orphanage where Patsy had grown up with no hope and no confidence and strangle everyone in it. Patsy wanted to know what time Sean Walsh had left, because she saw him walking around up on the quarry path at all hours. He had looked distraught, she reported, as if he had something in his mind.

Benny wanted to know no more of this. She changed the topic. Were there lights on in Eve's cottage? she wanted to know.

'Yes, it looked lovely and cosy. She had a little Christmas crib in the window with a light in it. And there was a tree too, a small tree with lots of things hanging on it.'

Eve had told Benny about the crib, a gift from the

convent, and every single nun had made a decoration for the tree as well. Angels with pipe cleaners and coloured wool. Stars made out of foil wrapping paper, little pom-pom balls, little figures cut out of Christmas cards and given a stiff cardboard backing. Hours of work had gone into those presents.

The Community was alternatively proud and sad that Eve had moved to her own home. But they had grown used to her being in Dublin. In those first weeks they had missed her running through the convent, and sitting up in the kitchen talking to them.

And as Mother Francis said it was only at the other end of the garden.

Mother Francis never said that to Eve herself. She always stressed that the girl must come and go, using the ordinary path when she wished. It was her house and she must entertain whom she liked.

When Eve asked about having a party, Mother Francis said she could have half the county if she pleased. Eve admitted ruefully that she seemed to be having half of Dublin. Because of her boasting they all thought Knockglen was the place to be.

Mother Francis said that this was only the truth and wondered how Eve was going to cope. She wondered what Eve was going to do about food for half of Dublin.

'I've brought a lot of stuff. Clodagh and Benny are going to come in on St Stephen's Day and help'.

That's great. Don't forget Sister Imelda would always love to be asked to make pastry.'

'I don't think I could . . .'

'You know, I believe they eat sausage rolls all over the world, including Dublin. Sister Imelda would be honoured.'

Clodagh and Benny were up at the cottage early.

'A soup, that's what you want,' Clodagh said firmly.

'I don't have a big pot.'

'I bet the convent does.'

'Why did I take this on, Clodagh?'

'As a housewarming. To warm your house.' Clodagh was busy counting plates, making lists and deciding where they would put coats. Benny and Eve watched her with admiration.

'That one could rule the world if she was given a chance,' Eve said.

'I'd certainly make a better stab at it than the eejits who are meant to be in charge,' said Clodagh cheerfully.

The Hogans were surprised to see Sean Walsh come in through the gate of Lisbeg on St Stephen's Day.

'We didn't ask him again, today?' Annabel asked, alarmed.

'I didn't, certainly. Benny may have.' Eddie sounded doubtful.

But nobody had invited Sean Walsh. He had come to have a discussion with Mr Hogan about business. He had taken a long walk last night up round the quarry and he had sorted everything out in his head. Sean Walsh had a proposition to put to Mr Hogan, that he should be taken on as a partner in the firm.

He realised that there wasn't sufficient cash flow to make him a more attractive salary offer. The only solution would be to invite him to be a full partner in the business.

Mario looked on as Fonsie backed the station wagon up to the door and loaded the record player into the back.

'We go back to the peace and quiet?' he asked hopefully.

Fonsie didn't even bother to answer. He knew that nowadays anything Mario said was more in the nature of a ritual protest than a genuine complaint.

The café was unrecognisable from the run-down place it was when Fonsie had arrived in town. Brightly painted, cheerful, it was attracting all kinds of clientele that would never have crossed its doorstep in the old days. Fonsie had seen that there was an opportunity for morning coffee for an older set, and he had gone all out to get it. This was the time of day when the younger set, the real customers, were tied up at school or working, so the place was almost empty.

Fonsie played old-style music and watched with satisfaction while Dr Johnson's wife, and Mrs Hogan, Mrs Kennedy from the chemist and Birdie Mac all took to call in for a coffee that was cheaper than Healy's Hotel in an atmosphere that was distinctly less formal.

And as for the youngsters, he had plans for a magnificent juke box which would pay for itself in six months. But there would be time enough to explain that to his uncle later. In the meantime he just said that he was lending the player they had to Eve Malone for her party.

'That's a better place to play it than here,' Mario grumbled. 'Up on the quarry is good. It will only deafen the wild birds that fly around in the air.'

'You won't stay too late at this party now, will you?' Benny's father was looking at her over his glasses.

It made him look old and fussy. She hated him peering like that. Either look through them or take them off, she wanted to shout with a surge of impatience.

She forced a reassuring smile on to her face.

'It's the only party there's ever been in Knockglen, Father, you know that. I can't come to any harm, just up at the back of the convent garden.'

'That's a slippy old path through the convent.'

'I'll come back by the road then, down through the square.'

'It'll be pitch dark,' her mother added. 'You might be better coming through the convent.'

'I'll have plenty of people to come back with me. Clodagh or Fonsie, Maire Carroll even.'

'Maybe I could walk up that way myself about the time it would be ending. Shep, you'd like a nice late-night walk wouldn't you?'

The dog's ears pricked up at the thought of any kind of walk.

Please let her find the right words. The words that

would stop her father walking out in the dark out of kindness and peering through the window at Eve's party, wrecking it for everyone, not only Benny.

Please could she say the right thing that would stop him in this foolish well-meant wish to escort her safely home.

Nan would know how to cope with this. What would Nan do? Nan always said stick as close to the truth as possible.

'Father, I'd rather if you didn't come up for me. It would make me look a bit babyish, you know, in front of all the people from Dublin. And it's the only party that's ever been given in Knockglen and maybe the only one that ever will be. Do you see how I don't want to be taken there and collected as if I were a child?'

He looked a bit hurt, as if a kind offer had been refused.

'All right, love,' he said eventually. 'I was only trying to be helpful.'

'I know, Father, I know,' she said.


This Christmas Nan's father had been worse than usual. The festive season seemed to bring him no cheer. The boys were almost immune to him. Paul and Nasey spent very little time in Maple Gardens.

Emily tried to excuse him. She spoke of him apologetically to Nan.

'He doesn't mean it. If you knew how full of remorse he is after.'

'I do,' Nan said. 'I have to listen to it.'

'He'll be so sorry he upset us. He'll be like a lamb today.' Em pleaded for understanding.

'Let him be like anything he likes, Em. I'm not going to be here to look at it. I'm going to the races.'

She had rehearsed this outfit over and over. It seemed to be just right. The cream camel-hair suit with the brown trimmings, the hat that fitted so perfectly into the blonde curly hair. A small, good handbag and shoes that would not sink in the mud. She went to the races on the bus, along with other Dubliners going on a day out.

But while they talked form and record and likely outsiders, Nan Mahon just sat and looked out of the window.

She had very little interest in horses.

It didn't take her long to find him, and position herself in a place where she could be seen. She stood warming her hands at one of the many coal braziers placed around the enclosure. She appeared to concentrate very much on the heat as she saw him from the corner of her eye.

'How lovely to meet you again, Nan Mahon,' he said. 'Where are your supporting group of ladies?'

'What do you mean?' Her smile was warm and friendly.

'It's only I never see you without a great regiment of women in tow.'

'Not today. I came with my brothers. They've gone to the Tote.'

'Good. Can I bear you off to have a drink?'

'Yes. I'd love that, but just one. I must meet them after the third race.'

They went into the crowded bar, his hand under her elbow guiding her slightly.

There were smiles here and there and people calling to him. She felt confident that she was their equal. There were no pitying looks. Not one of those people would ever know the kind of house she had left this morning to get here on the bus. A house where drink had been spilled, where a lamp had been broken, where half the Christmas pudding had been thrown against the wall in a drunken rage. These people accepted Nan as an equal.

Eve looked around her little house with pleasure.

The oil lamps were lit and they gave a warm glow. The fire burned in the grate.

Mother Francis had left what she called a few old bits and pieces around the place. They were exactly the kind of thing that Eve wanted. A big blue vase in which she could put the wild catkins she had gathered. A handful of books to fill a corner shelf. Two slightly cracked china candlesticks for the mantelpiece, an old coal scuttle polished and burnished.

In the kitchen on the old range there were saucepans which must have come from the convent. Nothing much useful had been left from her parents' time.

Only the piano. Sarah Westward's piano. Eve ran her fingers over it and wished yet again that she had paid attention and tried to learn when Mother Bernard had been giving her lessons. Mother Francis had wanted so much for Eve to share what must have been a great love of music. Her mother had a piano stool stuffed with sheet music, and books and scores in a cupboard. They had been neatly tidied and kept free of damp by Mother Francis over the years.

When the piano tuner came to the school he was always asked to do a further chore and had been led through the kitchen gardens up the path to the piano which he always told Mother Francis was twenty times better than anything they had in the music room of St Mary's.

'It's not ours,' Mother Francis used to say.

'Then why am I tuning it?' he used to ask every year.

Eve sat down at the fire and hugged herself.

As in so many things, Mother Francis had been right. It was very nice to have a place of your own.


The Hogans had decided not to talk to Benny yet about Sean Walsh's proposition. Or ultimatum.

It had been very courteously couched, but there was no question about it. If he were not invited to be a partner in the business he would leave, and it would be known why he left. Nobody in Knockglen would think that he had been fairly treated. Everyone knew what his input had been, and how great his loyalty.

Sean did not need to spell out what would be the future for the business if he were allowed to leave. As it was, he was the one holding it together. Mr Hogan had no real business sense in terms of what today's customers wanted. And old Mike in the shop wasn't going to be any help to him in that regard.

They would talk to Benny about it, but not now. Not since she had put herself out to be polite and courteous to him during the Christmas meal. She might flare up again and they didn't want to risk that.

'Has Sean been asked to the party above in Eve's cottage?' Eddie asked, although he knew that there was no question of the boy having been invited.

'No, Father.'

To Benny's relief the telephone rang. But it was startling to have someone call at nine o'clock in the evening. She hoped that it wasn't Jack to say he wasn't coming.

Benny answered it. Nan Mahon was on the line, pleading, begging that she could come to stay tomorrow night for the party. Nan had said that she didn't think she would be able to come to Knockglen when the party was first mentioned. What had changed her mind? A lot of things, apparently. She would explain everything when she arrived. No, she wouldn't need to be met on the bus. She'd be getting a lift. She'd explain all that later too. No, no idea what time. Could she say she'd see Benny at the party?

Next morning, on the day of the party, Benny went up early to Eve's cottage to tell her the news.

Eve was furious.

'What does she think she's doing, announcing her arrival like some bloody old king from the olden days?'

'You did ask her to the party,' Benny said mildly.

'Yes, and she said no.'

'I don't know what *you're* bellyaching about. It's just

416

one more for the party. I'm the one who was dragging beds all night with Patsy and checking that there's no dust on the legs of the furniture in case Nan does a household inspection.'

Eve didn't know why she was annoyed. It was, on the face of it, unreasonable. Nan was her friend. Nan had lent her that beautiful red skirt for the dance. Nan had advised Eve on everything from how to put on eyeliner to putting shoe trees in every shoe every night. The others would be delighted to see her. It would make the party go with an even bigger swing. It was strange that she felt so resentful.

They sat having coffee in the kitchen of Eve's home, the two of them puzzling out who was giving Nan a lift. Benny said it couldn't be Jack because he was coming in a car with Aidan and Carmel and Sean. They knew it wasn't with Rosemary Ryan and Sheila, still deadly rivals and driving discontentedly with Bill Dunne and Johnny O'Brien.

Benny was thinking about Jack and how after tonight surely Rosemary and Sheila would have to give up their hopes of him, once they had seen how he and Benny felt about each other. To say straight out that he had missed her. To say it on the phone on Christmas Day. It was the most wonderful thing that could have happened.

Eve's brow was furrowed. She wished she could think that Nan was just coming for the party. She felt sure that it was in order to wangle an invitation to Westlands. Which she would not get from Eve, and that was for sure and for certain.

*

Heather came to call wearing her hacking jacket and little hard hat.

'You look as if you've just got off a horse,' Eve said.

'I have,' and Heather proudly showed her the pony tied to the gate.

It was eating some of the bushes within its reach. Eve leaped up in panic. Those were her only decoration, she said, and now this terrible horse was hoovering it all up. Heather laughed, and said nonsense, her beautiful pony was only nuzzling. He wouldn't dream of eating anything between meals. Benny and Eve went out and stroked the grey pony, Malcolm, the light of young Heather's life. They kept away from the mouth with the big yellow teeth and marvelled at how fearless Heather seemed to be. Heather had come to help. She thought she would be useful in setting up the games and was very perplexed when there seemed to be no games to set up. No ducking for apples like at Hallowe'en. Heather wanted a party where they had advertisements all cut out of papers, just the words. The thing that was being advertised was cut out. Everyone had a pencil and paper and the one who got most of them right won.

In desperation they suggested she blow up balloons. That pleased her. She had plenty of breath, she said proudly. As she sat in an ever-increasing heap of green, red and yellow balloons Heather asked casually if Simon had been invited to the party.

'No, it's not really his kind of party,' Eve said. 'And besides, he'd be very old for it.'

She wondered why she was making excuses for not inviting this man for whom she had felt nothing but dislike all her life. But then who could ever have foreseen the way things would turn out? That she would be very fond of his younger sister, and that she would have been settled in this house where she had vowed never to live. The day might well come when her cousin Simon Westward could cross this door, but not for a long time yet.

Jack Foley was recognised as the expert on Knockglen. He had been there before, after all. He knew Benny's house. He had been given clear instructions on how to get to the quarry road. You came in like the bus to the square and took a hilly path that had no signpost on it, but looked as if it were leading to a farmhouse.

There was another way through the convent, but you couldn't take the car and Eve had been adamant that there was to be no horseplay anywhere near her nuns.

Aidan wanted them to go and have a look at the convent first. He stared out of the passenger seat at the high walls and the big wrought-iron gate.

'Imagine being brought up in a place like that. Isn't it a miracle that she's normal?' he said.

'But *is* she normal?' Jack wanted to know. 'She does appear to fancy you, which doesn't augur well for her state of mind.'

They wound their way up the perilous track. The curtains were pulled back in the cottage and they could see firelight, and oil lamps, a Christmas tree and balloons.

'Isn't it gorgeous?' breathed Carmel, whose plans for the future when Sean was an established businessman now widened to include a small country cottage for weekends.

Jack liked it too.

'It's away from everywhere. You could be here and nobody know a thing about it.'

'Unless of course the sounds of "Good Golly, Miss Molly" were coming out of every window,' Aidan Lynch said happily, leaping from the car and running in to find Eve.

Clodagh had brought a clothes rail and hangers up from the shop. It meant that Eve's bed wouldn't be swamped with people's garments and there would be room for the girls to sit at the little dressing table to titivate themselves.

Benny was in there doing a final examination of her face when she heard Jack's voice. She must not run out and fling herself into his arms as she wanted to. It was more important than ever now that she let him make the first move. A man like Jack used to having girls throw themselves at him would not want that.

She would wait, even if it killed her.

The door of Eve's bedroom opened. It was probably Carmel, coming in to dab her face and say something cosy about Sean.

She looked in the mirror and over her shoulder she saw Jack. He closed the door behind him and came over to her, leaning his hands on her shoulders and looking at her reflection in the mirror.

'Happy Christmas,' he said in a soft voice.

She smiled a broad smile. But she was looking at his eyes, not her own, so she didn't know how it looked. Not too broad and toothy, she hoped.

Clodagh had covered a strapless bra in royal blue velvet to look like one of those smart boned tops, and then put a binding of the same material down a white cardigan.

Naturally Benny had worn a blouse under it when she left Lisbeg, but the blouse had been removed and was folded neatly to await the home journey.

He sat on the edge of Eve's bed, and held both her hands.

'Oh, I really missed you,' he said.

'What did you miss?' She didn't sound flirtatious. She just wanted to know.

'I missed telling you things, listening to you telling things. I missed your face, and kissing you.' He drew her towards him, and kissed her for a long time.

The door opened and Clodagh came in. She was dressed from head to foot in black lace with a mantilla and a high comb in her hair. She looked like a Spanish dancer. Her face was powdered dead white and her lips were scarlet.

'I was actually coming to see if you wanted any assistance with your dress, Benny, but it appears you don't,' Clodagh said, without seeming the slightest confused by the scene she had walked in on.

'This is Clodagh,' mumbled Benny.

Jack's face lit up as it did when he was introduced to any woman. It wasn't that he was eyeing them up and down. He didn't even try to flirt with them. He liked women. Benny remembered suddenly that his father was like that too. At the big party in their house Dr Foley had been pleased to greet each new girl who was presented to him. There was nothing but warmth and delight in his reaction. So it was with Jack. And tonight when all the others arrived he would be the same.

It must be a wonderful thing to be so popular, she thought, to be able to please people just by being there.

Clodagh was explaining to Jack how she had got the lace in an old trunk upstairs in the Kennedys' house. Mrs Kennedy had told her she could go and rummage there and she had found marvellous things altogether. In return she had made Mrs Kennedy four straight skirts with a pleat in the back. It was amazing with all the plumage available that some people still wanted to dress like dowdy sparrows.

Jack put his arm around Benny's shoulders.

'I've hardly seen any sparrows in Knockglen. You're all pretty exotic birds to me.'

Together with his arm around her shoulder and followed by Clodagh in her startling black and white they came out of Eve's room and, in full view of Sheila and Rosemary, of Fonsie and Maire Carroll, of Bill Dunne and Johnny O'Brien, they joined the party.

Without Benny Hogan having to manoeuvre it one little bit, they joined the party as a couple.


There never had been a party like it. Everyone agreed on that. From Fonsie's wonderful solo demonstrations to the whole place on its feet, from Guy Mitchell and 'I Never Felt More Like Singing The Blues'. The soup had been a magnificent idea. Bowl after bowl disappeared, sandwiches, sausage rolls and more soup. Eve served it from the big convent cauldron, her face flushed and excited. This was her house. These were her friends. It couldn't be better.

Only during the supper did she remember that Nan hadn't arrived.

'Perhaps she didn't get a lift after all.' Benny was on a cloud of her own.

'Did we tell her how to find the house?'

'Anyone in Knockglen would tell her where you live.' Benny squeezed Eve's arm. 'It's going wonderfully isn't it?'

'Yes. He can't take his eyes off you.'

'I don't mean that. I mean the party.'

Benny did mean that of course as well. Jack had been at her side all night. He had had a few dances with the others as a matter of form, but for the most of the night he was with her, touching, laughing, dancing, holding, swaying, including her in every conversation.

Rosemary Ryan watched them with some bewilderment for the first few dances.

'I didn't know anything about you and Jack,' she said, as she and Benny were having a glass of punch.

'Well, I did tell you I met him from time to time in the Annexe.'

'That's right. You did.'

Rosemary was quite fair-minded. Benny had said she

was meeting Jack. If Rosemary read nothing into it then it was her own fault.

'You do look very well,' she said grudgingly, but again struggled to be just. 'Have you lost a lot of weight or put on more make-up or what?'

Benny didn't even react. She knew that whatever it was, Jack seemed to like it. And he didn't care who else knew. Benny had thought that somehow it would have had to be a secret about them.

Aidan asked Eve for a pound of sugar.

'What do you want that for?'

'I read that if you put it in the carburettor of a car, then the car won't start.'

'How about trying to find some discovery that would make it start? That seems to me to be the better invention,' Eve said.

'You're wrong. I want Jack's father's car never to start again. Then we can stay here in this magical place and never go away.'

'Yeah, terrific. And I'll have to put up Sean and Carmel for the night as well,' Eve said.

'If I stayed, would you take me to meet the nuns tomorrow?' Aidan asked.

Eve told him that there was no question of his staying, at any time, but least of all now when Mother Clare was below watching every move. Or indeed maybe outside in the fuchsia bushes with a torch, for all they knew. But she was glad that he liked the place. And when the weather got finer, he might come and spend a whole day. Aidan said they would probably be spending much of their adult life here. During the long vacations when he was called to the Bar. They would want to escape here with the children, away from the loud booming voices of his parents.

'And what about my job?' Eve asked, entertained in spite of herself by the fantasy.

'Your job will of course be to look after me, and our eight fine children, using your university education to give them a cultured home background.'

'You'll be lucky, Aidan Lynch.' She pealed with laughter.

'I have been lucky. I met you, Eve Malone,' he said, without a trace of his usual joky manner.


Bill Dunne was the first to see Nan when she came in the door. Her eyes were sparkling and she took in the scene around her with delight.

'Isn't it wonderful?' she said. 'Eve never said it was anything like this.'

She wore a white polo-necked jumper and a red tartan skirt, under a black coat. She carried a small leather case with her, and asked to be shown to Eve's bedroom.

Benny called to the kitchen to let Eve know that Nan was here.

'Bloody hell, we've finished the soup,' Eve said to Aidan.

'She won't expect it, not at this hour,' he soothed her.

It was a late hour to arrive. Eve had thought she heard

a car pull away down the track a few moments ago, but she had told herself she was imagining it.

Still, someone must have left Nan at the door. It was raining outside and Nan looked immaculate. She could not have climbed up that path in this weather.

Eve put some sausage rolls and sandwiches on a plate, and took them through the sitting room, skirting Fonsie and Clodagh, who were doing such a spirited rendering of the Spanish Gypsy Dance that everyone had formed a circle to clap and cheer. She knocked on the door of her own bedroom in case Nan was changing, but she was sitting down at the dressing table exactly as she was; Rosemary Ryan was sitting on the bed, telling the mystery-of-the-year story. Jack Foley and Benny Hogan, of all people, were inseparable.

'Did you know?' Rosemary was asking insistingly.

'Yes, sort of.' Nan didn't sound as if it mattered very much. Her mind seemed to be elsewhere.

Then she saw Eve. 'Eve, it's fabulous. It's a jewel. You never told us it was like this.'

'It's not always like this.' Despite herself, Eve was pleased. Praise from Nan was high praise.

'I brought you something to eat . . . in case you were changing,' she said.

'No, I'm all right like this.' Nan hadn't thought of changing.

She was of course all right in whatever she wore. It wasn't very dressy. All the others had put on the style. Parties weren't so run of the mill that you went in a jumper and skirt. But on Nan it looked beautiful.

They all went into the room. Nan loved it. She was busy stroking everything, the polished oil lamps, the wonderful wood in those shelves, the piano. Imagine having a piano of your own. Could she see the little kitchen?

Eve took her through and down the stone step. The place was covered with pots and pans and debris. There were boxes and bottles and glasses. But Nan saw only things she could praise. The dresser, it was wonderful. Where did it come from? Eve had never asked. And that lovely old bowl. It was the real thing, not like horrible modern ones.

'I'm sure a lot of those things came from your mother's home,' she said. 'They have a look of quality about them.'

'Yes, or maybe they bought them together.' Somehow Eve felt defensive about her father, and the thought that there could be no look of quality attached to him.

Nan said she was too excited to eat. It was marvellous to be here. Her eyes were dancing. She looked feverish and restless. Everyone in the room was attracted to her, but she was aware of none of them. She refused any offer to dance, saying she had to take it all in. And she wandered around touching and admiring, and sighing over it all.

She paused by the piano and opened it to look at the keys.

'Weren't we all very unlucky that we never learned to play?' she said to Benny. It was the first time Benny had ever noticed Nan Mahon sounding bitter.

'Are you ever going to dance, or is this tour of inspection going to go on all night?' Jack Foley asked her.

Suddenly Nan seemed to snap out of it. 'I'm being appallingly rude, of course,' she said, looking straight at him.

'Now, Johnny,' Jack said to Johnny O'Brien. 'I knew that all you had to do was wake her out of the trance, and it would work. Johnny says he's been asking you to dance for ten minutes and you can't even hear him.'

If Nan was disappointed that Jack had not been inviting her to dance there was no way that anyone would have known. She smiled such a smile at Johnny that it almost melted him into a little puddle on the floor.

'Johnny, how lovely,' she said, and put her arms straight around his neck.

They were playing 'Unchained Melody', a lovely slow smoochy number. Benny was so pleased that Jack hadn't left her for Nan just as Fonsie had put that one on. It was one of her favourite songs. She had never dreamed that she would dance to it, here in Knockglen with the man she loved, who had his arms wrapped around her, and seemed to love her too. In front of all her friends.

They put more turf and logs on the fire, and when one of the oil lights flickered down, nobody bothered to replace it.

They sat around in groups or in twosomes, the evening drawing to a close.

'Can anybody play that beautiful piano?' Nan asked.

Amazingly Clodagh said that she could. Fonsie looked

at her in open admiration. There was nothing that woman couldn't do, he told people proudly.

Clodagh settled herself at the keys. She had a repertoire that staggered them. Frank Sinatra numbers that they all joined in, ragtime solos, and she even got people to sing solos.

Bill Dunne startled them all by singing 'She Moved Through the Fair' very tunefully.

'That was a well-kept secret,' Jack said to him as they clapped him to the echo.

'It's only when I'm out of Dublin and can't be sent up by all you lot that I'd have the courage,' Bill said, red with pleasure from all the admiration.

Everyone said that Knockglen had not been properly praised up to this, and now that they knew where it was they'd be regular visitors. Fonsie told them to come earlier next time, when it was opening time in Mario's, soon to be Ireland's premier stylish café. Trends had to start somewhere and why not Knockglen?

Eve was sitting on the floor next to one of her two rather battered armchairs; on Clodagh's advice they had draped bedspreads over the shabby furniture. It looked exotic in the flickering light.

She thought she should get up and make more coffee for the departing guests, but she didn't want it to end, and the way Aidan had his arm around her and was stroking her, he didn't want to make any move to go either.

Nan sat on a tiny three-legged stool, hugging her knees.

'I met your grandfather today,' she said suddenly to Eve.

Eve felt a cold shock run through her. 'You did?'

'Yes. He really is a charming old man, isn't he?'

Benny felt she wanted to move away from Jack's arm and go over and support Eve physically. In some way she wanted to be a barrier between her and what Nan was saying.

Please may Eve not say anything brittle or hurtful. Let her just mumble for the moment. Let there not be a scene now to end the party on a sour note.

Eve might have read her mind.

'Yes. How did you meet him?' Although she knew. She knew only too well.

'Oh, I met Simon at the races yesterday and we got talking. He offered me a lift if I was going to this part of the world. So we got here a bit early . . . and, well, he took me to Westlands.'

If they had got here so bloody early, Eve thought, then Nan might have been on time rather than turning up when the supper was finished.

She didn't trust herself to say any more. But Nan had in no way finished with the subject.

'You could really see what he must have been like before. You know, very upright and stern. It must be terrible for him to be like that in his chair. He was having his tea. They serve it beautifully for him. Even though he's sometimes not able to manage it.'

She had been there since tea time. Since five o'clock and

she hadn't even bothered to come next or near them until after nine in the evening. Eve felt the bile rise in her throat.

Nan must have sensed it. 'I did keep asking Simon to drive me up here, but he insisted on showing me everything. Well, I suppose you've been over it dozens of times.'

'You know I haven't.' Eve's voice was dangerously calm.

Only Benny and Aidan who knew her so well would have got the vibrations.

Aidan exchanged a glance with Benny. But there was nothing he could do.

'Well, you must, Eve. You must let him take you all through the place. He's so proud of it. And he describes it so well, not boasting or anything.'

'Where's this?' Sheila always liked to hear of places that were splendid and people that were important.

'Eve's relations, up at the big house. About a mile over . . . that way . . . is it?' Nan pointed with her arm.

Eve said nothing. Benny said that it was more or less that way. Benny also wondered did anyone want coffee, but they didn't. They wanted to sit dreamily with low music on the player and to chat. And they wanted Nan to have the floor. There was something about the way her face was lit up by the fire and by the place she was talking about . . . they wanted her to go on.

'He showed me all the family portraits. Your mother was very beautiful, wasn't she, Eve?' Nan spoke in open admiration. There was nothing triumphalist about her having been there, about her having been taken on a tour and shown the picture that had not been shown to Eve on her one visit.

Nan had always said that Eve should bury her differences. Nan would have thought that Eve knew what her mother looked like.

'You must have had quite a tour.' The words nearly choked her.

'Oh yes. The trouble was getting away.'

'Still, you managed it,' Aidan Lynch said. 'Fonsie, if we're not going to be given cells in the convent for the night, which I was distinctly promised, I think we should have something to loosen up our limbs for the journey home. What would you suggest, man?'

Fonsie had long realised that Aidan was a fellow spirit. He leaped to his feet and flipped through a few record covers.

'I think it comes down to a straight contest between Lonnie Donegan "Putting on the Style" and Elvis being "All Shook Up" man,' he said after some thought.

'Man, let's not insult either of those heroes. Let's have them both,' Aidan said, and he went around the room clapping his hands at people to get them going.

Benny had followed Eve to the kitchen.

'She doesn't understand,' Benny said. Eve clutched hard with both her hands at the sink.

'Of course she does. How often have we talked about it?'

'Not to her. Seriously not to her. With Nan we usually pretend things are fine. Otherwise she gets you to change them. Remember?'

'I'll never forgive her.'

'Yes, of course you will. You'll forgive her this minute, otherwise it will change everything about the party. It was the most wonderful party in the world. Truly.'

'It was.' Eve softened. Inside she saw Aidan beckoning to her.

Everyone was on the floor. Benny went back. Jack and Nan were dancing, laughing happily, neither of them knowing that anything was amiss.

## 14

Dear Mr and Mrs Hogan,

Thank you very much for my lovely visit to Knockglen. You were both so hospitable to me I felt very welcome. As I said to you, I think your house is beautiful. You have no idea how lovely it is to come and stay in a real Georgian house. Benny is very lucky indeed.

You very kindly asked me if I would come back again some time. Nothing would give me more pleasure. My regards to Patsy, also, and thank her for the lovely breakfast.

Yours sincerely,
Nan Mahon

Eddie Hogan said to his wife that there were some people in life for whom it was a real pleasure to do the smallest thing, and that Benny's friend Nan was one of them.

Annabel agreed completely. They had never met a more charming girl. And such perfect manners too. She had given Patsy half a crown when she was leaving. She was a perfect lady.

Dear Kit,

The more I think of it, the more I realise that it was ridiculous of me to assume that I could just walk in years later and take up as if nothing had happened. Considering the way I treated you and how little I gave you and Frank over the years you would have had every reason to throw me out on my ear.

But you were very calm and reasonable, and I'll always be grateful for that.

I just wanted you to know that I have always had an insurance policy for you, in case anything happened to me, so that you and our son might have had something good to remember me by. I wish you all the luck and happiness that I didn't bring to you myself.

Love, Joe

Kit Hegarty folded the letter from the man that everyone else had called Joe. She had never called him anything but Joseph. Meeting him had been so different to the way she thought it would have been. She had intended to hurl everything at him if she ever saw him again. But in fact he was just like a distant friend who was down on his luck. He gave no address. She couldn't even acknowledge the letter.

Dear Mother Francis,

My sincerest thanks for being invited to spend the Holy Feast of Christmas with you and the Community in St Mary's. Thank you also for arranging the lift back to Dublin with your friend Miss Pine. An outspoken person, but no doubt a good Christian with a heavy cross to bear in that niece that she has.

I was very pleased to see that Eve Malone had settled down and begun to repay some of the work our Order has put into her education. It was gratifying to see that she studies so hard.

Your sister in Christ,
Mother Mary Clare

Mother Francis smiled grimly as she read the letter, particularly the part about how they had 'invited' Mother Clare. But it was wonderful that she had been able to forewarn Eve of the surprise visit that Mother Clare had intended to pay. Mossy Rooney had come along quietly with his cart and removed all the bottles and boxes. The cottage was flung open to the winter air to clear the fumes of smoke and drink from the previous night.

Mother Clare, to her great rage, had discovered Eve sitting blamelessly studying instead of what she had hoped to find as the aftermath of a party, and would have found had it not been for Mother Francis.

Dear Sean,

As you asked me to do I am confirming in writing

that I intend to invite you to become a partner in Hogan's Gentleman's Outfitters. I shall arrange with Mr Gerald Green of Green and Mahers, Solicitors, to come to Knockglen and we will formalise the details early in the New Year.

I look forward to a successful partnership in 1958.

Yours sincerely,

Edward James Hogan

Mrs Healy read the letter carefully, word by word, and then nodded approvingly at Scan Walsh. It was never any harm getting these things in writing, she told him, with the best will in the world people could always go back on what they said. And not a word against Eddie Hogan. He was the nicest man you'd meet in a day's walk, but it was time someone realised Sean Walsh's worth, and acknowledged it.

Eddie Hogan died on a Saturday at lunch time. After he had finished his cup of tea and queen cake, he stood up to go back to the shop.

'If Sean has his way, there'll be no closing for lunch . . .' he began, but he never finished the sentence.

He sat down on the sofa with his hand to his chest. His face was pale and when he closed his eyes his breathing was strange. Patsy didn't need to be asked to run across the road for Dr Johnson.

Dr Johnson came in his shirt sleeves. He asked for a small glass of brandy.

'He never takes spirits, Maurice, you know that!' Annabel's hand was at her throat in fear. 'What is it? Is it a kind of fit?'

Dr Johnson sat Annabel Hogan down on the chair. He handed her the brandy.

'Sip it slowly, Annabel, that's the girl.'

He saw Patsy with her coat on as if to go for Father Ross.

'Just a little drop at a time. It was totally painless. He never knew a thing.'

The doctor beckoned Patsy over.

'Before you get the priest, Patsy, where's Benny?'

'She's in Dublin for the day, sir. She went up to meet Eve Malone. They were going to a special lecture, I think she said.'

'Get Eve Malone to bring her back,' said Dr Johnson. He had managed to take a rug and cover the figure of Eddie Hogan, who lay on the sofa looking for all the world as if he were taking a quick nap before he went back to the shop.

Annabel sat rocking to and fro, moaning in disbelief.

Dr Johnson went to the door after Patsy.

'No need to tell that bag of bones in the shop yet.'

'No sir.'

Dr Johnson had always disliked Sean Walsh. He could almost see him picking one of the best black ties from the stock and combing his thin lank hair. He could visualise him putting on the correct expression of grief before he came to offer his condolences to the widow, and her daughter.

Whenever they found her.

Benny and Jack walked hand in hand over Killiney Hill. It had been one of those cold, crisp winter afternoons, which was going to end soon. Already they could see the lights of Dunlaoghaire twinkling far below them, and then the great sweep of Dublin Bay.

They would meet Aidan and Eve later in Kit Hegarty's house. Kit had promised them all sausages and chips before they went into the town on the train to the L and H. Tonight the notion was going to be about Sport, and Jack half threatened to speak. He said he didn't know whether he needed huge encouragement and masses of support, or if it would be easier to speak one night on his own when there were no friends to hear him make a fool of himself.

Not since the great dance before Christmas had Benny been able to spend a night in Dublin. Jack had been increasingly impatient.

'What am I going to do with my girl always miles away? It's like having a penfriend,' he had complained.

'We see each other in the day.' But her throat had narrowed in fear. He sounded cross.

'What's the use? It's at night I need you to go to things.'

She had wheedled this Saturday by pretending there was a lecture, and asking if she could tack the night on as well.

And she had another worry. He was very insistent that she go for a weekend to Wales with him.

His team were going to play a friendly match. There would be lots of people going. He really wanted her to go.

'It's not normal,' he had fumed. 'Anyone else could go. Rosemary, Sheila, Nan, they all have families who'd realise that if they're old enough to have a university education they're old enough to be let out on a simple boat trip for two days.'

She hated him saying her family weren't normal. She hated them for not being normal enough to let her go.

Soon it was more dark than it was day. They came down the springy turf together and walked along the Vico Road looking down at Killiney Bay, which people said was meant to be as beautiful as the Bay of Naples.

'I'd love to go to Naples,' Benny said.

'Maybe they'll let you when you're about ninety,' Jack grumbled.

She laughed, though she didn't feel like it.

'Race you down to the corner,' she said, and laughing they ran down to the railway station where they caught a train to Dunlaoghaire.

As soon as Kevin Hickey opened the door to them Benny knew something was wrong.

'They're in the kitchen,' he said, refusing to meet her eye. Behind him she saw the tableau of Kit and Eve and Aidan waiting to give them some very bad news.

It was as if everything had stopped. The sound of the traffic outside, the clocks ticking, the seagulls over the harbour.

Benny walked forward slowly to hear what they were going to tell her.

Shep seemed to be in everyone's way, all the time. He was looking for Eddie, and there seemed to be no sign of him. Almost everyone else in Knockglen seemed to be in and out of Lisbeg, but no sign of the master.

Eventually he went out and lay down beside the hen house; only the hens were behaving normally.

Peggy Pine arranged two big trays of sandwiches. She also asked Fonsie to collect drink from Shea's.

'I think your man is going to get some at Healy's.'

'Well, your man will be too late then,' Peggy said, taking ten pound notes from her till. 'We'll have paid cash. There's nothing he can do about that.'

They smiled at each other. The one bright spot in a dark day being the thought of besting both Sean Walsh and Mrs Healy at the same time.

By tea time everyone in the town knew. And everyone was shocked. By no standards was Eddie an old man, they speculated happily. Fifty-two at most, at the very most. Maybe not even fifty. The wife was older. They tried to work it out. And not a man for the drink, and not a day sick. Hadn't he and his wife taken to going on healthy walks recently? Didn't that show you that your hour was marked out for you and it didn't really matter what you did, you couldn't put it off once it came.

And such a gentleman. Never a harsh word out of him. Not a one to make a quick shilling here and there, he'd not hurry a farmer who hadn't paid a bill for a while. Not one to move with the times, the windows of Hogan's hadn't

441

changed much in all the time he was there. But such a gentleman. So interested in everyone who came in and their family and their news. All the time in the world for them. And he kept poor Mike on there too, long after he might have needed him.

The prayers that were added on to the family rosary that evening for the repose of Eddie Hogan's soul were prayers that were warm and genuine. And the prayers that people said were hardly needed. A man like Eddie Hogan would have been in Heaven by two o'clock.


Eve had managed to ward off Sean Walsh's attempts to come to Dublin to collect Benny.

She had also managed to say that Benny was at a lecture where it was impossible to disturb her, because it was a kind of field trip. Nobody knew where they had gone. They would have to wait until she came home at six o'clock.

'They're never bringing her father to the church tonight?' Eve had said.

It was unthinkable that Benny would not be there when her father's body was brought to lie overnight in Knockglen parish church.

'They might have done, if they had known where to find Benny.' Sean sounded aggrieved.

Jack said he'd get his father's car.

'They might need it.' Benny's face was wan and empty. 'They might need it for something important.'

'There's nothing more important than this,' said Jack.

'Will we go with them?' Aidan Lynch asked Eve.

'No,' Eve said. 'We'll go down by bus tomorrow.'

She could hardly bear to look at Benny's face as she sat looking unseeingly in front of her.

From time to time she said 'Dead' in a low voice, and shook her head.

She had spoken to her mother on the phone, her mother had sounded sleepy, she said. That too seemed hard to accept.

'They gave her a sedative, to calm her down. It makes her feel sleepy,' Kit explained.

But none of it made any sense to Benny, no matter what tablet you took. It couldn't make you feel sleepy. Not when Father had died. Died. No matter how many times she said it, it wouldn't sink in.

Mr Hayes next door drove them in to the Foleys' house.

Jack's mother was at the door. Benny noticed that she wore a lovely woollen suit with a cream blouse underneath. She had earrings on, and she smelled of perfume.

She gave Benny a hug of sympathy.

'Doreen has packed you a flask of coffee and some sandwiches for the car journey,' she said.

She made it sound as if Knockglen were at the other side of Europe.

'We're both very, very sorry,' she said. 'If there's anything at all we can do . . .'

'I think I'd better get her on the road.' Jack cut short the sympathies.

'Were they going out somewhere tonight?' Benny asked.

'No. Why?'

He was negotiating the early Saturday evening traffic in Dublin, and trying to get out towards the Knockglen road.

'She looked all dressed up.'

'No, she didn't.'

'Is she like that all the time?'

'I think so.' He was surprised, glancing over at her.

She sat in silence for a while, staring ahead. She felt very cold and unreal.

She wished over and over the most futile wish. That it could be this morning. If only it were eight o'clock this morning.

Her father had said that it was going to be a nice bright day.

'Isn't it a pity you have this lecture now. You could have had a great day here in Knockglen, and maybe yourself and Shep would have come up and got me out of the shop early for a bit of a walk!'

If only she had the time again. There'd have been no lies about lectures that didn't exist. There'd have been no shame at accepting his praise for her eagerness to study.

She'd have cancelled everything, just to have been there, to have been with him when he began to leave his life.

She didn't believe it was so instant that he didn't know. She would like to have been in the room.

And for her mother too. Mother, who never had to make a decision of her own . . . being alone to handle everything.

Benny's eyes were dry but her heart was full of shame that she hadn't been there.

Jack couldn't find any good words. Several times he almost had the right thing. But always he stopped.

He couldn't bear it any longer. He pulled into the side of the road. Two lorries hooted at him angrily, but he was parked now up on a grass verge.

'Benny, darling,' he said, and put his arms around her. 'Benny, please cry. Please cry. It's awful to see you like this. I'm here. Benny cry, cry for your father.'

And she clung to him and wept and wept until he thought that her body would never stop shaking with the sobs and the grief.

They were all like characters in a play, Benny thought. People moving off stage and on stage all evening. One moment she would look and there was Dekko Moore talking earnestly in the corner, the small tea cup and saucer looking ridiculous in his large hands. Then she would glance again and in that corner Father Ross was standing mopping his brow as he listened to the visions of poor Mr Flood and wondered how best to cope with them.

In the scullery Mossy Rooney stood not wanting to form part of the main gathering that spread through the whole house, but ready when Patsy called him to help. On the stairs sat Maire Carroll whom Benny had so disliked at school. Tonight, however, she was sympathetic and full of praise for Benny's father. 'A very nice man with a word for everyone.'

Benny wondered wildly what kind of a word her father would have been able to dredge up for the charmless Maire Carroll.

Her mother sat in the middle, accepting the sympathy, and she was the most unreal figure of all. She wore a black blouse that Benny had never seen before. She worked out that Peggy must have produced it from the shop. Mother's eyes were red, but she was calmer than Benny would have thought possible, considering.

The undertakers had told her that Father was lying upstairs. Jack went up with her to the spare room, where candles burned and everything seemed to have been miraculously tidied and covered. It didn't look like the spare bedroom at all. It looked like a church.

Father didn't look like Father either. One of the nuns from St Mary's was sitting there. It was something they did, go around to people's houses when someone died and sit there by the body. Somehow it made people more calm and less frightened to see the figure of a nun keeping guard.

Jack held her hand tightly as they knelt and said three Hail Marys by the bed. Then they left the room.

'I don't know where you're going to sleep,' Benny said.

'What?'

'Tonight. I thought you could stay in the spare room. I forgot.'

'Darling, I have to go back. You know that. I have to take the car back for one thing . . .'

'Of course, I forgot.'

She had thought that he would be there with her, standing beside her for everything.

He had been such a comfort in the car, when she had wept on his shoulder. She had begun to assume that he would always be there.

'I'll come back for the funeral. Obviously.'

'The funeral. Yes.'

'I should go soon.'

She had no idea what time it was. Or how long they had been home. Something inside her told her that she must pull herself together now. This minute, and thank him properly for his kindness. She must not allow herself to be a drag.

She walked him out to the car. It was a blowy night now, the dark clouds were scudding across the moon.

Knockglen looked very small and quiet compared with the bright lights of Dublin they had left . . . some time ago. She didn't know how long ago.

He held her close to him, more a brotherly hug than any kind of kiss. Perhaps he thought it was more suitable.

'I'll see you on Monday,' he said softly.

Monday.

It seemed so far away. Imagine her having thought he was going to stay for the weekend.


Eve and Aidan came on Sunday.

They walked from the bus down the main street.

'That's Healy's Hotel. Where I wanted you to stay.'

'Until I reminded you I am an impoverished student,

who has never spent a night in a hotel in my life,' Aidan said.

'Yes, well . . .'

She showed him the Hogans' shop with the black-rimmed notice in the window. She told him about how nice Birdie Mac in the sweet shop was, and how horrible Maire Carroll in the grocery was. From time to time Aidan turned and looked back up at the convent. He had wanted to be invited there first, but Eve had refused. They hadn't come on a social call, she said, they had come to help Benny. There would be time later to meet Mother Francis and Sister Imelda and everyone.

They passed Mario's café, which even when closed on a Sunday radiated cheer, and life and excitement.

They turned the corner at the end of the street and went to Benny's house.

'It's awful only going to people's houses when they're dead,' Aidan said suddenly. 'I'd like to have come here when he was alive. Was he nice?'

'Very,' Eve said. She paused with her hand on the gate.

'He never saw any bad in anyone, and he never saw anyone grow up either. He always called me Little Eve. He always thought Benny was nine, and he saw no harm in that Sean Walsh, who'll be lording it inside.'

'Will I deal with Sean Walsh, make verbal mincemeat of him?' Aidan asked eagerly.

'No, Aidan, thank you, but that wouldn't be what's required.'

*

It was an endless day, even with Eve and Aidan there. Benny had a headache that she thought would never leave her. There had been so many wearying encounters. Mrs Healy for example, wanting to know if there was any way she had offended the family.

No? Well, she was certainly glad to hear that, because she had been so ready and eager to supply the drink that would be needed and then was told that her participation would not be necessary. And then Benny had to cope with old Mike from the shop. There had been words said, words that Mr Eddie had not meant the way that Mr Walsh thought he had meant them.

Mr Walsh? Yes, Mike had been told that it wasn't fitting for a partner to be called Sean any more, even though Mike had been head tailor when Sean Walsh had come in as a schoolboy.

Benny had been coping with Dessie Burns who was in that perilous state of being off the jar but threatening to go back on to it at any moment because if there was one thing a man should not be it was doctrinaire, and with Mario who said that in Italy people would cry, cry and cry again over the death of a good man like Eddie Hogan, not just stand in his house talking and drinking.

And then the church bells began to toll. So often in Lisbeg they heard the bells and it just meant the angelus, or time for Mass, or someone else was being brought to the church. Benny put on her black lace mantilla and walked with her mother behind the coffin up the street,

449

where people came to their doors and to stand outside their businesses on the cold Sunday afternoon.

And as she walked past their shop her heart grew heavier. It would be Sean's shop from now on. Or Mr Walsh as he would want people to call him.

She wished she could talk to her father about old Mike and ask him what was going to happen. The procession paused momentarily outside Hogan's. And then moved on. She could never talk to her father again about his shop or about anything. And he was powerless now to do anything about the shop he had loved so much.

Unless of course she were to do something herself to try and sort it out.


Aidan Lynch was introduced to Mother Francis.

'I have appointed myself guardian of Eve's morals while she is at university,' he said solemnly.

'Thank you very much.' Mother Francis was formerly grateful.

'I hear nothing but good of the way you brought her up. I wish I'd been left to a convent.' His smile was infectious.

'There might have been more problems with you,' the nun laughed.

Mother Francis had thought it was very sensible for Aidan Lynch to spend the night in Eve's cottage, while Eve slept at the convent. Everyone liked the thought of Eve being back under their roof again, and her bedroom was going to be there for ever. This had been a promise.

Eve showed Aidan how to rake the range.

'I think when we're married we might have something more modern,' he grumbled.

'No, surely with the eight children we can have them stoking it, going up the chimney even.'

'You don't take me seriously,' he said.

'I do. I just believe in child labour, that's all.'

Back in the convent, having cocoa with Mother Francis in the kitchen, it was impossible to believe that she had ever left these walls.

'A very nice young man,' Mother Francis said.

'But basically a beast of course, like you told us all men were, ravening beasts.'

'I *never* told you that.'

'You hinted at it.'

They were more like sisters these days than mother and daughter. They sat companionably in the warm kitchen and talked of life and death and the town and Mr Flood's visions and how hard everything was on poor Father Ross. Because if the vision was as true as Fatima and everybody believed it, why could they not make the leap of imagination, and believe it might all be true in Knockglen?

Possibly because Mr Flood the butcher was such an unlikely person to be visited by a holy nun in a tree. Or even on the ground according to Mother Francis.

The funeral Mass was at ten o'clock. Benny and her mother and Patsy went to the church in the mourners' car provided by the undertaker.

451

As she led her mother up the aisle to sit in the front row, Benny was aware of the people who had come to pay their respects. Farmers had come yesterday, in their Sunday suits, they would be out in their fields on a weekday morning. Today she saw men in suits, commercial travellers, suppliers, people from two parishes away. She saw father's cousins, and her mother's brothers. She saw standing in a comforting crowd her own circle of friends.

There was Jack, so tall that everyone in the church must have seen him. He wore a black tie and he turned round to see them coming. It was almost like being at a wedding, where people turn around to see the bride . . . the thought came and went.

Bill Dunne had come too, which was very nice of him, and Rosemary Ryan. They stood beside Eve and Aidan, their faces full of sympathy.

And Nan was there, in a black blazer and a pale grey skirt. She wore gloves and carried a small black bag. Her mantilla looked as if it had been made by a dress designer to sit in her blonde hair. Everyone else wore a mantilla that looked like a rag, or a headscarf. Clodagh wore a hat, though. A big black straw hat. It was her only concession to mourning colours. The rest of her outfit was a red and white striped coat dress, considerably shorter than Knockglen would have liked.

But then it was hard to please Knockglen since there was also disapproval for Fonsie's coat – a long one like de Valera would wear except it had a huge velvet collar and small finishings of fake leopard fur at the pockets, collars and cuffs.

Mother looked very old and sad. Benny glanced at her from time to time. Sometimes a tear fell on Mother's missal, and once or twice Benny leaned over and wiped it away. It was as if Mother hadn't noticed.

Mercifully, Sean Walsh had not presumed upon them too much. Startled by the rebuff over obtaining supplies from Healy's Hotel, he had been more cautious in his overtures than Benny had dared to hope. He had not sat anywhere near them now in the church, in the role of a chief mourner. She must keep her head and not let him take over. His style was so different to her father's, his humanity so little in comparison.

Benny wished she had someone who could talk it through with her, someone who really understood. Her glance fell on Jack Foley, whose face was stony in its sympathy. But she knew she wouldn't burden him with it.

The tedious in-fighting over a small shabby country shop. Nobody would bother Jack Foley with all that.

Not even if she loved him, and he loved her.

Outside the church, the people of Knockglen talked to each other in low voices. They commented on the group of young people down from Dublin. Must be friends of Benny, they deduced.

'Very handsome-looking couple that tall boy and the blonde girl. They're like film stars,' Birdie Mac said.

Eve was nearby.

'They're not a couple,' she heard herself saying. 'The tall boy is Jack Foley . . . he's Benny's boyfriend. He and Benny are a couple.'

She didn't know why she said it, or why Birdie Mac looked at her so oddly. Perhaps she had just spoken very loudly.

Or it didn't seem suitable to talk of Benny having a boyfriend at a time like this.

But in fact she thought Birdie didn't believe her.

As they walked to the open grave past the headstones Eve stopped and pointed out a small stone to Aidan.

'In loving memory of John Malone' it said.

It was nicely kept, weeded and with a little rose tree.

'Do you do this?' he asked.

'A bit, mainly Mother Francis, wouldn't you know it.'

'And your mother?'

'Across the hill. Over in the Protestant graveyard. The posh one.'

'We'll go and see hers too,' he promised.

She squeezed his hand; for one of the few times in her life she was without words.

They were very good to her, all Benny's friends. They gave her great support. They were courteous to the people of Knockglen and helpful back at the house after the funeral.

Sean Walsh thanked Jack for coming, as if Jack were there somehow as an act of respect to Hogan's Outfitters. Benny gritted her teeth in rage.

'Mr Hogan would have been very honoured by your presence,' Sean said.

'I liked him very much when I did meet him. I came to tea here with Benny months and months ago.' He smiled at her warmly, remembering the day.

'I see.' Sean Walsh, to Benny's disappointment, now did see.

'You didn't stay overnight, did you?' Sean asked loftily.

'No, I didn't. I came down this morning. Why?'

'I heard that one of Benny's friends did stay, up in the cottage on the quarry.'

'Oh, that was Aidan.' Jack was easy. If he was tired of Scan and this pointless conversation he didn't show it, but he managed to manoeuvre Benny away.

'That's the creep, isn't it?' he whispered.

'That's who it is.'

'And he had notions of you.'

'Only notions of the business, which he more or less got without having to have me as well.'

'Then he lost the best bit,' Jack said.

She smiled dutifully. Jack was going to be off soon, she knew. She had heard him tell Bill Dunne that they had to be out of Knockglen by two at the latest. He had asked Bill to make the move.

She made it easy for him. She said that he had been a tower of strength, and everyone had been wonderful to come all that distance. She begged him to get on the road while there was still plenty of daylight.

They were all going to squeeze into Bill Dunne's car.

There had been four coming down, but they were going to try and fit Eve and Aidan in as well.

Benny said that was terrific, rather than have them just hanging on waiting for a bus.

She smiled and thanked them without a quiver in her voice.

It was the right way to be, she could see Jack looking at her approvingly.

'I'll ring you tonight,' he promised. 'About eight. Before I go out.'

'Great,' she said, eyes bright and clear.

He was going out. Out somewhere on the night of her father's funeral.

Where could he be going on a Monday night in Dublin?

She waved at the car as it went around the corner. It didn't matter, she told herself. She wouldn't have been there anyway. Last Monday night when Father was alive and well, Benny Hogan would have been safely back in Knockglen by eight o'clock.

That's the way things had always been, and would always be. She excused herself from the group of people downstairs, saying she was going to lie down for twenty minutes.

In the darkened room she lay on her bed and sobbed into her pillows.

Selfish tears too, tears over a handsome boy who had gone back to Dublin smiling and waving with a group of friends. She cried for him as much as for her father, who lay under heaps of flowers up in the graveyard.

She didn't hear Clodagh come in and pull up a chair. Clodagh still wearing her ludicrous hat, who patted Benny's shoulders and soothed her with exactly the words she wanted to hear.

'It's all right, it's all right. Everything will sort itself out. He's mad about you. Anyone can tell. It's in the way he looks at you. It's better he went back. Hush now. He loves you, of course he does.'

There was an enormous amount to do.

Mother was very little help. She slept a lot of the time, and dozed off, even in a chair. Benny knew that this was because Dr Johnson had prescribed tranquillisers. He had said she was a woman who had focused her whole life around her husband. Now that the centre had gone she would take a while to readjust. Better let her get used to things gradually, he advised, not make any sudden changes or press her for decisions.

And there were so many things to decide, from tiny things like thank-you letters, and taking Shep for a walk, and Patsy's wages, to huge things like had Sean Walsh been made a partner yet, and could the business survive, and what were they going to do for the rest of their lives without Father?

Mr Green, the solicitor, had come to the funeral, but said that there would be ample opportunity for them to discuss everything in the days that followed. Benny hadn't asked him whether he meant Sean Walsh to be in on the discussions or not.

It was something she wished she had said at the time. Then it would have been a perfectly acceptable question as someone distressed and not sure of what was going on. Afterwards it looked more deliberate, and as if there was bad feeling. Which there wasn't – except on a personal level.

It was extraordinary how many of Nan's sayings seemed to be precisely appropriate for so many situations. Nan always said that you should do the hardest thing first, whatever it was. Like the essay you didn't want to write, or the tutor you didn't want to confront with an unfinished project. Nan was always right about everything.

Benny put on her raincoat on the morning after the funeral and went to see Sean Walsh in the shop.

The first thing she had to do was to avoid old Mike, who started to shuffle up to her with every intention of finishing the conversation he had begun in her house. Briskly and loudly so that Sean could hear she said that she and her mother would be very happy to talk to Mike later, but for the moment he would have to excuse her, she had a few things she wanted to get settled with Sean.

'Well, this is nice and businesslike.' He rubbed his hands together in that infuriating way, as if he had something between his palms that he was trying to grind to a powder.

'Thank you for everything, over the weekend.' Her voice was insincere. She tried to put some warmth into it. He *had* stood long hours greeting and thanking. It wasn't relevant that she hadn't wanted him there.

'It was the very least I could do,' he said.

'Anyway, I wanted you to know that Mother and I appreciated it.'

'How *is* Mrs Hogan?' There was something off-key about his solicitude, like an actor not saying his lines right.

'Fairly sedated at the moment. But in a few days she will be herself again and able to participate in business matters.'

Benny wondered, did Sean have this effect on other people? Normally, she never used words like 'participate'.

'That's good, good.' He nodded sagely.

She drew a deep breath. It was something else Nan had read. That if you inhaled all the air down to your toes and let it out again it gave you confidence.

She told him that they would arrange a meeting with the solicitor at the end of the week. And until then perhaps he would be kind enough to keep the shop ticking over exactly as he had been doing so well over the years. And out of respect to her father she knew that there would be no changes made, no changes *at all*; her head inclined towards the back room where old Mike had gone fearfully.

Sean looked at her astounded.

'I don't think you quite realise . . .' he began. But he didn't get very far.

'You're quite right. I *don't* realise.' She beamed at him as if in agreement. 'There are whole areas of the way this business has been run, and the changes in it that are planned and under way, that I know nothing about . . . that's what I was saying to Mr Green.'

'What was Mr Green saying?'

'Well, nothing, obviously, on the day of a funeral,' she said reprovingly. 'But after we have talked to him then we should all talk.'

She congratulated herself on her choice of words. However often he played the conversation over to himself again he wouldn't be able to work out whether he was included in the conversation with the lawyer or not.

And he would not discover the huge gap in Benny's own information.

She didn't know whether in fact he was a partner in the business yet, or whether the deed of partnership might not have been signed.

She had a distinct feeling that her father had died before matters were completed, but another even stronger feeling, that there was a moral obligation to carry out what had been her father's wishes.

But Benny knew that if she were to survive in the strange clouded waters that she was now entering, she must not let Sean Walsh know how honourably she would behave to him. Even though she disliked and almost despised him, she knew that Sean had earned the right to be her father's successor in the firm.

Bill Dunne said to Johnny O'Brien that he half thought of asking Nan Mahon to the pictures.

'What's stopping you?' Johnny asked.

What was really stopping him, of course, was the thought that she would say no. Why invite rejection? But she wasn't going out with anyone else. They knew that. It was odd, considering how gorgeous she was. You'd think half the men in college would want to take her out. But perhaps that was it. They *wanted* to, and yet did nothing about it.

Bill decided to invite her.

Nan said no, she didn't really like the cinema. She was regretful, and Bill didn't think she had closed the door.

'Is there anything you would like to go to?' he asked, hoping he wasn't making himself too humble, too pathetic.

'Well, there is . . . but I don't know.' Nan sounded doubtful.

'Yes? What?'

'There's a rather posh cocktail party at the Russell. It's a sort of pre-wedding do. I'd like to go to that.'

'But we weren't invited.' Bill was shocked.

'I know.' Nan's eyes danced with excitement.


'Bill Dunne and Nan are going to crash a party,' Aidan said to Eve.

'Why?'

'Search me.'

They thought about it for a while. Why go to a place where you might be unwelcome? There were so many places where Nan Mahon could just walk in and everyone would be delighted. She looked like Grace Kelly, people said, confident and beautiful without being flashy. It was a great art.

'Maybe it's the excitement,' Aidan suggested.

It could be the fear of being caught, the danger element like gambling.

Why else would you want to go to a wedding party with a whole lot of horsey people from the country, neighing and whinnying? Aidan asked.

Once Eve knew it was that kind of party she knew immediately why Nan Mahon wanted to go. And why she needed someone very respectable and solid like Bill Dunne to go with her.

Jack Foley thought it was a marvellous idea.

'That's only because you don't have to do it,' Bill grumbled.

'Oh, go on. It's easy. Just keep smiling at everyone.'

'That would be all right if we all had your matinée-idol looks. Advertising toothpaste all over the place.'

Jack just laughed at him.

'I wish she'd asked me to escort her. I think it's a great gas.'

Bill was doubtful. He should have known there would be trouble involved once he had dared to ask out someone with looks like Nan Mahon. Nothing came easy in life.

And it was all so mysterious. Who on earth would want to go to a thing like that, where they'd know nobody and everyone else knew everyone?

Nan wouldn't explain. She just said that she had a new outfit and thought it would be a bit of fun.

Bill offered to pick her up at home, but she said no, they'd meet in the foyer of the hotel.

The new outfit was stunning. A pale pink sheath dress with pink lace sleeves. Nan carried a small silver handbag with a silk rose attached to it.

She came in without a coat.

'Better in case we have to make a quick getaway,' she giggled.

She looked high and excited, like she had looked when she came into Eve's party in Knockglen. As if she knew something nobody else did.

Bill Dunne was highly uneasy going up the stairs, loosening his collar with a nervous finger. His father would be furious if there was any trouble.

There was no trouble. The bride's people thought they were friends of the groom, the groom's thought they were on the bride's side. They gave their real names. They smiled and waved and because Nan was undoubtedly the most glamorous girl in the room it wasn't long before she was surrounded by a group of men.

She didn't talk very much, Bill noticed. She laughed and smiled and agreed, and looked interested. Even when asked a direct question she managed to put it back to the questioner. Bill Dunne talked awkwardly to a dull girl in a tweed dress who looked over at Nan sadly.

'I didn't know it was meant to be dressy-uppy,' she said.

'Ah. Yes, well.' Bill was trying to imitate Nan's method of saying almost nothing.

'We were told it was a bit low key,' the tweed girl complained. 'Because of everything, you know.'

'Ah yes, everything,' Bill mumbled desperately.

'Well, it's obvious isn't it? Why else wouldn't they wait until spring?'

'Spring. Indeed.'

He looked over her head. A small dark-haired man was talking to Nan. They looked very animated, and they hardly seemed to notice that anyone else in the room existed.

Lilly Foley looked at herself in the mirror. It was hard to believe that the lines would not go away. Not ever.

She had been used to little lines when she was tired or strained. But they always smoothed out after rest. In the old days.

In the old days, too, she didn't have to worry about the tops of her arms, whether they looked a little crêpey and even a small bit flabby.

Lilly Foley had been careful about what she ate since the day her glance had first fallen on John Foley. She had been thoughtful, too, about what she wore, and even, if she were honest, about what she said.

You didn't win the prize and keep it unless you lived up to the role.

That's why it was heartbreaking to think that big overgrown puppy dog of a girl Benny Hogan should think that she had a chance with Jack. Jack was so nice to her, he had his father's manners and charm. But obviously he couldn't have serious notions about a girl like that.

He had driven her to Knockglen and gone to the funeral out of natural courtesy and concern. It would be sad if the child got ideas.

Lilly had been startled to hear Aidan Lynch talking of Benny and Jack as if they were a couple.

At least Benny had the sense not to keep telephoning him like other girls did.

She *must* realise that there could be nothing in it.


Benny sat at the kitchen table and willed the phone to ring. She was surrounded by papers and books.

She intended to understand all about the business before talking to Sean and Mr Green at the end of the week. She could ask no help and advice from old Mike in the shop and her mother was not likely to be any help either. Benny had bought a box of black-bordered writing paper. She had listed the people who sent flowers, hoping that her mother would write a short personal note to each of them. She even addressed the envelopes.

But Annabel's hand seemed to feel heavy and her heart listless. She never managed more than two letters a day. Benny did them herself eventually. She ordered the mortuary cards, with little pictures of her father, and prayers on them which people would keep in their missals to remind them to pray for his soul. It was Benny, too, who had ordered the black-rimmed cards printed with a message of gratitude for the sympathies offered.

Benny paid the undertakers, and the gravediggers, and

the priest, and the bill in Shea's. She paid everyone in cash as she had drawn a large sum from the bank in Ballylee. Fonsie had driven her there in his van.

'Wait till we get Knockglen on the map,' Fonsie had said. 'Then we'll have a bank of our own, not having to wait till the bank comes on Thursdays as if we were some one-horse wild west outpost.'

The man in the bank in Ballylee had been most sympathetic, but also slightly uneasy about advancing the sum.

'I'm meeting Mr Green the solicitor on Friday,' Benny reassured him. 'Everything will be put on a proper footing then.'

She hadn't imagined the look of relief on the banker's face.

She realised that she hadn't the first idea about how her father had run his business all these years, and she had only had a few days to find out.

As far as she could see it was a matter of two big books and a till full of pink slips.

There was the takings book. Every item was entered in that as it was received. Some of them were pitiably small. The sale of collar studs, sock braces, shoehorns, shoe polishing brushes.

And then there was the lodgement book, a big brown leather volume with a kind of window in the front of it. It was ruled in three columns: cheques, cash and other. Other could mean postal orders or in one case dollars from a passing American.

Each Thursday her father had queued up with others when the bank came to town. The bank signature at the end of each week's lodgement was the receipt and acknowledgement that the money had been put in the account.

In the till there were always pink raffle tickets, books that had been sent on spec by Foreign Missions, ideal for tearing off to write out what had been taken out. Each time there was a sum listed and a reason. 'Ten shillings: petrol.'

It was Wednesday, early-closing day. She had lifted both books from the shop and put them into a large carrier bag.

Sean had remonstrated with her, saying that the books never left the premises.

Benny had said nonsense. Her father had often pored over the ledgers at home, and her mother wanted to see them. It seemed a small comfort at a time like this.

Sean had been unable to refuse.

Benny didn't even know what she was looking for. She just wanted to work out why the business was doing badly. She knew that there would be seasonal highs and lows. After the harvest when the farmers got paid for the corn they all came and bought new suits.

She wasn't looking for discrepancies, or falsification.

Which was why she was so surprised when she realised that the takings book and the lodgement book didn't match up. If they took so much a week, then that much should have been lodged, apart from the small pink tickets called drawings from the till, which were very insignificant.

But as far as she could see by reading it and adding everything laboriously, there was a difference between what was taken and what was lodged, every single week. Sometimes a difference of as much as ten pounds.

She sat looking at it with a feeling of shock and despair. Much as she disliked him and wished him a million miles away from Knockglen, she did not even want to think for a moment that Sean Walsh had been taking money from her father's business. It was so unlikely, for one thing. He was such an over-respectable person. And for another, if he was to be made a partner why steal from his own business? And most important of all, if this had been going on for months and months, and maybe years, why was Sean Walsh living in threadbare suits in a cramped room two floors above the shop? She sat numbed by the discovery, and hardly heard the telephone ring.

Patsy answered it and said that a young man was looking for Benny.

'How are you?' Jack was concerned. 'How's everything?'

'Fine. We're fine.' Her voice sounded far away.

'Good. You didn't ring.'

'I didn't want to be bothering you.' It was still unreal. Her eyes were on the books.

'I'd like to come down.' He sounded regretful, as if he were going to say he couldn't. She didn't want him here anyway. This was too huge.

'No, heavens no. Please.' She was insistent, and he knew it. He seemed cheered.

'And when will you come back to me?'

She told him she should have things sorted out in some way by next week. Maybe they could meet for coffee in the Annexe on Monday.

Her lack of pursuit was rewarded. He really *did* seem sorry not to see her.

'That's a long time away. I miss you, you see,' he explained.

'And I miss you. You were wonderful, all of you, to come to the funeral.'

When he was gone from the phone he went from her mind too.

There was nobody she could ask about the books.

She knew that Peggy, Clodagh, Fonsie and Mario would understand. As would Mrs Kennedy, and many other business people in the town.

But she owed it to the memory of her father not to reveal him as an incompetent bungler, and she owed it to Sean Walsh not to mention a word of her suspicion until she knew it was true.


'Why won't you let me take you home?' Simon asked Nan after dinner.

It was the second time they had met that week after the extraordinary coincidence of their meeting at the cocktail party.

Nan looked at him and spoke truthfully.

'I don't invite anyone home with me. I never did.'

She sounded neither apologetic nor defiant. She was saying it as a fact.

'Might one ask why?'

She smiled at him mockingly. 'One might, if one was rather pushing and curious.'

'One is.' He leaned across the table and patted her hand.

'What you see is the way I am, the way I see myself. And how I feel and the way I am always going to be. Were you, or anyone to come home with me, it would be different.'

For Nan it was a long speech about herself. He looked at her with surprise and some admiration.

He realised that she was from somewhere in North Dublin. He knew her father was in building. He had thought that perhaps they lived in a big nouveau-riche house somewhere. They must have money. Her clothes were impeccable. She was always at the best places. He felt quite protective about her wish to keep her home life to herself, and her honesty in saying that this was what she was doing.

He told her gently that she was a silly. He didn't feel ashamed of *his* home, a falling-down, crumbling mansion in Knockglen, a place that had seen better days, where he lived with underpaid retainers, a senile grandfather and a pony-mad little sister. It was a pretty weird background to introduce anyone into. Yet he had invited her there after Christmas. He held his head on the side quizzically.

Nan was not to be moved. It was not a pleasure for her

to bring her friends home. If Simon felt uneasy about this, then perhaps they had better not see each other again.

As she had known he would, he agreed to dismiss the matter from their conversation and their minds.

In a way he was actually relieved. It was better by far than being paraded at a Sunday lunch and having expectations raised.

Heather was very bad at needlework at school. But after a conversation with Dekko Moore, the harness maker in Knockglen, she had decided that she should try to be good at it. He said that she might have a future for herself making hunting attire for ladies, and that they could be sold through Pine's or Hogan's.

It was Heather's project for the new term to learn to sew properly.

'It's awful, things like cross stitch, not real things like clothes,' she grumbled to Eve. It was Heather's twelfth birthday and the school allowed her to spend the evening out with a relation just as long as she was back by eight.

They had a birthday cake in Kit's house and everyone clapped when she blew out the candles. The students liked Heather, and her overwhelming interest in food.

They discussed the teaching of sewing in schools and how unfair it was that boys never had to learn cross stitch.

'At least you don't have to make big green knickers with gussets in them like we did at school,' Eve said cheerfully.

'Why did you have to make those?' Heather was fascinated by the tales of the convent.

Eve couldn't remember. She thought it might have had something to do with wearing them over their ordinary knickers and under their tunics when they were doing handstands. Or maybe she was only making that up. She really didn't know. She was annoyed with Simon for not taking his sister out on her birthday and only sending her a feeble card with a picture of a crinoline lady on it. There were hundreds of nice horsey birthday cards around that he could have got.

But more than that, she was worried about Benny. There was some problem, some worry about the business. Benny had said she couldn't talk about it on the phone, but she'd tell all next week.

It was something she had said at the end that wouldn't go out of Eve's mind.

'If you ever say any prayers, Eve, prepare to say them now.'

'What am I to pray for?'

'Oh, that things will turn out all right.'

'But we've been praying for that for years,' Eve said indignantly. She wasn't going to start praying for unspecified things, she told Benny.

'The Wise Woman would leave them unspecified for a bit,' Benny had said.

Benny didn't sound very wise or very happy.

'Simon's got a new girlfriend,' Heather said chattily. She knew Eve was always interested in such tales.

'Really? What happened to the lady from Hampshire?'

'I think she's too far away. Anyway this one's in Dublin, so Bee Moore told me.'

Ah, Eve thought, that's going to be one in the eye for our friend Nan Mahon and her notions.

Then the thought came to her suddenly. Unless of course it *is* Nan Mahon.

## 15

Benny returned the account books to the shop very early
on the following morning. She took Shep with her for the
outing. The dog looked around hopefully in case Eddie
might come out of the back room beaming and clapping
his hands, delighted to see his dear old dog arriving for a
visit.

She heard a footstep on the stair and realised that she
had not been early enough. Sean Walsh was up and
dressed.

'Ah, Benny,' he said.

'I should hope so too. We wouldn't want anyone else
letting themselves in. Where'll I leave these for you, Sean?'

Was she imagining it or did he eye her very closely? He
took both books and laid them in their places. It was a
good three quarters of an hour before the shop opened.

The place smelled musty and heavy. There was nothing
about it that would encourage you to spend. Nothing that
would make a man feel puckish and buy a bright tie or a
coloured shirt when he had always worn white. She

looked at the dark interior and wondered why she had never taken the time to notice these things when her father was alive, less than a week ago, and talk to him about them.

But she knew why. Almost immediately she answered her own question. Her father would have been so pleased to see her taking an interest, it would have raised his hopes again. The whole subject of a union with Sean Walsh would have been aired once more.

Sean watched her looking around.

'Was there anything in particular . . .?'

'Just looking, Sean.'

'There'll have to be great changes.'

'I know.' She spoke solemnly and weightily. That was the only language he understood, heavy pontificating phrases. But she thought a look of alarm came into his eyes as if her words had been menacing.

'Did you find what you were looking for in the books?' His glance never left hers.

'I wasn't looking for anything, as I told you I just wanted to familiarise myself with the day-to-day workings before I met Mr Green.'

'I thought your mother wanted to see them.' His lip curled a little.

'She did. She understands much more than any of us realised.'

Benny didn't know why she had said this. Annabel Hogan knew nothing of the business that her dowry had helped to buy. She had deliberately stayed away from it, thinking it to be a man's world where the presence of a woman would be an intrusion. Men didn't buy suits and get measured in a place with a woman around it.

Suddenly Benny realised that this had been the tragedy of her parent's life. If only her mother *had* been able to get involved in the shop, how different things would have been. They would have shared so much more, their interest in Benny would not have been so obsessive. And her mother, in many ways a sharper, more practical person than Eddie Hogan, might have spotted this discrepancy, if such it was, and headed it off long ago. Long before it looked as serious as it looked now.

Emily Mahon knocked on the door of Nan's bedroom and came in carrying a cup of tea.

'Are you sure you don't want any milk in it?'

Nan had taken to having a slice of lemon instead. It was puzzling for the rest of the family, who poured great quantities of milk in their tea which they drank noisily from large mugs.

'It is nice, Em. Try it,' Nan urged.

'It's too late for me to change my ways, and no point in it either – not like you.'

Emily knew that her daughter had found a special person at last.

She knew from the amount of preparation that went on in the bedroom, from the new clothes, the wheedling money from her father and mainly from the sparkle in Nan's eyes.

On the bed lay a small petal hat. It matched exactly the wild silk dress and bolero in lilac trimmed with a darker purple. Nan was going to the races today. An ordinary working day for most people, a studying day for students, but a day at the races for Nan.

Emily was on late shift; they had the house to themselves.

'You'll be careful, love, won't you?'

'How do you mean?'

'You know what I mean. I don't ask you about him because I know you think it's bad luck, and we wouldn't want to be meeting him anyway, lowering your chances. But you will be careful?'

'I haven't slept with him, Em. I haven't a notion of it.'

'I didn't mean only that.' Emily had meant only that, but it seemed a bit bald to hear it all out in the open. 'I meant, careful about not neglecting your college studies, and not going in fast cars.'

'You meant sleeping, Em,' Nan laughed affectionately at her mother. 'And I haven't, and I won't, so relax.'

'Are you and I going to keep teasing each other for ever, or will we give in to ourselves and go to bed together soon?' Simon asked Nan as they drove to the race meeting.

'Are we teasing each other? I didn't notice.'

He looked at her admiringly. Nothing threw her. She was never at a disadvantage.

And she looked really beautiful today. Her photograph would probably be in the papers. Photographers always looked for somebody classy as well as the ladies with silly hats. His companion was exactly the girl they would seek out.

They got stuck with a lot of people as soon as they went into the Enclosure. At the parade ring Molly Black, a very bossy woman with a shooting stick, looked Nan up and down with some care. Her own daughter had once been a candidate for Simon Westward's interest. This was a very different type of girl for him to parade. Handsome certainly. A student by all accounts, living in Dublin, and giving nothing away whatsoever about herself or her background.

Mrs Black moaned about the decree from Buckingham Palace abolishing the debutantes' presentation at Court.

'I mean, how will anyone know who anyone is once that goes?' Molly Black said, staring at Nan with gimlet eyes.

Nan looked around for Simon, hurt he wasn't at hand. She resorted to her usual system, answering a question with another.

'Why are they abolishing it, really, do you think?'

'It's obvious. You have to be presented by someone who was herself presented. Some of these are on rather hard times, and they take a fee from really dreadful business-men to present their ghastly daughters. That's what caused it all.'

'And did you have someone to be presented?' Nan's voice was cool and her manner courteous.

She had hit home.

'Not my immediate family, no, obviously,' said Mrs Black, annoyed. 'But all one's friends, one's friends' children. It was so nice for them, such a good system. They met like-minded people until all this crept in.'

'But I suppose that it's easy to tell like-minded people, to recognise them, do you think?'

'Yes it is, quite easy.' Molly Black was gruff.

Simon was at her elbow again.

'Having a most interesting conversation about doing the Season with your little friend here,' Mrs Black said to him.

'Oh good.' Simon moved them away.

'What a battle-axe,' he said.

'Why do you bother with her then?'

'Have to.' He shrugged. 'She and Teddy are everywhere. Guarding their daughters from fortune hunters like myself.'

'Are you a fortune hunter?' Her smile was light and encouraging.

'Of course I am. You've seen the house,' he said. 'Come and let's have a very large drink and put a lot of money we can't afford on a horse. That's what living is all about.'

He took her by the arm and led her across the grass through the crowds into the bar.

The meeting with Mr Green was very low key. It was held in Lisbeg. Benny had woken her mother up enough to attend by strong coffee and a stern talking-to.

Her mother must not ask that things be put off, or postponed until later. There was no later, Benny insisted.

Hard as it was on all of them, they owed it to Father to make sure that things didn't end in a giant muddle.

Benny had begged her mother to recall any conversations about Sean's partnership. The letter existed, the letter saying that the intention was there. Had there been anything at all that made her think it had been formalised?

Wearily, Annabel said that Father had kept saying there was no need to rush things, that they'd wait and see, that everything got done in time.

But had he said that about things in general, or about Sean's partnership?

She really couldn't remember. It was very difficult for her to remember, she complained. It seemed such a short time ago Eddie Hogan had been alive and well and running his own business. Today he was buried and they were meeting a solicitor to discuss business dealings that she knew nothing of. Could Benny not be more patient and understanding?

Patsy served coffee in the drawing room, aired and used now because of the stream of sympathisers who had filled the house. There were just the three of them. Benny said they would telephone Sean Walsh and ask him to join them after a suitable period.

Mr Green told them what they already knew, which was that the late Mr Hogan, despite numerous reminders, suggestions and cautions, had made no will. He also told them what they didn't know, which was that the Deed of Partnership had been drawn up and prepared ready for signature, but it had not been signed.

Mr Green had been in Knockglen as was his wont on four Friday mornings in January, but on none of these occasions had Mr Hogan approached him with a view to signing the document.

On the one occasion that Mr Green had reminded him of it, the late Mr Hogan had said that he still had something to think about.

'Do you think he had discovered anything that made him change his mind? After all he did write that letter to Sean before Christmas?' Benny was persistent.

'I know. I have a copy of the letter. It was sent to me in the post.'

'By my father?'

'I rather think by Mr Walsh.'

'And there were no hints or feelings . . . Did you get any mood that the thing was wrong, somehow?'

'Miss Hogan, you'll have to forgive me for sounding so formal, but I don't deal in the currency of feelings or moods. As a lawyer I have to deal in what is written down.'

'And what is written down is an intent to make Sean Walsh a partner, isn't that right?'

'That is correct.'

Benny had no proof, only an instinct. Possibly in the weeks before his death her father too had noticed that they seemed to be lodging less than they took. But there had been no confrontation. Had there been a face-to-face accusation he would have told his wife about it, and Mike in the workroom would have heard every word.

Perhaps her father had been waiting to find proof, so this is what she too must do.

Like her father she would ask to delay the partnership agreement, by saying that it was hard to know who should be the parties to it.

Mr Green, who was a cautious man, said that it was always wise to postpone any radical change until well after a bereavement. They agreed that now would be the time to have Sean Walsh to the house.

Fresh coffee was brought in when Sean arrived.

He explained that he had closed the shop. It was impossible to allow Mike to remain in control. He was a man who had given untold service in the past, no doubt, but as Mr Hogan used to say, poor Mike wasn't able for a lot in today's world.

Her father used to say that, Benny remembered, but he had said it with affection and concern. He had not said it with the knell of dismissal echoing around it.

The arrangement was that for the moment everything would carry on as it was. Did Sean think they needed to employ somebody on a temporary basis? He said that all depended.

Depended on what? They wondered. On whether Miss Hogan was thinking of abandoning her university studies and coming to work in the shop with him. If that were to happen there would be no need to employ a casual.

Benny explained that nothing was further from her father's dreams. Her parents were both anxious that she should be a university graduate, but she would nonetheless take a huge and continuing interest in the shop. She almost kicked her mother into wakefulness and a few alert statements that she would do the same thing.

Very casually and with no hint of anything being amiss, Benny asked if the very simple book-keeping system could be explained to them. Laboriously Sean went through it.

'So what's in the takings books should be more or less as what's in the lodging book each week.' Her eyes were round and innocent.

'Yes. Give or take the drawings,' he said.

'Drawings?'

'Whatever your father took out of the till.'

'Yes. And the little pink slips, they say what those were, is that right?'

'When he remembered.' Sean's voice was sepulchral and he sounded as if he were trying not to speak ill of the dead. 'Your father was a wonderful man, as you know, but forgetful in the extreme.'

'What might he have taken money out for?' Benny's heart was cold. There would never be any proof, not if this was believed.

'Well, let me see.' Sean looked at Benny. She was wearing her best outfit, the new skirt and bolero top that she had been given as a Christmas present.

'Well, maybe for something like your clothes, Benny. He might have taken money out to pay for an outfit without remembering to sign a drawing slip.'

She knew now that she was defeated.

\*

Kevin Hickey said that his father was coming up from Kerry and wondered could Mrs Hegarty recommend a good hotel in Dunlaoghaire?

'God, Kevin, you pass a dozen of them yourself every day,' Kit said.

'I think he wanted your choice rather than mine.'

Kit suggested the Marine, and she booked it for him.

She supposed that Kevin's father would like to see the house where his son lived all through the academic year, and urged the boy to bring him round for a cup of tea during his visit.

Paddy Hickey was a big, pleasant man. He explained that he was in machinery in the country. He had a small bit of land, but there wasn't the streak of a farmer in any of them. His brothers had all gone to America, his sons had all done degrees in something, but none of them in agriculture.

Like all Kerry men he said he put a great emphasis on education.

Kit and Eve liked him. He talked easily about the boy of the house who had died, and asked to see a picture of him.

'May he rest in peace, poor young lad who never got a chance to know what it was like down here,' he said.

It was awkward but affecting. Neither Kit nor Eve felt able to say anything in reply.

He thanked them for giving his son such a good home, and encouraging him to study.

'No hope he's getting anywhere with a fine-looking young girl like yourself?' he asked Eve.

'Ah no, he wouldn't look at me,' Eve said, laughing.

'Besides, she has a young law student besotted about her,' Kit added.

'That must leave you lonely here sometimes, Mrs Hegarty,' he said. 'When all the young folk go out of an evening.'

'I manage,' Kit said.

Eve realised that the man was revving up to ask Kit Hegarty out. She knew that Kit herself was quite unaware of this.

'You do manage,' Eve said. 'Of course you do. And people want you everywhere, but I'd love you to go out and be silly, just once.'

'Well, talking of being silly,' said big Paddy Hickey, 'I don't suppose there's a chance you'd accompany a poor, lonely old Kerry widower out for a night on the town.'

'Well, isn't that *great*,' cried Eve, 'because we're all going out tonight, every single one of us.'

Kit looked startled.

'Come back for her about seven o'clock, Mr Hickey. I'll have her ready for you,' Eve said.

When he was gone Kit turned on Eve in a fury.

'Why are you behaving like that? Cheap and pushy. It isn't at all like you.'

'It's not like me for *me*, but by God I'd need it for you.'

'I can't go out with him. I'm a married woman.'

'Oh yes?'

'Yes, I am. No matter what Joseph did in England I'm married anyway.'

'Oh, belt up, Kit.'

'*Eve!*'

'I mean it. I really do. Nobody's asking you to commit adultery with Kevin's father, you great fool, just go out with him, tell him about your living encumbrance across the channel if you want to. I wouldn't personally, but you will. But don't throw a decent man's invitation back in his face.'

She looked so cross that Kit burst out laughing.

'What'll I wear?'

'That's more like it.' Eve gave her a big squeeze as they went upstairs to examine both their wardrobes.


'I was wondering would you consider Wales a sort of break . . .' Jack asked Benny hopefully.

'No, it's too soon.'

'I just thought it could be a change. They always say that's a good thing.'

Benny knew what he meant. She longed to go to Wales with him. She longed to be his girl, on a boat sailing out from Dunlaoghaire to Holyhead. She longed to be sitting beside him on a train, and meeting the others and being Benny Hogan, Jack Foley's girl, with everything that that implied.

And she knew that a change could clear her head of the thoughts and the suspicions that buzzed around in it.

She had tried to get her mother to make a visit. To go to her brothers and their wives. They had been very solicitous at the funeral. But Annabel Hogan told Benny sadly that they had never approved of her marrying Eddie all those years ago, a man younger than she was with no stake in any business. They had thought she should have done better for herself. She didn't want to go to stay in their homes, large country places, and tell them tales of a marriage which had worked for her but which they had never thought anything of.

No, she would stay in her home and try to get used to the way things were going to be from now on.

But Benny didn't want to explain all this to Jack. Jack wasn't a person to weigh down with problems. The great thing was that he seemed so glad to see her. He took no notice of the admiring glances coming at him from every corner of the Annexe. He sat on his hard wooden chair and drank cup after cup of coffee. He had two fly cemeteries, but Benny said she had gone off them. In fact her whole being cried out for one, but she was eating no cakes, bread puddings, chips or biscuits. If she had not had Jack Foley to light up everything for her, it would have been a very dull life indeed.


Nan was delighted to see Benny back at lectures.

'I had no one to talk to. It's great to see you again,' she said.

Despite herself, Benny was pleased.

'You had Eve. Lord, I envy the two of you being here all the time.'

'I don't think Eve is too pleased with me,' Nan confided. 'I've been going out with Simon, you see, and she doesn't approve.'

Benny knew that was true: Eve did not approve, but then it would have been the same with anyone who went with Simon. She felt that he should have made some effort to make provisions for his cousin once he was old enough to understand the situation.

And she felt that Nan had been sneaky. Eve always claimed that Benny had been dragged to the Hibernian with the express purpose of making the introduction. Benny thought that was impossible, but there were some subjects on which Eve was adamant.

'And where does he take you?' Benny loved to hear Nan's cool comments on the high life that Simon Westward was opening up.

She described the back bar in Jammet's, the Red Bank, the Baily and Davey Byrne's.

'He's so much older, you see,' Nan explained. 'So most of his friends meet in bars and hotels.'

Benny thought that was sad. Imagine not going to where there was great fun, like the Coffee Inn, or the Inca or the Zanzibar. All the places she and Jack went to.

'And do you like him?'

'Yes, a lot.'

'So why do you look so worried? He obviously likes you if he keeps asking you to all these places.'

'Yes, but he wants to sleep with me.'

Benny's eyes were round. 'You won't, will you?'

'I will, but how? That's what I'm trying to work out. Where and how.'

*

Simon as it turned out had decided where and how. He had decided that it was going to be in the back of a car parked up the Dublin mountains. He said it was awfully silly to pretend they both didn't want it.

Nan was ice cool. She said she had no intention of doing anything of the sort in a car.

'But you do want me?' Simon said.

'Yes, of course I do.'

'So?'

'You have a perfectly good house where we can be comfortable.'

'Not at Westlands,' Simon said.

'And most definitely not in a car,' said Nan.

Next day Simon was waiting at the corner of Earlsfort Terrace and Leeson Street as the students poured out at lunch time, wheeling bicycles or carrying books. They moved off to digs, flats and restaurants around the city.

Nan had said no, when Eve and Benny asked her to come to the Singing Kettle. Chips for Eve and black coffee for strong-willed Benny.

They didn't see her eyes dart around as if she knew someone would be waiting for her.

They didn't notice as Simon stepped out and took her hand.

'How amazingly crass I was last night,' he said.

'Oh, that's perfectly all right.'

'I mean it. It was unpardonable. I wondered if you

might come down to a pretty little hotel I know for dinner and we might stay overnight. If you'd like to.'

'I'd like to, certainly,' Nan said. 'But sadly I'm not free until next Tuesday.'

'You're making me wait.'

'No, I assure you.'

But she was indeed making him wait. Nan had worked out the safe period, and next Tuesday was the earliest she dared go to bed with Simon Westward.

Clodagh was sitting in her back room sewing. She had a glass door and could see if there was a customer who needed personal attention. Otherwise her aunt and Rita, the new young girl they had taken on, could manage fine without her.

Benny came in and sat beside her.

'How's Rita getting on?'

'Fine. You've got to choose them – quick enough to be of some use. Not so quick that they'll take all your ideas and set up on their own. It's the whole nature of business.'

Benny laughed dryly. 'I wish someone had told that to my father ten years ago,' she said ruefully.

Clodagh went on sewing. Benny had never brought up the subject of Sean Walsh before. Even though it had been a matter of a lot of speculation in the last weeks. Just after Christmas there had been talk of him becoming a partner. Those who drank in Healy's Hotel said Mrs Healy spoke of it very authoritatively. Clodagh, since the day she had been barred from Healy's, made it her business to find out everything that went on there, and all subjects discussed at its bar.

She waited to hear what Benny had to say.

'Clodagh, what would happen if Rita was taking money from the till?'

'Well, for a start I'd know it at the end of the day, or else the end of the week.'

'You would?'

'Yes, and then I'd suggest cutting off her hands at the wrists, and Aunt Peggy would say we should just sack her.'

'And suppose you couldn't prove it?'

'Then I'd be very careful, Benny, so careful you wouldn't believe it.'

'If she had put it in a bank someone would know?'

'Oh yes. She wouldn't have put it in a bank, not around these parts. It would have to be in cash somewhere.'

'Like where?'

'Lord, I'd have no idea, and I'd be careful I didn't get caught looking.'

'So you might have to let it go if you couldn't prove it.'

'Crucifying as it would be, I might.'

Benny heard the warning in her voice. They both knew they were not talking about the blameless Rita out in the shop. They each realised that it would be dangerous to say any more.

Jack Foley said he'd ring Benny when he got to Wales. They were staying in a guest house. He was going to share a room with Bill Dunne, who was going for the laugh and a beer.

'You won't need me at all,' Benny had said, laughing away her disappointment that she couldn't be there.

'Fine though Bill Dunne is and everything, I don't think there's much comparison. I wish you were coming with me.'

'Well, ring me from the height of the fun,' Benny said.

He didn't ring. On night one, or night two, or night three. Benny sat at home. She didn't take her mother up to Healy's Hotel to try out one of their new evening dinners, at Mrs Healy's invitation.

Instead she stayed at home and listened to the clock ticking and to Shep snoring and to Patsy whispering with Mossy while her mother looked at the pictures in the fire and Jack Foley made no phone call from the height of the fun.


Nan packed her overnight bag carefully. A lacy nightie, a change of clothes for the next day, a very smart sponge bag from Brown Thomas, with talcum powder and a new toothbrush and toothpaste. She kissed her mother goodbye.

'I'll be staying with Eve in Dunlaoghaire,' she said.

'That's fine,' said Emily Mahon, who knew that wherever Nan was going to stay it was not with Eve in Dunlaoghaire.


Bill Dunne ran into Benny in the main hall.

'I'm meant to bump into you casually and see how the land lies,' he said.

'What on earth do you mean?'

'Is our friend in the doghouse or isn't he?'

'Bill, you're getting worse than Aidan. Talk English.'

'In plain English, your erring boyfriend, Mr Foley, wants to know if he dares approach you, he having not managed to telephone you.'

'Oh, don't be so silly,' Benny said, exasperated. 'Jack knows I'm not that kind of girl, going into sulks and moods. He knows I don't mind something like that. If he couldn't phone he couldn't.'

'Now I see why he likes you so much. And why he was so afraid that he'd upset you,' Bill Dunne said admiringly. 'You're a girl in a million, Benny.'

Heather Westward didn't really like the thought of Aidan coming on their outings, but that was before she got to know him. Soon Eve complained that she liked Aidan more than she liked Eve. His fantasy world was vastly more entertaining than her own.

He told Heather that he and Eve were going to have eight children, with ten months between each child. They would marry in 1963 and keep having children until late 1970.

'Is that because you're Catholics?'

'No, it's because I want something to occupy Eve during my first hard years at the Bar. I shall be in the Law Library all day and night in order to make money for all the Knickerbocker Glories that these children will demand. I shall have to work at night in a newspaper as a sub-editor. I have it all worked out.'

Heather giggled into her huge ice cream. She wasn't absolutely sure if he was being serious. She looked to Eve for confirmation.

'That's what he thinks now, but actually what's going to happen is that he's going to meet some brainless little blonde who'll flutter long lashes at him and giggle, and he'll forget all about me and the long-term plan.'

'Will you mind?' Heather spoke as if Aidan weren't there.

'No, I'll be quite relieved really. Eight children would be exhausting. Remember how Clara felt with all those puppies?'

'But you wouldn't have to have them all at the same time?' Heather took the matter seriously.

'Though it would have its advantages,' Aidan was reflective. 'We'd get free baby things, and you could come and help with the babysitting, Heather. You'd change four while Eve changed the other four.'

Heather laughed happily.

'I wouldn't want a brainless little blonde, honestly,' Aidan said to Eve. 'I'm no Jack Foley.'

Eve looked at him, astonished. 'Jack?'

'You know, the Wales outing. It's all right. It's all right, Benny's forgiven him. Bill Dunne says.'

'She's forgiven him for not phoning her. She doesn't know anything about a brainless blonde that should be forgiven.'

'Oh . . . I don't think it was anything really . . .' Aidan backtracked.

Eve's eyes glinted.

'Well, only a ship that passed in the night, or the evening, a blonde, silly Welsh ship. I don't know, for God's sake. I wasn't there. I was only told.'

'Oh, I'm sure you were told, and all the gory details.'

'No, really. And Eve, I wouldn't go and say anything to Benny.'

'I'm her friend.'

'Does that mean you will or you won't?'

'It means that you'll never know.'


Nan settled herself into Simon's car.

'You smell beautiful,' he said. 'Always the most expensive of perfumes.'

'Most men don't recognise good perfume,' she complimented him. 'You're very discerning.'

They drove out of Dublin south through Dunlaoghaire, past Kit Hegarty's and past Heather's school.

'That's where my sister is.'

Nan knew this. She knew that Eve went there on Sundays when Simon did not. She knew Heather was unhappy there and would much prefer a day school within reach of her beloved pony and dog and the country life she loved so much, pottering around Westlands. But she didn't let Simon know that she knew any of this.

With Simon she was determined to play it cool and distant. To ask little and seem to know little of his family and home life, so that he would not feel justified in prying into hers. Later, when she had really captivated him, then it would be time for him to get answers to his questions.

And by then he would know her well enough to realise that a drunken father and a messy family would form no part of the life that she led.

She believed that she had flirted with him for long enough and that she was timing it right to go to this hotel with him tonight.

She had looked the hotel up in a guide book, and knew all about it. Nan Mahon would not arrive anywhere, even at a hotel to lose her virginity, unprepared and uninformed about the social background of the place.

He smiled at her, a crooked lopsided smile. He really was most attractive, Nan thought, even though he was smaller than she would have chosen. She didn't wear her really good high-heeled shoes when she was out with him. He was very confident of her, as if he had known that this day would come sooner rather than later.

In fact that thought must have been on his mind.

'I was very glad when you agreed to come to dinner and let us spend a whole evening together instead of rushing away at a taxi rank,' he said.

'Yes, it's a lovely place, I believe. It has marvellous portraits and old hunting prints.'

'Yes. How do you know that?'

'I can't remember. Someone told me.'

'You haven't been here with any of your previous boyfriends?'

'I've never been to a hotel with *anyone*.'

'Come on now.'

'True.'

He looked slightly alarmed. As if the thought of what lay ahead was now more arduous and complicated than he had supposed. But a girl like Nan would not go ahead with something like this unless she intended it.

And when she said she had never been to a hotel with a chap, she might be speaking the literal truth. But a girl like this must have had some kind of experience, whether it was in a hotel bedroom or a sand dune. He would not face that problem until he had to.

There were candles on the table, and they sat in a dark dining room with heavy oil paintings of the hotelier's stern ancestors.

The waiter spoke respectfully like an old retainer, and they seemed to recognise Simon, and treat him with respect.

At the next table sat a couple. The waiter addressed the man as 'Sir Michael'. Nan closed her eyes for an instant. In many ways being here was better than being in Westlands. He had been right.

It was like a stately home, and they were being treated like the aristocracy. Not bad for the daughter of Brian Mahon, builders' provider and drunk.

Nan had not been telling him any lies, Simon realised with surprise and some mild guilt. He was indeed the first man she had gone to a hotel with in any sense of the word. She lay there with the moonlight coming through the curtains and catching her perfect sleeping face. She really was a very beautiful girl, and she seemed to like him a lot. He drew her towards him again.

Benny knew that Sean Walsh's partnership could not be postponed for ever. If only she could get her mother to take an interest in the matter. Annabel woke heavy and leaden from a sleep that had been gained through tablets. It took her several hours to shake off the feeling of torpor.

And when she did the loneliness of her position came back to her. Her husband dead before his time, her daughter gone all day to Dublin and her maid about to announce an engagement to Mossy Rooney, and only holding up the actual date out of deference to the bereavement in the family.

Dr Johnson told Benny that these things took time. Sometimes a lot of time, but eventually, like Mrs Kennedy in the chemist's, if the wife could be persuaded to take an interest in the business they would recover.

Dr Johnson looked as if he were about to say something and thought better of it.

He had always hated Sean Walsh. Benny wondered could it have been about him?

'The problem is Sean, you see,' she began tentatively.

'When was it not?' Dr Johnson asked.

'If only Mother was in the shop and properly there, taking notice . . .'

'Yes, I know.'

'Do you think she'll ever be able to do that? Or am I just running after a pipe dream?'

He looked affectionately at the girl with the chestnut hair, the girl he had watched grow from the chubby toddler into the big awkward schoolgirl and now fined down a bit he thought, but still by anyone's standards a big woman. Benny Hogan may have had more comforts than some of the other children in Knockglen whose tonsillitis and chicken pox and measles he had cured, but she never had as much freedom.

Now it looked as if the chains that bound her to home were growing even stronger.

'You have your own life to live,' he said gruffly.

'That's not much help, Dr Johnson.'

To his own surprise he heard himself agreeing with her.

'You're right. It isn't much help. And it wasn't much help saying to your mother, "Stop grieving and try living". She won't listen to me. And it was no help at all, all those years ago, telling Birdie Mac to put her mother into a home, or telling Dessie Burns to go to the monk in Mount Mellary who gets people off the jar. But you have to keep saying these things. Just to stay sane.'

As long as she had known him Benny had never known Dr Johnson make such a speech. She stared at him open-mouthed.

He pulled himself together. 'If I thought it would get that long drink of water, Sean Walsh, out of your business and miles from here, I'd give Annabel some kind of stimulant to keep her working in there twelve hours a day.'

'My father had an undertaking to make Sean a partner. We'll have to honour it.'

'I suppose so.' Dr Johnson knew that this was so.

'Unless there was any reason my father didn't sign the deed.' She looked at him beseechingly. It was the smallest hope in the world that Eddie Hogan might have confided his suspicions to his old friend Maurice Johnson. But no. With a heavy heart she heard Dr Johnson say gloomily that he didn't know any reason.

'It's not as if he was the kind of fellow who'd ever be caught with his hands in the till. He hasn't spent tuppence on himself since the day he arrived.'

Sean Walsh was having his morning coffee in Healy's. From the window he could see if anyone entered Hogan's.

Mike could cope with an easy sale, or measuring a regular customer. Anything more difficult would have to be monitored.

Mrs Healy sat beside him. 'Any word of the partnership?'

'They're going to honour it. They said so in front of the solicitor.'

'So they might. It should be done already. Your name should be above the shop, for all to see.'

'You're very good to have such a high opinion of me . . . um . . . Dorothy.' He still thought of her as Mrs Healy.

'Nothing of the sort, Sean. You deserve to make more of yourself. And be seen to be what you are.'

'I will. One day people will see. I move slowly. That's my way.'

'Just as long as you're moving, not standing still.'

'I'm not standing still,' Sean Walsh assured her.


'When can I see you again?' Simon said as he dropped Nan off outside University College.

'What do you suggest?'

'Well, I'd suggest tonight, but where could we go?'

'We could go for a drink anywhere.'

'But afterwards?'

'I'm sure you know some other lovely hotels.' She smiled at him.

He did, but he couldn't afford them. And he couldn't take her to Buffy and Frank's place where he stayed when he was in Dublin. And she wasn't going to take him to her home. A car seemed out of the question, and Westlands was off limits as far as he was concerned.

'We'll think of something,' he promised.

'Goodbye,' Nan said.

He looked after her with admiration. He hadn't met a girl like this in a long time.


'Benny, you look awful. You haven't even combed your hair,' Nan said.

'Thanks a bundle, that's all I need.'

'It *is* what you need, actually,' Nan said. 'You've got the most handsome man in college panting after you. You can't turn up looking like a mess.'

'I'll comb my hair then,' Benny said ungraciously.

The most handsome man in college was not panting

after her. He was looking like a guilty sheep, every time he met her he apologised for the whole Wales thing. Benny had said he must forget it, these things happened. And she wasn't making an issue of it, so why should he?

She had even arranged to stay in town this Friday, and suggested they have an evening together. She had asked Eve if they could stay in Dunlaoghaire. She had told Patsy that she would be gone and she had explained to her mother that she needed one night a week in Dublin. That everyone got over a loss in their own way, and her way had to be spending time with her friends.

Her mother's eyes, dull and listless, had clouded as if this was one further blow.

Worst of all Jack said that Friday wasn't a good night for him. They had a meeting in the rugby club, and then they'd all go for a drink afterwards.

'Make it another night,' he said casually. Benny had wanted to smack him very hard. He was as thoughtless as any child.

Why did he not realise how hard it was for her to arrange anything at all? Now she had to go and unpick everything she had arranged. Eve, Kit, Patsy, her mother. Bloody hell, she wouldn't. She'd stay in Dublin anyway that night and maybe go to the pictures with Eve and Aidan. They had asked her often enough, and to have a curry afterwards.

They were still whistling the theme tune of *Bridge on the River Kwai* when they arrived at the Golden Orient in

Leeson Street. They met Bill Dunne coming out of Hartigan's, and he joined them for the meal.

Aidan took them through the menu as an expert.

Everyone was to order something different, then they could taste four dishes and become curry bores.

'But we all like kofta,' Eve complained.

'Too bad. The mother of my children is not going to be a one-dish lady,' Aidan said.

'Where's Jack?' Bill Dunne enquired.

'At a rugby club meeting.' Benny spoke casually.

She thought she saw the boys exchange glances, but decided that she was imagining it. All that watching of Sean Walsh made her see glances and looks where none existed.

Jack Foley rang, very cross, on Saturday.

'I believe there was a great outing last night. The only night of the week I couldn't get away,' he said.

'You never told me. You always said Fridays were marvellous nights in Dublin.' Benny was stung by the injustice of it all.

'And so they were for some, Bill Dunne was telling me.'

'What night *are* you free next week, Jack? I'll arrange to stay in town.'

'You're sulking,' he said. 'You're sulking over the Wales thing.'

'I told you, I understand that you didn't have time to ring me. I am *not* sulking over a phone call.'

'Not the phone call,' he said. 'The other thing.'

'What other thing?' asked Benny.

Nan and Simon met three times without being able to do what they both wanted to do, which was to make love.

'What a pity you don't have a little flat in town,' he said to her.

'What a pity you don't,' she countered.

What they really needed was a small place where nobody would see them, somewhere they could steal in and out of.

It needn't be in Dublin. It could be miles away. Petrol was no problem. Apparently Simon put it all down for the farm. It was complicated, but it was free.

He just needed to be back in Knockglen to fill up.

Nan remembered Eve's cottage by the quarry.

She had seen where Eve put the key under a stone in the wall. Nobody went there. Except sometimes a nun to keep an eye on the place. But the nun wouldn't be keeping an eye on the place at night.

There were only lights in one cottage. Nan remembered that this was the one where a silent man called Mossy lived. She had heard Benny and Eve talking about him once.

'That's the man our Bee Moore wanted for herself, but some other took him away,' Simon said, smiling loftily at his local knowledge.

Nan had brought a pair of sheets, pillowcases and two towels. Plus her sponge bag, this time with soap as well. They must leave no trace of their visit.

Simon couldn't understand why they didn't just ask Eve. Nan said this was not even remotely possible. Eve would say no.

'Why? You're her friend. I'm her cousin.'

'That's why,' Nan said.

Simon had shrugged. They were here, so what did it matter? They dared not light the fire or the range. They brought the bottle of champagne to bed immediately.

Next morning it was very chilly.

'I'll have to bring my primus stove if I can find it,' Simon said shivering.

Nan folded the sheets and towels carefully and put them into the bag.

'Can't we leave them here?' he asked.

'Don't be ridiculous.'

Washed briskly in cold water, but as yet unshaven, Simon examined the cottage for the first time.

'She has some nice things here,' he commented. 'That came from Westlands, definitely.' He nodded at the piano. 'Does Eve play?'

'No, I don't think so.'

He touched other things. This was definitely from the house, and that might have been. He seemed to know even though he was only a child when his aunt had begun the ill-advised marriage, and started to live in this cottage instead of a Big House similar to the one she grew up in.

He laughed at a statue in place of honour on the mantlepiece.

'Who's he, when he's at home?' he said looking at a china figure of a man with a crown and a globe and a cross.

'The Infant of Prague,' Nan replied.

'Well, what's he doing on display like this?'

'Probably one of the nuns gave it to her. They do come and clean the house. Why not leave it there to please them when you don't have to look at it yourself?' Nan asked.

He looked at her admiringly. 'You're a businesswoman as well as everything else, Nan Mahon.'

'Let's go,' she said. 'It would be terrible to be caught first time.'

'You think there'll be others?' he teased.

'Only if you get your primus stove going,' she laughed.

On the first floor of Hogan's the rooms were big and high-ceilinged. That was where the family that owned the shop formerly used to live. It was where Eddie Hogan and his bride lived for the first year of their marriage. They had bought Lisbeg just before Benny was born.

The rooms on that first floor were still filled with lumber. To the furniture which was already stacked there came extra lumber, old rails not used in the shop, bales empty now of material, boxes. It was not a pretty sight.

The rooms where Sean Walsh had had his home for going on ten and a half years were on the floor above that.

A bedroom, another room which could be a sitting room, and a very old-fashioned bathroom with a geyser that looked like a dangerous missile.

\*

Benny had not been up there since she was about eight or nine.

She remembered her father saying that he had asked Sean would he like a key to his own area. But Sean had been insistent that he did not.

If he had taken the money he would not have hidden it in his own rooms, since that was the first place that would be searched if it ever were found out. It would be pointless for her to search. Pointless and dangerous. She had not forgotten Clodagh's heavy warning.

Things would be quite bad enough if Sean Walsh were not made a partner. There would be an outrage in Knockglen if he were wrongfully accused of stealing from her father. Benny did not relish the thought of hunting in his private rooms for some evidence. But she felt so sure that there must be something, perhaps in the form of a post office book from some faraway branch.

In the beginning as she had ploughed through her father's simplistic and even then not very thorough book-keeping methods, she had only *suspected* that Sean must be taking away a sum of money each week. But now she knew it. She knew it because of one simple lie he had told.

When she had tried to ask him to explain the system of drawing slips in front of Mr Green, she had asked for an example. Sean Hogan had pointed to the outfit she wore and suggested that Benny's own clothes might be something that her father drew money from the till to pay for. The thought had raised a lump in her throat.

Until she had looked at the cheques that were returned

with the bank statement. Her father had paid for every single garment he had bought for her. Clothes she had liked, clothes she had hated, each one paid for in Pine's by cheque with his slanting writing.

She wished it were all over. That Sean had been unmasked, and that he had left town. That her mother had recovered her spirit and gone in to run the business. And most of all that someone would tell her exactly what had happened in Wales.

Simon brought his primus stove. Nan brought two pretty china candlesticks, and two pink candles.

Simon brought a bottle of champagne. Nan brought two eggs, and herbs, and bread and butter. She brought some instant coffee powder too. She made them a glorious omelette in the morning.

Simon said it made him feel so excited they should go straight back to bed.

'We've just remade it with all her things, silly,' Nan said. Nan never referred to Eve by name.

After a time Simon stopped calling her Eve as well.

'Where does that daughter of yours spend the nights?' Brian Mahon asked.

'You were very drunk a couple of times, Brian. I think she was frightened. She goes out to her girlfriend, Eve, in Dunlaoghaire. They all get on together, that Eve and Benny down in Knockglen. They're her friends. We should be glad she has them.'

'What's the point of rearing children and having them stay out at night?' he grumbled.

'Paul and Nasey often don't come home. You never worry about them.'

'Nothing could happen to them,' he said.

'Nor Nan either,' Emily Mahon said, with a small silent prayer.

Nan was out three nights a week at least nowadays.

She did hope most fervently that nothing would happen to her beautiful golden daughter.

Mossy Rooney saw lights there one evening. He walked straight by.

Eve Malone must have come home quietly for a night, he thought to himself.

None of his business.

The very next day Mother Francis asked him if he would do a job on the guttering at the cottage. She came up to show him where it was falling away.

'Eve hasn't been back for weeks, the bold child,' Mother Francis scolded. 'If it wasn't for yourself and myself, Mossy, the place would fall down around her ears.'

Mossy kept his peace.

Eve Malone might have wanted to come back to her house without letting the nuns know.

Sean Walsh walked the quarry road at night. It was a place you didn't meet many people. It left him free to think of his plans, his hopes, his future. It was a space where he could consider Dorothy Healy and the interest she showed in him. She was several years older than him. There was no denying that. He had always thought in terms of marrying a much younger woman. A girl in fact.

But there were advantages in a union with an older woman. Eddie Hogan had done so after all. It had never hurt his prospects. He had been perfectly happy in his life, limited though it was. He had fathered a child.

Sean's thoughts were in a turmoil as he passed the cottage. He wasn't really aware of his surroundings.

He thought he heard music coming from inside. But he must have been imagining it.

After all, Eve wasn't at home and who else would be in there at midnight playing the piano?

He shook his head and tried to work out what length of time Mr Green the solicitor had in mind when he spoke about the regrettably snail-like process of the law.

Dr Johnson pulled his prescription pad across the desk. Mrs Carroll had always been a difficult person. He felt that she needed the services of Father Ross more than himself, but was it fair to dump all the neurotic moaners on to the local priest and call the whole thing a religious crisis?

'I know I'm not going to be popular for saying so, Dr Johnson, but I have to say what's true. That cottage up in the quarry is haunted. That woman died roaring and her poor halfwitted husband, God be good to him, may have taken his own life, God bless the mark afterwards. No wonder a house like that is haunted.'

'Haunted?' Dr Johnson was weary.

'No soul died at peace there. No wonder one of them comes back to play the piano at night,' she said.

Heather rang Westlands. She was coming home next weekend. Bee Moore said that was grand, she'd tell Mr Simon.

'I'll be going to tea with Eve in her cottage,' Heather said proudly.

'I wouldn't fancy that myself. People say it's haunted,' said Bee Moore, who had heard that for a fact.

Heather and Eve sat making toast by the fire in the cottage. They had long toasting forks that Benny had found for them.

She said there were amazing things on the first floor of Hogan's shop, but she didn't like to denude the place entirely in case bloody Sean *was* going to be a partner. So she had just brought something he could hardly sue for through every court in the land.

'Is it definite about the partnership?' Eve wanted to know.

'Some time, when you have about thirty-five hours . . .'

'I have.'

'Not now.'

'Do you want me to go away? I could go out to the pony,' Heather said.

'No, Heather, it's a long, long story, and it would

depress me telling it and depress Eve listening to it. Stay where you are.'

'Right.' Heather put another of Sister Imelda's wonderful tea cakes on the toasting fork.

'Anything new though?' Eve thought Benny looked troubled.

But Benny shook her head. There was a resigned sort of look on her face that Eve didn't like. As if Benny wanted to get into a big fight over something and lacked the energy.

'I could help. Like the old days. The Wise Woman would let two people tackle it.'

'The Wiser Woman might give in to the inevitable.'

'What does your mother say?'

'Very little.'

'Benny, will you have a toasted cake?' Heather's solution for nearly every crisis.

'No. I'm fooling myself that if I don't eat, this fellow will like me more and stop going off with Welsh floozies.'

Eve sighed heavily. So someone had told her.

They cycled along cheerfully, Eve saluting almost everyone they passed. Heather knew no one. But she knew fields that would have donkeys at the gate, and a gap in the hedge where you could see a mare and two foals. She told Eve about the trees and their leaves and how her nature scrapbook was the only thing she was any good at. She wouldn't mind school work if it was all to do with pressing flowers and leaves and drawing the various stages of a beech tree.

Eve thought how odd it was about two first cousins, with only seven years between them, living only a mile and a half apart, never having met, and one knowing every person who walked the road and the other every animal in every farm.

It was strange to ride up the ill-kept ridge-filled drive of Westlands with the young woman of the house.

Even though she was no outsider, coming to ask for a handout, Eve still felt odd and out of place.

'We'll go in through the kitchen.' Heather had thrown her bicycle up against the wall.

'I don't know . . .' Eve began. Her voice was an almost exact copy of Heather's when lunch at the convent was suggested.

'Come on,' Heather said.

Mrs Walsh and Bee Moore were surprised to see her, and not altogether pleased.

'You should have come in at the front when you had a guest,' Mrs Walsh said reprovingly.

'It's only Eve. We had lunch in the kitchen of the convent.'

'Really?' Mrs Walsh's face expressed very clearly that Eve had been unwise to receive the daughter of the Big House so poorly. The very least that might have been arranged was lunch in the parlour.

'I told her you made great shortbread,' Heather said hopefully.

'We must make up a nice little box of it some time.' Mrs Walsh was polite, but cold. She definitely didn't want Eve

Malone on her patch. From inside the house, Eve heard someone playing a piano. 'Oh, good,' Heather said, pleased. 'Simon's home.'

Simon Westward was charming. He came forward with both his hands out to Eve.

'Lovely to see you here again.'

'I didn't really intend . . .' She wanted terribly to tell him that she had no intention of being a casual visitor to his house. She must make him understand that she was doing it to please a child, a lonely child, a lonely child who wanted to share the place with her. But those words were hard to find.

Simon probably had no idea of what she was trying to say.

'It's great you're here now, it's been far too long!' he said.

She looked around her. This was not the drawing room she had been in on her first visit. It was another, south-facing room, with faded chintz and old furniture. A small desk stuffed with papers stood in the corner, a large piano near the window. Imagine one family having so many rooms and enough furniture to fill them.

Enough pictures for their walls.

Her eyes roamed around the portraits, hoping to find the one of her mother. The one she had not known existed.

Simon had been watching her. 'It's on the stairs,' he said.

'I beg your pardon?'

'I know Nan told you. Come, and I'll show it to you.'

Eve felt her face burn. 'It isn't important.'

'Oh, but it is. A painting of your mother. I didn't show it to you that first day because it was all a bit strained. I was hoping you'd come again. But you didn't, and Nan did, so I showed it to her. I hope you're not upset.'

'Why should I be?' Her fists were clenched.

'I don't know, but Nan seemed to think you were.'

How dare they talk about her! How *dare* they, and whether or not she was upset.

With tears stinging at the back of her eyes, Eve walked like a robot to the foot of the stairs where hung a picture of a small dark woman, with eyes and mouth so like her own she felt she was looking in a mirror.

She must have so little of her father about her, if there was so much of Sarah Westward there already.

Sarah had her hand on the back of a chair, but she didn't look relaxed and at peace. She looked as if she were dying for it all to be over so that she could get away. Somewhere, anywhere.

She had small hands and big eyes. Her dark hair was cut short, as the thirties fashion would have dictated. But looking at her you got the feeling that she might have preferred it shoulder length and pushed behind her ears. Like Eve's.

Was she beautiful? It was impossible to know. Nan had only said that she was in order to let Eve know that she had seen the picture.

Nan. Nan had walked around this house, as a guest.

'Has Nan been back here since then?' she asked.

'Why do you say that?'

'I just wondered.'

'No. That was the only day she was at Westlands,' he said.

There was something slightly hesitant about the way he said it, but yet she knew it was the truth.

Out in the kitchen they were getting a grudging afternoon tea ready. Eve thought that the food they were eating this day would never end, but Heather was loving it and it would be a pity to spoil it for her now.

Eve admired the pony and the way Heather had cleaned its tack. She admired Clara's puppies and refused the offer of one as guard dog.

'It would be good to look after your property,' Heather tried to persuade her.

'I'm not there often enough.'

'That's all the more reason. Tell her, Simon.'

'It's up to Eve.'

'I'm hardly ever there. Only the odd weekend. A dog would die of loneliness.'

'But whoever *is* there could walk him.'

Heather held an adorable little male puppy up for inspection. It was seven-eighths labrador, she explained, all the best, but with a little of the silliness taken out.

'No one but me, and Mother Francis from time to time.'

'Does she sleep there?' Heather asked.

'Heavens no. So you see, no need for a guard dog.'

She didn't think to ask why Heather supposed the nun might sleep in her little cottage. She just assumed it was part of Heather's continuing ignorance of convent life. And she didn't notice any change of expression in Simon's face.

Mrs Walsh came to tell them that tea was served in the drawing room.

Eve walked in to meet her grandfather for the second time in her life.

The grandfather that Nan Malone had told everyone was so charming and such a wonderful old man. She felt herself pushing her shoulders back, and taking those deep breaths that Nan said were so helpful if you had to do something that was a bit stressful. As if Nan would know!

He looked about the same. Possibly a bit more alert than on the previous occasion. She had heard that he had been taken ill on Christmas Day, and that Dr Johnson had been summoned, but that it had all passed.

It was touching to see Heather, the child who had grown up with him and who loved him as part of the only life she knew, sit beside him, nestling in to him and helping him with his cup.

'No need to cut up the sandwiches for you today, Grandfather. They're absolutely tiny. It must be to impress Eve.'

The old man looked across at where Eve sat awkwardly in a hard-backed and uncomfortable chair. He looked at her long and hard.

'You remember Eve, don't you?' Heather tried.

There was no reply.

'You do, of course, Grandfather. I was telling you how good she's been to Heather, taking her out of school . . .'

'Yes, yes indeed.' He was cuttingly distant. It was as if someone told him that a beggar on the street had once been a fine hard worker.

She could have just smiled and let it pass. But there was something about the way he spoke which went straight to Eve's heart. The temper that Mother Francis had always said would be her undoing bubbled to the surface.

'Do you know who I am, Grandfather?' she said in a loud, clear voice. There was a note of challenge in her voice that made them all look at her, startled, Heather, Simon and the old man. Nobody helped him out.

He would have to answer now or mumble.

'Yes. You are the daughter of Sarah and some man.'

'The daughter of Sarah and her husband Jack Malone.'

'Yes, possibly.'

Eve's eyes blazed. 'Not possibly. Definitely. That was his name. You may not have received him here, but he was Jack Malone. They were married in the parish church.'

He raised his eyes. They were the same dark almond-shaped eyes that they all had, except that Major Westward's were smaller and narrower.

He looked hard at Eve. 'I never doubted that she married the handyman Jack Malone. I was saying that it is possible he was your father. Possible, but not at all as definite as you believe . . .'

She was numb with shock, the words filled with hate

seemed to make no sense. His face, slightly lopsided, was working with the effort of speaking clearly and making himself understood.

'You see, Sarah was a whore,' he said.

Eve could hear the clock ticking.

'She was a whore with an itch, an itch that many handymen around the place found it easy to satisfy. We lost so many good grooms, I remember.'

Simon was on his feet in horror. Heather sat where she had been, on the little footstool, the one with beaded trimming at her grandfather's feet. Her face was white.

He had not finished speaking.

'But let us not think back over unpleasant times. You may indeed be the child of the handyman Jack Malone. If you wish to believe that, then . . . that is what you must believe . . .'

He reached for his tea. The effort of speaking had exhausted him. His cup shook and rattled against the saucer.

Eve's voice was low, and because of that all the more menacing.

'In all my life there has only been one thing I was ashamed of. I was ashamed that my father used a religious occasion, the funeral of my mother, to call down a curse on you. I wished he had more respect for the people who had come down to mourn. I even thought that God might have been angry with him for it. But now I know he didn't curse you hard enough, and his wish wasn't answered. You have lived on full of hate and bile. I will never look

519

on your face again. And I will never forgive you for the things you said today.'

She didn't pause to see how the others took her departure. She walked straight out of the door, and through the big hall into the kitchen. Without speaking to Mrs Walsh or to Bee Moore she let herself out of the back door. She got on her bicycle and without a backward glance cycled down the rutted avenue that led from her grandfather's house.

At the window of the drawing room Heather stood, tears pouring down her face.

When Simon came to comfort her she pummelled him with her fists.

'You let her go. You let her go. You didn't stop him. Now she'll never be my friend again.'


Dearest Benny, dearest, dearest Benny,

Do you remember those shaking tempers I used to get at school? I thought they had passed over like spots do, but no. I was so desperately and hurtfully insulted by that devil in a wheelchair out in Westlands that I am not normal to speak to, and I'm going back to Dublin. I haven't told Mother Francis about the row, and I won't tell Kit, or Aidan. But I will tell you when I'm able. Please forgive me for running off, and not meeting you tonight. I've asked Mossy to take this note in to you, but honestly it's the best thing.

See you on Monday.

Love from a very distraught Eve

When Mossy handed her the note Benny first thought it was from Sean Walsh, that it was some kind of threat or instruction to back off her investigations.

She was deeply upset to hear of a row bad enough to send Eve away in one of her very black moods. Sorry, too, because that nice child would be caught in the middle of it.

And selfishly she was sorry, because she had hoped to spend the evening telling Eve all about her ever-growing belief that Sean Walsh had been salting away money and to ask her advice about where they should look for it.

When Eve let herself into the house, Kevin Hickey was in the kitchen.

'Not out, wowing the girls on a Saturday night, Kevin?' she said.

She had promised herself that she would be a professional. This was her job, this house her place of work. She would not allow her personal anger to rub off on the guests.

Kevin said, 'I did have a sort of a plan, but I thought I'd hang around.' He nodded with his head, indicating upstairs towards Kit's room.

'She's had some bad news, apparently. Her old man died in England. I know she hated him, but it's a shock all the same.'

Eve came into the dark room with two cups of tea and sat beside the bed. She knew Kit would not be asleep.

Kit lay, head propped up by pillows and cushions,

smoking. Through the window the lights of Dunlaoghaire harbour were glinting and shining.

'How did you know I needed you?'

'I'm psychic. What happened?'

'I'm not sure. An operation. It didn't work.'

'I'm very sorry,' Eve said.

'She said it was very unexpected, the operation, that he had no idea that there was anything wrong with him. That if ever he were to die she was to ring me and say he had no idea there was anything wrong.'

'Who said all this?'

'Some landlady. He had given her fifty pounds in an envelope and said it was for her.'

Eve was silent. It was all curious and complicated and messy, like everything Joseph Hegarty seemed to have touched in his life.

'What's worrying you, Kit?'

'He must have known he was dying. That's why he came back. He must have wanted to spend the last few weeks here. And I didn't let him.'

'No, didn't he make a big point about that? He didn't know.'

'He *said* that because of the insurance.'

'The what?'

'Insurance policy. He's done what he never did in his life, he's made sure I'm provided for.'

Eve felt a big lump in her throat.

'They're going to bury him in England next weekend. They're extraordinary over there. Funerals aren't the next day. It's at a weekend so people could get there. Will you come with me, Eve? We could go on the boat.'

'Of course I will.'

Dear Heather,

I have to go to a funeral in England. Kit's ex-husband died. She needs me to go with her. That's why I won't be there on Sunday. Nothing to do with other things. See you the weekend after. Maybe Aidan will come as well.

Just so that you know it's urgent, otherwise I'd come.

Love, Eve

Heather read the letter silently at breakfast. Miss Thompson, who was the only nice teacher in Heather's opinion, looked at her.

'Everything all right?'

'Yes.'

Miss Thompson shrugged and left her alone. You couldn't push adolescent girls for confidences they didn't want to give.

She's never coming again, Heather said to herself over and over. She said it during morning prayers, during mathematics and during geography. Soon it became like the refrain of a song you can't get out of your mind. 'She's never coming again.'

Miss Thompson didn't remember about the letter, but she did say that she had noticed Heather was extremely quiet and withdrawn during the week. And she went back over it all, as they all had to on Friday night when Heather Westward didn't turn up for supper, and couldn't be found anywhere on the school premises. And she had not turned up at home. It had to be admitted by all those who didn't want to believe it, that Heather had run away from school.

## 16

As soon as Simon heard that Eve Malone had gone to England he said that was where they would find Heather.

Eve had not acknowledged his note of apology and explanation that his grandfather's hardening of the arteries made him unstable and unreliable and therefore someone whose opinions and views were best ignored.

Simon wondered had the note been too formal? He had told Nan about it, and to his surprise she had been critical of him. Normally she had been so cool, unruffled and giving so little of herself or her views.

'Why was it such an awful letter?' he asked anxiously.

'Because it sounds icy, like your grandfather.'

'It wasn't meant to be. It was meant to be low key, to try and bring down the temperature.'

'It did that all right,' Nan agreed.

On Friday when the school had been in touch he rang Nan.

'You know what you were saying about the letter . . . do you think that's why she took Heather?'

'Of course she didn't take Heather.' Nan was dismissive.

'So where is Heather then?'

'She ran away because you were all so awful.'

'Why don't you run away then?' He sounded petulant.

'I like awful people. Didn't you know?'

The schoolgirls were frightened. Nothing like this had ever happened before. They were all being asked extraordinary questions. Had they seen anyone come into the school, had they seen Heather leave with anyone else?

Her school coat was gone, her hated school beret left on the bed. Her pyjamas and sponge bag, her book of pressed flowers, her snaps of the pony and Clara and her puppies had disappeared. They were normally on display beside her bed where other girls had pictures of their families.

Heather's classmates were asked had she been upset? They hadn't noticed.

'She's very quiet really,' said one of them.

'She doesn't like it here,' said another.

'She's not much fun. We don't take much notice of her,' said the class bully.

Miss Thompson's heart was heavy.

There had been no sign of Heather on the bus. Mikey said he knew her well. A big thick lump of a child as square as a half door. Of course he'd have noticed her.

She would have had eleven shillings at the most, and possibly a lot less. Heather was known to spend a few pennies on sweets.

By the time Simon arrived at the school they had called the guards.

'Is it really necessary to have the police?' he said.

The headmistress was surprised. 'Since she hasn't gone home and you could throw no light on anywhere she might be . . .'

Miss Thompson looked at Simon with some dislike.

'And we have assumed that there was nothing for her to run home to apart from her pony and her dog, and she didn't go there anyway, so we thought you would have wanted us to call in the guards. It would be the normal thing for anyone to do, the normal thing to do.'

Simon looked at her miserably. Until now he hadn't realised how far from normal poor Heather's life had been.

He would make it up for her, when they got her back from England, which was undoubtedly where Eve had taken her.

At the guest house in Dunlaoghaire, the guards and Simon found three students holding the fort. Mrs Hegarty had gone to England to a funeral. Eve Malone had gone with her. Yes, of course they had left an emergency number where they could be contacted.

Mrs Hegarty had said she would ring anyway next morning to see if they had managed their breakfasts.

It was now eleven o'clock on a Friday night. The mail boat would not yet have arrived at Holyhead. Mrs

Hegarty would not be in London until seven in the morning. She and Eve would take the mail train to Euston.

There was a discussion about telephoning the police in Wales to look for Heather.

There was some doubt on the part of the two guards who were busy taking down details.

'You're absolutely sure this is where your sister is, sir?' they asked again.

'There's nowhere else she could be.' He was sure of that.

'Did anyone see Mrs Hegarty and Miss Malone off at the boat?' one guard asked.

'I did.' The boy who said he was Kevin Hickey, veterinary student, was spokesman.

'And were they accompanied by a twelve-year-old girl?'

'You mean Heather?'

Simon and the guards had not explained the purpose of their enquiries.

'Was she with them?' Simon asked.

'Of course not. That's the problem. Eve was worried because she was going to this funeral. She was afraid Heather wouldn't understand that she simply *had* to go away.'

Eve had left a box of chocolates which she had instructed Kevin to deliver to the school on Sunday, with a note from Eve.

'Could you give them to her, if you're connected?' he asked Simon.

They asked to see the note.

It was simple and to the point: 'Just to show I haven't forgotten you. Next week, *you* choose where we go. Love, Eve.'

Simon read it and for the first time since his sister's disappearance had been discovered tears came to his eyes.

On Saturday morning there could hardly have been anyone in Knockglen who didn't know about it. Bee Moore had done her fair share of telling, and Mr Flood, who had been one of the early recipients of the news, had been out consulting with the nuns in the tree, but finding to his disappointment that there was no heavenly message about Heather.

'I had hoped she might have been in heaven. Well, her kind of Heaven,' he said, remembering that he mustn't lose sight of the fact that the Westwards were Protestants.

Dessie Burns said there'd be a fine reward for anyone who found her, and mark his words she was kidnapped, and what's more kidnapped by someone in the know.

Paccy Moore said that the chances of being kidnapped by anyone in the know were slim. If you knew anything about the Westwards you'd know they could hardly pay their bills. If the poor child had been kidnapped it was by some gombeen Dubliner who thought that she was wealthy because she had a posh accent and came from a big house.

Mrs Healy said to Sean Walsh that they'd be singing a different song up at Westlands now. They had always been so distant and different, and things that happened to ordinary people never happened to them.

Sean wondered why she had turned against them. And

Mrs Healy said it wasn't a matter of that so much as being slightly peeved. Mr Simon Westward had implied that he would be having the most important of people to stay at the hotel in the near future, if they had evening dinners. Mrs Healy had put on those dinners, but Mr Westward had never partaken.

'But other people have,' Sean Walsh said. 'You've made your profit on them, that's all that matters.'

Mrs Healy agreed, but you didn't like to be hopping and jumping like people in a gate cottage just for the whims of the aristocracy.

She said as much to Mrs Kennedy from the chemist who looked at her thoughtfully, and said that it was a sad thing to have a hard heart when there was a child's life at stake, and Mrs Healy changed her tune drastically.

Clodagh told the news to Peggy Pine. Clodagh thought that a man in a raincoat had offered poor Heather a whole box of chocolates in Dunlaoghaire harbour.

Mario said that all the men of Knockglen should go out and beat the hedges with sticks looking for her.

'You see too many bad films,' Fonsie complained.

'Well, where do you think she is, Mister Smartie Pants?' Mario enquired.

'I see too many bad films too. I think she went for that bloody horse of hers, and rode off into the sunset.'

But it was one of the many theories that didn't hold up because the pony was still up at Westlands.

Peggy Pine went up to the convent to talk to Mother Francis.

'Eve was on the phone from London,' Mother Francis said. 'I could hear her grinding her teeth from there. Apparently they thought she had taken Heather with her. I dread to think what she'll do when she gets back.'

'But Eve would never have done that.'

'I know, but there was some kind of row up in Westlands last week. Needless to say Miss Malone didn't tell *me* anything about it . . . Lord, Peggy, where would that child be?'

'When you think about running away you think about running to somewhere you were happy.' Peggy Pine was thoughtful. It didn't get them much further.

Heather had never seemed to be all that happy anywhere.

Sister Imelda had started the Thirty Days Prayer. She said it had never been known to fail.

'The poor child. I never met a girl who was as appreciative. You should have heard her telling me how much she enjoyed toasting my tea cakes up in Eve's cottage.'

Suddenly Mother Francis knew where Heather was.

She reached into the gap in the wall and as she suspected the key wasn't there.

Mother Francis moved softly to the front door of Eve's cottage. It was closed. She peeped in the window and saw a large box on the table. There was something moving inside it, a cat she thought first, a black cat. Then she saw it was a bird.

A wing of black feathers came at an awkward angle out of the box.

Heather had found a wounded bird and had decided to cure it. Not very successfully, by all appearances. There were feathers and bits of torn-up newspaper everywhere.

Heather, flushed and frightened-looking, was trying to get a fire going. She seemed to be using only sticks and bits of cardboard. It would flare for a moment, and then die down.

Mother Francis knocked on the window.

'I'm not letting you in.'

'All right,' Mother Francis said unexpectedly.

'So there's no point in staying. Seriously.'

'I brought your lunch.'

'No, you didn't. It's a plot. You're going to rush me as soon as I open the door. You have people out behind the wall.'

'What kind of people? Nuns?'

'The guards. Well, maybe nuns as well, my brother. People from school.'

Mother Francis sighed. 'No, they all think you're in London. That's where they're looking for you as it happens.'

Heather stood on a stool and looked out of the window. There did not seem to be anyone else.

'You could leave the lunch on the step.'

'I could. But it would get cold, and I'll need the dish for Sister Imelda, and it means I don't get any.'

'I'm not coming home or anything.'

Mother Francis came in. She left a covered dish and the big buttered slices of bread on the sideboard.

She looked first at the bird.

'Poor fellow. Where did you find him?'

'On the path.'

Gently Mother Francis lifted the bird. She kept up a steady stream of conversation. It was only a young crow. The young often fell from the high trees. Some of them were quite clumsy. It was a myth to believe that all birds were graceful and could soar up in the air at will.

The wing wasn't broken, she told Heather. That was why the poor thing had been trying so hard to escape. It had just been stunned by the fall.

Together they felt the bird and smiled at the beating of the little heart and the anxious bird eyes not knowing what fate was in store for it.

Mother Francis gave it some bread crumbs, and then together they took it to the door.

After a few unsteady hops it took off in a low lopsided flight, just clearing the stone wall.

'Right, that's the wildlife dealt with. You get rid of all those feathers and newspapers and put back this box in the scullery. I'll see to lunch.'

'I'm still not going back, even if you did help me with the bird.'

'Did I say a thing about going back?'

'No, but you will.'

'I won't. I might ask you to let them know you're safe, but that's all.'

Mother Francis got the fire going. She explained to Heather about the dry turf, that stood leaning against the wall. She showed her how to make a little nest of twigs and get that going with a nice crackling light before putting on the turf. Together they ate Sister Imelda's lamb stew, and big floury potatoes, and dipped their bread and butter into the rich sauce.

There was an apple each and a piece of cheese for afterwards. Mother Francis explained that she couldn't carry much more, because the path was quite slippy and anyway she didn't want to arouse suspicion about where she was going.

'Why did you come for me?' Heather asked.

'I'm a teacher, you see. I imagine I know all about children. It's a little weakness we have.'

'There's nothing you can do.'

'Ah now, we never know that till we've examined all the possibilities.'

Eve rang Benny from England. She said she had spent more time making cross-channel phone calls than she had spent being any help to Kit. The whole thing was so infuriating she was going to tear off Simon Westward's affected little cravat and tie it round his thin useless neck and pull it hard until he was blue in the face and only when she saw his tongue and eyeballs protruding would she stop pulling.

'You're wasting time,' Benny said.

'I am. I suppose there's no news, is there?'

'Not that we've heard.'

'I've just had an idea where she might be. It's only an idea,' said Eve.

'Right. Who will I tell? Simon?'

'No, go on your own. Just go up as if you happened to be passing, and if the key isn't there you'll know she's inside. And Benny, you know how comforting you can be. She'll need that. Tell her I'll sort it out when I get back.'

On her way up the town Benny thought that she might buy some sweets. It would break the ice if Heather was there and needed to be talked out of the place. She had no money, but she knew that her credit would be good in Birdie Mac's.

As she passed the door of Hogan's she suddenly thought of the drawing slips. She could sign a pink piece of paper and write '£1 miscellaneous goods' on it. Why should she, from one business premises in the town, ask credit from Birdie in another?

Sean watched carefully.

'There, I think that's in order, isn't it?' she smiled brightly.

'You've taken a great interest in the mechanics of the business,' he said.

She knew he had something to hide. She *knew* it. But she must be careful. She continued in her same cheery tone.

'Oh well, one way or another, I'll have to be much more involved from now on,' she said.

He repeated the phrase with an air of wonder.

'One way or another?'

She shouldn't have said that. It implied that there might be doubt over his partnership. She had told herself so often to be careful. Best now to play the role of someone who was not the full shilling.

'Oh, you know what I mean, Sean.'

'Do I?'

'Of course you do.'

She almost ran from the shop. In and out of Birdie's and up to the square. She had better not go through the convent, even though it was quicker. The nuns would see her and ask her what she was up to.

Eve wanted this done on the quiet.


They had been over a lot of ground, Mother Francis and Heather Westward. The school in Dublin and the games and the other girls having lots of family coming to see them and houses to go to at weekends.

And how much Heather loved Westlands and how horrible Grandfather had been to Eve, and the fear that Eve might not come again.

And how nice it would be if there was a school that she could cycle to every day.

'There is,' Mother Francis said.

There were some areas that had to be argued through. Mother Francis said that there wouldn't be any effort made to convert Heather to Catholicism because the main problem these days was keeping those that were already in the flock up to the mark.

And there would be no idols of the Virgin Mary to bow down to and worship. There would however be statues of the same Virgin Mary around the school to remind anyone who wished to be so reminded of the Mother of God.

And there would be no need for Heather to attend religious doctrine classes, and she need have no fear that history would be taught with an emphasis on the Pope being always right and everyone else being wrong.

'What was it all about, the split?' Heather asked.

'The Reformation do you mean?'

'Yes. Was it about your side worshipping idols?'

'I think it was more about the Real Presence at Mass. You know, whether Communion is truly the Body and Blood of Jesus, or just a symbol.'

'Is that all it was about?' Heather asked, amazed.

'It started that way. But it developed, you know the way things do.'

'I don't think there should be all that much fuss then.'

Heather seemed greatly relieved that the doctrinal differences of three hundred years appeared to be so slight. They were just shaking hands on it when there was a knock on the door.

'You said you didn't tell anyone.' Heather leapt up in dismay.

'Nor did I.' Mother Francis went to the door.

Benny stood there with her speech ready. Her jaw dropped when she saw the nun and the angry little figure inside.

'Eve rang. She wondered whether Heather might have been here. She asked me to come and . . . and well . . .'

'Did you tell anyone?' Heather snapped out the question.

'No, Eve particularly said not to.'

The face relaxed.

Mother Francis said she had to be going now before the Community assumed that she too was a missing person and started broadcasting appeals for her on the wireless.

'Are they doing that for me?'

'Not yet. But a lot of people are very worried and afraid that something bad might have happened to you.'

'I'd better tell them . . . I suppose.'

'I could if you like.'

'What would you say?'

'I could say that you'll be back later this afternoon, that you'll be calling in to the convent to borrow a bicycle.'

She was gone.

Benny looked at Heather. She pushed the box of sweets over to her.

'Come on, let's finish it. We'll tear through it, both layers.'

'What about the man who fancies Welsh women, the one you're getting thin for?'

'I think it's too late.'

Happily they ate the chocolates. Heather asked about the school and who were the hard teachers and who were the easy ones.

Benny asked about her grandfather and whether he knew all the awful things he had said.

'Did she tell everyone?' Heather looked ashamed.

'Only me. I'm her great friend.'

'I don't have any great friends.'

'Yes, you do. You have Eve.'

'Not any more.'

'Of course you do. You don't understand Eve if you'd think a thing like that mattered. She didn't want to like you in the first place because she had all the bad memories about that old business years ago. But she did, and she always will.'

Heather looked doubtful.

'Yes, and you can have me, too, if you want me, and Eve's Aidan as a sort of circle of friends. I know we're way too old for you, but until you make your own.'

'And what about the man who goes off with thin Welsh people? Is he in the circle?'

'On the edges,' Benny said.

In a way that was more true than she meant it to be. She had met Jack twice during the week, and he had been rushing. There was a lot of training, and hardly any time to speak alone.

He had been very contrite about some still unspecified incident during the friendly match played in Wales. Some girls had come to the club, and it had all been a bit of fun, a laugh, nothing to it. Tales had been greatly exaggerated. In vain Benny tried to tell him that she had heard no tales so nothing could be made better or worse because there had been no stories to exaggerate.

Jack had said that everyone was entitled to a bit of fun, and he never minded her jiving away in Mario's when he wasn't around. It had been highly unsatisfactory.

There was an uneven number of sweets, so they halved the last one, a coffee cream.

They tidied up Eve's house and damped the embers of the fire. Together they left and replaced the key in the wall.

Mossy nodded to them gravely as he passed by.

'Who was that?' Heather whispered.

'Mossy Rooney.'

'He's broken Bee Moore's heart,' Heather said disapprovingly.

'Not permanently. She's going to be Patsy's bridesmaid when the time comes.'

'I suppose people get over these things,' Heather said.

Mother Francis handed Heather Eve's bicycle.

'Off you go. Your brother will be waiting for you. I said he should let you go home on your own pedals.'

The nun produced Heather's small bag of possessions, her nature book, her pyjamas, the photographs of the horse and dog and the small sponge bag. She had wrapped them neatly in brown paper and twine and clipped them on to the back of the bicycle.

Benny and Mother Francis watched her cycle off.

'You guessed! Eve always said you had second sight.'

'If I have then I'd say you have some big worry on your mind.'

Benny was silent.

'I'm not prying.'

'No, of course not.' Benny's murmur was automatic politeness.

'It's just being what people laughingly call out of the real world . . . I hear a great deal about what goes on amongst those who are in it.'

Benny's glance was enquiring.

'And Peggy Pine and I were school friends years ago, like you and Eve . . .'

Benny waited. Mother Francis said that if it was of any use to Benny she should know that Sean Walsh had enough money, from whatever source, to think himself able to buy one of the small cottages up in the quarry road. Cash deposit.

Benny's mother said that Jack Foley had rung. No, he hadn't left a message. Benny thought harsh things about Heather Westward for having taken her out of the house when the call came. And she wished that she had not run so readily to do Eve's bidding.

But then Eve would have done the same for her. And if he loved her and wanted to talk to her, he would ring again.

If he loved her.

Nan's mother came to say that there was a Simon Westward on the phone.

Nan's tone was cold.

'Did I give you my phone number?' she asked.

'No, but that's irrelevant. Heather's home.'

'Oh, I am glad. Where was she?' Nan was still wondering how he knew where to telephone. She had been adamant about not telling anyone how to contact her.

'She was in Eve's cottage, as it happens.'

It had been a distinct possibility that Nan and Simon might have been there also. The thought silenced them both for a moment.

'Is she all right?'

'She's fine, but I can't leave. I have to sort her out.'

Nan had been ironing her dress for the last hour. It had complicated pleats in the linen. Her hair was freshly washed and she had painted her toenails a pearly pink.

'Yes, of course you must stay,' she said.

'Oh good. I thought you'd be annoyed.'

'The main thing is that she's safe.'

There was no hint of the rage that Nan was feeling. His tone was so casual.

Simon said that apparently Heather had been very unhappy at the school in Dublin. Nan sighed. Eve had been saying this for months. Heather had probably been saying it for years, but Simon had not listened. There were just a few schools that were suitable for his sister and she would jolly well have to learn to like the one she was in. That had been his attitude.

'So maybe tomorrow?' He was confident and sure.

'Sorry?'

'Tomorrow, Sunday night. Things will have sorted themselves out here . . .'

'And?'

'And I was hoping you might come down . . . for the night?'

'Well, I'd love to.' Nan smiled. At last he had invited her. It had taken some time, but he was inviting her to Westlands. She would be given a guest room. She was going there as Mr Simon's young lady.

'That's marvellous.' He sounded relieved. 'You get the last bus. I'll go to the cottage and set things up for us.'

'The cottage?' she said.

'Well, we know Eve's in England.'

There was a silence.

'What's wrong?' he asked.

'Suppose Heather decides to call again?'

'No, by heavens, she'll get a strict talking-to about respecting other people's property.'

He saw no irony in this at all.

'I think not,' she said.

'Nan?'

She had hung up on him.


Joseph Hegarty had made a few, but not many, friends during his years in England. They had gathered to speak well of him after his funeral.

In the back room of a bar they sat, an ill-assorted group. A landlady who had been fond of him; whenever he didn't have the rent, he always did so many repairs around the house, it was twenty times better than having a lodger, she confided. Eve could see the pain in Kit's face. That Joseph Hegarty should be without the rent was bad enough, but that he should do plumbing and carpentry for a strange woman in England rather than in his own house in Dunlaoghaire was even worse.

If the barmaid was amongst the group she did not declare herself. The whole thing had such an unreal atmosphere about it, Eve felt that they were taking part in some play. Any moment the curtain would fall and they would all start talking normally again.

The only clue to why Joseph Hegarty might have stayed so long in this twilight world where he touched so little on people around him came from Fergus, a Mayo man, who said he was a friend.

Fergus had left a long time ago. There had been no row, no one thing that drove him out of his smallholding in the West of Ireland. He just felt one day that he wanted to be free and he had taken a train to Dublin, and then the boat.

His wife was now dead, his family grown. None of them wanted anything to do with him, and in many ways it was for the best. If he had gone back, he would have had to explain.

'At least Joe saw his son last summer. That was the great thing,' he said.

Kit looked up, startled.

'No, he didn't. Francis never saw him since he was a child.'

'But didn't he write to him and all?'

'No.' Kit's voice was clipped.

Eve went to stand beside Fergus the Mayo man at the bar later.

'So he did keep in touch with his son then?'

'Yes, I think I was out of order. The wife is very bitter. I shouldn't have said . . . I didn't know.'

'In time she'll be glad. In time I'll tell her properly. And maybe she'll want to talk to you.' She took out a diary and a pen. 'Where would you be . . . if we wanted to get in touch?'

'Ah, now, that's hard to say.' The look in the eyes of Fergus became wary. He wasn't a man who liked to plan too far ahead.

There was a discussion with the man from the insurance, and some documents to sign. Eve and Kit went to Euston and took the train to Holyhead.

For a long time Kit Hegarty looked out of the window at the land where her husband had lived for so long.

'What are you thinking about?' Eve asked.

'About you. You were very good to come with me. Several people thought you were my daughter.'

'I seem to have been on the phone most of the time.' Eve was apologetic.

'Thank God it turned out all right.'

'We don't know that yet. They're a weird bunch. They could send her back there. I hate being beholden to them, I really do.'

'You don't have to be,' said Kit. 'The first thing I'm going to do when I get the insurance money is to give you a sum. You can walk back up that avenue, and throw it back. Throw it on the floor.'

Patsy said that with all their talk about teaching them to work in a house, the orphanage had been very bad at teaching them to sew.

Mossy had said that his mother was expecting Patsy to have made a lot of things for her hope chest, like pillowcases, and hemmed them herself.

She was struggling away in the kitchen. The trouble was that often she pricked her fingers and the nice piece of linen got stained with blood.

'He's mad. Can't you buy grand pillowcases for half nothing up in McBirney's in Dublin?' Benny said indignantly.

But this wasn't the point. Apparently Mrs Rooney expected a suitable bride for Mossy to be able to turn a hem properly and sew dainty stitches. Patsy had to try harder and put up with all this nonsense because she had nothing else to bring to the marriage. No family, no bit of land, not even her father's name.

'Does it have to be hand done? Couldn't it be on a machine?' Benny was worse than useless, her own stitching was in big loops, irregular and impatient.

'What's the difference? We haven't a machine that works.'

'We'll ask Paccy to mend it. Let's look on it as a challenge,' Benny said.

*

Paccy Moore said that a horse with heavy hooves must have been using the sewing machine, and that if you had a fleet of highly paid engineers they wouldn't be able to put it back in working order. Tell the lady of the house to throw it out, was his advice. And surely they must have had an old one years ago, one of those nice firm ones that people like Benny and Patsy couldn't break.

They went sadly back to Lisbeg. There wasn't much point in telling the lady of the house anything. The listless manner hadn't changed. They *did* have an old sewing machine somewhere with a treadle underneath. Benny remembered seeing it once, even playing at it. But it was useless to talk to Mother. She would try to remember and then say that her headache was coming back.

But Benny hated to see Patsy, who had started life with so little, continue in this struggle to please.

'You see, I can't have bought ones, Benny. The old rip gives me the material herself, just to make sure.'

'I'll ask Clodagh to do them for you. She loves a challenge too,' said Benny.

Clodagh said they should both be shot for not knowing how to do a simple seam. She showed them on the machine.

'Go on, do it yourselves,' she urged.

'There isn't time for that. You do it and we'll do something in return for you. Tell us what you want us to do.'

'Ask my aunt to lunch and keep her there all afternoon. I want to rearrange everything in the shop: if I knew someone was looking after Peg I could get a gang in to

547

help me. When she comes back it'll be too late to change it.'

'When?'

'Thursday, early closing day.'

'And you'll do all these pillowcases and some sheets and two bolster cases?'

'It's a deal.'

Jack Foley said he was going to skip lectures on Thursday and they'd go to the pictures.

'Not Thursday. Any other day.'

'Bloody hell. Isn't that the day you don't have lectures?'

'Yes, but I have to go back to Knockglen. There's this great scheme . . .'

'Oh, there's *always* some great scheme in Knockglen,' he said.

'Friday. I can stay the night in Dublin.'

'All right.'

Benny knew she would have to do something to try and smooth down Jack's ruffled feelings. She was very much afraid it might involve doing something more adventurous in the car than they had done already.

As Patsy said, at least three times a day, men were the divil.

Nan had taken a risk in hanging up on Simon. She had also left the phone slightly off the hook in case he called again. She went angrily up to her room and lay on her bed. The freshly ironed dress hung on its hanger, her pink nails twinkled at her, she really should go out somewhere and get value from all this primping and preening.

But Nan Mahon didn't want to arrange a meeting with Bill Dunne, or Johnny O'Brien, or anyone. Not even the handsome Jack Foley, who had been prowling discontentedly since Benny was never around.

Benny. Simon must have got her telephone number from Benny. He had probably pleaded with her and said it was urgent. Benny was very foolish, Nan thought. A handsome man like Jack Foley should not be left on his own in Dublin. All very well to say that the Rosemary Ryans and Sheilas knew he was spoken for. But when it came to it people often forgot loyalties. In Dublin things were not more immediate than that.

'You're very cross,' Heather said.

'Of course I am. Why couldn't you have told us how awful it was?'

Heather had, many times, but nobody had listened. Her grandfather had looked away dreamily, and Simon had said everyone hated school. You just had to grin and bear it. Mrs Walsh had said that in her position Heather had to have a suitable education, meeting the people she would be meeting socially later on, not the daughters of every poor fellow down on this luck which is what you'd meet in a village school.

She hadn't expected Simon to be so annoyed. He had been on the phone to someone and had come back in a great temper.

'She hung up on me,' he had said, several times.

At first Heather had been pleased to see him distracted, but she realised that it wasn't making their conversation about her future any easier.

'Mother Francis will talk to you about the school,' she began.

'That's all that bloody woman wants. First they got Eve, and now they want you.'

'That's not true. They took Eve because nobody else wanted her.'

'Oh, they have *you* well indoctrinated, I can see that.'

'But who did want her, Simon? Tell me.'

'That's not the point. The point is that we have planned an expensive education for you.'

'It'll be much cheaper here, much. I asked. It's hardly anything.'

'No. You don't understand. It's not possible.'

'*You* don't understand,' Heather said, twelve years of age and confronting him with her fists clenched. As she told him that she would run away every single time she was sent back to that school, her eyes flashed and she reminded him suddenly of the way Eve had looked that day she came to Westlands.

Jack seemed to have got over his bad temper. On Thursday morning he took Benny to coffee in the Annexe. She ate a corner of one of his fly cemeteries in order to prevent him from overdosing on them, and being pronounced unfit to play in the next match.

He put his hand over hers.

'I am a bad-tempered boorish bear, or bearish boor, whichever you like,' he apologised.

'It won't be long now. I'll have everything sorted out, I swear,' Benny said.

'Days, weeks, months, decades?' he asked, but he was smiling at her. He was the old Jack.

'Weeks. A very few weeks.'

'And then you'll be able to romp shamelessly around Dublin with me, giving in to my every base wish and physical lust.'

'Something like that,' she laughed.

'I'll believe it when I see it,' he said, looking straight at her. 'You do know how much I want you, don't you?'

She swallowed, not able to find the right words. As it happened, she didn't need to. Nan had approached.

'Is this a Sean-Carmel impersonation, or can I join you for coffee?'

Benny was relieved. Jack went back to the counter to collect it.

'I'm not interrupting anything am I, seriously?' Nan was marvellous. You could actually ask her to take her coffee off and join another group. Nan wouldn't mind. She was a great apostle of the solidarity between girls. But in fact it was much better not to walk any further down the path of discussing sex.

'I wanted Benny to come to *Swamp Women* but she's stood me up,' Jack said, in a mock-mournful voice.

'Why d'ya not go to *Swamp Women* with the nice

gen'leman, honey?' Nan asked. 'I sho would in yore place.'

'Then come with me,' Jack suggested.

Nan looked at Benny, who nodded eagerly.

'Oh, please do, Nan. He's been talking about *Swamp Women* for days.'

'I'll go and keep him from harm,' Nan promised.

On their way to the cinema they met Simon Westward.

'Have you been avoiding me?' he asked curtly.

Nan smiled. She introduced the two men. Anyone passing by would have thought they made an extraordinarily handsome tableau standing there, two of them in college scarves, the third small, and very county.

'We're going to *Swamp Women*. It's about escaped women prisoners and alligators.'

'Would you like to join us?' Jack suggested.

Simon looked up at Jack, a long glance.

'No, thanks all the same.'

'Why did you ask him to come with us? Because you knew he wouldn't?' Nan asked.

'Nope. Because I could see how much he fancied you.'

'Only mildly, I think.'

'No, seriously, I think,' Jack said.

Because Nan knew that Simon would have turned to look after them, she took Jack's arm companionably.

Benny went back to Knockglen on the bus in high good humour. Jack was cheerful again. He did say he wanted her, he couldn't have been more explicit. And now she didn't even have to worry about him being left high and dry. Nan had gone to the silly film with him.

All Benny had to do now was keep Peggy Pine entertained while unmentionable things went on in her shop. She knew that Fonsie, Dekko Moore, Teddy Flood and Rita were all poised. Peggy must be kept off the scene until at least five o'clock.

When she got into Lisbeg Benny was pleased to see that Patsy had made a good soup, and there were plain scones to be served with it. Mr Flood had sent down a small leg of lamb, there was the smell of mint sauce made in a nice china sauce boat.

Mother wore a pale grey twinset with her black skirt, and even a small brooch at the neck. She looked more cheerful. Probably she needed company, Benny realised. She certainly seemed a lot less listless than on other days.

Peggy drank three thimblefuls of sherry enthusiastically, and so did Mother. Benny had never known Clodagh's aunt in better form. She told Mother that business was the best way to live your life, and that if she had her time, and her chances, all over again she would still think so.

She confided to them something that they already knew, which was that she had been Disappointed earlier in life. But that she bore the gentleman in question no ill will. He had done her a service in fact. The lady he had chosen did not have the look of a contented person. Peggy Pine had seen her from time to time over the years. While she in her little shop was as happy as anything.

Mother listened interested, and Benny began to have the stirrings of hope that Peggy might be able to achieve for Mother what she had not been able to do. Peggy might make Annabel Hogan rediscover some kind of reason for living.

'The young people are the hope, you know,' Peggy said.

Benny prayed that the transformation taking place in the shop at this moment would not be of such massive proportions as to make Peggy withdraw this view.

'Ah, yes, we've been blessed with Sean Walsh,' Annabel said.

'Well, yes, as long as you'll be in there to keep the upper hand,' Peggy warned.

'I couldn't be going in interfering. He did fine in poor Eddie's time.'

'Eddie was there to be a balance to him.'

'Not much of a balance I'd be,' Annabel Hogan said. 'I don't know the first thing about it.'

'You'll learn.'

Benny saw the dangerous trembling of her mother's lip. She hastened to come in and explain to Peggy that things were a little bit up in the air at the moment. There had been a question of Sean being made a partner and that should be cleared up before Mother went into the shop.

'Much wiser to go in before the deed is signed,' Peggy said.

To her surprise Benny saw her mother nodding in agreement. Yes, it did make sense to go in and be shown the ropes. It wouldn't look as if she were only going in afterwards to make sure they got an equal share.

And after all they might need more hands around the shop, so Sean if he was going to be a partner would prefer an unpaid one than someone who would need a wage. She told an astonished Benny and Patsy that she might go in on Monday for a few hours to see how the daily routine worked.

Peggy looked pleased, but not very surprised.

Benny guessed that she might have planned the whole thing. She was a very clever woman.


Nan and Jack came out of the cinema.

'It was terrible,' Nan said.

'But great terrible,' Jack pleaded.

'Lucky Benny. She's back in Knockglen.'

'I wish she didn't spend so much time there.'

They had a cup of coffee in the cinema café and he told her how hard it was to have a girlfriend miles away.

What would Nan do if she had a chap down in Knockglen, at the far end of civilisation?

'Well, I do,' Nan said.

'*Of course,* the guy in the cavalry twill and the plummy accent.'

But Jack had lost interest. He wanted to talk about Benny and how on earth they could persuade her mother to let her live in Dublin.

He wondered was there any hope that she could have a room in Nan's house? Nan said there was none at all.

They said goodbye at the bus stop outside the cinema. Jack ran for a bus going south.

Simon stepped out of a doorway.

'I wondered if you were free for dinner?' he said to Nan.

'Did you wait for me?' She was pleased.

'I knew you wouldn't see *Swamp Women* round a second time. What about that nice little hotel we went to in Wicklow? We might stay the night.'

'How lovely,' Nan said, in a voice that was like a cat purring.

It was a marvellous night in Knockglen.

Peggy Pine absolutely loved the changes in the shop. The new lighting, the fitting rooms, and the low music in the background.

Annabel Hogan had called on Sean Walsh and said that she hoped to come and join him in the shop on Monday and that would he be patient with her and explain things simply. She mistook his protestations as expressions of courtesy and insisted that she turn up at nine a.m. on the first day of the week.

Mossy Rooney said that his mother thought that Patsy was a fine person and would be very happy for them to go to Father Ross and fix a day.

And best of all Nan Mahon telephoned Benny and said that *Swamp Women* was the worst film she had ever seen, but that Jack Foley obviously adored Benny and wanted nothing but to talk about her.

Tears of gratitude sprang to Benny's eyes.

'You're so good, Nan. Thank you, thank you from the bottom of my heart.'

'What else are friends for?' asked Nan as she packed her little overnight bag and prepared to meet Simon for their visit to Wicklow.

Sean Walsh was in Healy's Hotel.

'What am I going to do?'

'Let her come in. She'll tire of it in a week.'

'And if she doesn't?'

'You'll have someone to help you to do the errands. It makes it harder for her to refuse you the partnership. She can't be avoiding your eye and the issue if she's working beside you.'

'You're very intelligent . . . um . . . Dorothy,' he said.

Rosemary Ryan knew what was going on everywhere. Eve said she was like those people during the war who had a map of where their troops were and their submarines and they kept moving them about like pieces on a board.

Rosemary knew Jack had been to the pictures with Nan. She was checking that Benny knew.

'Aren't you the silly-billy to go off and leave your young man wandering around unescorted?' Rosemary said.

'He wasn't unescorted for long. I sent him to the pictures with Nan.'

'Oh, you did. That's all right.' Rosemary seemed genuinely relieved.

'Yes, I had to go back to Knockglen and he had declared an afternoon off for himself.'

'You spend too long down there.' Rosemary was trying to warn her about something.

'Yes, well, I'm staying in town tonight. We're all going to Palmerston. Are you coming?'

'I might. I have ferocious designs on a medical student. I'll send out a few enquiries to know whether he'll be there or not.'

What could Rosemary be warning her about? Not Nan, that was clear. Everyone knew that Nan was besotted with Simon Westward. Sheila had given up on him. There was nobody else. Perhaps it was just that he was getting used to being on his own at social occasions. Perhaps by staying so long in Knockglen Benny was letting Jack think that he was free to ramble, and there might have been a bit of rambling, possibly the Welsh type of rambling . . . that she didn't know about. Benny dragged her mind back to Tudor Policy in Ireland. The lecturer said that it was often complicated and hard to pin down since it seemed to change according to the mood of the time. What else is new? Benny wondered. Jack, who had been so loving about her when talking to Nan, was annoyed again now.

He had thought she was going to stay in town for the weekend apparently and had made plans for Saturday and Sunday too. But Benny had to go back to prepare her mother for work on Monday. If he couldn't understand that what kind of friend was he? Eve would say he wasn't meant to be a friend. He was meant to be a big handsome hunk who happened to fancy Benny. But there had to be more to it than that.

Eve and Kit discussed plans.

They would put a hand basin in each bedroom, and build an extra lavatory and shower. That would stop the congestion on the landings in the morning.

They would have a woman to come in and wash on Mondays. They would have the house rewired; some of those electrical installations didn't bear thinking about.

They would be able to charge a little more if the facilities were that much better. But the real benefit would be they needn't keep students they didn't like. The boy who never opened his bedroom window, who had Guinness bottles under the bed and who had left three cigarette burns on the furniture would be given notice to mend his ways or leave. Nice fellows like Kevin Hickey could stay for ever.

For the first time in her life Kit Hegarty would have some freedom.

'Where does that leave me?' Eve asked lightly. 'You won't need me now.'

But she knew Kit did need her. So she spoke from a position of safety.

They had decided after reflection that the money would not be cast back on the drawing-room floor of Westlands. It would be put for Eve in a post office account. Ready to be taken out and thrown, the moment Eve wanted to.

*

They danced at the rugby club and Benny realised there were people who came here every Friday night and that all of them knew Jack.

'I love you,' he said suddenly as they sat sipping club oranges from bottles with straws. He pushed a damp piece of hair out of her eyes.

'Why?' she asked.

'Lord, I don't know. It would be much easier to love someone who didn't keep disappearing.'

'I love you too,' she said. 'You delight me.'

'That's a lovely thing to say.'

'It's true. I love everything about you. I often think about you and I get a great warm feeling all over me.'

'Talking about great feelings all over us, I have my father's car.'

Her heart sank. Once in the car it was going to be very, very hard to say no. Everything they had been told at school, and at the mission, and in all those sermons on purity, made it seem like a simple choice. Between sin and virtue. You were told that virtue was rewarded, that sin was punished, not only hereafter, but in this life. That boys had no respect for the girls who gave in to their demands.

But nobody had ever told anybody about how nice it felt, and how easy it would be to go on, and how cheap you felt stopping.

And about how you feared greatly that if you didn't go ahead with what you both wanted to do then there would be plenty more who would.

People of the temperament and lack of scruples up to now only discovered in Wales.

'I hope we didn't drag you away from each other too early.' Eve spoke dryly as they settled down to sleep in Kit Hegarty's.

'No, just in time, I think,' Benny said.

It had been the opportune demands of Aidan and Eve to let them into the car before they froze to death out of discretion.

'Why can't you stay the weekend?' Eve too seemed to be warning her about something. It was like a message that she was getting from everyone. She should stay around.

But there was no way that she could stay, no matter how great the danger. Things were at a crossroads in Knockglen.

'Have you a cigarette?' she asked Eve.

'But you don't smoke.'

'No, but you do. And I want you to listen while I tell you about Sean Walsh.'

They turned on the light again, and Eve sat horrified as the tale of the money and the suspicions and the partnership was unfolded.

The hopes that Benny's mother might find a life of her own in the shop, the support that would be needed. Eve listened and understood. She said that it didn't matter how much temptation was thrown into Jack Foley's path, some things were more important than others, and Benny had to nail Sean Walsh, no matter what.

Eve said she'd come down herself and help to search for the money.

'But we can't go into his rooms. And if we were to get the guards he'd hide it.'

'And he's such a fox,' Eve added. 'You'll have to be very, very careful.'

There was now a Saturday lunch-time trade at Mario's, toasted cheese slices and a fudge cake with cream. The place was almost full as Benny walked past.

She went in to admire Clodagh's drastic changes. There were half a dozen people examining the rails and maybe four more in the fitting rooms.

Between them Clodagh and Fonsie had brought all the business in the town to their doorstep. There were even people who might well have gone to Dublin on a shopping trip browsing happily.

'Your mother's in great form altogether. She's talking of shortening her skirts, and smartening herself up.'

'Mother of God, who'll shorten her skirts for her? You're too busy.'

'You *must* be able to take up a simple hem. Didn't you say you had a sewing machine somewhere?'

'Yes, but I don't know where it is in the lumber and rubble up in the shop.'

'Up in the Honourable Sean Walsh's territory?'

'No, he's right upstairs. The first floor.'

'Ah, get it out, Benny. Get someone to drag it down to your house. I'll come round for ten minutes and start you off.'

'It mightn't be working,' Benny said hopefully.

'Then your mother'll have to look streelish, won't she?'

Benny decided she'd go back to the shop and see if the machine really was there and looked in workable condition before she asked Teddy Flood or Dekko Moore or someone with a handcart to help her home with it.

Sean wasn't in sight in the shop. Only old Mike saw her go upstairs.

She saw the sewing machine behind an old sofa with the springs falling out. It couldn't have been used for nearly twenty years.

It looked like a little table. The machine part was down in it. Benny pulled, and up it came, shiny and new-looking as well it might be, considering how little use it had had. It was quite well made, she thought, with those little drawers on each side, probably for spools of thread and buttons and all the things that sewing people filled their lives with.

She opened one of the little drawers. It was stuffed with small brown envelopes, pushed up one against the other. It seemed an extraordinary way to keep buttons and thread. She opened one idly and saw the green pound notes, and the pink ten-shilling notes squeezed together. There were dozens and dozens of envelopes, old ones addressed to the shop, originally with invoices, each with its post mark. With a feeling of ice water going right through her body, Benny realised that she had found the money Sean Walsh had been stealing from her father for years.

She didn't remember walking home. She must have passed Carroll's and Dessie Burns' and the cinema as well as Pine's and Paccy's and Mario's. Maybe she even saluted people. She didn't know.

In the kitchen Patsy was grumbling.

'Your mother thought you must have missed the bus,' she said. Benny saw her preparing to put the meal on the table.

'Could you wait a few minutes, Patsy? I want to talk to Mother about something.'

'Can't you talk and eat?'

'No.'

Patsy shrugged. 'She's above in the bedroom trying on clothes that stink of mothballs. She'll run them out of the shop with the smell of camphor.'

Benny grabbed the sherry bottle and two glasses and went upstairs.

Patsy looked up in alarm.

In all her years in this house she had never been excluded from a conversation with the mistress and Benny. And never would she have believed that there was any subject that needed a drink being brought to the bedroom.

She said three quick Hail Marys that Benny wasn't pregnant. It was just the kind of thing that would happen to a nice big soft girl like Benny. Fall for a baby from a fellow who wouldn't marry her.

Annabel listened white-faced.

'It would have killed your father.'

Benny sat on the side of the bed. She chewed her lip as she did when she was worried. Nan had said she must try to get out of the habit. It would make her mouth crooked eventually. She thought about Nan for a quick few seconds.

Nan wouldn't pause to care about her father's business. Not if it was being robbed blind by everyone in it. It was both terrible and wonderful to be so free.

'I wonder if Father knew,' Benny said.

It was quite possible that he had his suspicions, but that being Eddie Hogan he had put them away. He wouldn't have opened his mouth unless he had positive proof. But it was odd that he had delayed the partnership deal. Mr Green had said he was surprised that it had not been signed. Could Father have had second thoughts about going into partnership with a man who had had his hand in the till over the years?

'Your father would not have been able to bear the disgrace of it all. The guards coming in, a prosecution, the talk.'

'I know,' Benny agreed. 'He'd never have stood for that.'

They talked as equals sitting in the bedroom that was strewn with the clothes Annabel had been trying on to wear on her first day in the shop. Benny didn't urge her to make decisions and Annabel didn't hang back.

Because they were equals they gave each other strength.

'We could tell him we know,' Annabel said.

'He'd deny it.'

They couldn't call the guards, they knew that. There was no way that they could ask Mr Green to come in, climb the stairs to the first floor and inspect the contents of the sewing machine. Mr Green wasn't the kind of lawyer you saw in movies who did this sort of thing. He was the most quiet and respectable of country solicitors.

'We could ask someone else to witness it. To come and see it.'

'What good would that do?' Annabel asked.

'I don't know,' Benny admitted. 'But it would prove it was there in case Sean were to shift it and hide it somewhere else. You know, when we speak to him.'

'*When* we speak to him?

'We have to, Mother. When you go in there on Monday morning, he has to be gone.'

Annabel looked at her for a long time. She said nothing. But Benny felt there was some courage there, a new spirit. She believed that her mother would face what lay ahead. Benny must find the right words to encourage her.

'If Father can see us, it's what he'd want. He'd want no scandal, no prosecution. But he wouldn't want you to stand beside Sean Walsh as a partner knowing what we know now.'

'We'll ask Dr Johnson to witness the find,' Annabel

Hogan said with a voice steadier than Benny would ever have believed.

Patsy said to Bee Moore that evening that you'd want to have the patience of a saint to work in Lisbeg these days. There was that much coming and going, and doors closed, and secrets, and bottles of sherry and no food being eaten and then food being called for at cracked times.

If this is what it was going to be like when the mistress went up into the shop then maybe it was just as well she was going to marry Mossy Rooney and his battle-axe of a mother and be out of it.

Patsy remembered Bee's former interest in Mossy and altered her remarks slightly. She said she knew she was very lucky to have been chosen by Mossy and was honoured to be a part of his family. Bee Moore sniffed, wondering again how she had lost him to Patsy. She said that things were equally confusing in her house. Everyone in Westlands seemed to have gone mad. Heather had started in St Mary's and was bringing what Mrs Walsh called every ragtag and bobtail of Knockglen back up to the house to ride her pony. The old man had taken to his bed, and Mr Simon was not to be seen, though it was reliably reported that he had been in Knockglen at least two nights without coming home. Where on earth could he have stayed in Knockglen if he hadn't come home to his own bed in Westlands? It was a mystery.

Maurice Johnson said that he was a man whom nothing

would surprise. But the visit of Annabel Hogan and her daughter, and its reason, caught him on the hop.

He listened to their request.

'Why me?' he asked.

'It's you or Father Ross. We don't want to bring the Church into it. It's involving sin and punishment. All we need is someone reliable.'

'Let's not delay,' he said. 'Let's go this minute.'

There were two customers in the shop when they went in. Sean looked up from the boxes of V-necked jumpers that he had opened on the counter.

There was something about the deputation that alarmed him. His eyes followed them as they went to the back of the shop towards the stairs.

'Is there anything . . . ?' he began.

Benny paused on the stairs and looked at him. She had disliked him ever since she had first met him, and yet at this moment she felt a surge of pity for him. She took in his thin greasy hair and his long white narrow face.

He had not enjoyed his life or enriched it with the money he had taken.

But she must not falter now.

'We're just going to the first floor,' she said. 'Mother and I want Dr Johnson to see something.'

She saw the fear in his eyes.

'To witness something,' she added, so that he would know.

\*

Dr Johnson went down the stairs quietly. He walked through the shop, his eyes firmly on the floor. He didn't return Mike's greeting. Nor did he acknowledge the figure of Sean standing there immobile with a box in his hands. He had said to the Hogans that he would confirm that in his presence they had removed upwards of two hundred envelopes each containing sums of money varying from five to ten pounds.

There had been no gloating in the downfall of a man he had never liked. He looked at the little hoard in tightly screwed-up envelopes. The man was buying himself some kind of life, he supposed. Had he thought of wine, or women, or song when he had stashed Eddie Hogan's money away? It was impossible to know. He didn't envy the two women and their confrontation, but he admired them for agreeing to do it at once.

They sat in the room and waited. They knew he would come upstairs. And both of them were weak with the shock of their discovery and the shame that they would have to face when Sean came up to meet them.

Neither of them feared that he would bluster or attempt to deny that it was he who had put the money there. There was no way now for him to say they had made it up. Dr Johnson's word would be believed.

They heard his step on the stair.

'Did you close the shop?' Annabel Hogan asked.

'Mike will manage.'

'He'll have to a lot of the time from now on,' she said.

'Have you something to say? Is there some kind of accusation?' he began.

'Let's make it easy,' Annabel began.

'I can explain,' Sean said.

They could hear the Saturday afternoon noises of Knockglen, people tooting their car horns, children laughing and running by, free from school since lunch time. There was a dog barking excitedly, and somewhere a horse drawing a cart had been frightened. They sat, the three of them, and heard him whinnying until someone calmed him down.

Then Sean began to explain. It was a method of saving, and Mr Hogan had understood, not exactly agreed, but acknowledged. The wages had not been great. It was known that Sean did the lion's share of the work. It had always been expected that he should build a little nest egg for himself.

Annabel sat in the high-backed chair, a wooden one they had never thought of bringing to Lisbeg. Benny sat on the broken sofa, the one she had pulled out to find the sewing machine. They hadn't rehearsed it, but they acted as a team, neither of them said a word. There were no interruptions or denials. No nods of agreement or shaking of the head in disbelief. They sat there and let him form the noose around his neck. Eventually his voice grew slower, his hand movements less exaggerated. His arms fell to his sides, and soon his head began to hang as if it were a great weight.

Then he stopped altogether.

Benny waited for her mother to speak.

'You can go tonight, Sean.'

It was more decisive even than Benny would have been. She looked at her mother in admiration. There was no hate, no revenge, in her tone. Just a simple statement of the position. It startled Sean Walsh just as much.

'There's no question of that, Mrs Hogan,' he said.

His face was white, but he was not now going to ask for mercy, or understanding, or a second chance.

They waited, to hear what he had to say.

'It's not what your husband would have wanted. He said in writing that he wanted me to become a partner. You have agreed that with Mr Green.'

Annabel's glance fell on the table full of envelopes.

'And there is no one to confirm or deny that this was an agreement.'

Benny spoke then. 'Father would not have liked the police, Sean. I know you would agree with that. So Mother and I are going along with what we are sure would be his wishes. We have discussed this for a long time. We think he would have liked you to leave this evening. And that he would like us to speak to no person of what has happened here today. Dr Johnson, as you need hardly say, is silent as the grave. We only asked him here to give substance to our request that you leave, without any fuss.'

'And what'll happen to your fine business when I leave?' His face had become crooked now. 'What's to become of Hogan's, laughing stock of the outfitting business? Will it have its big closing-down sale in June or in October? That's the only question.'

Agitated and with his features in the form of a smile he walked around rubbing his hands.

'You have no idea how hopeless this place is. How its days are numbered. What do you think you'll do without me? Have old Mike, who hasn't two brains to rub together, talking to the customers and God blessing them, and God saving them, like Barry Fitzgerald in a film? Have you, Mrs Hogan, who don't know one end of a bale of material from another? Have some greenhorn of an eejit serving his time from some other one-horse town? Is this what you want for your great family business? Is it? Tell me, is it?'

His tone was becoming hysterical.

'What did we ever do to you that makes you turn on us like this?' Annabel Hogan asked, her voice calm.

'You think you were good to me. Is that what you think?'

'Yes. In a word.'

Sean's face was working. Benny realised she had never remotely suspected that he could feel so much.

He told a tale of being banished upstairs to servant's quarters, being patronised and invited to break bread from time to time with the air of being summoned to a palace. He said that he had run the business single-handed for a pittance of a wage and a regular pat on the head. The cry that they would be lost without Sean Walsh was said often enough to render it meaningless. He said that his genuine and respectful admiration for Benny, the daughter of the house, was a matter of mockery, and had been thrown back in his face. He had been honourable and would have been proud to escort her to places even when she was not a physically beautiful specimen.

Neither Annabel nor Benny allowed a muscle to move in the face of the insults.

He had not intruded, imposed or in any way traded on his position. He had been discreet and loyal. And this was the thanks he was getting for it.

Benny felt a great sadness sweep over her. There was some sincerity in the way Sean spoke. If this was his version of his life, then this was his life.

'Will you stay in Knockglen?' she asked unexpectedly.

'What?'

'After you leave here?'

Something clicked then. Sean knew they meant it. He looked at them, as if he had never seen either of them before.

'I might,' he said. 'It's the only place I've really known, you see.'

They saw.

They knew there would be talk. A lot of talk. But on Monday the shop would open with Annabel in charge. They had only thirty-six hours to learn the business.

Mrs Healy agreed to see Sean in her office. Even given his usual pallor, she thought he looked badly as if he had just had a shock.

'May I arrange to have a room here for a week?'

'Of course. But might I ask why?'

He told her that he would be leaving Hogan's. As of now. That he would therefore be leaving his accommodation there. He was vague in the extreme. He parried questions about the partnership, denied that there had been any fight or unpleasantness. He said that he would like to transfer his belongings across the road at a time when half the town wouldn't be watching, like when they were gone home to their tea.

Fonsie saw him of course, saw him carrying one by one the four cardboard boxes that made up his possessions.

'Good evening, Sean,' Fonsie said gravely.

Sean ignored him.

Fonsie went straight back to tell Clodagh.

'I think I see a love nest starting. Sean Walsh was bringing twigs and leaves and starting to build it across in Healy's.'

'Was he moving across, really?' Clodagh didn't seem as surprised as she should be.

'In stealth and with lust written all over him for Dorothy,' Fonsie said.

'Well done, Benny,' said Clodagh, closing her eyes and smiling.

Maire Carroll had come up to the convent to ask for a reference. She was going to apply for a job in a shop in Dublin. As Mother Francis struggled to think of something to say about Maire Carroll that was both truthful and flattering, Maire revealed that Sean Walsh had been seen taking all his belongings and going to live in the hotel.

'Thank God, Benny,' Mother Francis breathed to herself.

Sunday was the longest day that any of them had worked. It had an air of unreality because the shutters were closed so that nobody should know they were there.

They would have looked a very strange crew to anyone who saw them. Patsy in her overalls scrubbing out the small room which had been filled with the results of a thousand cups of ill-made tea. Old Mike said that they took it in turns to make the tea and open the biscuits. The place had all the signs of it. The Baby Belling had been brought down from Sean's quarters upstairs. From now on there would be proper tea, and even soup or toast made.

Hogan's was going to change.

And to help it change, Peggy Pine and Clodagh were there, as was Teddy Flood.

To none of them had any explanation been given apart from the fact that Sean Walsh had left, and they were in need of some advice. Clodagh said one business was the same as another. If you could run one you could run the lot, and she always hoped she might be seconded to get a steel works or a car plant on its feet.

Mike, who had never been the centre of such attention, was asked respectful questions. It was the general opinion that Mike must be addressed slowly, and his answers weighed with the same deliberation that he gave them.

To fuss Mike would be counter-productive. Let him think there was all the time in the world.

Let him wander down no lanes of regret about Mr Eddie and no tight-lipped mutterings about the Sean Walsh who wanted to be called Mister.

Slowly they pieced it together, the way the business was run. The people who had credit, and those who didn't. The way the bills had been sent out, the reminders. The salesmen who came with their books for orders. The mills, the factories.

Haltingly Mike told it all. They listened and worked out the system, such as it was.

A thousand times Annabel Hogan cursed herself for not taking an interest and forming a part of the company when her husband was alive. Perhaps he would have liked it? It was only her own hidebound feelings that had kept her at home.

Benny wished that she had come to help her father. If only she could have had the time over again, then she would have spent Saturday afternoons here with him, learning about his life at work.

Would he have been proud of her and pleased that she was taking such an interest? Or would he have thought that she was a distraction in the all-male world of gentleman's outfitters? It was impossible to know. And anyway she had avoided the shop a lot because of Sean Walsh.

As they toiled on, working out which bales of material were which, Benny let her mind wander. Could her parents seriously have expected her to marry Sean just because he had been helpful in the business? And even worse, suppose she had gone along with their views? Promised herself to him, allowed his disgusting advances and been engaged to him now? Think then how impossible it would have been once they discovered his theft. The mean, grubbing, regular stealing from a kind employer who had wished him nothing but well.

Patsy had heated up the soup and served the sandwiches. They sat companionably and ate them.

'Is it wrong of us, do you think, to work on a Sunday?' Mike was fearful about the whole thing.

'*Laborare est orare*,' Peggy Pine said suddenly.

'Could you translate for those of us without the classical education, Aunt?' Clodagh asked.

'It means that the Lord thinks working is a form of prayer,' Peggy said, wiping away the crumbs and settling down to writing out proper sales tickets which Annabel could understand.

They had opened up the back door of the shop late on Saturday night so they could come and go by the lane at the rear of the premises.

The sun shone on the disused back yard with its rubbish and clutter.

'You could make a lovely conservatory here,' Clodagh said admiringly.

'What for?' Benny asked.

'To sit in, you clown.'

'Customers wouldn't want to sit down, would they?'

'Your mother and you.'

Benny looked blank.

'Well, you are going to live here, aren't you?'

'Lord no. We'll be living in Lisbeg. We couldn't live over the shop.'

'Some of us do, and manage fine,' Clodagh said huffily.

Benny could have bitten off her tongue. But there was no point in trying to take it back now.

Clodagh didn't seem a bit upset.

'Good for you if you can,' she said. 'I thought the object of all this was to try and turn this place around. You won't do that if you don't put some money into it. I assumed you were going to sell your house.'

Benny wiped her forehead. Was there ever going to be any end to all this? When could she get back to living an ordinary life again?

Jack Foley telephoned Benny from nine in the morning until noon.

'She can't be at Mass *all* bloody morning,' he grumbled.

Benny telephoned Jack at home.

She got his mother.

'Is that you, Sheila?' she asked.

'No, Mrs Foley. It's Benny Hogan.'

She heard that Jack was out and not expected back until late. He had left quite early.

'I thought he was down in your neck of the woods, actually,' Mrs Foley said.

She made it sound like a swamp with alligators in it. Like the film Benny hadn't seen.

She forced her voice to be light and casual. No message. Just to say that she had rung for a chat.

Mrs Foley said that she'd write it down straight away. She managed to make it sound as if the name of Benny Hogan would be added to a long list of those who had already telephoned.

It was over, and she longed to celebrate. Everything she had wanted for the shop since the day Father had died had been achieved. They had had huge support from their friends in Knockglen. Sean had been rendered unimportant.

It was a night of triumph, she wanted to tell Jack all about it. The awful bits and the funny bits, the look on Sean's face, Patsy making more and more tea, and sandwiches. Old Mike getting surges of energy like Frankenstein's monster. Peggy Pine showing her mother how to ring up a sale. She wanted to tell him that from now on she wouldn't be needed so desperately at home.

She would be free to spend several nights a week in Dublin. She had a terrible foreboding that she had left it all too late. That she had been away too long.

## 17

Brian Mahon said that it was great to be spending all that money paying fees for a university student when she didn't get up for her bloody lectures.

Emily said he should hush. That was unfair. Nan worked very hard, and it was rare the girl had a lie-in.

'When she *is* in the house it would be nice to see her, just now and again,' he said.

Nan told them that she stayed with Eve out in Dunlaoghaire, on the occasions when she didn't come home. Her father said it was a pity that woman in the guest house didn't pay her fees and buy her clothes for her.

But he had to meet a man who had come in on the boat to the North Wall. He'd been down in a dockers' pub. There was a deal about a consignment.

Emily sighed. There might be a deal about a consignment, but there would also be a day's drinking. When he had gone she went upstairs.

Nan was lying on her bed with her arms folded behind her head.

'Aren't you well?'

'I'm fine, Em. Honestly.'

Emily sat down on the stool opposite the dressing table.

There was something troubled in Nan's face, some look she had never seen before. It was surprise mixed with indecision.

Nan had never known either, not since she was a little girl.

'Is it . . . Simon?'

Normally Emily never mentioned his name. It was almost like tempting fate.

Nan shook her head. She told her mother that Simon was most devoted and attentive. He was down in Knockglen. She'd be seeing him for dinner tomorrow night. Emily was not convinced. She shook her head as she went downstairs, tidied away the breakfast things, put on her smart blouse and set out for work.

As she stood at the bus stop she wondered what was wrong with her daughter.

Back in her bedroom Nan lay and looked ahead of her. She knew there was no need to have sent the specimen to Holles Street Maternity Hospital. Her period was seventeen days late. She was pregnant.

Eve and Kit were up early. They had builders arriving and they wanted to show them from the beginning that this was a house with rules, a house like they had never known before.

They had left bags of cement and sand in the back yard

the night before. The name on the sacks was Mahon.

'You must tell Nan that we're putting a few shillings into her father's pocket,' Kit said.

'No, Nan wouldn't like to hear that. She doesn't want to be reminded of her father and his trade.'

Kit was surprised.

Nan always seemed remarkably unpretentious for such an attractive girl. You never caught her stealing a look at herself in the mirror, or blowing about the people she had been out with.

Eve had liked her so much at the beginning, but had been very resentful of Nan taking up with the Westwards.

'You're not still bearing a grudge against her because she went out with Simon Westward are you?'

'A grudge? Me?' said Eve, laughing. She knew that most of her life had been spent bearing grudges against the family that had disowned her.

And anyway Kit had used the wrong tense. Nan was still going out with Simon. Very much so.

Heather had been on the phone, squeaking with excitement about her life in the convent and how funny and mad and superstitious everyone was.

'I hope you don't *say* any of that,' Eve said sternly.

'No, only to you. And I have another secret. I think Simon's doing a line with Nan. She rings sometimes, and I know he goes off to meet her, because he packs a bag. And he doesn't come home at night.'

Eve was sure that Nan and Simon were Going All The Way. Simon wouldn't be remotely interested in a girl unless she would. It wasn't a sin for him anyway, and he wouldn't take Nan out, no matter how gorgeous she looked, unless he was getting value for it.

Because Eve knew very well that Nan was not someone her cousin Simon was going to bring home to Westlands.

When she telephoned it was as she had known it would be. The pregnancy test was positive.

Nan dressed carefully and left the empty house in Maple Gardens. She took the bus to Knockglen.

She walked past the gates of St Mary's Convent and looked up the long avenue. She could hear the sounds of children at play. How strange of Simon to let his sister stay there, amongst all the children of people who worked on the estate.

But from her own point of view it was good. It meant that he was tied more to Knockglen. She could come more frequently to the cottage. And there would be fewer crises about Heather being unhappy and running away from the school where she should be.

She couldn't remember clearly how far it was from the village to Westlands, but decided that it was too far to walk. Knockglen didn't have the air of a place that would have a taxi. She had heard so much bad about Healy's Hotel from Benny, Eve and Simon that she dared not risk asking them to arrange her a lift.

Nan would wait until a suitable car passed by.

A middle-aged man in a green car came into view. She hailed him and as Nan had known he would, he stopped.

Dr Johnson asked her where she was heading.

'Westlands,' she said simply.

'Where else?' the man said.

They talked about the car. He explained it was a Morris Cowley, the cheapest end of the Ford range. He'd love a Zodiac or even a Zephyr, but you had to know when to draw the line.

'I don't think you do,' said the beautiful blonde girl, whom Dr Johnson remembered seeing somewhere before.

She had a slightly high, excited look about her. He asked no questions about her visit.

She said that a lot of people were too timid, they didn't reach for things. He should reach for a Zephyr or a Zodiac, not assume that they were beyond his grasp.

Maurice Johnson smiled and said he would discuss the notion of reaching with his wife and with his bank manager. He could see neither of them agreeing with this view, but he would certainly present it.

He turned in the gates of Westlands.

'Were you going here anyway?' Nan asked, alarmed. She didn't want to clash with another visitor.

'Not at all. But a gentleman, even in a Morris Cowley, always sees a lady right to the door.'

She gave him a smile of such brightness, he thought to himself that men like Simon Westward who were knee high to a grasshopper had all the luck when it came to getting gorgeous women, just because they had the accent and the big house.

Nan looked up at the house. It wasn't going to be easy.

But then nothing that was important had ever been easy. She took three deep breaths, and rang at the door.

Mrs Walsh knew well who Nan Mahon was. She had heard the name on the telephone many times, and even though she discouraged Bee from gossiping, she knew that this girl, who had been in the house a couple of days after Christmas, was a friend of Eve Malone and Benny Hogan.

But just to keep things as they should be, she asked her name.

'Mahon,' Nan said, in a clear, confident voice.

Simon was coming out of the morning room anyway. He had heard the car pull up and draw away.

'Was that Dr Johnson, Mrs Walsh? He seems to have driven off without seeing Grandfather . . . ?'

He saw Nan.

His voice changed.

'Well, hallo,' he said.

'Hallo, Simon.'

She stood, very beautiful in a cream-coloured suit with a red artificial flower pinned to the lapel. Her handbag and shoes were the same red. She looked as if she were dressed to go out.

'Come in and sit down,' he said.

'Coffee, Mr Simon?' Mrs Walsh asked, but she knew she would not be needed.

'No thanks, Mrs Walsh.' His voice was light and easy. 'No, I think we'll be all right for the moment.'

He closed the door firmly behind them.

Aidan Lynch came up to Jack in the pub and said that Benny had taught him the Charleston.

It was really quite simple, once you learned to work the two legs separately.

'Yes,' Jack Foley said.

And it looked very snazzy, Aidan said, and possibly Benny should give up her notion of becoming a librarian, and be a teacher. After all anyone could check books in and out of a library, but not everyone could teach. Impart knowledge.

'True,' Jack Foley agreed.

And so, Aidan wondered, how much more was he going to have to go on making inane chat until they could get down to the point, the point being that he and Eve, who were so to speak Love's Young Dream of the university at the moment, leaving Sean and Carmel in the halfpenny place, wanted to know had there been a falling out between Benny and Jack?

'Ask her,' Jack said.

'Eve has. And she says no, it's just that she can never find you.'

'That's because she's always looking for me in Knock-glen,' Jack said.

'Have you been able to . . . you know?' Aidan was the old confiding mate now.

'Mind your own business,' Jack said.

'That means you haven't. Neither have I. Jesus, what do they teach them in these convents?'

'About people like us, I suppose.'

They forgot about women and talked about the match and the way that some people couldn't kick a ball out of their way if it was laid down in front of them.

Aidan hadn't any more information for Eve about Benny. But at least he could report that no new person had come on the scene.


'This is a surprise,' Simon said. The small narrow frown that was just a half line between his eyes showed it wasn't entirely a welcome surprise.

Nan had rehearsed it. No point in small talk, and fencing.

'I waited until I was certain. I'm afraid I'm pregnant,' she said simply.

Simon's face was full of concern.

'Oh no,' he said, moving towards her. 'Oh no, Nan no, you poor darling. You poor, poor darling.' He embraced her and held her close.

She said nothing. She felt his heart beat against hers. Then he drew her away, examining her face, looking to see how upset she was.

'How awful for you,' he said tenderly. 'It's not fair is it?'

'What isn't?'

'Everything.' He waved his hands expansively.

Then he went over to the window and ran his hands through his hair. 'This is awful,' he said. He seemed very upset.

They stood apart, Nan with her head on the piano,

Simon by the window, both of them looking out the long window at the paddock where Heather's pony stood and across at the fields where the grazing had been let and cattle moved slowly round.

Everything seemed like slow motion, Nan thought. Even the way Simon spoke.

'Will you know what to do?' he asked her. 'Will you know where to go?'

'How do you mean?'

'Over all this.' He waved a slow wave of his hand vaguely in the direction of her body.

'I came to you,' she said.

'Yes, I know, and you were right. Utterly right.' He was anxious she should know this.

'I never thought it could happen,' Nan said.

'Nobody ever does.' Simon was rueful, as if it happened all over the place, to everyone he knew.

Nan wanted to speak. She wanted desperately to say 'What do we do now?'

But she must give him no chance to say anything hurtful or careless that she would have to respond to angrily. She *must* leave silences. The expression was Pregnant Pauses, she thought with a little giggle that she fought back. Simon was about to speak.

'Nan, sweetheart,' he said, 'this is about as terrible as it can be. But it will all be all right. I promise you.'

'I know.' She looked at him trustingly.

And then her ears began to sing a little as he told her of a friend who knew someone and it had all been amazingly

588

simple, and the girl had said that it was much easier than going to a dentist.

And there had been no ill effects. Well, actually Nan had met the girl, but it wouldn't be fair to name names. But she was someone terribly bubbly and well-adjusted.

'But you don't mean . . .?' She looked at him, shocked.

'Of course I'm not going to abandon you.' He came towards her again and took her in his arms.

Relief flooded through her. But why had he talked about this silly bubbly woman who had been to have an abortion? Had he changed when he saw her stricken face?

Simon Westward stroked her hair.

'You didn't think I'd let you look after it all on your own, did you?' he said.

Nan said nothing.

'Come on now, we both enjoyed ourselves. Of course I'll look after it.'

He pulled away from her and took a cheque book out of a drawer.

'I don't know what this chap said, he did tell me a figure, but this should cover it. And I'll get the name and address of the place and everything. It's in England of course, but that's all for the best, isn't it?'

She looked at him unbelieving. 'It's your child. You know that?'

'Nan, my angel, it's not a child at all. Not a speck yet.'

'You do know that you were the first and there has been nobody else?'

'We're not going to upset ourselves over this, Nan. It

can't be between us. You know that, I know it, we've known it since we went into our little fling.'

'Why can't it be? You want to get married. You want an heir for this place. We get on well together. I fit in with your world.' Her voice was deliberately light.

But she was playing for everything in this plea. She never thought she would have had to beg like this. He had said he loved her. Every time they made love he called out how much he loved her. It was unthinkable that he was reaching for a cheque book to dismiss her.

He was gentle with her. He even took her hand.

'You know that you and I are not going to marry, Nan. You, of all people, so cool, so reasonable, so sensible. You know this. As do I.'

'I know you said you loved me,' she said.

'And so I do, I love every little bit of you. I don't deny it.'

'And this is love then? A cheque and an abortion?'

His face looked troubled. He seemed surprised that she took this view.

'And it wouldn't have mattered, I suppose, if my father was a rich builder instead of a shabby builder.'

'It has nothing to do with that.'

'Well, it certainly has nothing to do with religion. It's 1958 and neither of us believes in God.'

He opened her hand and pressed the folded cheque into it.

She looked at him in disbelief.

'I'm sorry,' he said.

She was still silent. Finally she said, 'I'm going back now.'

'How will you get home?' he asked.

'I was stupid enough to think I was coming home.' She looked around her, at the portraits on the wall, the piano, the view from the window.

Something about her face touched him. She was always so very, very beautiful.

'I wish . . .' he began, but couldn't finish the sentence.

'Do you know someone who would drive me back to Dublin?'

'I will, of course.'

'No. It would be too artificial. Someone else.'

'I don't really know anyone else . . . anyone that I could ask . . .'

'No. You do keep yourself to yourself. But I know what we'll do. I'll take your car just down to the square,' she said. 'There'll be a bus soon. You can collect it later in the day.'

'Let me at least . . .'

He moved towards her.

'No, please stay away from me. Don't touch me.'

He handed her the car keys.

'It needs a lot of choke,' he said.

'I know. I've been in it a great many times.'

Nan walked down the steps of Westlands. He watched from the window while she got into his car and drove away.

He knew that from the kitchen window Bee Moore and Mrs Walsh were watching and speculating.

He looked at her with admiration as she started his car and drove down the long avenue without looking back.

She left the keys in the car. Nobody would dare to steal the car of Mr Simon Westward in this feudal backwater. They'd all be afraid of crossing anyone at the Big House.

Mike was turning the bus. He'd be going back to Dublin in five minutes, he told her. She paid her fare.

'You could have got a return, it would have been cheaper.' Mike was always anxious to give people a bargain.

'I didn't know I'd be going back,' Nan said.

'Life's full of surprises,' said Mike, looking at this blonde girl in the cream and red outfit, who looked much too smart for this part of the world anyway.

Bill Dunne saw Benny come into the Annexe. She was looking around, hunting for Jack, but there was no sign of him. She stood in the line with the other students. If Jack had been there he would have kept a table, and she could have gone straight to join him.

Bill waved and said he had an extra coffee. In fact he hadn't begun his own, but it seemed a way of calling her over. She looked very well today, in a chestnut-coloured sweater, the exact colour of her hair, and a pale yellow blouse underneath.

Bill and Benny talked easily. If she was glancing around for Jack she never mentioned it. And he never showed that he noticed. Benny was so easy to talk to. They discussed banning the bomb and if it would ever work. Benny said she was afraid it was like asking boxers to tie one hand behind their backs, or saying we should go back to bows and arrows once they had invented gunpowder. They wondered would Elvis really join the US Army or was it just a publicity stunt? They talked of Jack Kerouac. Would every single person that he met On the Road have been interesting? Surely some of them must have been deadly bores.

The time flew, and they had to go back to lectures. If Benny was disappointed that Jack Foley hadn't turned up she showed no sign of it. But then women were known to be very good at hiding their feelings. Most people didn't know what they were up to half the time.

Rosemary saw everything and noted it all. She watched Bill and Benny chatting animatedly. They seemed like great friends. Perhaps he was consoling her about Jack. Rosemary had often thought that the feeling was unworthy, but she felt that Jack was too handsome for Benny. She thought it was like a mixed marriage. A Black and a White, a Catholic and a non-Catholic. You heard of those that did work. But the usual rule was that they didn't. It wasn't a view that anyone would agree with so she didn't express it. Anyway people might think she was after Jack Foley for herself. Which oddly enough was not true. She had met a very nice medical student called Tom. He wouldn't be qualified for years, which would give Rosemary time to be an air hostess or something with a bit of glamour in the meantime.

Sean Walsh stood on the Quays waiting for the bus back to Knockglen. He had stayed in a men's hostel in Dublin for five days to think things out. During the daytime he had walked through the menswear shops in Dublin trying to see himself working in any of them.

The prospect began to look less and less likely. He would not come armed with a reference. He would be unlikely to be taken on anywhere.

Little by little he began to realise how his horizons had narrowed. The idea of buying his own place, renovating a cottage up over the quarry, was now only a fantasy. The notion of standing at the door of his own business and watching the town walk by was not one he could hold any more in his dreams. His name would be over no premises in Knockglen, the town where he had lived for ten years, and which, when all was said and done, he thought of as home.

He was going to go back now with a proposition.

He saw a very good-looking girl get off the bus, a blonde girl in a cream suit with red trimmings. He recognised her as the friend of Eve and Benny. The girl who had been at Mr Hogan's funeral, and had been up at Westlands around Christmas time. She didn't acknowledge him. She looked as if her mind were set on something else entirely.

Sean got on to the bus and looked without pleasure at Mikey, a man who was over-familiar and with an unfortunate habit of referring to people's physical appearance.

'There you are, Sean, with a face as long as a wet week. Is it the return of the Prodigal we see?'

'I wish I understood what you mean, Mikey.'

'It's a reference to a story Our Lord told in the New Testament, Sean. A man like yourself nearly eating the altar in the church should know that.'

'I am well aware of the parable of the Prodigal Son, but since he was a man who spent his life in wrong-doing, I'm afraid I can't see the similarity.'

Mikey looked at Sean shrewdly. His wife had given him some highly coloured speculation about what might or might not have happened in Hogan's Outfitters. But obviously Sean Walsh had not run away.

'I was only wondering where the fatted calf was going to be killed, Sean,' Mikey said. 'Maybe they're basting it already down in Healy's Hotel.'

Nan let herself into the house that she had left that morning. She took off her cream suit and hung it carefully on a padded hanger. She sponged it lightly with lemon juice and water. She put shoe trees in her red shoes, and she rubbed her red leather bag with some furniture cream, before wrapping it carefully in tissue paper and placing it beside her other four handbags in a drawer. She put on her best college clothes, combed her hair and went out to stand for a second time at the bus stop across the road.

Mrs Healy had tidied up her office. She placed a big jug of

daffodils on the window and two small hyacinths in plastic bowls on the filing cabinet.

She had been to Ballylee to have her hair done.

The new corset was very well fitting. It managed to distribute the flesh very well. So well, in fact, that a tight skirt looked remarkably fine. She wore her high-necked blouse and cameo brooch. The ones reserved for special occasions.

And after all it would be a special occasion this afternoon. She knew that Sean Walsh was coming back today. And that he was going to make a proposal of marriage.

It was lunch time in the convent, and Mother Francis had her turn on dinner duty. That meant she walked up and down keeping order as the girls had their sandwiches. Then she supervised the tidying up of the hall, the careful cleaning and refolding of the greaseproof paper for tomorrow's packed lunch, the airing of the room and the quick exercise in the yard.

She saw a group of the girls explaining to Heather Westward the nature of rosary beads.

'Why do you call them a pair, there's only one?' Heather looked at the necklace of beads.

'They're always called a pair.' Fiona Carroll, the youngest of the badly behaved Carroll children from the grocery, was scornful.

'What does it mean "Irish Horn"?' Heather was interested.

'That's just what they're made from,' Siobhan Flood, the butcher's granddaughter, dismissed it.

'So what does it *do*?' Heather demanded, looking fearfully at the rosary beads.

She was not at all convinced that it did nothing, that you did things with it, you used it to pray with, that was all. That the spacings on the beads meant that you said ten Hail Marys and then stopped and said a Glory Be and then an Our Father.

'Like the Lord's Prayer?' Heather asked.

'Yes, but the proper way,' Fiona Carroll said, in case there should be any doubt about it.

They explained that the whole point was not to say one Hail Mary more than was needed. That was why they were made.

Mother Francis had an art of listening to one set of conversations while being thought to be in the middle of others. Her heart was heavy when she heard the explanations being given to the unfortunate Heather.

After all her teaching, this is what they thought. They thought the point of this beautiful prayer to Our Lady was never to let yourself say one more Hail Mary than was necessary.

Wouldn't a teacher be very foolish to think that anything ever got into their heads? Perhaps the Mother of God would be touched and pleased by the innocence of children. Mother Francis would, at this particular lunch time, have liked to take them out individually and murder them one by one.

Kit answered the phone at lunch time. It was Eve wanting to know if Benny could stay the night. She knew the answer would be yes, but between them there had always been courtesies like this.

Kit was pleased. She wanted to know was there a dance or an occasion?

'No, there's not.' Eve sounded worried. 'She said she wants her mother to get used to her being away from home.'

'And what about Jack Foley?'

'That's the question I wanted to ask and didn't,' Eve said.

Hogan's had closed for lunch. Annabel, Patsy and Mike adjourned to the back room and ate shepherd's pie and tinned beans. Mike said he hadn't felt as well in years. These midday dinners in the shop would build you up for the afternoon. Patsy said it was a grand, handy place to cook. They should move up here altogether.

Nan tried three pubs before she found them. It was nearly closing time. Almost the Holy Hour when the Dublin city pubs closed between half past two and half past three.

'Well, look who's here.' Bill Dunne was pleased.

'Caught you, Nan. You're on a pub crawl,' said Aidan.

Jack as always said the right thing. He said it was great to see her and what would she like?

Nan said she was sick and tired of studying and she had

come out to find a few handsome men to take her mind off her books. They were all flattered to think she had set out to look for them. They sat around her in an admiring circle.

She looked fresh in her pale green jumper with a dark green skirt and jacket. Her eyes sparkled as she laughed and joked with them.

'How goes the romance with Milord?' Aidan asked.

'Who?'

'Come on. Simon.'

'I haven't seen him for ages,' she said.

Aidan was surprised. Only last night Eve had been fulminating about it all.

'Did it end in tears?' Aidan knew that Eve would demand the whole story from him, not just half-said, half-understood bits of conversation.

'Not a bit. Nothing could come of it. We knew that. He's one world, I'm another,' Nan said.

'That's establishment baloney. Just because he's part of the crumbling classes,' Bill Dunne said.

'Exactly. And much as I know we should be nice to the crumbling classes, they're a bit hard to take,' said Nan.

Bill, Jack and Aidan realised immediately that this Simon was besotted with Nan, but that she had thrown him over because she couldn't go along with all that would be involved if she was to play the game as they wanted to play it at the Big House.

Aidan knew that Eve would be very pleased with this news. Jack knew that Nan was just saying what he knew already. Only a few weeks ago he had seen Simon approach Nan and beg to be taken back into her warmth, while she had been polite and distant. Bill Dunne was pleased that he could report to everyone else that Nan Mahon was in circulation again.

The barman mentioned that drinking-up time had long been exceeded. He looked stern, young law students weren't going to be much help to him if he got an endorsement on his licence.

Bill and Aidan drifted back to the university.

Jack dallied and spoke to Nan.

'I don't supppose you'd think of being really bad and coming to the pictures with me?'

'Lord no, more *Swamp Women*!'

'We could look at a paper.'

They bought an *Evening Herald*.

Nan said, 'What about Benny?'

'What about her?'

'I mean where is she?'

'Search me,' said Jack. There was nothing they could agree on. They walked slowly through the Green debating this one and that, heads close together inside the pages of the newspaper.

It took them a long time to get to Grafton Street. They still hadn't made up their minds. The pubs were open again now. The Holy Hour was well over.

'Let's have a drink and discuss it,' Jack suggested.

He had a Guinness. Nan had a pineapple juice.

Jack told her a long, sad saga about Benny never being

there. He said he knew things were difficult in Knockglen and that Benny was trying to get her mother started in the shop. But he wondered was she taking it all on her shoulders too much?

'She shouldn't stay holding her hand,' Nan agreed with him. She explained that she had never felt responsible for her mother, who went out to work every day and didn't need anyone to mind her.

Jack brightened. He had been afraid that he was being selfish. No, Nan told him, it was a sign of how much he liked Benny around that he missed her.

He warmed to this view. Take tonight for example. There was a club dance. Everyone brought a partner. And here would he be, Jack Foley, yet again with no partner.

He looked across at her suddenly.

'Unless, of course . . . ?'

'I wouldn't like to. Benny might . . . ?'

'Oh, come on. Benny won't mind. Didn't she ask us to go to the pictures together?'

Nan looked doubtful.

'You're not worried about your old pal Cavalry Twill, are you?'

'I told you, that's long forgotten. He's no part of my life.'

'Well then.' Jack was easy and somewhat cheered. 'Will we meet at the club?'

Carmel was on the Ladies' Committee. It involved helping to prepare the supper for the functions. Sean liked her to be involved. He was Treasurer of course, and very important. She was buying bread for the sandwiches when she met Benny, who was trying to turn her back on the sweet counter and make do with an apple.

'It's the Tiffin Bar that's almost reaching out its arms at me from the shelf,' Benny said. 'Thank God you came in. I was nearly going to buy it.'

'It'd be a shame to go back on the Tiffin now,' Carmel said.

Benny didn't like the feeling that seemed to hang unspoken that there had been years of wedging chocolate bars down her throat. She bought the apple unenthusiastically.

'It's a pity you're not going to be here tonight,' Carmel said. 'The party's going to be great. They've given us much more money than usual. We're going to have sponge flans filled with whipped cream and decorated with chocolate flake. Oh, sorry, Benny, but you're not here, so you won't be tempted anyway.'

'I am here as it happens. I'm staying with Eve,' Benny said.

'Great,' said Carmel warmly. 'See you tonight.'

'Ring him,' Eve said. 'Ring him and tell him you're in town.'

'He knows. He must know. I told him.'

'They never listen. Ring him.'

Benny said she'd have to talk to that woman, Jack's mother, who always made people sound as if they were

602

looking for autographs instead of trying to speak to her son. Eve said that was nonsense. Benny had only phoned the house once. She must ring now. Jack would be delighted.

From the house in Dunlaoghaire Benny eventually did phone.

'I'm sorry, but he's gone out to the rugby club. They're having some kind of party tonight. He said he'd be late back.'

'He can't have known you were in town,' Eve said.

'No.'

They sat at the kitchen table. Neither of them suggested that Benny should just dress up and go in to the club anyway.

Neither of them said it had all been the forgetfulness of men, and that Jack would be delighted to see her.

They concentrated instead on Kit Hegarty who was going out with Kevin Hickey's father.

'Don't cheapen yourself now, remember,' Eve warned.

'He won't respect you,' said Benny.

Kit said that it was wonderful to see the high moral tone of the younger generation. She was relieved to know that this was their attitude.

'It's not our attitude for ourselves. We have no restraint at all,' Eve assured her. 'It's only for you.'

'I wish we had no restraint,' Benny said gloomily. 'We might be better off.'


Annabel Hogan had brightened up the shop considerably by taking away some of the wooden panels and surrounds in the window. It did not look nearly so sepulchral and solemn. She had V-necked jumpers in several colours displayed on stands. For the first time a man coming into Hogan's might be able to browse and choose rather than knowing what he wanted before he came in the door.

It also meant that she could see out much more clearly, without having to peer.

She saw Sean Walsh walk into Healy's Hotel without a backward glance at the business where he had worked for so long.

She knew that he had left his belongings there while he went away to make his plans. Perhaps he had got a job somewhere and he had returned to collect his belongings. Peggy Pine had said that Sean had hopes of Mrs Healy. Annabel doubted it. Dorothy Healy was no fool. She would know quicker than most that Sean would not have left Hogan's as he did unless there had been an incident. He was no longer an aspiring merchant in the town.

'I'm no longer a person of substance in this town,' Sean Walsh said to Mrs Healy.

She inclined her head graciously. There had been a time when he thought he would have more to offer, something to bring to the request he was going to make. But circumstances had changed.

Her head was angled like a bird considering its options. Sean spoke of his admiration for her. The respect in which she was held. The potential in Healy's Hotel, a potential as yet not fully realised.

He said there was a need for an overseer, someone to look after the daily business, the nuts and bolts, while Mrs Healy's own flair was used where it was of most use in greeting the customers, and being a presence.

Dorothy Healy waited.

He spoke of his admiration, his gratitude for her interest in him and his career, the affection that he hoped he was correct in thinking had grown between them. He was sorrier than he could ever say that things had not worked out as he would have liked. He had always envisaged himself making this speech when he was a partner in a business and the owner of a small property on the Quarry Road.

He spoke a lot of the time with his head hanging, and addressed many of his remarks to Mrs Healy's knees. She gazed at his dead-looking hair, which would be perfectly all right if he used a good shampoo and went to a proper barber. When he looked up at her anxiously, his pale face working with the anxiety of his proposal, she smiled at him encouragingly.

'Yes, Sean?'

'Will you accept my proposal of matrimony?' he said.

'I shall be happy to accept,' said Dorothy Healy.

She saw some colour flood into his face and join the look of disbelief.

He reached out and touched her hand.

He didn't realise that he was a far likelier prospect now than he had been before.

Mrs Healy wanted no refurbished cottage up on a path by the quarry.

She wanted no connections with a dying clothing business across the road. She needed a man who could manage the heavy and duller side of the hotel for her. And she knew, since Sean Walsh must have been thrown out because he was found with his hand in the till across the road, that he would have to be careful in his new employ.

She had him where she wanted him now.

'I don't know what to say,' he said.

But as the afternoon became evening they found a lot to say. Plans were made, big plans and little plans. A jeweller in Ballylee would be visited for a ring. Father Ross would be consulted about a date. Sean would visit Dublin and buy three suits off the peg, since he was a stock size. Sean would be declared the Manager as of Monday. He would live in the new building which had been erected at the back. Sean hadn't been aware of its purpose. He had thought it some kind of store house. Together they looked at it. It had all the makings of a fine family house.

As if Mrs Healy had known that this would happen one day.


Paddy Hickey was a fine dancer. And he said Kit was light as a feather.

'It was the hand of God that directed my son to your house,' he said.

'That and the notice I have up in the university,' Kit replied.

'Will you come down to Kerry with me?' he asked.

She looked at his big square handsome face. He was an

honourable man, who wouldn't run away from her.

'I might, one day, go down and see the place you're from,' she said.

He had told her that his family was reared. That Kevin was the youngest lad. That his place was grand and modern, the kitchen had the best Formica in it, and you could eat your dinner off the tiled floor.

He said he had nice neighbours and relatives who knew all about Mrs Hegarty the widow in Dublin who had given such a home to Kevin.

'I'm only a recent widow,' Kit said.

'Well, I didn't know that, until you told me, and they need never know it, and I suppose Joe Hegarty would be pleased to know that someone was looking after you.'

'I never called him Joe, in all the years. I never called him that,' she said almost wonderingly.

'Maybe that was part of it all,' said Kevin Hickey's father, who had every intention of making this woman his wife.


The mournful sound of the fog horn boomed around Dunlaoghaire harbour. Eve was so used to it now that she hardly heard it any more.

But she stirred and looked at her clock with the luminous hands. It was half past three.

She listened. Benny didn't seem to be breathing the way a sleeping person does. She must be lying there awake.

'Benny?'

'It's all right. Go back to sleep.'

Eve turned on the light. Benny was propped up against her pillows in the small camp bed. Her face was tear-stained.

Eve swung her legs out of the bed and reached for her cigarettes.

'It's just that I love him so much,' wept Benny.

'I know, I know.'

'And he must have gone off me. Just like that.'

'It's a misunderstanding. For God's sake, if he was going with anyone else we'd know.'

'Would we?'

'Of course we would. You should have rung earlier. You'd have saved yourself all this. You'd be out somewhere in a steamy car trying to keep your clothes on you.'

'Maybe I kept them on me too much.'

'Stop blaming yourself. You always think it's your fault.'

'Would you tell me if you knew? Really and truly would you tell me? You'd not keep it from me to be kind?'

'I swear I'd tell you,' Eve said. 'I swear I'd not let you be made a fool of.'


The party was great. Carmel was in the kitchen most of the time and so didn't see the way Jack Foley and Nan Mahon danced together. And how they found everything funny, and hardly talked to anyone else.

Carmel was busy washing plates when Jack Foley got Nan's coat and took her home.

'I'm honoured to be allowed to take you home. Bill Dunne and the boys say you never tell them where you live.'

'Maybe I don't want *them* to know,' Nan said.

They sat outside the door of Maple Gardens and talked. The light of the street lamp on Nan's face made her look very beautiful. Jack leaned across and kissed her.

She didn't move away when he bent over to kiss her. Instead she clung to him eagerly.

It was very easy to kiss and hold Nan Mahon. She didn't move away and pull back just as you were feeling aroused. He stroked her breast through the lilac silky dress she wore under her coat.

His voice was husky. There was no other sensation outside this car.

When she did pull away she spoke to him, cool and unruffled and different to the woman he had held in his arms, pliant, eager and wrapping herself close to him.

'Jack, don't you think we should talk about Benny?'

'Nope.'

'Why not?'

'She's not here.' He realised that it sounded too harsh, too dismissive. 'What I mean is that anything between Benny and me has nothing to do with this.' He reached for her again.

She leaned over and kissed him on the nose.

'Goodnight, Jack,' she said, and vanished. He saw her let herself into the house and the door close behind her.

\*

It was the same ritual of hanging up the clothes, sponging them and brushing them.

Cleaning her face with cream and doing her stretching exercises. Though she might have to change those exercises. Nan lay in her bed and thought about the events of the day. She laid her two hands on her stomach where a lab report had proved what she knew already. That a child was beginning to grow. She did not think about Simon Westward. She would never think about him again, no matter what happened.

She lay in the bedroom that she and her mother had decorated over the years, the years when they told each other Nan was like a princess, and that she would leave Maple Gardens and find a prince.

Her first attempt had not been very successful.

Nan stared ahead of her unseeingly and thought out the options.

She did not want to go to this person and have something that was less important than tooth extraction. She did not want the sordidness of it, the shabby end of something that had been important. She didn't think it was a speck, as Simon had said. But she didn't believe it was a baby either.

If it were done, then it would all be over, the slate would be clean, she could continue with her studies.

She looked over at her desk. She didn't enjoy them. They took up too much time. They ate into the hours she should have been grooming herself, and preparing for the places to go. She found no great joy sitting in those large musty chalk-smelling halls, or the cramped tutorial rooms. She wasn't academic. Her tutor had told her more than once that she would not make the Honours group. What was the point of struggling on doing a pass degree while the kudos was on the Honours students?

She could go to England and have the child. She could have it adopted. Take less than a year out of her life. But why have a child to give it away? Go through all that just to make some anonymous couple's dream come true?

If she lived in a remote country village in the West of Ireland, the community might have excused a beautiful girl falling for the Squire and bringing up his child, ashamed but still accepted.

In parts of working-class Dublin, an unexpected child would have been welcomed in the family. The child would grow up believing its granny was its mother.

But not in Maple Gardens. It was the beginnings of respectability for the Mahons and their neighbours. And for Nan and Em it would be the end of the dream.

It looked as if a lot of the options weren't really options after all.

It was too early for morning sickness. But she didn't take any breakfast.

Em looked at her anxiously.

'You'll be seeing Simon this evening, is that right?' she asked, hoping to see Nan's face light up.

But she was disappointed.

'I haven't seen Simon for weeks and weeks, Em.'

'But I thought you said . . .'

'I'm saying now, and I want you to remember it, I haven't been going out with Simon Westward since after Christmas.'

Emily Mahon looked at her daughter astonished.

But there was something about the set of Nan's jaw that made it seem very important.

Emily nodded, as if she had taken the instruction to heart. It didn't make it any easier to understand. Either Nan had been lying when she told her of the outings to smart places with Simon, or else she was lying now.

Jack came into the Annexe. Benny waved eagerly from a table. She had been holding a chair against all comers, by draping her scarf and her books all over it.

She looked so glad to see him and a lurch of guilt shook him.

Nobody had reported his long hours dancing with Nan to her anyway; he was slightly afraid that Carmel might have seen it as her duty to make sure that Benny was informed.

But Benny's eyes were shining with pleasure to see him.

'How was the party?'

'Oh, you know, these things are always the same. Everyone was fine, very cheerful.' There had been two wins to celebrate, some fine playing and thanks to Sean they were in funds. He told her all those details and little about the night itself.

'It was a pity you couldn't have been in Dublin.'

'But I was. Remember I said it would be early-closing day and Mother was going to have a rest and an early night.'

'I'd forgotten,' Jack admitted.

There was a pause.

'And of course you didn't know about the party.'

'Well, I did, because I ran into Carmel when she was shopping for it. And she told me.'

She looked unsure. He felt a heel, not just for holding Nan so close last night, but because Benny had thought he mightn't have asked her.

'I'd have loved you to have been there. I just forgot. Honestly, I'm so used to your not being here. What did you do?'

'I went to the pictures with Eve.'

'You should have rung me.'

'I did, but it was too late.'

Jack hadn't even looked at the message pad this morning. His mother would have written the names of anyone who called.

'Ah, Benny, I'm very sorry. I'm stupid.' He banged his head as if it were wood.

He seemed very sorry.

'Well, no harm done,' she said.

'I ran into Nan. And since she wasn't doing anything I asked her to come instead. I think she quite enjoyed it.'

Benny's smile was broad. Everything was all right. He had genuinely forgotten. He wasn't trying to tell her anything. He wasn't wriggling out. He would have loved her to have been with him last night.

Thank God he had met Nan and invited her.

Now she had nothing to worry about.

## 18

Jack woke suddenly with his heart pounding. He was in the middle of a very violent dream. It was so real it was hard to shake it off. Benny's father, Mr Hogan, was standing at the top of the quarry pushing the black Morris Minor belonging to Dr Foley over the edge.

Mr Hogan had red burning coals where his eyes should be, laughing while the car bounced to the bottom of the quarry with a crash.

It was the crash that had jerked Jack awake.

He lay there, panting.

Beside him lay Nan, sleeping innocently, her hands folded under her face, a little smile on her lips.

They lay in Eve's cottage, the place he had come for a party just after Christmas.

They had needed somewhere to go, Nan said. This was a perfectly safe place. Nobody ever passed by. The key was in the stone wall.

Nan had been wonderful. So cool and practical, saying

they must bring a spirit lamp and perhaps their own sheets and towels.

Jack would never have thought of that. She said they should keep the curtains very tightly drawn and leave the car hidden in the square lest anyone see it. There was a place behind the bus shelter where nobody would think to look.

She was naturally observant.

She had said that she never thought it was possible that she could desire someone so much.

He had been worried about everything of course, but she said that it would be all right. The alternative was just to go on being a tease. She wanted to love him completely and honestly. It had been so wonderful, compared with that girl in Wales, which had all been just rushed and quick and awkward. Nan's beautiful body was magical in his arms. She seemed to love everything as much as he did.

It must have been awful for her the first time, but she had made no complaint. What excited him most was her calm exterior when they met in college. The cool Nan Mahon looking fresh and immaculate was the same girl who wrapped herself around him and gave him an ecstasy that he had not known could exist.

This was their third visit to the cottage.

He had still not spoken to Benny.

It was just that he didn't know what to say.

There was going to be an Easter Pageant at the school. Heather wanted to take part.

'We told your brother that you wouldn't be involved in religious instruction,' Mother Francis explained.

'But this isn't religion. It's drama. It's only a play,' Heather pleaded.

It had been an exercise in spirituality intended to give the children some feeling of the message of Easter by re-enacting the Passion of Our Lord. Mother Francis sighed.

'Well, who'll explain it to your brother? Will you, or will I?'

'I don't think we'll bother him about it. He's like a weasel. Could I be Hitler, please, Mother, please!'

'Could you be *who*?'

'Um . . . Pontius Pilate. I got confused . . .'

'We'll have to see. But first I will have to discuss it with Mr Westward.'

'It's too late,' said Heather triumphantly. 'He's gone to England today. To Hampshire. To look for a wife.'


Mossy Rooney cleared out the back of Hogan's shop, and made the derelict yard look as if it had always intended to be a garden. Benny and her mother decided they must put flowers and even shrubs in it.

Mossy said that they could even have a bit of a garden seat. The place was nice and sheltered.

Patsy had told him that if the mistress had an ounce of sense she'd sell Lisbeg and move into the shop good and proper. There was plenty of room in it, and why did she want to be rattling around like a tin can in a big empty house?

If they were in the shop it would be easier for Patsy to come and do a bit of daily work. It wouldn't be as heavy and constant as looking after a big house where nobody lived. Annabel Hogan had not admitted it to herself yet, but as she stood beside Benny watering in the fuchsias that they had taken at Eve's request from the cottage, she began to think that it might be the wisest course.

In a way it would be nice just to walk upstairs and be home. Or be able to stretch out your feet on the sofa.

But time enough to think of that later. There was more than enough to sort out already.

Benny had been careful not to make the first floor, the lumber room where they had found the money in the sewing machine, a place they didn't visit. Bit by bit she managed to get rid of what had to go. Very gradually she started to ferry things up from Lisbeg. Little by little she and Patsy were transforming that big room into a place where it would be quite possible to sit and spend an evening. They took a wireless, some chairs that did not have the springs protruding. They polished a shabby old table and put place mats on it. Soon they were having their meals up here. Shep spent more time nosing around the lane, prowling the small garden which he regarded as his own exercise yard, and sitting proprietorially in the shop, than he did lording it over an empty Lisbeg.

Soon the shop was beginning to feel like home.

Soon Benny would be able to feel more free.

Dekko Moore asked Dr Johnson was there a chance that Mrs Hogan might part with Lisbeg?

Very often customers came in to him, people from big places, loaded down with money, and they often enquired were there any houses of a certain style going to come up on the market.

'Give them a few months, yet,' Dr Johnson said. 'I imagine they'll be moved up above by the end of the summer, but you wouldn't want to rush them.'

Dekko said it was extraordinary the way things had gone already. He had gone into the shop to buy a pair of socks the other day, and he had spent a fortune.

Nan and Jack ran down the track from the quarry walk to the square. The Morris Minor was hidden behind the bus shelter. For the third time they were lucky nobody was about. It was only six thirty in the morning. The car started and they were on the road to Dublin.

'One morning it won't start. And then we're for it,' Jack said, squeezing her hand.

'We're very careful. We won't be caught,' she said. She looked out of the window, as they sped past the fields and farms on their way to Dublin.

He sighed, thinking of the nights and early mornings they had spent in Eve Malone's small bed.

But a part of him felt almost sick at the risk they were taking. Eve would kill them if she knew they were using her house like this. Knockglen was a village. Someone must see them sooner or later. Knockglen was much more than a village. It was Benny's home town.

Benny.

He tried to put her out of his mind. He had managed to see her only with other people for the last two weeks. Since this amazing explosive thing with Nan had begun. He didn't think that Benny noticed. He made sure that Bill or Aidan or Johnny was there, or else he called over people to join them.

They never went to the pictures alone; on the hard-fought nights that Benny was able to stay in Dublin he made sure they went out in a group. He tried not to include Nan with them, though sometimes Benny brought her along.

Nan told him that she accepted exactly what he said, that whatever happened between them had nothing to do with Jack and Benny. They were two different worlds.

Yes, he had said that in the heat of the moment, but when he saw Benny's trusting face, and laughed at her funny remarks . . . when she turned out on a cold after-noon to watch him at a practice match, when she offered to help Carmel with the sandwiches, when he realised that he actually wanted to be with her alone and to touch her the way he touched Nan, then he felt confused.

It was easy to say that your world was compart-mentalised. But in real life it wasn't easy.

Nan must be much more mature than all of them if she could accept that what Jack felt for her was a huge and almost overpowering passion. It had everything to do with desire and very little to do with sharing a life. They didn't talk much in the car, while with Benny they would both find the words stumbling over each other.

Jack felt a great sense of anxiety as the traffic began to build up a little on the road and they approached Dublin. Nan told him nothing of her home and family.

'How do they let you stay out all night?' he had asked.

'How do yours let you stay out all night?' she had replied.

The answer was simple. That he was a boy. Nothing terrible could happen to him, like getting pregnant.

But he didn't say it. He didn't dare to say it out of politeness, and out of superstition.

Nan watched fields turn into first factory premises and then housing estates. They would soon be home. She would ask him to leave her at the corner of Maple Gardens. As soon as his car had disappeared, Nan would go to the bus stop.

She would come into college early and get herself ready for lectures.

Not that her heart was in them. But she couldn't go home. Her father thought she was staying with Eve Malone in Dunlaoghaire, instead of sneaking into Eve's cottage in Knockglen.

It would confuse and worry her mother. Let Jack go home to his house with hot water and clean shirts, and a mildly perplexed mother and maid putting bacon and egg on the table. He had nothing to worry about, a lover and a patient loving girlfriend. From what you read in books it was what all men wanted.

Nan bit her lip as they drove along in silence. She would have to tell him very soon. She could see no other way out.

That night when she lay on her bed she examined the options. This was the only one that looked as if it might possibly work.

She was not going to think about Benny. Jack had said that was his business. It had nothing to do with what was between them. Nan didn't really believe that. But he had said that it was up to him to cope with. She had enough to worry about.

She could not confide in one single person because there was nobody alive who would condone what she was about to do. For the second time in a month she was going to have to tell a man that she was pregnant. And with the unfairness of life, the second one who had no duty or responsibility would probably be the one to do the right thing.

Mossy's mother said that May was nice for a wedding. Paccy Moore said they could have the reception in the room behind his shop. After all, his sister Bee was being the bridesmaid, and Patsy didn't have a home of her own.

It wasn't what Patsy had hoped. The guests coming through the cobbler's shop. But it was either that or let it be known she was coming in with nothing to her mother-in-law's house and have the gathering there.

What she would really have liked was to be able to use Lisbeg, and have the reception in the Hogans' house, but it didn't look likely. The master would only be four months gone. The mistress and Benny spent that much time above in the shop they would have little time and energy to spare for Patsy. She was getting a dress at Pine's. She had been paying for it slowly since Christmas.

Clodagh told Benny about Patsy's hopes. 'It may be impossible, I'm not suggesting you do it, it's just that you'd hate to hear afterwards and not have realised.'

Benny was very grateful to be told. It was bad of them not to have thought of it in the first place. They had assumed that all the running would be made by Mossy's side and didn't even think of suggesting a venue.

Patsy's joy knew no bounds. It was one in the eye for Mossy's mother. She began to get the wedding invitations printed.

'And how's your own romance?' Clodagh enquired. 'I believe he was down here the other night.'

'God, I wish he had been. I *think* it's going all right. He's always coming looking for me and suggesting this and that, but there's a cast of thousands as well.'

'Ah well, that's all to the good. He wants to show you to his friends. And he has friends. That lunatic across the road there has no friends except people who sell pinball machines and juke boxes. I could have sworn I saw him at Dessie Burns' getting petrol.'

'Who? Fonsie?'

'No, your fellow. Oh well, I suppose there's dozens of

handsome blokes in college scarves getting petrol in Morris Minors.'

'It's not only Mr Flood who's seeing visions,' Benny said to Jack next day. 'Clodagh thought she saw you getting petrol in Knockglen the other night.'

'Would I have come to Knockglen and not gone to see you?' he asked.

It was a ridiculous question. It didn't even need an answer. She had only brought it up to show him that he was a person there, that he had an identity.

He breathed slowly through his teeth and remembered the shock that he and Nan had got when he realised the petrol gauge was showing empty. They had to fill up there and then. There would be nowhere open when they made their dawn escape.

Another very near miss. He wouldn't tell Nan about it. He hoped Benny wouldn't.

Sean Walsh was taking his early morning walk. These days he was accompanied by the two unattractive Jack Russell terriers with whom he would be sharing his home. They were less yappy and unpleasant if they were wearied by this harsh morning exercise.

He had ceased to look at the houses with the resentment and longing that he had once felt.

Things had turned out very much better than he would have dared to hope.

Dorothy was a woman in a million.

From Eve Malone's cottage he saw two figures emerge. The early sunlight was in his eyes and he couldn't see who they were.

They ran hand in hand, almost scampered down the way that led to the square. He squinted after them. They both looked vaguely familiar. Or perhaps he was imagining it. They must be Dublin people who had rented or borrowed the cottage.

But where were they going?

It was much too early for a bus. There had been no cars in the square.

It was a mystery, and that was something Sean Walsh didn't like at all.


Lilly Foley spoke to her husband about Jack.

'Three nights last week, and three again this week, John. You'll have to say something.'

'He's a grown man.'

'He's twenty. That's not a grown man.'

'Well, it's not a child. Leave him be. When he's passed over for a team, or fails an exam, *that's* the time to talk to him.'

'But who could he be with? Is it the same girl, or a different one each time?'

'It's a fair distance on the old milometer, I notice, whoever it is.' Jack's father laughed roguishly.

He had found a receipt for petrol from Knockglen. It must be that big girl Benny Hogan. Which was a turn-up for the books, and where on earth did they go? Her father had died, but her mother was strict. Surely she wouldn't have been able to entertain Jack in her house?

Heather rang Eve. 'When are you coming home? I miss you.'

Eve felt absurdly flattered.

She said she'd come soon, next weekend or the weekend after.

'It doesn't have to be the weekend.'

Eve realised that was true. It didn't.

She was free to leave any afternoon. She could travel on the bus with Benny. She'd have tea with Mother Francis and the nuns and then take Heather up to the cottage. She'd hear at first hand how the plans for the Easter Pageant were going. She could go to see Benny's mother and admire the changes in Hogan's. She could call at Mario's to end the evening. Knockglen was full of excitement these days. She might go tomorrow, but she had better check it wasn't a night that Benny was coming to town. It would be silly to miss her.

Benny said they'd skip a lecture and meet on the three o'clock bus. That way they'd have a bit of time. They had sandwiches in the place that the boys liked. The pub with the relaxed view about the Holy Hour.

Aidan, Jack and Bill were there. Rosemary had called in to borrow ten shillings. She needed to have a hair-do in a very good place. Tom the medical student had been harder to pin down than she had hoped. It was time for heavy remedies now, like new hairstyles.

Nobody felt like work, but Eve and Benny refused the offer of being taken to play some slot machines in an amusement arcade.

'I'm getting the bus,' said Benny.

'Goodbye, Cinderella.' Jack blew her a kiss. His eyes were very warm. She must have been mad to worry about him.

Benny and Eve left the pub.

Aidan said that he felt sure those two would be up all night and maybe bopping till dawn in Mario's.

'What?' Jack spilled some of his drink.

He hadn't realised that Eve was going back to her cottage. He had arranged to meet Nan on the Quays at six o'clock. They had been planning to go to the very same place.

Nan Mahon walked briskly down towards the river. Her overnight bag contained the usual sheets, pillowcases, candlesticks, breakfast and supper materials. Jack just brought a primus stove and something to drink.

But this time Nan had packed a bottle of wine as well. They might need it. Tonight was the night she was going to tell him.

Heather was overjoyed to see Eve. As she went through the school hall she called her over excitedly. There was a rehearsal in progress, and she was wearing a sheet. Heather Westward was playing Simon of Cyrene, the man who helped Jesus to carry his cross.

It was something that Knockglen would not have believed possible a few short weeks ago.

'Are you coming to cheer me on when we do it for real?' Heather wanted to know.

'I don't think cheering you on is what Mother Francis had in mind . . .'

'But I'm one of the good people. I help him. I step forward and lighten his burden,' Heather said.

'Yes. I'll certainly come and support you.'

'You see, I won't have any relations here like everyone else has.'

Eve promised that she would be there when the pageant was performed. She might even bring Aidan so that Heather would have two people. Eve Malone knew very well what it was like to be the only girl in the school who had nobody to turn up with a cake for the sale of work or with applause for the pageants and the plays. That had been her lot all during her years in St Mary's.

She let Heather get back to rehearsal and said she'd see her later in the cottage. It was time to talk to Mother Francis.

Eve said she had to go down to Healy's Hotel to have a cup of coffee so that she could get a close-up look at Love's Young Dream, Dorothy and Sean, Great Lovers of our Time. Mother Francis said she wasn't to be making a jeer out of them. Everyone was being very restrained, and Eve must be the same.

Hadn't it turned out better than anyone dared to hope? Mother Francis said sternly, and Eve realised that she must have known or suspected something of the secret Benny had told her, the missing money and the terror of the confrontation.

But if she did, it would never be discussed.

Up in her own cottage, waiting for Heather to come pounding up the convent path, Eve looked round.

There was something different. Not just the way things were placed. Mother Francis came here often. She polished and she dusted. Sometimes she rearranged things. But this was different.

Eve couldn't think what it was. It was just a feeling that someone else had been there. Staying there, cooking even. Sleeping in her bed. She ran her hand across the range. Nobody had used it. Her bed was made with the neat corners she had learned at school.

Eve shivered. She was becoming fanciful. All those stories about the place being haunted must have got to her. But on a bright April evening this was ridiculous.

She shook herself firmly and started getting the fire going. Heather would need toast within minutes of her arrival.

Later, down in Healy's Hotel, Eve saw Sean. In his dark manager's suit.

'Might I be the first to congratulate you?' she said.

'That's uncommonly gracious of you, Eve.'

Eve enquired politely about when they intended to marry. Was courteously interested in the expansionist plans for the hotel, the honeymoon that would include the

Holy Cross and the Italian lakes, and enquired whether Mrs Healy was around so that she could express her congratulations and pleasure personally.

'Dorothy is having a rest. She does that in the early evenings,' Sean said, as if he were describing the habits of some long extinct animal in a museum.

Eve stuffed her hand into her mouth to stop any sound coming out.

'I see you've decided to capitalise on your property,' Sean said.

Eve looked at him blankly.

'Let your cottage out to people.'

'No, I haven't,' she said.

'Oh, I'm sorry.'

She thought he was manoeuvring the conversation to a point where he would ask her to rent it to him or to let it to someone he knew.

A feeling of revulsion rose in her throat. She decided that this must be nipped in the bud. Sean Walsh must be left under no illusion that her home could be let to anyone, not even to anyone for money.

'No, I'm sorry for speaking so sharply, Sean. It's just that I never intend to. I'm keeping it for myself and my friends.'

'Your friends. Yes,' he said.

Suddenly he realised who he had seen coming out of Eve's cottage. It was that blonde girl he had seen several times before, most recently getting off the Knockglen bus, on the Quays in Dublin.

And the man. Of course he remembered who he was. He was Benny's boyfriend. The doctor's son.

So *that* little romance hadn't lasted long. And there had been precious little said about its being over.

He smiled a slow smile. There was something about it that made Eve feel very uneasy. That was twice this afternoon she had got goosebumps. She must be getting very jumpy. Aidan was right. Eve Malone was a deeply neurotic woman. She felt an overwhelming urge to be away from Sean Walsh and out of his presence.

She jumped up and started to hasten out of the hotel.

'You'll pass on my good wishes to Mrs Healy.' She tried to say Dorothy, but somehow the word wouldn't form in her mouth.

The traffic was bad on the Quays. Jack saw Nan but he couldn't attract her attention. She was leaning against the wall, and looking down into the Liffey. She seemed many miles away.

Eventually by hooting and shouting he managed to make her hear him. She walked threading her way confidently between the parked cars in the traffic jam. He thought again how beautiful she was, and how hard it was to resist these nights with her. However, he would have to resist it tonight. His heart nearly stopped when he realised how near they had been to discovery. In future they would have to check and double-check that Eve was not going home mid-week.

It was terrifying enough that time they had seen the man

631

with the dogs, the tall thin fellow that Benny hated so much, the one there had been all the fuss over about getting him to leave.

Nan slipped into the car easily and laid her overnight bag on the back seat.

'Change of plan,' he said. 'Let's have a drink and discuss it.'

It was always something that made Benny smile, that phrase. Nan didn't know it.

'Why?'

'Because we can't go down there. Eve's going home.'

'Damn!' She seemed very annoyed.

'Isn't it lucky we discovered?' He wanted to be congratulated on the amazing accident that made Aidan reveal this to him.

'Isn't it unlucky that she chose tonight of all nights to go down there?'

Jack noticed that Nan never referred to Eve by name.

'Well, it *is* her house,' he said with a little laugh.

Nan didn't seem amused.

'I really wanted to be there tonight,' she said. Even frowning she looked beautiful.

Then her face cleared. She suggested this lovely hotel in Wicklow. It was absolutely marvellous. Very quiet and people didn't disturb you. It was exactly where they could go.

Jack knew the name. It was a place his parents had dinner sometimes. It was much too expensive. He wouldn't be able to afford it and he told her so.

'Do you have a cheque book?'

'Yes, but not enough money in the bank.'

'We'll get the money tomorrow. Or I will. Let's go there.'

'And stay the night. Nan, we're not married. We can't.' He looked alarmed.

'They don't ask for your wedding certificate.'

He looked at her. She changed her voice slightly.

'I've heard of people who've been there, and stayed the night. There was no problem.'

As they drove out south past Dunlaoghaire they saw the house where Eve lived with Kit Hegarty.

'Why on earth can't she be there tonight?' Nan said.

Jack thought it would certainly be a lot cheaper for everyone if she were.

He dreaded the thought of writing a cheque that bounced in this hotel, and having to face his mother and father when it all came out.

He wished that Nan could just have faced the fact that this was one night they would have to put off. Benny would have been most agreeable and understanding.

He wished he didn't keep thinking of Benny at times like this. It was as hypocritical as hell.


Benny and Eve met in the square next morning. They sat in the shelter and waited for Mikey to arrive with the bus.

'Why do we call this a square?' Eve asked. 'It's only a bit of waste ground really.'

'That's until the young tigers get their hands on it. It might be a skating rink next week,' Benny laughed.

It was true that Clodagh and Fonsie were tireless in their efforts to change Knockglen. They had even frightened other people into improving their businesses.

Fonsie had gone to Flood's and said that if ever he owned a fine frontage like that he'd have the lettering repainted in gold. Mr Flood, terrified that somehow it would be taken from him unless he lived up to this young man's expectations, had the signwriters in next day. Clodagh had stood in Mrs Carroll's untidy grocery and chatted about the food inspectors who were closing shops down all over the place. It was amazing what a coat of paint and a spring clean did to fool them. All the time she pretended she was talking in the abstract. But she could have told Mossy Rooney that he would be called in next day, as indeed he was.

Clodagh told Mossy to put up a fitting for an awning without being asked. Dessie Burns was now stocking various colours of big canvas blinds. Clodagh and Fonsie were going to have their town looking like a rainbow before they finished.

'I suppose they'll get married,' Eve said.

'Clodagh says never. There's too many nuptials coming up, she says we'll be sick of weddings. Mrs Healy and Mr Walsh, Patsy and Mossy, and Maire Carroll home from Dublin with a fiancé already, I gather, unlike the two of us who were very slow off the mark.'

They were giggling as usual when they got on the bus. Nothing had changed since they were schoolgirls.

Rosemary was full of smiles. The hair-do had been highly successful, she said. Benny had lent her three shillings. It was counted meticulously back to her. Tom had been very impressed.

'It looks a bit flattened,' Benny said, examining the hair-do.

'Yes, I know,' Rosemary said delightedly. 'I owe Jack a shilling. Will you give it to him for me?'

Benny said she would. She'd be seeing him in the Annexe anyway.

Sean and Carmel had a table. Benny joined them with Jack's shilling clutched in her hand so that she wouldn't forget to give it to him.

'Jack was looking for you everywhere this morning,' Sean said. Benny was pleased.

'He went and stood outside a Latin lecture, he thought it was yours, but it was Baby Latin.'

'Oh, I'm not Baby Latin,' Benny said proudly. She was just one step above it. Everyone in First Arts had to do some kind of Latin in their first year. Mother Francis would have killed her if she had gone into the easy option.

Bill Dunne joined them.

'Jack said if I saw you, to say that he'll meet you at one o'clock in the main hall,' Bill said. 'Though if you want my personal opinion you wouldn't touch him with a bargepole. He hasn't shaved. He's like a bear with a sore head. He's not worthy of you.'

Benny laughed. It made her feel as high as a kite when Bill Dunne said things like this in front of everyone. It confirmed somehow that she was Jack's girl.

'He's not coming here now, then.' She had been looking at the door.

'Him come anywhere? I asked him about cars and all for the outing to Knockglen after Easter. He said not to talk to him about cars, outings or Knockglen or he'd knock my head off.'

Benny knew that Bill was dramatising it all, so that he could cast himself in the role of the beautifully mannered nice person and Jack the villain.

Since this was different to the way things were, everyone knew it was a joke. She smiled at Bill affectionately. She knew Jack was longing for the great weekend in Knockglen. It would be even better than Christmas.

Everyone had been planning it for ages. Sean had been collecting money from people, a shilling now and a shilling then. The fund was building up.

There would be a gathering in Eve's, in Clodagh's, and very possibly something upstairs in Hogan's. The rooms were so big and with high ceilings they positively called out to have a party. Benny had been sounding her mother out. And the signs looked good.

She was pleased that Jack was looking for her.

For the past few weeks he had never wanted to see her on her own.

Benny hoped that he might want them to go off to lunch together, like that time ages ago when they had gone to Carlo's.

Maybe she should take *him* there for a treat. But she'd wait and see his mood. She didn't want to be too pushy.

Bill was right. Jack *did* look very badly. Pale and tired as if he hadn't slept all night. He still looked just as handsome, maybe even more so. There was less of the conventional College Hero and more of the lead player in some film or theatre piece.

Yes, Jack Foley looked as if he were in a play.

And he spoke as if he were in one too.

'Benny, I have to talk to you. Where can we go that's away from all these people?'

She laughed at him good-naturedly.

'Hey, you were the one who said the main hall at one o'clock. I didn't choose it. Did you think it would be deserted and just the two of us?'

The crowds swarmed past them in and out, and just standing around in groups talking, duffle coats over arms now, scarves loosely hanging. The weather was getting too warm for them, but they were the badge of being a student. People didn't want to discard them entirely.

'Please,' he said.

'Well, would you like to go to Carlo's, you know that lovely place we went . . .'

'*No.*' He almost shouted it.

Everywhere else would be full of people they knew.

637

Even if they were to sit in St Stephen's Green, half the university would pass by on its way to stroll down Grafton Street at lunch time.

Benny was at a loss, and yet she knew she had to make the decision.

Jack looked all in.

'We could sit by the canal?' she suggested. 'We could get apples for us and some stale bread in case we see the swans.'

She looked eager and anxious to please him.

It seemed to distress him still further.

'Oh, Jesus, Benny,' he said, and pulled her towards him. A flicker of fear came and went. She felt something was wrong, but then she was always feeling that and it never was.

There was a place near one of the locks where they often sat. There was a bit of raised ground.

Benny took off her coat and laid it down for them to sit on.

'No, no, we'll ruin it.'

'It's only clay. It'll brush off. You're as bad as Nan,' she teased him.

'It's Nan,' he said.

'What is?'

'She's pregnant. She found out yesterday.'

Benny felt a jolt of shock for her friend. At the same time she felt the sense of surprise that Nan of all people had been going all the way with Simon Westward. Nan. So cool and distant. How had she made love properly?

Benny would have thought that she would have been the last person on earth to have found herself in this position.

'Poor Nan,' she said. 'Is she very upset?'

'She's out of her mind with worry,' he said.

They sat in silence.

Benny went over the whole awfulness of it in her mind. A university career in ruins, a baby by the age of twenty. And possibly from the look of sympathy on Jack's face a problem about Simon Westward.

Eve would have been right about him.

He would never marry Nan Mahon from the North Side of Dublin, a builder's daughter. And beautiful though she was, the fact that she had given in to him would make him less respectful of her than ever.

'What's she going to do? I suppose she's not going to get married?'

She looked at Jack.

His face was working with emotion. He seemed to be struggling for words.

'She *is* getting married.'

Benny looked at him, alarmed. This wasn't normal speech.

He took her hand, and held it to his face. There were tears on his face. Jack Foley was crying.

'She's getting married . . . to me,' he said.

She looked at him in disbelief.

She said absolutely nothing. She knew her mouth was open and her face red with fright.

He was still holding her hand to his face.

His body was shaking with sobs.

'We have to get married, Benny,' he said. 'It's my baby.

## 19

Eve was in the Singing Kettle when she saw Benny at the door. At first she thought that Benny was going to join them and was about to pull up another chair.

Then she saw her face.

'See you later,' she said hastily to the group.

'You haven't finished your chips.' Aidan was amazed. Nothing could be that pressing.

But Eve was out in Leeson Street.

She drew Benny away from the doorway where they were in the main path of almost everyone they knew.

Then, leaning against the iron railings of a house, Benny began to tell her the tale. Sometimes it was hard to hear the words, and sometimes she said the same words over and over again.

Like that he said he loved her, he loved Benny. He really did and he wouldn't have had this happen for the world. But there was nothing else that could be done. The announcement would be in the *Irish Times* on Saturday.

Eve looked across the road and saw a taxi letting

someone off at St Vincent's Private Nursing Home. She dragged Benny through the traffic and pushed her into the back of it.

'Dunlaoghaire,' she said briskly.

'Are you girls all right?' The taxi driver watched them in the mirror. The big girl looked particularly poorly, as if she might get sick all over his car.

'We have the fare,' Eve said.

'I didn't mean that,' he began.

'You did a bit.' They both grinned.

Eve said to Benny that she should rest. There'd be plenty of time to talk when they got home.

Kit was out. She was shopping for a new outfit for Easter when she was going to Kerry as a guest of Kevin Hickey and his father.

They had the kitchen to themselves. Benny sat at the table and through a blur saw Eve prepare a meal for them. She noticed her small thin hands cut deftly through the cold cooked potatoes and trim the rinds from rashers of bacon. She saw thin fingers of bread dipped in a beaten egg.

'I don't want any of this,' Benny said.

'No, but I do. I left my whole lunch in the Kettle, remember?'

Eve took a bottle of sherry from inside a cornflake packet.

'It's to hide it from the drinky students,' she explained.

'I'm not having any.'

'Medicinal,' Eve said, and poured out two huge tumblers for them as she placed the big white plates of comfort food in front of them.

'Now start at the very beginning and tell me slowly. Start from when you sat down on the coat by the canal, and don't tell me that he loves you or I'll get up and throw every single thing that's on this table on the floor and you'll have to clear it up.'

'Eve, please. I know you mean to help.'

'Oh, I mean to help all right,' said Eve. Benny had never seen her face looking so grim. Not in all that long war she had waged with the Westwards, not in the fight with Mother Clare or in her hospital bed had she seen Eve Malone's face so hard and unforgiving.

They talked until the shadows got longer. Benny heard Kit let herself in. She looked around at the untidy kitchen and the half-finished sherry bottle.

'It's all right,' Eve said gently, 'she'll understand. I'll do a quick clear-up.'

'I should be going for my bus.'

'You're staying here. Ring your mother. And Benny . . . she'll ask are you seeing Jack. Tell her you don't see Jack any more. Prepare her for it being over.'

'It needn't be over. He doesn't want it to be over. He says that we have to talk.'

Kit came to the door and looked around in surprise. Before she could make any protest Eve spoke.

'Benny's had a bit of a shock. We're coping with it the

best we can, by eating most of tomorrow's breakfast. I'll go up to the huckster's shop and replace it later.'

Kit knew a crisis when she saw one.

'I have to hang up my finery. See you in half an hour to prepare supper. That's if there's any of that left.'

She nodded encouragingly and disappeared.

Annabel Hogan said that was fine. She had a lot of work to do in the shop. It would save them making a supper. She and Patsy would just get something from Mario's. Benny thought bitterly of all the nights she had left Jack Foley to his own devices in Dublin while she had trundled wearily home to keep her mother company. Now she was less in the way staying in Dublin.

'Are you going out with Jack?' Mother asked.

Despite Eve's warning, Benny couldn't do it. She couldn't tell her mother that it was over. Even to say it meant it might be true.

'Not tonight,' she said brightly. 'No, tonight I'm just going out with Eve.'

Benny lay on Eve's bed and bathed her eyes with cold water while Eve served the supper downstairs. The curtains were drawn and she could hear the clatter of plates and cutlery below. Kit had looked in briefly with a cup of tea. She had made no attempt to cheer her or sympathise. Benny could see why she must be such a restful person to live with.

She dreaded the bucketfuls of sympathy that Mother

would pour on her, the endless wondering and speculating and ludicrous little suggestions. Maybe if you wore paler colours or darker colours, perhaps if you went round to his house to talk to his mother. Men like girls who get on well with their mothers.

She wouldn't tell Mother that Nan was pregnant. It demeaned them all somehow.

It put everything on a different level.

They walked, Benny and Eve, for what seemed and felt like hours and miles.

Sometimes they argued, sometimes Benny stopped to cry again. To say that Eve wouldn't be so harsh if only she could have seen Jack's face, and Eve would tighten her lips and say nothing. As they walked up the Burma Road and into Killiney Park, Benny said that it was all her fault. She hadn't understood how a man needs to make love. It's a biological thing. And when they sat by the obelisk and looked down on the bay she said that Jack Foley was the most dishonest cheating man in the whole world, and why in God's name did he keep saying he loved her if he didn't?

'Because he did love you. Or thought he did,' Eve said. 'That's the whole bloody problem.'

It cheered Benny that Eve could find some ray of hope and sincerity in the whole thing. She thought that Eve had set her heart against him.

'I'm not against him,' Eve said softly. 'I'm only against the idea of your thinking that somehow you'll get him back.'

'But if he still loves me . . .'

'He loves the idea of you, and hates hurting you. That's totally different.'

Eve put her small hand over Benny's. She wished she had better words, softer ones. But she knew that Benny mustn't sleep a night in false hopes. She pointed out that there was very little hope in a situation where one party was explaining things to an unbelieving family in Donnybrook and another in Maple Gardens.

'Why didn't I sleep with him? Then we'd be explaining things tonight in Knockglen.'

When it was dark and they got back to Dunlaoghaire, Eve said Benny should have a bath.

'I don't feel like going to bed.'

'Who said anything about that? We're going out, on the town.'

Benny looked at her friend as if she were mad. After these hours of listening and appearing to understand she must have had no realisation of how Benny felt, if she suggested going out.

'I don't want to meet anyone now. I don't want to be taken out of myself.'

Eve said that wasn't the object of the outing. They were going to go everywhere and meet everyone. They were going to talk about Jack and Nan before it became gossip, and long before it appeared as an engagement announcement in the papers. Eve said that it was the only thing that could be done now. Benny must be seen to hold her head high. She didn't want to live with the sympathy vote for the rest of her life. She didn't want to be written off as someone who was let down. Let nobody be the one to tell Benny the news. Let Benny be the one to tell it everywhere.

'What you are asking is ridiculous,' Benny asked. 'Even if I could do it, everyone would still see through me. They'd know I was upset.'

'But they would never think you had been made a fool of,' Eve said, eyes burning. 'The one good thing about Jack that came out of all this is that he told you first. He told you before he told his mates and asked them for advice. He gave you the story before he gave it to his parents, to the chaplain. You must use that advantage.'

'I don't like to . . . and I suppose I keep hoping that his parents won't let him.'

'They will. When they hear the sound of shotguns coming from Nan's family and moral responsibility from the clergy. And he's a man of twenty. In a few months he won't even have to ask them.'

It was a shadowy night. She only remembered patches of it. Bill Dunne asking was it an April Fool? He couldn't believe that Jack was going to *marry* Nan Mahon. If he was going to marry anyone it should have been Benny. He said that three times in front of Benny.

Three times she answered brightly that she was far too busy becoming a tycoon in Knockglen and trying to get an Honours BA to get married.

Carmel held her hand too tightly and too sympathetically.

Benny wanted to snatch it away, but she knew Carmel meant well.

'It could be all for the best, and we'll still be seeing lots of you, won't we?'

Sean said that he could be knocked over with a feather. And how was Jack going to manage as a married man, with all those years ahead of him? Perhaps he was going to give up his degree and go straight into his uncle's firm as an apprentice. And where were they going to live? The whole thing was startling in the extreme. Had Jack given any indication of what he was going to live on? And presumably a family was planned. Fairly imminently. Hence the haste. Had Jack given Benny any idea of what he was going to live on? Through clenched teeth Benny said that he hadn't.

Johnny O'Brien said he wondered where they'd done it. It gave the lie to the fact that you couldn't get pregnant in a Morris Minor.

When they lay exhausted in their beds in Dunlaoghaire, Benny said sarcastically that she hoped that Eve had found the evening worthwhile, and that it had served her purposes.

'Most certainly it has,' Eve said cheerfully. 'Firstly, you're so tired that you'd sleep standing up, and secondly you've nothing to dread going in tomorrow. They know you've survived the news. They've seen you surviving.'

Aengus Foley had a toothache. He had been given whiskey on a piece of cotton wool. But not much sympathy and no attention. His mother's voice had been sharp as she asked him to go to bed, close the door and realise that pain had to be borne in this life. It wasn't permanent, it would go, probably at the precise moment they took him to Uncle Dermot the dentist.

They seemed to want to talk to Jack interminably in the sitting room. Twice he had come down to hear what it was all about, but the voices were low and urgent, and even the phrases that he could hear he couldn't understand.

John and Lilly Foley were both white with fury as they stood in their drawing room listening to their eldest son describe how he had ruined his life.

'How could you have been so stupid?' his father said over and over again.

'You can't possibly be a father, Jack, you're only a child yourself,' said his mother with tears coming down her face. They begged, they pleaded, they cajoled. They would visit Nan's parents, they would explain about his career. How it couldn't be ruined before it had begun.

'What about *her* career? That has been ruined no matter what happens.' Jack's voice was flat.

'Do you want to marry her?' his father asked, exasperated.

'I don't want to marry her now, in three weeks' time, obviously I don't. But she's a wonderful girl. We made love. I was the one who wanted to, and now we have no other option.'

The pleas began again. She might like to go to England, and give the child for adoption. A lot of people did that.

'It is my child. I'm not going to give it to strangers.'

'Forgive me, Jack, but do we know that it is your child? I have to ask you this.'

'No, you don't have to ask me, but I'll answer you. Yes, I'm absolutely certain that it's my child. She was a virgin the first night I slept with her.'

Jack's mother looked away in disgust.

'And are we also absolutely sure that she *is* pregnant? It's not just a false alarm? A frightened young girl. These things can happen, believe me.'

'I'm sure they can, but not this time. She showed me the report from Holies Street. The lab test was positive.'

'I don't think you should marry her. Truly I don't. She's not even someone you've been going out with for a long time. Someone you've known, that we've all known, for years.'

'I met her on the first day in college. She's been in this house.'

'I'm not saying that she's not a very lovely girl . . .' Jack's father shook his head. 'You're shocked now and frightened. Leave it. Leave it for a few weeks.'

'No, it's not fair on her. If we say we'll wait she'll think I've been persuaded to change my mind. I'm not going to let her think that.'

'And what do her parents think of all this mess . . . ?'

'She's telling them tonight.'

Brian Mahon was sober. He sat at his kitchen table wordless as Nan in an even tone explained to her father, mother and two brothers that she would be getting married to Jack Foley, a law student, in three weeks' time.

She saw her mother twist her hands and bite her lip. Em's dream lay broken into a thousand pieces.

'You'll do nothing of the sort,' Brian Mahon roared.

'I think it would be better for everyone if I did.'

'If you think . . . I'm going to let you . . .' he began, but stopped. It was all bluster anyway. The damage had been done.

Nan sat looking at him cool and unflustered, as if she were telling him that she was going to the cinema.

'I suppose you knew all about this.' He looked at his wife.

'I deliberately didn't tell Em, so that you couldn't accuse her of covering things up,' Nan said.

'And by God there's plenty to cover. He's put you up the pole, I suppose.'

'Brian!' Emily cried.

'Well, if he has, he'll pay good and proper, for whatever we decide to do.' He looked foolish as he sat there angry and red-faced, trying to be the big man in a situation over which he had no control.

'You'll decide nothing,' Nan said to him coldly. 'I decide. And our engagement will be in the *Irish Times* on Saturday morning.'

'Janey Mac, the *Irish Times*,' Nasey said. It was the poshest of the three papers, not often seen in the Mahon household.

'While you're living in my house . . . I tell you that I make decisions.'

'Well, that's just it. I won't be living here much longer.'

'Nan, are you sure that this is what you want to do?'

Nan looked at her mother, faded and frightened. Always living her life in the shadow of someone else, a loud drunken husband, a mean-spirited employer at the hotel, a beautiful daughter whose fantasies she had built up.

Emily would never change.

'It is, Em. And it's what I'm going to do.'

'But university . . . your degree.'

'I never wanted one. You know that. We both know that. I was only going there to meet people.'

They talked, mother and daughter, as if the men didn't exist. They spoke to each other across the kitchen, across the broken dream, without any of the accusations or excuses that would be the conversation of most girls in this situation.

'But it wasn't a student you were going to meet. Not this way.'

'The other didn't work, Em. The gap was too wide.'

'And what do you expect us to do, coming home with this kind of news . . . ?' Brian wanted to put a stop to the conversation that he didn't even understand.

'I want to ask you a question. Are you prepared to put on a good suit and behave well for four hours at a wedding, without a drink in your hand, or are you not?'

'And if I'm not?'

'If I even *think* you're not, we'll go to Rome and get married there. I will tell everyone that my father wouldn't have a wedding for us.'

'Go on, do that then,' he taunted her.

'I will if I have to. But I know you, you'd like to blow and blow and boast to your pals and the people you sell supplies to that your daughter's having a big society wedding. You'd like to hire the clothes, because you're still a handsome man and you know it.'

Emily Mahon looked at her daughter in amazement. Unerringly she had gone for the right targets. She knew exactly how to make her father give her a wedding.

Brian would think of nothing else. No expense would be spared.

'Go home with her for the weekend,' Kit urged Eve.

'No, she has to do it on her own.'

Knockglen was quick to judge, and it was important who began to spread the story. If Benny was there saying to people that her romance with Jack Foley was a thing of the past, then no serious whispers would begin. Benny was going to have to live with enough this summer without having to live with the pity of Knockglen as well. Eve was an expert on avoiding the pity of Knockglen.

Mother was still in the shop. It was after seven, and Benny had only looked in automatically and seen her there. Benny let herself in with the key she carried on her key ring.

'Glory be to God, you put the heart across me.'

Annabel Hogan was standing on a chair trying to reach something that had slid away on the top of a cupboard. Annabel was hoping that it was some nice rolls of paper with the name Hogan's on it. Eddie had bought it years ago, but it had proved impractical to cut. It hadn't been thrown out. It might be up here covered with dust.

Benny looked up at her animated face. Perhaps when people were older they did recover from things. It was impossible to believe that this was the same listless woman who had sat by the fire with the book falling from her hand. Now she was lively and occupied, her eyes were bright and her tone had light and shade.

Benny said she was bigger, she'd reach. And true, there it was, rolls of it. They threw it down on the floor. Tomorrow they would dust it, see if it was usable.

'You look tired. Was it a busy day?' Mother asked. It had been a day of heartache to walk the corridors and sit in lectures while the rumour about Jack and Nan spread like a forest fire. Sheila actually came and offered her sympathy as one would for a bereavement. Several groups had stopped speaking as Benny approached.

But Eve had been right. Better let the other story spread too, the news that Benny was not wearing mourning. That she had been able to talk about it cheerfully. There had been no sign of either Nan or Jack in college. Benny kept thinking that Jack was going to appear by magic, all smiles, tucking his arm into hers, and that the whole thing would have been a bad dream.

654

Mother knew none of this, of course. But she did realise that Benny looked worn out.

She thought she knew just what would cheer her up.

'Come up and look at what Patsy and I were doing today. We've pulled around a lot of the furniture on the first floor. We thought it would be grand for your party before we get the place painted. Then you could make as much mess as you liked without having to worry about it . . . you could even have some of the boys stay here and the girls stay at Lisbeg . . .'

Benny's face was stony. She had forgotten the party. The great gathering planned for the weekend after Easter. She and Jack had talked of little else as they sat with their groups of friends over the last weeks. And all the time, every night possibly, he was saying goodbye to her and making love with Nan.

She gave a little shudder at how she had been deceived, and how he had said with his eyes full of tears that he couldn't help himself, and he was sorrier than he could ever say. She walked wordlessly up the stairs behind her mother and listened to the animated conversation about the party that would never be.

Gradually her mother, noticing no response, let her voice die away.

'They are still coming, aren't they?' she said.

'I'm not sure. A lot of things will have changed by then.' Benny swallowed. 'Jack and Nan are going to get married,' she said.

Her mother looked at her open-mouthed.

'What did you say?'

'Jack. He's going to marry Nan, you see. So things might change about the party.'

'Jack Foley . . . your Jack?'

'He's not my Jack any more. Hasn't been for some time.'

'But when did this happen? You never said a word. They can't get married.'

'They are, Mother. The engagement will be in tomorrow's *Irish Times*.'

The look on her mother's face was almost too much to bear. The naked sympathy, the total incomprehension, the struggling for words.

Benny realised that Eve was probably right in this harsh face-saving exercise. Bad as it was now, it would be worse if she had said nothing and her mother had found out through someone else. Like today in college, it was over now, the shock and the pity and the whispering. They couldn't continue indefinitely if Benny seemed to be in the whole of her senses. What was very hard was this pretence that she and Jack had been just one more casual romance, with no hearts broken at the end of it.

'Benny, I'm so sorry. I can't tell you how sorry I am.'

'That's all right, Mother. You were always the one to say that college romances come and go . . .' The words were fine, but the tone was shaky.

'I suppose she's . . .'

'She's very excited, certainly, and . . . and . . . everything.'

If her mother said the wrong thing now she would lose the little control she still held on to. Please let Mother not embrace her or say something about the fickleness of men.

Being in business for a few weeks must have taught Annabel a great deal about life.

There were just a few headshakes at the modern generation, and then a suggestion that they go home for tea before Patsy sent a search party out to look for them.

After supper she called on Clodagh. She moved restlessly around, picking things up and putting them down again as they talked. Clodagh sat and stitched, watching her carefully.

'Are you pregnant?' Clodagh asked eventually.

'I'm not the one who is, unfortunately,' Benny said. She told the tale. Clodagh never put down her needle. She nodded, and agreed, and disagreed and asked questions. At no time did she say that Jack Foley was a bastard, and that Nan Mahon was worse to betray her friend. She accepted it as one of the things that happen in life.

Benny grew stronger as she spoke. The prickling of her nose and eyes, the urge to weep, had faded a little.

'I still believe that it's me he loves,' she said timidly at the end of the saga.

'It might well be,' Clodagh was matter-of-fact. 'But that's not important now. It's what people do is important, not what they say or feel.'

She sounded so like Eve, so determined, so sure. In the most matter-of-fact way she said that Jack and Nan would probably make no better or no worse a fist of getting married and having a child than most people did. But that's what they would be. A couple with a child. And then another and another.

Whether Jack still loved Benny Hogan was irrelevant. He had made his choice. He had done what was called the decent thing.

'It was the right thing,' Benny said, against her will.

Clodagh shrugged. It might have been, or it might not, but whatever it was it was the thing he had done.

'You'll survive, Benny,' she said comfortingly. 'And to give him his due, which I don't want to do at this moment, he wants you to survive. He wants the best for you. He thinks that's love.'

Late that night at the kitchen table Patsy said that all men were pigs and that handsome men were out and out pigs. She said he had been well received and made welcome in this house, and that he was such a prize pig he didn't know a lady when he saw one. That Nan wasn't a lady for all her fine talk. He'd discover that when it was too late.

'I don't think it was a lady he wanted,' Benny explained. 'I think it was more a lover. And I wasn't any use to him there.'

'Nor should you have been,' Patsy said. 'Isn't it bad enough that we're going to have to do it over and over when we're married, and have a roof over our heads. What's the point in letting them have it for nothing before?'

It seemed to shed a gloomy light on the future that lay

ahead for Patsy and Mossy. It was almost impossible to imagine other people having sex, but depressing to think that Patsy was dreading it so much.

Patsy poured them more drinking chocolate and said that she wished Nan not a day of luck for the rest of her life. She hoped that her baby would be born with a deformed back and a cast in its eye.

*The engagement is announced between Ann Elizabeth (Nan), only daughter of Mr and Mrs Brian Mahon, Maple Gardens, Dublin and John Anthony (Jack), eldest son of Dr and Mrs John Foley, Donnybrook, Dublin.*

'I saw the *Irish Times* this morning.' Sean Walsh had made it his business to exercise the two Jack Russells up and down the street until he met Benny.

'Oh yes?'

'That's a bit of a surprise, isn't it?'

'About Princess Soraya?' she asked innocently. The Shah of Persia was about to divorce his wife. There had been a lot about it in the press. Sean was disappointed. He had hoped for a better reaction, a hanging of the head. An embarrassment even.

'I meant your friend getting married?'

'Nan Mahon? That's right. You saw it in the paper. We didn't know when they'd be making it official.'

'But the man . . . she's marrying your friend.' Sean was totally confused now.

'Jack? Of course.' Benny was bland and innocent.

'I thought you and he . . .' Sean was lost for words.

Benny helped him. They had indeed been friends, even walking out . . . as people might put it. But college life was renowned for all the first-year friendships, people moved around like musical chairs. Sean looked at her long and hard. He would not be cheated of his moment of victory.

'Well, well, well. I'm glad to see that you take it so well, Benny. I must say that when I saw them here, around Knockglen, I thought it was a . . . well, a little insensitive, you know. But I didn't say anything to you. I didn't want to upset anybody.'

'I'm sure you didn't, Sean. But they weren't here. Not here around Knockglen. So you were mistaken.'

'I don't think so,' said Sean Walsh.


She thought about the way he said it. She thought about Clodagh having seen Jack at Dessie Burns' petrol pump. She thought about Johnny O'Brien wondering where they did it. But it was beyond belief. *Where* could they have gone? And if Jack loved her, how could he have come back to her home town to make love to someone else?


Somehow the weekend passed. It was hard to remember that when the phone rang it wouldn't be Jack. It was hard when Fonsie talked about the party to realise that nobody would come to it. It was hard to believe that he wouldn't be waiting in the Annexe with eyes dancing, waving her over, delighted to see her.

The hardest thing was to forget that he had said on the banks of the canal that he still loved her.

It was easy for Eve and Clodagh to dismiss that. But Benny knew Jack wouldn't have said it unless he meant it. And if he did still love her none of the other business made sense.

She didn't even allow herself to think about meeting Nan. The day would come, probably next week, when she would have to see her.

There had been conflicting stories. Nan was going to continue and finish her degree, while her mother did the babysitting. Or that Nan was going to leave immediately. That she was out already flat hunting. Benny had kept the cutting from the newspaper. She read it over and over to make it have some meaning.

John Anthony. She had known that. And even more, like that the name he took at Confirmation was Michael, so his initials were JAM Foley. She hadn't known that Nan would have been baptised Ann Elizabeth. Probably Nan had been a pet name when she was a beautiful little baby. A baby who could get what she wanted. All the time.

Perhaps she hadn't been able to get Simon Westward, and so she had taken Jack instead. How unfair of Simon not to want Nan. That's what must have happened. Benny raged at him, and his snobbery. Nan was exactly the kind of person who would have livened up Westlands. If only that romance had continued then none of this would have happened.

Benny stood behind the counter in the shop, in order to

free her mother and Mike for earnest discussions on new cloth. Heather Westward came in in her St Mary's uniform.

She had come in to buy a handkerchief for her grandfather. It was a treat because he was so ill, and it would cheer him up. Was there one for under one and six? Benny found one, and wondered should it be wrapped up for him? Heather thought not. He wouldn't be able to open the wrapping paper, maybe just a bag.

'He mightn't even know what it is, but he's not well, you have to do something?' She looked at Benny for approval.

Benny thought she was right. She handed over the handkerchief for the old man who had shouted at Eve and called Eve's mother a whore.

He might have done the same if Simon had married Nan.

Suddenly with a jolt Benny wondered if Nan had slept with Simon.

Suppose she had. Just suppose that she had, then this baby might be his, and not Jack's after all.

Why hadn't she thought of it before?

The whole thing that looked as if it could never be solved might, in fact, have a solution after all.

She looked wild-eyed at the thought of it. She saw Heather watching her in alarm.

She *must* say it to Jack. She had to. He couldn't be forced to marry someone he didn't love, when it might not be his child. No matter that he had slept with Nan. Benny would forgive him. Like she had forgiven him over that business in Wales. It wouldn't matter, just as long as he loved her.

But the feeling of excitement, the ray of hope, died down. Benny realised that she was clutching at straws. That Jack and Nan must have had this discussion. She wished she could remember how long ago it was that Nan had been talking enthusiastically about Simon, but if it was over for ages . . . then there was no hope.

And anyway Jack wouldn't be foolish enough . . .

He'd know, wouldn't he? Men always did. That's why you had to keep your virginity until you married, so that they'd know it was the first time.

No, it was just a mad, wild hope.

But suppose she believed it to be true. It would only lead to a huge confrontation, and almighty indignation if she were to suggest it to Jack. Imply that Nan was passing off someone else's child on him.

The thought had better go back to where it came from.

Heather was still in the shop. She seemed to be hovering as if about to ask a favour.

'Is there anything else, Heather?'

'You know the Easter Pageant. Eve and Aidan are going to come. It's on Holy Thursday. I was wondering would you like to come too? As part of my group.'

'Yes, yes I will, thank you.' Her mind was still far away.

'I'd have forced Simon to come, but he's in England. He mightn't even be back for Easter.'

'What's he doing there?'

'Oh, they think he's going to ask this woman to marry him. She's got pots and pots of money.'

'That would be nice.'

'We could get the drainage and the fencing done.'

'Would you mind, someone else coming in there?'

'No, I'd hardly notice.' Heather was practical.

'And this romance with the lady in England . . .' Benny enquired. 'Has it been going on for a while or is it new?'

'For ages,' Heather said. 'It's about time they made some move.'

So that was that. The wild little hope that Simon could be drawn into the whole business seemed to have faded.

Benny looked distant and abstracted. Heather had been about to tell her that there had been some great row with Nan. That Nan had come to Westlands about four weeks ago all dressed up and there had been words in the Morning Room and she had driven Simon's car to the bus and wouldn't let him come with her.

Heather remembered the date, because it was when they were casting for the Easter Pageant and she had been very nervous. If she had told Benny then, Benny would have realised that it was the very same day as the party in the rugby club. The one she hadn't gone to, but Nan had. The very night it had all begun.

Nan went to Sunday lunch at the Foleys' to meet the family. She was immaculately dressed, and Lilly thought that they would have no apologies or explanations to make for her on grounds of appearance. Her stomach was flat, and her manner was entirely unapologetic.

She came up the steps of the large Donnybrook house as of right, not as the working-class girl who had been taken advantage of by the son of the house. She spoke easily and without guile. She made no effort to ingratiate herself.

She paid more attention to Dr Foley than to his wife, which would have been the appropriate attitude of any intelligent girl coming to the house.

She was pleasant, but not effusive to Kevin, Gerry, Ronan and Aengus. She didn't forget their names or mix them up, but neither did she seek their approval.

Lilly Foley watched her with dislike, this cunning, shrewd girl with no morals who had ensnared her eldest son. There were few ways she could fault the public performance. The girl's table manners were perfect.

At coffee afterwards in the drawing room, just the four of them, Nan spoke to them with such a clear and unaffected stance that both of Jack's parents were taken aback.

'I realise what a disappointment all this must be to you, and how well you are covering this. I want to thank you very much.'

They murmured, startled words denying any sense of disappointment.

'And I am sure that Jack has told you my family are all much simpler people than you are, less educated, and in many ways their hopes for me have been realised rather than crushed. If I am to marry into such a family as yours.'

She went on to explain to them the kind of ceremony

that she would like to provide and for which her father would pay. A lunch for perhaps twenty or thirty people in one of the better hotels. Very possibly the one where her mother worked in the hotel shop.

There would be minimum speech-making because her father was not a natural orator, and she thought that she would wear an oyster satin coat and dress instead of a long, white dress. She would hope that some of Jack's and her friends would attend. On her side she would provide two parents, two brothers, two business associates of her father and one aunt.

When Jack took her away on their journey for afternoon tea in Maple Gardens, John and Lilly Foley exchanged glances.

'Well?' she said.

'Well?' he answered.

He filled the silence by pouring them a small brandy each. It was never their custom to have a drink like this in the afternoon, but the circumstances seemed to call for it.

'She's very presentable,' said Jack's mother grudgingly.

'And very practical. She had the Holies Street report in her handbag, left open for us to see in case we were going to question it.'

'And very truthful about her own background.'

'But she never said one word about loving Jack,' Dr Foley said with a worried frown.

In Maple Gardens the table was set for tea. A plate of biscuits with sardines on them, another with an egg mayonnaise. There was a bought swiss roll and a plate of Jacob's USA assortment. Nasey and Paul were in navy suits and shirts. Brian Mahon wore his new brown suit. It hadn't cost as much as it should have because he had been able to give the man in the shop a few cans of paint for his own house. Cans of paint that hadn't cost anything in the first place.

'There's no need to tell all that to Jack Foley when he arrives,' Emily had warned.

'Jesus Christ, will you stop nagging at me? I've agreed to stay away from the jar until after they've been and gone, which is a fine imposition to put on a man who's going to lash out for a fancy society wedding. But still, give you lot an inch and you take a bloody mile . . .'

Jack Foley was a handsome young fellow. He sat beside Nan during afternoon tea. He tried a little of everything. He thanked Mr Mahon for the generous plans for the wedding. He thanked Mrs Mahon for all her support. He hoped Paul and Nasey would be ushers in the church.

'You'd hardly need ushers for that size of a crowd,' said Nasey, who thought twenty people was the meanest he'd ever heard of.

'Who's going to be your best man?' Paul asked.

Jack was vague. He hadn't thought. One of his brothers, possibly.

He felt awkward asking Aidan, what with the whole Eve and Nan friendship. And Bill Dunne or Johnny . . . it was all a bit awkward, to be honest.

He turned to Nan. 'Who'll be the bridesmaid?' he asked.

'Secret,' Nan said.

They talked about places to live, and flats. Brian Mahon said that he'd be able to give them the name of builders who did good conversion jobs if they found an old place and wanted to do it up.

Jack said that he would be working in his uncle's office, first as a clerk, and then as an apprentice. He was going to take lessons in book-keeping almost at once, in order to be of some use in there.

Several times he felt Nan's mother's eyes on him, with a look of regret.

Obviously she was upset about her daughter being pregnant, but he felt it was something more than that.

As Nan talked on cheerfully of basements in South Circular Road, or top-storey landings in Rathmines, Emily Mahon's eyes filled with tears. She tried to brush them away unseen, but Jack felt that there was some terrible sorrow there, as if she had wanted something very different for her beautiful daughter.

When they had gone Brian Mahon loosened his collar.

'You can't say too much against him.'

'I never said anything against him,' Emily said.

'He had his fun and he's paying for it. At least that's to his credit.' Brian was grudging.

Emily Mahon took off her good blouse and put on her old one automatically. She tied an apron around her waist and began to clear the table. She could puzzle for a thousand years and never understand why Nan was settling for this.

Nan and she had never wanted cheap bedsitters, student flats, cobwebby conversion jobs. For years they had turned the pages of the magazines and looked at the places where Nan might live. There was never a moment when they planned a shotgun marriage to a student.

And Nan was adamant about saying that her relationship with Simon Westward was long over. And had never been serious. She was almost too adamant when she was telling her mother how long it had been over.

Brian changed into his normal clothes for going to the pub.

'Come on, lads, we'll get a pint and talk normally for a while.'

Emily filled the sink with hot water and did the washing-up. She was very worried indeed.

Jack and Nan sat in his father's car.

'That's the worst over,' she said.

'It'll be fine,' he assured her.

She didn't believe the worst was over, and he didn't believe everything would be fine.

But they couldn't admit it.

After all, it was there in black and white in the paper. And the chaplain would be able to give them a date very shortly.

Aidan Lynch said that Sundays weren't the same without Heather.

Eve said that he had been invited to watch Heather in a

sheet helping Our Lord to carry his burden. Next week, on Holy Thursday, could he bear to come? Aidan said he'd love it, it would count as his Easter Duty. Would they bring a First Night present for Heather?

Eve said that he was worse than Heather. The thing was meant to be some kind of religious outpouring, not a song and dance act. Still it was great that he'd come down, and he could even stay the night in the cottage.

'It'll make up for us not having the party,' Eve said.

'Why won't we have the party?' Aidan asked.

Rosemary was sitting in the Annexe with Bill and Johnny. She was telling them that Tom, her medical boyfriend, had very healing hands. She refused to listen to ribald jokes on the subject. She said that she had an unmerciful headache and he had massaged it right away.

'I'm very sorry that there'll be no party now, down in Knockglen,' she said. 'I was looking forward to Tom coming and meeting you all properly.'

'Why won't there be a party?' asked Bill Dunne.

'I never heard anything about it being off,' said Johnny O'Brien.

Jack was not at his lectures now. He hadn't officially given up, but he was in his uncle's office all day. Learning the ropes. Aidan was going to meet him at six o'clock.

'He has time to go out and drink pints, has he?' Eve said disapprovingly.

'Listen, he hasn't been sent to Coventry. He's not in

disgrace. He's just getting married. That's not the end of the earth,' Aidan said.

Eve shrugged.

'And what's more, I'm going to be his best man, if he asks me.'

'You're not!' She was aghast.

'He's my friend. He can rely on me. Anyone can rely on a friend.'

Nan made an appearance in college. She went to a ten o'clock lecture and then joined the crowds streaming down the stairs to the Annexe.

There was a rustle as they saw her coming to join the queue.

'Well, I'm off now,' Rosemary said under her breath to Carmel. 'If there's one thing I can't bear, it's the sight of bloodshed.'

'Benny won't say anything,' Carmel whispered back.

'Yes, but have you seen Eve's face?'

Benny was trying to calm Eve down. It was ridiculous to say that Nan didn't have a right to show her face in college. Benny begged Eve not to make a scene. What had been the point of urging her to get over everything publicly if Eve was going to ruin it all now?

'That's quite right,' Eve said suddenly. 'It was just a surge of bad temper.'

'Well, why don't you go now, in case it surges again?'

'I can't, Benny. I'd be afraid you'd be so bloody nice and

ask her all about the wedding dress and offer to knit bootees.'

Benny squeezed her friend's hand. 'Go on, Eve, please. I'm better on my own. I won't do any of that. And anyway she won't join us.'

Nan went to another table. She drank her coffee with a group she knew from another class.

She looked across at Benny, who looked back.

Neither of them made a gesture or mouthed a word. Nan looked away first.


Nan lay on her bed. Jack was going out with Aidan, which surprised her. She thought that there would be a heavy boycott from Eve's side of things.

But men were easier, more generous at forgiving. Men were more generous at everything. She lay with her feet raised on two cushions.

If Em had been a different kind of mother, she would have pursued the question she had been skirting around. Emily Mahon knew that her daughter was carrying Simon Westward's child. What she didn't know was why she, the princess, was going to let this one mistake spoil a lifetime of planning. Emily would suggest going to England, having the child adopted, and starting all over again.

The pursuit, the quest, the path to a better life. But Em didn't know that Nan was tired. Tired and weary of pretending. And that for once she had met someone, a good and honest person, who didn't have a life plan . . .

a system of passing black as white. That's what she had been doing. Like Simon had been passing as rich.

Jack Foley was just himself.

When told that a child was his he accepted that it was. And when it was born, it would be theirs. She could leave university. She had made a good impression on the Foley parents. She could see that. There was a small mews at the end of their garden. In time it would be done up, in more time they would live in a house similar to his parents'. They would entertain, they would have dinner parties, she would keep in touch with her mother.

It would all be a great sense of peace compared to the never-ending contest. The game where the goalposts kept moving, and the rules changing.

Nan Mahon was going to marry Jack Foley, not just because she was pregnant, but because at the age of almost twenty she was tired.

Kit Hegarty had a lemon-coloured suit and a white blouse for her trip to Kerry.

'You need some colour to go with it. I keep forgetting we can't ask Nan.'

'Have you spoken to her at all?' Kit asked.

'Nope.'

'God, you're a tough girl. I'd hate to make you my enemy.'

The Hayes next door had come in to wish Kit well. Ann Hayes said what she needed was a big copper-coloured brooch and she had the very thing at home.

Mr Hayes looked at Kit admiringly.

'Lord bless us, Kit, but you're like a bride,' he said.

'Stop putting so much hope in this. It's only an outing.'

'Your Joseph would have been glad for you to meet another fellow. He often said.'

Kit looked at him startled. Joseph Hegarty would have said little to the Hayes, he hardly knew them.

She thanked him, but said as much.

'You're wrong, Kit. He did know us. He sent us letters for his son.'

Eve's heart chilled. Why did this man have to tell Kit now?

'He wanted to keep in touch with his boy. He wrote every month, giving his address as he moved on from place to place.'

'And Francis read these?'

'Frank read them all. He went to see him last summer when he was canning peas in England.'

'Why did he never say, why did neither of them ever say?'

'They didn't want to hurt you. The time wasn't right to tell you.'

'And why is the time right now?'

'Because Joe Hegarty wrote to me before he died. He wrote to say that if you met a good man I was to explain that you must never worry about having deprived your son of his father. Because you didn't.'

'Did he know he was going to die?'

'Sure, we're all going to die,' said Mr Hayes, as his wife

came back in and pinned the brooch on Kit Hegarty's lapel.

Kit smiled, unable to speak. It was something she had been worrying a lot about lately. When she saw how close Paddy Hickey was to his sons, she wondered had she done wrong letting Francis grow up without knowing a father?

She was glad that it had been explained in front of Eve. It showed how much Eve was part of the family.

The Hayes were going to keep an eye on the house for two weeks. The outing was going to be much longer than Kit had first thought when it had been described as a weekend. And Eve would be down in Knockglen. Kit was delighted they had decided to go ahead with their party. It would be a further betrayal to admit that there could be no party now. That the stars had gone.

When Carmel's Sean had been organising the finances, he had given some money to Jack as an advance. Jack was the one with most access to a car. Jack could get them a reduction through a wine merchant. He had been the one who was going to bring the drink. But obviously everything had changed now. And no one liked to remind Jack that he was already in possession of eleven pounds of the communal money.

Carmel's Sean suggested they should forget it. The other boys agreed. Jack had quite enough on his plate without reminding him that he owed the kitty eleven pounds.

*

Heather was wonderful in the pageant.

Aidan, Eve and Benny were enormously proud of her. She was a stockier, more solid, Simon of Cyrene than was normally shown by artists, but then surely they would have pulled from the crowd someone strong to help in the journey up the hill of Calvary.

Mother Francis had always urged the children to make up their own words.

Heather had been adept at this.

'Let me help you with that cross, Jesus, dear,' she said to Fiona Carroll, who was playing Our Lord with a sanctimonious face.

'It's a difficult thing to carry going uphill,' Heather added. 'It would be much easier on the flat, but then they wouldn't see the Crucifixion so well, you see.'

There was tea and biscuits in the school hall afterwards and Heather was greatly congratulated.

'It's the best Easter ever,' she said, with her eyes shining. 'And Eve says I can be a waitress at her party, next week, so long as I go home before the necking starts.'

Eve looked at Mother Francis sadly. A grown-up look of collusion, of admitting how children would hang you. Heather was unaware of anything amiss.

'Will your friend be here again?' she asked Benny.

'Which one?'

'The man that took to fancying Welsh girls for a bit, but came back.'

'He went off again,' Benny said.

'Better leave him to go then,' Heather advised. 'He sounds a bit unreliable.'

Standing there in her sheet, in the middle of the party, Heather had no idea why Eve, Aidan and Benny got such a fit of hysterical laughter, and had to wipe the tears out of their eyes. She wished she knew what she had said that was so funny, but she was glad anyway that it had pleased them all so much.

Everyone was delighted to be going to Knockglen. Not for just a party, but for a series of outings.

They would arrive on the Friday after six o'clock, when there would be drinks in Hogan's, and then they would all adjourn to Mario's for the evening. There were bunk beds and sofas and sleeping bags for the boys in Hogan's shop; the girls were going to stay in Eve's and Benny's houses. Then there would be a great trek to Ballylee for lunch and a walk in the woods on Saturday and back for the main event, the proper party in Eve's cottage.

They all said that the one at Christmas would take some beating. Eve said it would be better than ever now. An April moon, and the blossom out on the hedges and grass instead of mud around. There would be wild flowers all over the disused quarry, it would look less like a bomb site than it had done in winter. No one would slip on the mucky paths this time. They wouldn't need to huddle by the fire.

Sister Imelda was as usual aching to be asked to help with the cooking.

'It's no fun for you, Sister, if you can't see them enjoying it,' Eve pleaded.

'It's probably just as well I don't see all that goes on up there. It's enough for me to be told they like it.'

'If Simon and the woman from Hampshire come home that weekend, are you going to ask them?' Heather asked.

'No,' said Eve.

'I thought you only hated Grandfather. I thought you and Simon got on well enough.'

'We do.' Eve was dry.

'If he had married Nan, would you have come to the wedding?'

'You ask an awful lot of questions.'

'Mother Francis says we should have enquiring minds,' Heather said primly.

Eve laughed heartily. That was true. Mother Francis *had* always said it.

'I might have, if I'd been asked. But I don't think your brother would ever have married Nan.'

Heather said it would all depend whether Nan had money or not. Simon couldn't marry anyone poor because of the drainage and the fencing.

He had thought that Nan's father was a wealthy builder in the beginning. She heard a lot of this from Bee Moore, but Bee always had to stop when Mrs Walsh came in because Mrs Walsh didn't like gossip.

Heather was helping to tidy up the cottage garden. They had a big sack, which they were filling with weeds. Mossy would take it away later.

They worked easily, the unlikely friends and cousins, side by side.

Eve said that maybe they shouldn't talk too much about Nan over the weekend. She was going to marry Jack Foley shortly. Neither of them would be here. There was nothing hush-hush, just better not to bring the subject up.

'Why?' Heather asked.

Eve was a respecter of the enquiring mind. As they dug the dandelions and slashed back the nettles, she told an edited version of the story. Heather listened gravely.

'I think you're taking it worse than Benny,' she said eventually.

'I think I am,' Eve agreed. 'Benny fought all my battles for me at school. And now there's nothing I can do for her. If I had my way, I'd kill Nan Mahon. I'd kill her with my bare hands.'

The night before they were all due to arrive, Benny lay in bed and couldn't sleep.

She would close her eyes and think that a lot of time had passed, but when she saw the luminous hands of the little pink clock she realised that it had only been ten minutes.

She got up and sat by her window. Out in the moonlight she saw the shape of Dr Johnson's house opposite, and the edge of Dekko Moore's, where young Heather said she was going to work as a harness maker.

What had Benny wanted when she was Heather's age, twelve? She had grown out of the wish for pink velvet dresses and pointed shoes with pom-poms. What had she wanted? Maybe a crowd of friends, people that she and Eve could play with without having to be home at a special time. It wasn't very much.

And they had got it, hadn't they? A whole crowd coming down from Dublin to herself and Eve. How little you knew when you were twelve. Heather Westward wouldn't want to be a harness maker when she was twenty. She'd forget that this is what she had wanted now.

She couldn't get Jack out of her mind tonight. The weeks in between had passed by without touching her. His face was just as clear as it always was, and never more clear than when he had cried on the canal bank and told her he still loved her and that he wouldn't have had this happen for all the world.

She wondered what he and Nan talked about. Did Nan ever tell him how she had helped Benny to put on make-up, and to use good perfume? How Nan had advised Benny to hold in her tummy and push out her chest?

But it was madness to suppose that they ever talked about her at all.

Or to suppose that either of them even remembered that they had been intending to spend this weekend in Knockglen.

'What are you going to wear?' Clodagh asked her next morning.

'I don't know. I've forgotten. I can't get interested. Please, Clodagh, don't nag me.'

'Wouldn't dream of it. See you at Mario's tonight then.'

'What about up above the shop first, that's where we're starting.'

'If you can't be bothered to get dressed for it, why should I be bothered to go?'

'Damn you to Hell, Clodagh. What'll I wear?'

'Come into the shop and we'll see,' said Clodagh, smiling from ear to ear.

By six o'clock they were coming up the stairs, exclaiming and praising. The huge rooms, the high ceilings, the lovely old windows, the davenport, the marvellous frames on the old pictures.

It was like Aladdin's Cave.

'I'd live here if I were you,' Bill Dunne said to Benny's mother. 'Not that your own house isn't terrific . . .'

'I'm half thinking about it,' Annabel Hogan said to him.

Benny felt her heart soar. The groundwork was beginning to pay off. She was afraid to smile too much. Clodagh had sewed her into a very tight country-and-western-type bodice. She looked as if she were going to take out a guitar and give them a song. Johnny O'Brien said that she looked utterly fantastic. Fabulous figure, out-in-out, he said, showing her with his hands. Jack must be mad, he said helpfully.

They were all in high form to cross the street to rock the night away in Mario's.

Eve nudged Benny as Sean Walsh, Mrs Healy and the two Jack Russells went for an evening constitutional around the town.

Mario was delighted to see them, rather over-welcoming, Fonsie thought, until he heard that Mr Flood had been in with a message from the nun in the tree saying that his café was a den of vice and must not only be closed down, but should be exorcised as well.

Any company other than Mr Flood looked good to Mario at the moment.

Fonsie's new juke box, which Mario secretly thought looked like the product of a diseased mind, spat out the music. The tables were pushed back and those who couldn't fit in the café watched and cheered from outside.

With a mixture of regret and amazement Mario looked back on the days before his sister's son had come to work with him. The peaceful poverty-stricken days when his till hardly ever rang and most people couldn't have told you there was a chip shop and a café in Knockglen.

On Saturday Benny and Patsy fried a breakfast for Sheila, Rosemary and Carmel. Then they went up to the shop and did the same for Aidan, Bill, Johnny and the man who was always called Carmel's Sean.

'I do have an identity of my own,' he grumbled when Benny called out to know if Carmel's Sean would like one egg or two.

'In this town if your name is Sean, you'd be wise to give yourself some other handle,' Benny said. Patsy got a fit of the giggles. It was magical to be able to mock Sean Walsh in these very premises.

Slowly the day took shape. The journey to Ballylee

began. Never had the countryside looked lovelier. Benny turned round in the car twice to point things out to Jack. She wondered would it take her long to remember he wasn't there. And wouldn't ever be there again.

Bill Dunne and Eve got separated from the others as they walked up to see an old folly. A summer house facing the wrong way that a family even more unused to the land than the Westwards were had built.

'Benny's fine over all this Jack business, isn't she?' Bill asked, looking for confirmation.

'Hasn't she plenty of fellows looking for her attention? Of course she's fine.' Eve was burning loyal.

'Has she?' Bill seemed disappointed.

He told Eve that nothing had ever surprised him as much. Jack was inclined to talk, the way fellows do, the way girls did too amongst each other, he supposed. He never mentioned a word about Nan. Oh, he used to complain that Benny was a convent girl through and through which presumably meant she wouldn't go to bed with him, despite all his blandishments, and that she wasn't in Dublin enough. But not till the night of the rugby club party did Jack even go out with Nan, he knew that for a fact.

'That was only a few weeks ago,' Eve said, surprised.

'Yes, didn't the other business happen very quick?' Bill shivered in case talking about it might make him the putative father of someone's child.

'Well, it only takes once, that's what they always say.' Eve's voice was light.

'That must have been all it was.' Bill was sympathetic.

Eve changed the subject. Bill's line of thinking was dangerously near to her own. That the pregnancy had happened too suddenly.

She had not been able to pinpoint Jack and Nan's first encounter until now, and that night was only a few weeks ago. It was the night she and Benny had gone to the pictures in Dunlaoghaire. Even with Benny's poor mathematics, that was surely too soon for anything to have happened and be confirmed. Surely they would know this. Surely Jack's father, a doctor, would know?

And that meant something almost impossible to believe. It meant that Nan Mahon was pregnant with someone else's child, and had taken Benny's Jack to be its father.

Her mind was racing, but the race came to an abrupt end. The engagement was announced. The marriage date was fixed. This is what Nan and Jack were going to do. It wasn't a melodrama of blood tests and confrontations. It would go ahead, no matter what.

To cast any suspicions would only raise Benny's hopes again and break her heart further.

And then there was the possibility that she could be wrong. Eve had never been sure where Simon and Nan could have made love, and had been forced to dismiss the possibility that they ever had. Westlands was out, Maple Gardens was out, so was a car. Simon had no money for hotels. Nan had no friends. None at all except Benny and Eve. She was having great difficulty in finding anyone to be her bridesmaid.

Eve had been forced reluctantly to believe that they might not have been lovers at all. Which was disappointing, as it meant there was no chance of being able to blame the pregnancy on Simon.

But then if there had been any possibility of doing that, surely Nan would have done it. She wouldn't have let a chance like that pass by.

But there had been no tales of any rows with Simon. According to all accounts, or to Nan's account, the friendship had ended amicably a long time ago.

'You're muttering to yourself,' Bill Dunne criticised her.

'It's my only unpleasant habit. Aidan says it's a tiny flaw in an otherwise perfect character. Come on, I'll race you up to the folly.'

She wanted no more of these buzzings in her mind.

The house looked beautiful. It had been well worth it to have Mossy give the door a coat of paint. And the garden was a tribute to Heather's and Eve's hard work. Heather was inside in a white chef's hat made for her by Clodagh, and a butcher's apron. It seemed excessive for passing plates of savouries, but she felt important in it. The dusk was turning to darkness. The stars were coming out in the clear sky.

Figures came up the path to the party. Teddy Flood, Clodagh Pine, Maire Carroll and her new fiancé, Tom, the medical student that Rosemary had such ferocious designs on. A few more from college who were just coming for the night rather than making a whole weekend out of it.

Aidan was explaining that tomorrow was called Low Sunday and that this was probably prophetic. With the amount they had eaten, drunk and danced, low would be exactly how they would feel.

'Keep the drink moving will, you?' Eve said. 'I have to carve this beast.'

They had a huge joint of pork boned and rolled by Teddy Flood for them. He said you'd be able to cut it like butter. Honestly, it would be like carving a swiss roll. But Eve didn't want to make a mess of it. She closed the door behind her so that she could be on her own in the kitchen.

And as she prepared the place for herself, the huge carving dish, something that Benny had found in the shop, the plates that were heating in the bottom of the range, she was concentrating so hard that she didn't hear the door open and two extra guests arrive.

Carrying bottles of wine and cans of beer, in came Jack and Nan.

Rosemary was the nearest to the door and therefore the first to see them. She let her arm drop from Tom's shoulder where it had rested all evening to mark clearly lines of possession.

'My God,' she said.

Jack smiled his easy smile. 'Not exactly. Just his deputy,' he said.

Carmel was nuzzling Sean on a bench close by. 'You didn't say they were coming,' she accused Sean in a whisper.

'I didn't bloody know,' Sean hissed back.

Johnny O'Brien was doing a complicated tango step with Sheila.

'Hey, it's the black sheep,' he called happily.

Sheila whirled around to see if she could see Benny. She was just in time to see Benny look up from where she and Bill Dunne were sorting out records. And to see the colour go out of Benny's face as she dropped three of the EPs straight from her hands.

'Thank God for the passing of the seventy-eights,' said Fonsie, whose record collection would have been the loser.

'There's a surprise,' Bill said.

Even though the music of 'Hernando's Hideaway' was thumping and thudding itself all round them, Nan and Jack must have felt the silence and the chill.

Jack's legendary smile came to his rescue.

'Now, come on, did you think I'd forgotten I said I'd get the drink?' he laughed. He had put it down on the floor, his hands were wide apart, being held out helplessly in the little gesture Benny knew and loved.

It *must* have been a dream. All of it, and now that he was back it was over.

She felt herself smiling at him.

And he saw the smile. All the way across the room.

'Hallo, Benny,' he said.

Now everyone could feel the silence. Everyone except the Johnson Brothers, who were singing 'Hernando's Hideaway'. Clodagh had dressed Benny in black and white for the party. A big black corduroy skirt, a white blouse with a black velvet trim. She looked flushed and happy at the moment that Jack saw her.

He was walking over to her.

'How's your mother and the shop?'

'Fine, going great. We had a party there last night.' She spoke too quickly. She looked over his shoulder. Aidan Lynch had taken the bottles of wine from Nan and laid them on the table. Clodagh was trying to explain to Fonsie out of the corner of her mouth.

Johnny O'Brien, who could always be relied on to say something, if not the right thing, came over and punched Jack warmly on the arm.

'It's great to see you. I thought you were barred,' he said.

Aidan poured Jack a drink. 'Jack the lad!' he said. 'Like old times.'

'I thought it would be silly to act as if there was a feud or something.' Jack looked only mildly anxious that he had done the right thing.

'What feud would there be?' Aidan asked, looking nervously over at where Nan stood beside the door, hardly having moved since she came in.

'Well, that's what I thought. Anyway I couldn't make off with all the money for the jar.'

They both knew it had nothing to do with the drink.

'How are things?' Aidan asked him.

'Fine. A bit unreal.'

'I know,' said Aidan, who didn't know and couldn't

possibly imagine it. He thought it safer to move to different waters.

'And your uncle's office?'

'Crazy. They're all so petty, you wouldn't believe . . .' Jack had his arm upon a tall chest of drawers and was talking easily. Benny had moved slightly away. She felt very hot and then very cold. She hoped she wasn't going to faint. Perhaps she could get some air.

Then she realised that Eve didn't know they were here. She must go into the kitchen and tell her.

Aidan had realised this at the same time. He had moved Fonsie in to talk to Jack and headed Benny off at the kitchen door.

'I'll do it,' he said. 'Come in to rescue me if I'm not out in an hour and there's no sign of supper.'

She gave a watery smile.

'Are you all right?' he asked, concerned.

'I'm okay.' For Benny that was like saying she was terrible. Aidan looked around him and caught Clodagh's eye. She moved over to join them.

As Aidan went into the kitchen, Clodagh said, 'She can stand there at the bloody door all night. She's got some nerve coming here, I tell you. She got short shrift from me.'

'What?'

'She said, "Hallo, Clodagh", nice as pie. I looked through her. She said it again. "Do I know you?" is what I said.' Clodagh was pleased with her repartee.

'People will have to speak to her.'

'Let them. I'm not going to.'

And indeed Nan did seem curiously isolated, while Jack was the centre of his mates.

Benny looked across the room. Nan's face, serene and beautiful as ever, looked around her in that interested, slightly questioning way. She gave no sign that she might feel unwelcome, ungreeted. She looked perfectly at ease standing just where she had come in, when Aidan had removed the wine bottles from her arms.

Benny looked at Nan as she had done so often, admiringly. Nan knew what to say, how to behave, what to wear. Tonight she was in yet another new outfit, a very flowery print, all mauve and white. It looked so fresh, you'd think it had come straight off a shop rail five minutes ago, not from a long car drive.

Benny swallowed. For the rest of her life, Nan would drive in a car with Jack, sit beside him sharing all the things that *she* had once shared. Tears of disappointment came into her eyes. Why had she not done as he asked, taken off her clothes and lain down beside him, loved him generously and warmly, responded to him, instead of buttoning herself up and moving away and saying they should be going home?

If it were Benny who was pregnant, surely he would have been pleased and proud.

He would have explained to his parents, and to her mother as he had done for Nan. Big tears welled up in her eyes at her own foolishness.

Nan saw and came towards her.

'I haven't been avoiding you,' Nan said.

'No.'

'I was going to write to you, but then we never wrote each other letters, so that would be artificial.'

'Yes.'

'And it's hard to know what to say.'

'You always know what to say.' Benny looked at her. 'And you always know what to do.'

'It was never intended to be like this. I assure you.' There was something in Nan's voice that sounded phony. Benny realised with a shock that Nan was lying. Perhaps it was intended to be like this. That this was exactly the way Nan had planned it.

In the kitchen Eve was white-faced.

'I don't believe you,' she said to Aidan.

'Put those things down.' He looked at the carving knife and fork in her hand.

'Well, they're getting out. They're getting straight out of my house, let me tell you.'

'No, they're not, Eve.' Aidan was unexpectedly firm. 'Jack is my friend, and he is not going to be ordered out. It was always planned that he'd come here . . . he brought the drink.'

'Oh, don't be a fool,' Eve blazed. 'Nobody wanted the bloody drink. If he was that worried about it couldn't he have sent it . . . they're not welcome here.'

'They're our friends, Eve.'

'Not any more. Not now.'

'You can't keep up these things for ever. We've got to

get back to normal. I think they were absolutely right to come.'

'And what are they doing inside? Lording it over everyone?'

'Eve, please. These people are your guests, our guests in a way since you and I are a couple. Please don't make a scene. It would ruin the party for everyone. They're all behaving fine in there.'

Eve went over and put her arms around Aidan.

'You're very generous, much nicer than I am. I don't think we'll work as a couple.'

'No, you're probably right. But could we sort that one at another time, not just when they're going to have their supper?'

Bill Dunne came through the kitchen to go to the bathroom.

'Sorry,' he said, as he saw Aidan and Eve in each other's arms. 'You wouldn't know where to put yourself these days.'

'All right,' Eve conceded, 'just so long as I don't have to talk to her.'

Benny was dancing with Teddy Flood when Eve went into the room. Jack was talking to Johnny and Sean. He was as handsome and assured as ever. He looked delighted to see her.

'Eve!'

'Hallo, Jack.' Unenthusiastic, but not rude. She had made a promise to Aidan. Hospitality must never be abused.

'We brought you a vase, a sort of glass jug. It would be nice for all the daffodils and everything,' he said.

It was a nice jug. How did someone like Jack Foley do the right thing so often? How did he know she had daffodils? He hadn't been here since Christmas, when there was nothing but holly in bloom.

'Thanks. That's lovely,' she said. She moved around the room, emptying ashtrays, making spaces where the plates could be put down.

Nan stood on her own on the edge of a group.

Eve couldn't bring herself to say any words of greeting. She opened her mouth, but she couldn't find anything to say. She went back to the kitchen and stood at the table leaning on both hands. The rage she felt was a real thing, you could almost take it out of her and see it, like a red mist.

She remembered how Mother Francis, and Kit Hegarty, and many a time Benny, had warned her that this temper wasn't natural. It would only hurt her in the end.

The door opened, and Nan came in. She stood there in her fresh flowery print, the breeze from the window slightly lifting her blonde hair.

'Listen, Eve . . .'

'I won't, if you don't mind. I have a meal to prepare.'

'I don't want you to hate me.'

'You flatter yourself. Nobody hates you. We despise you. That's different altogether.'

Nan's eyes flashed now. She hadn't expected this.

'That's a bit petty of you, isn't it? A bit provincial? Life goes on. Aidan and Jack are friends . . .'

She looked proud and confident. She knew she held all the winning cards. She had broken all the rules and yet she had won. Not only was she able to take away her only friend's boyfriend, find somewhere, the Lord knew where, to sleep with him, and then get him to agree to marry her, she was also expecting everything to remain the same as it had been in their social life.

Eve said nothing. She looked at her dumbfounded.

'Well, say something, Eve,' Nan was impatient. 'You must be thinking something. Say it.'

'I was thinking that Benny was probably your only friend. That of every one of us she was the only one who just liked you for being you, not just for being glamorous.'

Eve knew that this was pointless. Nan would shrug. If she physically didn't shrug her shoulders, she would mentally. She would say that these things happened.

Nan would take, she would take everything she saw. She was like a child crawling towards a shining object. She took just by instinct.

'Benny's better off. She'd have had a lifetime of watching him, of wondering.'

'And you won't?'

'I'll cope.'

'I'm sure you will, you've coped with everything.'

Eve realised she was shaking. Her hands were trembling as she filled the jug with water and started to arrange a bunch of flowers that someone else had brought.

'I chose that for you,' Nan said.

'What?'

'The vase. You don't have one.'

Suddenly Eve knew where Jack and Nan had spent their nights together. Here in this house, in her bed.

They had driven to Knockglen, come up the track, taken her key and let themselves in. They had made love in her bed.

She looked at Nan aghast. That was why she had had the feeling that someone had been in the house. The strange undefined sense of someone else's presence.

'It was here, wasn't it?'

Nan shrugged. That awful dismissive shrug. 'Yes, sometimes. What does it matter, now . . .?'

'It matters to me.'

'We left the place perfect. No one would ever know.'

'You came to my house, to my bed, to take Benny's Jack in my bed. In Benny's town. Jesus Christ, Nan . . .'

Now Nan lost her temper, utterly.

'By God, I'm sick of this. I am sick of it. This Holy Joe attitude, all of you desperate to do it, playing around the edges, not having the guts or the courage, confessing it, titillating everyone still further . . .'

Her face was red and angry.

'And don't talk to me about this cottage . . . don't talk as if it was the Palace of Versailles. It's a damp, falling-down shack . . . that's what it is. It hasn't electricity. It has a Stanley Range that we couldn't light for fear you'd find the traces. It has leaks and draughts, and it's no wonder they say the place is haunted. It feels haunted. It smells haunted.'

'Nobody says my house is haunted.' There were tears of rage in Eve's eyes.

Then she stopped. People had said that they heard someone playing the piano here at night.

But that was ages ago. Jack didn't play the piano. It must have been before Jack.

'You brought Simon here too, didn't you?' she said.

The memory of Simon playing the piano at Westlands came back to her. That day she had gone up there with Heather, the day the old man had cursed at her and called her mother a whore. Nan said nothing.

'You brought Simon Westward to my bed, in my house. You knew I'd never have let him over the doorstep. And you brought him in here. And then, when he wouldn't marry you, you tricked Jack Foley . . .'

Nan was suddenly pale. She looked around her at the door to the room where the others were dancing.

The music of Tab Hunter on the record player.

'Young love, first love . . .'

'Take it easy . . .' Nan began.

Eve had picked up the carving knife. She started to move towards her, the words came tumbling out. She couldn't control them if she tried.

'I will *not* take it easy. What you have done, by Christ, I won't take it easy.'

Nan wasn't near enough to reach the handle of the door to the sitting room. She backed away, but Eve was still moving towards her, eyes flashing and the knife in her hand.

'Eve, stop!' she cried, moving as fast as she could out of range. She lurched against the bathroom door so hard that the glass broke.

Nan fell, sliding down on the ground, and the broken glass ripped her arm. Blood spurted everywhere, even on to her face.

The dress with the mauve and white print became crimson in a second. Eve dropped the knife on the floor. Her own screams were as loud as Nan's as she stood there in her kitchen amid the broken glass, the blood and the meal ready to be served, and the sound of everyone joining in the song in the room next door.

'Young love, first love, is filled with deep emotion.'

Eventually someone heard them and the door opened.

Aidan and Fonsie were in first.

'Whose car is nearest?' Fonsie asked.

'Jack's. It's outside the door.'

'I'll drive it. I know the road better.'

'Should we move her?' Aidan asked.

'If we don't she'll bleed to death in front of our eyes.'

Bill Dunne was great at keeping everyone back out of the kitchen. Only Jack, Fonsie and of course Tom, the medical student, in case he knew something the rest of them didn't, were allowed in. Everyone else should stay where they were, the place was too crowded already.

They had opened the back door. The car was only a few yards away. Clodagh had brought a rug and clean towels from Eve's bedroom. They wrapped the towel around the arm with the huge, gaping wound.

'Are we pushing the glass further in?' Fonsie asked.

'At least we're keeping the blood in,' Aidan said.

They looked at each other in admiration. Jokers yes, but when it came to the crunch, they were the ones in charge.

Benny sat motionless in the sitting room, her arm around Heather.

'It's going to be all right,' she kept saying, over and over. 'Everything's going to be all right.'

Before he got into the car Aidan came over to Eve.

'Don't let anyone go,' he warned. 'I'll be back very soon.'

'What do you mean?'

'Don't let them crawl away because they think it's expected. Give them something to eat.'

'I can't . . .'

'Then get someone else. They need food anyway.'

'Aidan!'

'I mean it. Everyone's had too much to drink. For God's sake feed them. We've no idea who'll be in on top of us now.'

'What do you mean?'

'Well, if she dies, we'll have the guards.'

'Die! She can't die.'

'Feed them, Eve.'

'I didn't . . . she fell.'

'I know, you fool.'

Then the car, with Jack, Fonsie, Aidan and a still hysterical Nan, left.

Eve straightened herself up.

'I think it's ludicrous myself, but Aidan Lynch says we should all have something to eat, so could you clear a little space and I'll bring it in,' she said.

Stricken, they obeyed her. Even though they would never have suggested it, it was exactly the right thing to do.

Dr Johnson looked at the arm and phoned the hospital.

'We're bringing someone in, severed arteries,' he said crisply. The three white faces of the boys looked at him as he hung up.

'I'll drive her,' he said. 'Just one of you. Which one?'

Fonsie and Aidan stood back, and Jack stepped forward. Maurice Johnson looked at him. His face was familiar. A junior rugby player, he had been in Knockglen before. In fact Dr Johnson had a feeling that he was meant to be Benny Hogan's boyfriend. There had been talk that she was walking out with a spectacularly handsome young man.

He wasted no time speculating. He nodded to Fonsie and Aidan and drove out of his gate.

It was an endless Sunday. The whole of Knockglen had heard that there had been a terrible accident and an unfortunate girl from Dublin had slipped and fallen, cutting herself on a glass door.

Dr Johnson had been quick to say that there wasn't any horseplay and everyone seemed to him to be stone cold sober. In fact he had no idea whether this was true or not, but he couldn't bear the tongues to wag, and Eve Malone to get further criticism for things that were beyond her control.

Dr Johnson also told everyone in sight that the girl would recover.

And recover she did. Nan Mahon was out of danger on the Sunday night. She had received several blood transfusions and there had been a time when her heartbeat had slowed down, causing alarm. But she was young and healthy. It was wonderful, the recuperative powers of the young.

Some time on the Monday night, she miscarried. But the hospital was very discreet. After all, she wasn't a married woman.

## 20

It was summer before Jack Foley and Nan Mahon had the conversation they knew that they would have to have. After her stay in the hospital in Ballylee she had gone back to Dublin.

That was at her insistence. She had seemed so agitated that Dr Johnson agreed.

Jack still worked in his uncle's office, but he studied for his first-year examination as well. There was, unspoken, the thought that he might return and do his degree in Civil Law. Aidan kept the notes from lectures.

Aidan and Jack met a lot, but they never talked about what was uppermost in their minds. Somehow it was easier to chat and be friends if they didn't mention that.

Brian Mahon wanted to sue. He said that by God people were always suing his customers for harmless jackass incidents. Why shouldn't they get a few quid out of it? That girl had to have some kind of insurance, surely?

Nan was very weak but her wound was healing, the livid red scar would fade in time.

Since she had never said aloud to her family that she was pregnant she did not have to report that this was no longer the case. She lay long hours in the bed where she had lain full of dreams.

She would not let Jack Foley come to see her.

'Later,' she had told him. 'Later, when we are able to talk.'

He had been relieved. She could see that in his eyes. She could also see he wished it to be finished, over, so that he could get on with his life.

But she wasn't ready yet. And she had had terrible injuries. He owed her all the time she needed to think about things.

'There's no sign of your fiancé,' Nasey said to her.

'It's all right.'

'Da says that if he leaves you now because of your injuries, we can sue him for breach of promise,' Nasey said.

She closed her eyes wearily.

Heather told over and over the story about the fall and the blood. She knew she would never have such an audience again. They hung on her every word. Heather aged twelve had been at a grown-ups' party wearing a chef's hat, and had seen all the blood. Nobody had taken her home or said she wasn't to look. She didn't tell them that she had felt dizzy and had cried into Benny's chest most of the time. She didn't tell them that Eve had sat white-faced, saying nothing for hours.

Eve took a long time to get over the night. She told only three people about having had the carving knife in her hand.

She told Benny, and Kit and Aidan. They had all said the same thing. They told her she hadn't touched Nan, she was only gripping it. They told her that she wouldn't have, that she would have stopped before she got near her.

Benny said that you couldn't be someone's best friend for ten years and not know that about them.

Kit said she wouldn't have anyone living in the house unless she knew what they were like. Eve would shout and rage. She wouldn't knife someone.

Aidan said the whole business was nonsense. She had been gripping that knife all evening. Hadn't he asked her to put it down himself? He said the future mother of his eight children had many irritating qualities, but she was not a potential murderess.

Gradually she began to believe it.

Little by little she could go into her kitchen and not see in her mind's eye all that blood and broken glass.

Soon the strained look began to leave her face.

Annabel Hogan said to Peggy Pine that they would never know the full story of the night above in the cottage, no matter how much they asked. Peggy said that it was probably better not to ask any more. To think on more positive things like Patsy's wedding, like whether she should sell Lisbeg and move in over the shop. Once people heard that it might be for sale there were some very positive enquiries, and figures that would make poor Eddie Hogan turn in his grave.

'He'd turn with pleasure,' Peggy Pine said. 'He always wanted the best for the pair of you.'

It was the right thing to say. Annabel Hogan began to look at the offers seriously.

Benny found the summer term at University College was like six weeks in another city. It was so different to everything that had gone before. The days were long and warm. They used to take their books to the gardens at the back of Newman House in St Stephen's Green and study.

She always meant to ask about these gardens and who looked after them. They belonged to the university, obviously. It was peaceful there and unfamiliar. Not like almost every other square inch of Dublin, which she associated with Jack.

Some nights she stayed with Eve in Dunlaoghaire, other nights they both went home on the bus together. There was a divan couch in Eve's cottage; sometimes she spent the night up there. Mother, absorbed with plans and redecoration, seemed pleased that Benny had Eve to talk to. They called it studying, but in fact it was talking; as fuchsias started to bud, as the old roses began to bloom, the friends sat and talked. They spoke very little about Nan and Jack and what had happened. It was too soon, too raw.

'I wonder where they went,' Benny said once, out of the blue. 'A couple of people said they saw them here in Knockglen, but where could they have stayed?'

'They stayed here,' Eve said simply.

She didn't have to tell Benny that it was without her permission, and that it had broken her heart. She saw tears in Benny's eyes.

There was a long silence.

'She must have lost the baby,' Benny said.

'I expect so,' Eve said.

She found herself thinking unexpectedly of the curse her father had laid on the Westwards.

And how so many of them had indeed had such bad luck.

Could this have been more of it? A Westward not even to survive till birth?

Mr Flood was referred to a new young psychiatrist, who was apparently a very kind young man. He listened to Mr Flood endlessly, and then prescribed his medication. There were no more nuns in trees. In fact, Mr Flood was embarrassed that he should ever have thought there were. It was decided that it should be referred to as a trick of the light. Something that could happen to anyone.

Dessie Burns said that what was wrong with the country was this obsession with drink. Everyone you met was either on the jar or off the jar. What was needed was an attitude of moderation. He himself was going to be a moderate drinker from now on, not all this going on tears or going off it totally. The management in Shea's said that it all depended on your interpretation of the word moderation, but at least Mr Burns had cut out the lunch-time drinking and that could only be to everyone's advantage.

Knockglen was cheated of the wedding of Mrs Dorothy Healy and Mr Sean Walsh. It was decided, they told people, that since the nuptials would be second time around for Mrs Healy and since Sean Walsh had no close family to speak of, they would marry in Rome. It would be so special, and although they would not be married by the Holy Father they would share in a blessing for several hundred other newly married couples.

'They couldn't rustle up ten people between them who'd come to the wedding,' Patsy told Mrs Hogan.

Patsy was thrilled by the decision. It would mean that her own wedding would now have no competition.

Eve was surprised to get an invitation to Patsy's wedding. She had expected just to go to the church to cheer her on. She realised that of course she and Patsy would be neighbours, up on the quarry path. She assumed that Mossy's mother had heard dire reports of the goings-on at the party, and would look on her as a shameless hussy who gave drunken parties. Eve didn't realise that Mossy told his mother as little as he told anyone else. She was getting increasingly deaf, and since she only knew about the world what he told her, she knew remarkably little.

She knew that Patsy was a good cook, and didn't have a family of her own to make demands, so Patsy would be free to look after Mossy's mother in her old age.

Mother Francis saw Dr Johnson passing the school in his car. She was looking out of the window as she often did when the girls were doing a test and thinking about the town. How she would hate to leave Knockglen, and go to another convent within the Order. Every year in summer the changes were announced. It was always a relief to know that she had another year where she was. Holy Obedience meant that you went without question where Mother General decided.

She hoped unworthily each year that Mother Clare would not be sent to join them. She didn't exactly pray that Mother Clare would be kept in Dublin, but God knew her views on that. Any day now they would know. It was always an unsettling couple of weeks waiting for the news.

She wondered where Dr Johnson was going, what a strange demanding life, always out to see someone being born or die or go through complicated bits in between.

Major Westward was dead when the doctor arrived. He closed the eyes, pulled a sheet over the head and sat down with Mrs Walsh. He would phone the undertakers and the Vicar, just to alert them, but first someone had better find Simon.

'I telephoned him this morning. He's on his way from England.'

'Right then. Not much more that I can do.' He stood up and reached for his coat.

'Not much loss,' he said.

'I *beg* your pardon, Dr Johnson?'

He had looked at her levelly. She was a strange woman. She liked the feeling of being in the Big House, even though it was Big rather than Grand. She would probably stay if Simon brought home a bride, grow old here, feel that her own state had been ennobled by her contact with these people.

It wasn't fair of him to be snide about the dead man. He had never liked old Westward, he had thought the man arrogant and ungiving to the village that was on his doorstep. He had found the disinheriting of Eve Malone beyond his comprehension.

But he must not tread on the sensibilities of other people. His wife had told him that a thousand times.

He decided to change his epitaph.

'Sorry, Mrs Walsh, what I said was, "What a loss, such a loss." You'll pass on my condolences to Simon, won't you?'

'I'm sure Mr Simon will telephone you, Doctor, when he gets back.'

Mrs Walsh was tight-lipped. She had heard very well what he had said the first time.

Jack Foley's parents said that he was behaving most

unreasonably. What were they to think, or indeed to say? Was the wedding on or was it off? Obviously since the urgency had gone out of it and the three-week run-up time had been and gone, they could assume that she was no longer pregnant. Jack had snapped and said he couldn't possibly be expected to discuss all this with them at this early stage while Nan was still convalescing.

'I think we can be expected to know whether you now have reason to call off this rushed marriage.' His father spoke sharply.

'She had a miscarriage,' he said. 'But nothing else is clear.'

He looked so wretched they left him alone. After all their main question had been answered, the way they hoped it would be.

Paddy Hickey proposed to Kit Hegarty at a window table in a big Dunlaoghaire hotel. His hands were trembling as he asked her to marry him. He used formal words, as if a proposal was some kind of magic ritual and wouldn't work unless he asked her to do him the honour of becoming his wife.

He said that all his children knew he was going to ask her, they would be waiting, hoping for a yes, like himself. He spoke so long and in such flowery tones that Kit could hardly find a gap in the speech to say yes.

'What did you say?' he asked at length.

'I said I'd love to and I think we'll make each other very happy.'

He got up from his side of the table and came round to her, and in front of everyone in the restaurant dining room he took her in his arms and kissed her.

Somehow, even in the middle of the embrace he felt that people had laid down their cutlery and their glasses to look at them.

'We're going to get married,' he called out, his face pink with pleasure.

'Thank God I'm going off to the wilds of Kerry, I'd never be able to come in here again,' said Kit, acknowledging the smiles and handshakes and even cheers of the other diners at the tables around them.

Simon Westward wondered could his grandfather possibly have known how inconvenient was the day he took to die. The arrangements with Olivia were at a crucial stage. He did not need to be summoned to a sick bed. But on the other hand, he would be in a better position to talk to her once he was master of Westlands in name as well. He tried to feel some sympathy for the lonely old man. But he feared that he had brought a lot of his misery on himself.

So, it mightn't have been easy to welcome Sarah's ill-matched husband, a handyman, to the house, but he should have made some overtures of friendship to their child.

Eve would have been a good companion for all those years. Petted and fêted in the Big House, she would not have developed that prickling resentment which was her hallmark as a result of being banished.

He didn't like thinking about Eve. It reminded him uncomfortably of that terrible day in Westlands when the old man had lashed out all around him.

And it reminded him of Nan.

Somebody had sent him a cutting from the *Irish Times,* with the notice of her engagement. The envelope had been typed. At first he thought it might have been from Nan herself, and later he decided that it was not her style to do that. She had left without a backward glance. And as far as he could see from his statement, had not cashed that cheque. He didn't know who had sent the newspaper cutting. He thought it might have been Eve.

Heather asked Mother Francis, would Eve be coming to their grandfather's funeral?

Mother Francis said that somehow she thought not.

'He used to be very nice once, he got different when he got old,' she said.

'I know,' Mother Francis said. Her own heart was heavy. Mother Clare was going to be sent to Knockglen. It was all very well for Peggy Pine to urge Mother Francis to take the whip hand, and to show her who was master, and a lot of other highly unsuitable instructions for religious life. It was going to disrupt the Community greatly. If only there was some kind of interest, some area she could find for Mother Clare to be hived off.

'Are you in a bad humour, Mother?' Heather asked.

'Oh, Lord, child, you really are Eve's cousin. You have exactly the same way she had of knowing when anything was wrong. The rest of the school could tramp past and never know anything.'

Heather looked at her thoughtfully.

'I think you should put more faith in the Thirty Days Prayer. Sister Imelda says it's never been known to fail. She did it for me when I was lost, and look at how well it turned out.'

Mother Francis sometimes worried about how Heather had latched on to some of the more complicated aspects of the Catholic faith.


Nan asked Jack to meet her.

'Where would you like?' he asked.

'You know Herbert Park. It's quite near you.'

'Is that not too far from you?' They were curiously formal.

If anyone saw this handsome couple walking there they would have assumed that this was another summer romance, and smiled at them.

There was no ring to give back. There were very few arrangements to unpick.

She told him that she was going to London. She hoped to do a course in dress designing. She wanted to be away for a while. She didn't really know exactly what she did want, but she knew what she didn't want.

She talked flatly, with no light and shade in her voice. Jack fought down the guilty, overwhelming surge of relief, that he was not going to have to marry this beautiful dead girl and spend the rest of his life with her.

When they left the small park with its bright rows of flowers and the pit-pat of people playing tennis they knew that they would probably never see each other again.

The day dawned bright and sunny for Patsy's wedding. Eve and Benny were there to help her dress. Clodagh would be down to see that those two clowns didn't get anything wrong.

Paccy Moore was going to give her away. He had said that if she wanted someone with a proper leg he wouldn't be a bit insulted, and he might make a bit of clatter with the iron going up the church, but Patsy would have no one else.

His cousin Dekko was going to be the best man, and his sister Bee the bridesmaid. It gave the appearance of a family.

The best silver was out despite Patsy saying that a couple of Mossy's cousins might be light-fingered. There was chicken and ham, and potato salad, and a dozen different types of cake, and trifle and cream.

It would be a feast.

Clodagh had plucked Patsy's eyebrows and insisted on doing a make-up.

'I wonder would there be a chance that my mother might see me up in Heaven?' Patsy said.

For an instant, none of the three girls could find an answer. They found it too moving to think that Patsy would need the support of a mother she had never known, and her easy confidence that this woman was in Heaven.

Benny blew her nose loudly.

'I'm sure she can see you, and she's probably saying you look lovely.'

'God, Benny, don't blow your nose like that in the church. You'd lift half the congregation out of their seats,' Patsy warned.

Dr Johnson was driving the party up to the church.

'Good girl, Patsy,' he said, as he settled Paccy and the bride into the back of his Morris Cowley. 'You'll tear the sight out of the eyes of that old rip above.'

It was exactly the right remark, the partisan response to show Patsy that she was on the winning team, that Mossy's mother wouldn't even be a starter in the race.

Dessie Burns had abandoned moderation that morning. He tried to wave a cheery greeting at them from his front door, but it wasn't easy with a bottle in one hand and a glass in the other. He somehow went into a spin and fell down. Dr Johnson looked at him grimly. That would be his next call, stitching up that eejit's head.

It was a great wedding. Patsy had to be restrained several times from clearing up or going to the kitchen to bring out the next course.

They were waved away at four o'clock.

Dekko was going to drive them to the bus, but Fonsie said he had to drive to Dublin anyway, so he'd take them to Bray.

'Fonsie should be canonised,' Benny said to Clodagh.

'Yes, I can see his statue in all the churches. Maybe they'd even make this a special place of pilgrimage for him. We'd outsell Lourdes.'

'I mean it,' Benny said.

'Don't you think I don't know?' A rare look of softness came into Clodagh's face.

That night Mother asked Benny if she'd mind if they sold Lisbeg.

She knew she mustn't appear too eager. But she said thoughtfully that it was a good idea, there'd be money to build up the shop. It was what Father would have liked.

'We always wanted you to be married from here. That's the only thing.'

The signs of Patsy's wedding were still everywhere, the silver ornaments from the cake, the paper napkins, the confetti, the glasses around the house.

'I don't want to get married for a long, long time, Mother. I mean that.' And oddly she did.

All that pain she had felt over Jack seemed much less now.

She remembered how she had ached all over at the very thought of him and how she had wanted to be the one leaving to walk up the church to a smiling Jack Foley.

That ache was a lot less painful now.

Rosemary said that they should have a party in Dublin just to show that it wasn't only the socialites in Knockglen who could organise things. A barbecue maybe, the night their exams were over, down by White Rock, on the beach, between Killiney and Dalkey.

They'd have a huge fire, and there'd be sausages and lamb chops and great amounts of beer.

Sean and Carmel would not be in charge this time. Rosemary would do the food, and her friend Tom would collect the money. The boys started contributing.

'Will we ask Jack?' Bill Dunne said.

'Maybe not this time,' said Rosemary.

Eve and Benny were going to share a flat next year. The digs in Dunlaoghaire would be closed. They were very excited and kept looking at places now before the vacation so that they'd be ahead of the posse in September.

They were full of plans. Benny's mother would come and stay, maybe even Mother Francis might come and visit. There had been wonderful news from the convent. Mother Clare had broken her hip. Not that Mother Francis *called* it wonderful news, but it did mean that Mother Clare would need to be near a hospital and physiotherapy, and all the stairs and the walking in St Mary's wouldn't be advisable. Mother Francis was in the middle of the Thirty Days Prayer when this happened. She told Eve that it was her biggest crisis of faith yet. Could the prayer be *too* powerful?

As they left one flat they had been examining, they ran into Jack.

He looked at Benny.

'Hallo, Jack.'

Eve said she had to go, seriously, and she'd see Benny later out in Dunlaoghaire. She was gone before they could say anything.

'Would you come out with me tonight?' he asked her.

Benny looked at him. Her eyes went all around the face that she had loved so much, every line, every fold of the skin so dear to her.

'No, Jack, thank you.' Her voice was gentle and polite. She was playing no games. 'I'm going out already.'

'But that's just with Eve. She won't mind.'

'No, it's impossible. Thanks all the same.'

'Tomorrow then, or the weekend?' His head was on one side.

Benny remembered suddenly the way that his mother and father had stood on the steps of their house that night. His mother watchful and wondering.

Little things that she had learned during the past month about the Foleys made her think that this was always the way things were.

Benny didn't want to wonder and watch over Jack for the rest of her life. If she went out with him now, it would be so easy. They would be back to where they had been before. In time Nan would be forgotten like the incident in Wales had been sort of forgotten.

But she would always worry about the next one.

The next time she just wasn't around, ever smiling, always ready. It was too much to ask.

'No.' Her smile was warm.

His face was surprised and sad. More sad than surprised.

He began to say something.

'I only did what . . .' Then he stopped.

'I never meant it to . . .' He stopped again.

'It's all right, Jack,' Benny said. 'Honestly, it's all right.'

She thought she saw tears in his eyes and looked away quickly. She didn't want to be reminded of that day on the canal bank.

The firelight danced and they threw more and more logs on. Aidan had said he wondered were he and Eve leaving the conception of their eight children too late; and she assured him that they weren't, it would be wrong to rush these things. He sighed resignedly; he had known she would say this.

Rosemary was flushed and pretty, and Tom paid her the most extravagant compliments; Johnny O'Brien was in disgrace because he had whirled a blazing log and it had set fire to a great bowl of punch. The blaze had been spectacular, but the drink severely diminished.

Fonsie and Clodagh had come up from Knockglen. It would be a long time before anyone forgot their dazzling jive display on the big flat rock.

Sean and Carmel nuzzled up to each other as they had done from the beginning of time, Sheila from the law faculty had a new hair-do and a happier smile. Benny wondered why she hadn't liked her so much in the old days.

It was all over Jack, probably. Like everything had been.

The clouds that had been in front of the moon scudded past and it was almost as bright as daylight.

They laughed at each other, delighted. It was as if someone had shone a huge searchlight over them, then more clouds came and made it discreet again.

They were tired now from singing and from dancing to the little record player Rosemary had provided. They only wanted to sing something gentle.

Not anything that would make Fonsie start to dance again. Someone started the song about 'Sailing Alone on Moonlight Bay'. Everyone groaned because it was so awful and old-fashioned, but everyone sang it because they knew the words.

Benny was leaning half against a rock and half against Bill Dunne, who was sitting beside her. Bill was so enjoying the night, and was looking after her, getting her nice bits of burned sausage on a stick and some tomato ketchup to dip it in. Bill was a great friend. You wouldn't have to spend the night worrying if he was having a good time or too good a time.

She was thinking how comfortable he was when she saw Jack coming down the steps.

It was very dark and to the others it might just have looked like a figure in the distance. But she knew it was Jack coming to join the summer party. Asking to belong again.

She didn't make any move. She watched him for a long

time; sometimes he stopped in the shadows, as if doubtful of his welcome.

But Jack Foley would never be doubtful for long. He would know that these were his friends. The long winding steps were quite a distance from the rocks where they sat around their fire. Probably not very far, but it seemed a long time for him to cross the sand.

Long enough for her to realise how often she had seen his face everywhere. She used to see his face smiling and frowning. She used to see it like Mr Flood saw visions, up in trees and in the clouds. She used to see it in the patterns of leaves on the ground. When she woke and when she slept there was no other image in the foreground, and not because she summoned it there. It just wouldn't go away.

That was the way it had been for a very long time, when things were good and when things were bleak.

But tonight she would have difficulty in seeing his face. She would have to wait until he came into the firelight to remember what he looked like. It was oddly restful.

They were still in full voice when someone saw Jack. The song didn't stop. They were all exaggerating the words anyway, and laughing. A few people waved to him.

He stood on the edge.

Jack Foley on the edge of things. Nobody waved him into the centre of the group. He smiled around him, glad to be back. His nightmares brushed away, his sins, he hoped, forgiven. He seemed happy to be part of the court again. Not even his worst enemy would ever have accused him of having wanted to be king. That's just the way it had turned out.

Across the fire his eyes sought Benny. It was hard to know what he was asking her. Permission to be there? Pardon for everything that had gone before? Or the right to come and hold her in his arms?

Benny smiled the big, warm smile that had made him fall in love with her. Her welcome was real. She looked lovely in the light of the flames, and she did what no one else had done. She pointed him to where the drink was, where the long sticks lay for cooking the food. He opened a beer and moved slightly towards her. That had been encouragement, hadn't it?

There wasn't much room on the rug where she sat leaning against Bill Dunne and the craggy bit of rock.

Nobody moved over to make space. They assumed he would sit down where he was.

After a few moments Jack Foley did that. Perched on a rock. On the edge.

Bill Dunne, who had his arm lightly around Benny's shoulder, didn't take it away because she hadn't moved as he had thought she might.

The song was over and someone had started 'Now is the Hour'. They sang in exaggerated poses and mimes, in funny accents and pretence of huge passion. Benny looked into the fire.

It was peaceful here. There would be other nights like this. More like floating along than racing along. And as she saw the sticks move and huge showers of sparks fly up to the sky over the dark hills, she couldn't see Jack's face.

All she could see were the flames and the sparks, and the long shadows out over the sand, and the edge of the sea with tiny bits of white coming in over the stones and the beach.

And the friends, all the friends sitting in a great circle, looking as if they were going to sing for ever.

Since they were into sentimentality, Fonsie said, they shouldn't overlook 'For Ever, and Ever, my Heart will be True'.

The voices soared up to the sky with the smoke and the sparks and nowhere in the sky did Benny Hogan see the face of Jack Foley.

And Benny sang with the others, knowing that Jack Foley's face was somewhere with all the faces around the fire, not taking over the whole night sky.

# Light a Penny Candle

## Maeve Binchy

Evacuated from Blitz-battered London, Elizabeth White is sent to stay with the O'Connor family in Kilgarret, Ireland. It is the beginning of an unshakeable bond between Elizabeth and Aisling O'Connor, which endures over twenty turbulent years of change and chaos, joy and sorrow, soaring dreams and searing betrayals . . .

With warmth, wit and great compassion, Maeve Binchy tells a magnificent story of two women, bound together in a friendship that nothing can tear apart – not even the man who threatens to come between them forever.

'Maeve Binchy! I've loved her stories and have
since *Light a Penny Candle*.'
Tom Hanks

'The ideal doorstopper to occupy long, dark evenings.'
*Daily Mail*

arrow books

# *Echoes*

## Maeve Binchy

Growing up in a quiet seaside town, Clare O'Brien and David Power shout their hearts' desires into the echo cave, praying their destinies will carry them far away from Castlebay.

Years later, their paths cross again. David, following in his father's footsteps, is studying medicine and Clare has won a scholarship to University College.

But eventually Castlebay will draw them back and, against a backdrop of empty grey skies, sea-spray and howling winds, this drama of ambition, betrayal and love will reach its turbulent conclusion.

'Wonderfully warm and involving.'
Katie Fforde

'Chronicled with tenderness and wit.'
*Sunday Times*

arrow books